Ou

DIANA ANTHONY
writer, who lives in New York with her husband
and young son. *Out of a Dream* is her second
major novel, which follows the success of her
Once a Lover.

Available in Fontana by the same author

Once a Lover

DIANA ANTHONY

Out of a Dream

FONTANA PAPERBACKS

First published by Fontana Paperbacks 1984

Made and printed in Great Britain by
William Collins Sons & Co. Ltd., Glasgow.

FOR R.D., WITH MUCH LOVE

"Our birth is but a sleep and a forgetting . . ."
William Wordsworth, *"Ode on Intimations of Immortality"*

PROLOGUE.

BOSTON. 1951.

The gun had been cold to the touch when she'd dropped it into her bag and started off into the snowstorm that blew and blew and was likely to blow forever in her loveless world. All day long, snow sifted through the bare branches of the oak trees and on to the steeples and rooftops of the old waterfront city. It clung to the coats of tailored women and lined the hat brims of tall men entering the chic, but out-of-the-way restaurant, always in pairs, always together, at this dusky, after-work hour of five p.m.

Shivering at her post outside the restaurant, she had never felt so devoutly alone.

She turned up her mink collar against the shock of cold that seemed to have no proper place in her life – reared as she had been in sunny, high-windowed rooms, in the grace of an old Puritan family and its godly riches – the cold that would never go away, arising as it did from some secret chamber of the heart.

Until today, she had not known of her vocation for sorrow.

Once more, she forced herself to focus on the attractive couple at the corner table. The rose tint of the diamond-paned window by which she was framed lent the other woman a chromatic young glow as though she had been painted there, her auburn hair spreading in gilded waves over her shoulders like a Renaissance Virgin's. The man clasped her hands in his own, and pressed fervid kisses upon them. His lips moved as though in prayer. Love leapt between their fingertips, a palpable electricity, so that the woman watching outside could almost hear it crackle.

A sudden rage stirred within her like an unborn child. The numbness of shock had been better than this new sensation.

7

Now she must begin to feel.

With two shaking fingers she lifted the sheer black netting of her hat veil.

Her husband looked different to her. He was different with that woman beside him, the blue ice of his eyes thawed, the grudging mouth easy with a smile. She had seldom seen that smile bless her, could not reconcile this stranger with the quietly angry man she knew.

These last few months, when he had begun reeling in at late hours, reckless with his passion, generous in his disdain, when the phone calls were hushed and hurried, when his gentleness made her cry out for the first days, the early days, she had suspected his guilty transformation into the man at the corner table. Nevertheless, it had taken her this long to summon up the mortal courage to confront him. After all, in her case, betrayal was inevitable, wasn't it?

The circumstances of their marriage, fragile and forced beyond mutual feeling, dependent on crumbling social rites, had seen to that. She was only eighteen when she was told she was pregnant and he was bound to marry her. How she had aged since then!

Their families had ordered it in the tidy, dignified way upper-class Boston families do. Out of duty, he had been good to her and the child. A child herself, she had begun to hope it would work after all. And now this.

She tried her fingers inside the kid gloves, for the blood in the veins seemed to have stopped flowing. Dully, she unclasped her handbag and felt for the pistol she had put there in a dream.

Then, she opened the door to the pub he would never have taken her to, and walked into the warmth and light, from which, by an act of illicit love, she had been forever cast . . .

PART I

MICHELLE

Chapter One

WINTER
198–

That day in New York City was bitter with ice and snow and Northern winds blowing down the channels from Canada. Penn Station, the echoing cavern on busy Sixth Avenue, inhaling and exhaling its daily horde of travellers, who stamped their boots at the entrance, unfurled umbrellas, puffed smoke clouds, blinking at the radiant white world beyond the doors of the great terminal.

All along the street, holiday shoppers trampled down the snow, their chins swaddled in mufflers, their bodies hunched against the gale-force winds that funnelled up from glass and concrete chasms along the Avenue of the Americas. Abandoned newspapers whirled about their booted ankles like black and white kites and little piles of debris went spinning off into the frosty air.

The young woman with a soft sweep of champagne-coloured hair, and a floor-length vanilla fox coat wandered up out of the station, a fabulous apparition, lost even to herself.

Patrolman Joe Cerretti had his eye on her for a while before he went over to investigate. At first, he'd thought she was just another suburban hausfrau, with too many hours on her hands and too little attention from her husband, already tanked by noon, and looking for a bite of the Big Apple.

But then instinct told him this woman was different. She reminded him of a poem he'd read in school, the one about 'She Walks in Beauty Like the Night . . .' He remembered that one because he'd had to write it out twenty-five times for the sin of leaving his Religion homework at home. Anyway, there was something extravagently fragile, even classy, about this one. Like one of those porcelain figurines his Grandmother Virgilina brought back from Firenze, with the etched white faces and the rosebud bodices you could never touch with your clumsy boy's hands.

He decided she would smell like something flowery and old-fashioned, maybe lavender. Connie used to hang lavender pomander balls in all the cupboards at home. He always liked that. It made the house in Bayside seem richer and more refined. He'd have to tell her to buy them again, and to get rid of those damn rubber vegetables in the dining room fruit bowl . . .

Hell, it was cold! He chafed his raw, red hands. A harried mother with twins asked for directions to Macy's, distracting his attention. When Cerretti had a chance to look up again, the pretty lady was still there, gliding like a ghost, up and down the street.

He moved in closer for a better look. It was only then he realized that the woman's exquisite face was locked in a frieze of pure terror.

'Hey, lady, you all right? Need some help?' He didn't want to startle her; she might break or something.

Without a word, the woman stretched her hands to his blue tunic and tumbled into his arms.

Then the white cloud of her fur coat burst open and a cold tremble of diamonds took the officer's breath away. She must have been decked out in a hundred thousand dollars worth of rocks: watery diamond bracelets, long shivering necklaces with gold clasps, multicoloured rings that flashed blindingly in the winter daylight. Cerretti was no expert, but he'd seen enough hot ice to know the real thing.

Had she stolen it all? He searched for the jeweller's hallmark by which important pieces might be traced. However, they were of such vintage that the name or names had been rubbed off with the usage of years. They looked to be heirlooms.

10

He'd have to send out a missing person bulletin, he thought, distracted by the shimmer of stones.

'You shouldn't be walking around here with all this stuff. It's not safe, this part of town . . .'

Her violet eyes were furtive.

Maybe simple questions . . . 'What's your name? Where are you from? Don't you have a handbag? How about credit cards? I can take you home if I know your address from a credit card.'

Curiosity-seekers were beginning to gather in knots around the pair. Standing closer to her protectively, Cerretti decided the woman was dazed from an accident of some sort, and not drunk at all, for she had the clean breath of a baby. A quick search of her pockets turned up no identification. It did turn up five thousand dollars in cash.

The unknown woman held her hand to her side and favoured her left leg. When she winced in pain, the cop stared down and sure enough, beneath the luxurious fur and designer dress, her right leg was darkening with bruises.

Of course, he'd been right about the accident. She'd probably wandered away from the scene, leaving her bags behind. 'You're in pain?'

Cerretti slowly became aware of the burgeoning crowd. 'All right, all right, break it up!' he growled. 'The floor show's over.' He'd have to get her to a hospital.

Supporting her weight with one arm, he flipped open his walkie-talkie and called for an ambulance. She was feather-light in his arms, lighter than he'd ever imagined a woman could be.

Minutes later, an ambulance careened into view. The woman looked at him accusingly as he helped her in.

The next few hours passed with Cerretti pacing the halls of Bellevue, flashing back to the woman, her diamonds, her skin . . . It was like when you have a fever and the same thought keeps running through your mind, over and over, like an animal stuck on a treadmill in some science experiment.

11

Then the word came. They'd found only a few superficial bruises. But there was something wrong with this silent woman that a regular doctor couldn't fix. She would have to be kept here under observation.

Cerretti knew he couldn't let this happen. Not to her. He felt responsible now for finding her and her inarticulate pain, her sad beauty, cast up at the gates of his city like the pearl of great price. He searched for a name, a place he'd heard about where rich people go to be cured of their expensive head problems. 'Graft' something . . . Graff-Lowell, that was it, New York City Hospital's famous Clinic where all the celebrities flocked to dry out or put their breakneck lives on hold for a while. It fit his thwarted sense of refinement. No batty Bellevue, no vomit-smelling City emergency rooms for her. This blonde beauty belonged in a palace like Graff-Lowell. It would probably have pristine white walls and large, opalescent vases filled with hothouse blooms. No one would ever talk above a whisper, and the meals would be served on a silver tray. Graff-Lowell, right. He liked the name. It had a high-priced ring.

But how could he get her in there? The doctors, white-gowned and clean-smelling, passed him in the halls. Cerretti knew many of them. Whom did he know at Graff-Lowell?

The one with the old eyes and silver hair, Dr Beckstein. A good man, he'd put in more gratis hours at the City Hospital than the law demanded. He'd call Dr Beckstein and talk him into taking on the 'Jane Doe'.

A quick call to the generous Dr Beckstein and Cerretti took the patient in hand.

When he and his charge stepped into the arriving squad car, the blonde woman clung to his arm with a child's trusting hand. She sparkled in the dimness of the car, she or all those oversized rocks that would be neatly bagged and filed away for her at the headshrinker's hotel – until the day of her release into society, when she might finally pay for her own hospital care.

'Graff-Lowell,' Cerretti told the cop at the wheel, and he couldn't resist a knowing smile.

12

That afternoon, Joshua Free felt all the things a veteran journalist is no longer supposed to feel: passionate curiosity, fierce excitement, even an obscure desire. He did not, in any case, feel objective about the little drama he had just seen unfolding on the snowy street.

Free hadn't managed to get a good look at the lady, just a tantalizing flash of creamy fur coat over a glide of thigh, but it was enough of an erotic image to arrest him in mid-step, as he passed the snowbound portals of Penn Station.

With the rest of the crowd, he surged towards the stopped ambulance, but the police were warning everyone back.

'What happened?' he shouted to the closemouthed cop, when he'd got close enough.

'Nothing, move along.'

Josh flashed his press badge. 'I'm Josh Free, the owner of the *Globe*.

With a grudging face, the officer spoke. 'Just a Jane Doe.'

'Pretty nice threads for a Jane Doe.'

The cop shrugged his shoulders and the ambulance screamed away.

Josh had to laugh to himself. Just imagine if anyone from the *Globe* found out that Josh Free, king of the fastest growing newspaper chain in the country, with scores of journalistic fiefdoms at his command, had used his noon constitutional (it was impossible for him to sit two hours together behind his custom-made *faux marbre* desk, gift of a Saudi princeling, and loyally rumoured by his staff to be the largest of its kind in the world. Motion was his business. Some would say, his madness.) to chase an ambulance.

Old habits die hard.

Back in Tampa, with his shoestring budget news daily, he'd chased not only ambulances, but limousines, press agents and leads of any size or seriousness. It was a wonder he ever got an edition out at all. After all, what did he know about running a journal? He'd come cocky from a real estate agency, where he'd broken records with his first year's sales, to buying up and investing, to starting his own daily. If it weren't for T.J., Carter and some of the other real newspapermen, he would have folded in a flash. As it was, he'd tripled his personal fortune in two years, become a journalistic legend in five, married and divorced a sinfully beautiful *Vogue* model, moved his headquarters to New York, and today, had his editorial hand in every major political cause on the globe.

Maybe his success had something to do with his credo that 'Knowledge is Power'. A reader, he always told his reporters, wants to know 'why' things happen, *how* does the world get into the state it's in? Knowing *that* gives some measure of control to the little man and woman, a kind of cosmic comfort. Thus, Josh Free was heavy on the editorial page, urged his people to dig beyond the 'when, where' rubrics, and on to the 'whys.' From there, it was just a short hop, skip and jump to humanitarian jaunts – from helping displaced persons in Middle Eastern Wars in their search for a home, to feeding the famine-stricken in Africa, to funding anti-nuclear, pro-peace candidates in his own country's elections.

UNICEF had already cited him for his special kindness to the world's children.

Big doings for a little boy from Tampa, the minister's blue-eyed boy, Joshua Jefferson Free, who had once fancied himself an aeroplane pilot. Not a well-fed airline company man, ferrying floral-shirted tourists to distant summer isles, but something lean, elegant and dangerous out of the earliest era of aviation. A barnstormer in a Bleriot, or a WWI ace, with a scarf of white silk streaming behind his ear as he saluted the downed Prussian foe. Unable to realize that dream, he had, instead, walked romantically tall through his life in the corridors of business, doing outsized deeds, as men in boy's heroic stories do.

The divorce had been of heroic proportions too, with an outsized settlement and years of regret to follow, leaving Josh Free so damned dissatisfied, so hungry all the time that he kept up with Nicole, just to see if maybe he was the one who'd made a mistake. All he ever saw, though, was what he'd been missing.

At first, Nicole had found it exciting when her new husband took a call from an Israeli General in the small hours of the morning, and had to hop a plane before breakfast. Then she became angry when what seemed like the whole teeming world began to intrude into their bedroom, via the telephone. And then she was just indifferent, drifting away from Josh, in one of her filmy couture gowns, on the winds of adultery and bad faith.

'I'm leaving you,' she said that afternoon, when fresh from disembarking from the Concorde, Josh had found her at the door of their penthouse apartment, with her bags packed and her guard up.

Her rich russet hair tumbled down her back and she was wearing the pale green Chanel suit, the colour of young almonds, they'd given her on one of her more generously produced shoots. She blazed with beauty and disappointment.

'In case you're interested, I'm determined to marry again as soon as possible. Unlike you, I like knowing where I'm going to be the next day. I like roots. I like individuals, as opposed to the masses. You, Josh, you're married to the masses, you belong to history, like some goddam Abraham Lincoln or something! I can't compete with the masses, Josh, there's just too damn many of them. Besides, it's their love that really turns you on – not mine.' She kissed him on the cheek, as she brushed by. When her hand was on the knob of the door, she turned. 'Bye bye. My attorney will be contacting you.'

'But, Nicole . . .' It was so hard to defend himself against the truth. He said the only thing a man can say at such moments. 'I love you.'

'I'm sure you think you do, Josh,' she said without anger. 'But you see, my darling, you don't know the first thing about it. You've never let me or any other woman come anywhere near you. You're the Statue of Liberty, Josh, calling in the tired, the poor, the downtrodden. Embrace *them*, Josh. Take *them* to bed at night. It's what you want.'

He put his hand on her shoulder, tenderly, in shock.

'Good bye, Josh.' She went out the door, into her new life.

Josh, standing on the icy pavement in front of Penn Station, clapped his gloved hands together. Brr, it was getting colder. This woman he'd just caught a glimpse of, the 'Jane Doe', she was built like Nicole, long, lean and surpassingly lovely. He remembered the first time he'd seen his wife. She'd just stepped off a bus on 59th St in Manhattan, her portfolio in hand, and Josh felt it was a kind of natural miracle that had transformed the hard-knock city for him in an instant. Like when the light hits your eye a certain way and you see auras shining around everything. Or when a gutter puddle turns into a spot of rainbow with the sun. Nicole was his lady, and his relentless energy had swept her into his life, with very little regard for emotional consequences on either side.

He put Nicole, resolutely, from his mind, and, following a final abortive attempt at conversation with the cop – all he could get out of him was the information that the woman was headed for Bellevue – Josh started back for his pressing appointment in the city room, a few blocks away. That was the trouble with being a big-shot executive, you ended up doing everything but the nuts and bolts reporting you loved.

With a buzz of cold air, he stomped into the skyscraper offices of the *Globe* full of plans. He crooked his index finger, as he barrelled through his outer office.

Straight, dark Doria Sevenstars glided up from her desk, her glorious black hair streaming all the way down to her waist, her skin a certain shade of apricot. Doria looked out at the workaday world through the dusky, unfathomable eyes of her mother's proud tribe. In the presence of Ms Sevenstars it was thus easy to see why even the haughty Conquistadors had reserved a special fascination for the Seminole women. Her face glowed warm like Aztec copper as she waited for her boss to speak.

But as usual, Josh scarcely nodded a greeting, dismissing such amenities as a patent sign of weakness in a man of power. It had never once occurred to him to pamper his assistant of five thriving years, anymore than he would think to pamper his right arm.

16

The trouble was there always seemed to have been a Ms Sevenstars gracing his outer office as though she'd been issued with the gold key to his executive suite or the cat-at-the-cream purr of his first Mercedes sedan. Gradually, over the years, Free had come to expect those daily miracles she worked so well – the towers of business letters that melted away under her nimble fingers, her wheat-tone office kept spruce and sparkling with model efficiency, the hanging spider plant tirelessly spinning its green tendrils at the plate-glass window, a paradigm of health.

That Sevenstars was beautiful too, seemed only right and proper in her boss's mind. That mane with the sheen of black satin, parted in the middle and flowing down either side of her pre-Columbian face. A certain charming quirkiness to her movements that had its own special reasons and rhymes. An infectious set of moods and an answer for everything – but her long bout of undeserved loneliness. A woman, like most women, of whom it could be said, she was eternally surprised by the nature of her own destiny.

However, these endearing traits had no personal significance for him, as Josh Free held to the strict separation of 'Church and State;' 'Church' being *affaires de coeur,* and would only worship at a woman's feet if she were standing at a respectable distance from his own backyard.

As for Doria herself, a five-year fixation on the whims and wonders of her rugged young boss had given her an extrasensory feel for what he required, even before he fully grasped it himself. Being half in love with him didn't hurt rapport either. She was the very seismograph of his soul. It was obvious to Doria this particular blustery afternoon, that Josh had hatched another Good Idea during his daily stroll. He would probably tell her to get the odious McShane on it.

'Get McShane on it,' Josh was saying in his Florida twang. 'See if he can dig up a real good human interest story on this woman.'

'Yes, Sir.' Doria's narrow face never once betrayed the adoration in which she held Joshua Free. That would be unprofessional, and Doria Sevenstars was above all a professional. It was her efficiency which had catapulted her to this giddy pinnacle of trust in the *Globe* organization, and she would never jeopardize her position with a display of schoolgirl emotions.

Shaking out her superb black fringe of hair, Doria came from around her desk.

Josh had shucked off his heavy fur coat, the colour of an after-sex smoke, and called her name.

'Doria.'

She'd brought her pad into his office. He was lying in wait behind the door.

'I thought you'd never get here.' He raised his arm above her head, and leaned it against the door, shutting it. She was caught.

'What would you say,' his ultramarine eyes travelled all over her willing body, so that she felt naked and hot and hungry as a wolf, 'if I told you I want to take you right now on my newly-shampooed office rug?'

'I'd say,' Doria gasped, as his warm, wet tongue lapped into her ear, 'that you're the boss, and can do whatever you . . .'

Doria never finished her sentence because she was watching her buttons magically opening, one by one, her clothes strewn by invisible hands all over the floor.

She was down to her champagne-satin camisole and tap pants. Not to be outdone in eagerness, she tugged at his heavy silver Western belt, let her fingers play at the feathery pelt exposed in the vee of his custom-made pure white shirt.

Now he slipped his strong arm around her waist, locking her in, and drew her down to the very carpet they'd been talking about.

She could feel his sinuous muscular weight flowing all the way down her body. She shivered. Her pelvis tingled as he tasted her like a delicacy.

He tarried in the silken hollow of her throat, roughly yanked down the spaghetti straps of the skimpy camisole, and cupping her breasts, played with their dark rosettes. His hands smoothed their way down her stomach, where he kneaded her glowing flesh until she burned at her epicentre, for his entry.

18

In a delirium, she ran her own hands down his back, to the taut crease of his buttocks. He moaned softly.

They rammed into one another with a wild energy, and they laughed out loud with the massive pleasure of it, the pure animal open-throated roar of it.

Doria had her man . . .

Just then, Josh Free reared up from behind his mammoth desk. Doria sighed. That delectable scene had been just another daydream.

'And damn it, Doria, why do I have to be the one to think of these things?' Josh was stalking about his plushly carpeted office, done up proud in serpentine green and mica black by a world-famous designer's own hand. The designer, it was rumoured, subsequently had a nervous breakdown. 'Where's my crack staff, hmm? Then they have the nerve to come crying to me that it's silly season, a slow news day. Bull! To a real reporter, it's never a slow news day in New York City!'

A familiar cry. A man fundamentally alone, who always walked a step ahead of his companions, Josh Free was proud of his proven skill at sounding excitement. And openly scornful of those who weren't quite as good. Like the time he'd just bought up his first failing East coast newspaper, with the money made on his brilliant real estate deals. He'd needed a major story to kick off the paper's debut, needed it desperately. So he got himself invited to a diplomatic reception in New York City, one he had no business being at, befriended the Pope's ethnic cook by exchanging culinary lore, and gained a Papal audience that way. It was thus the upstart Josh Free who broke the story that the Pope would be visiting a certain Eastern bloc country for the first time in history with an inflammatory message for that nation's Communist regime. The New York papers had eaten their hearts out with envy, not to say embarrassment.

Josh just laughed, grew richer and more influential with every unorthodox move into the highflying circles of international power. It was said he loved the challenge of the impossible more than anything, with the exception, perhaps, of a beautiful, and willing, always willing, woman.

19

Suddenly, Doria's back went up. She didn't even have to look to know the reason why. A face flat as a Sunday morning pancake, sprinkled with freckles like blueberries in the batter. Slitted silicon chips for eyes. An indelible sneer like a painter's mistake . . .

Tom Joad McShane (his mother had been a great fan of the late Henry Fonda) with features crumpled as his ancient grey flannel suit, had come into the office, and was polluting the space before her desk.

T.J., who was built compact and low to the ground like a tough little Skye terrier, was a bachelor with more pet peeves than a letters to the editors column. Among his long list: the hated yogurt-eaters, Brooke Shields-clones, and the entire 'Me' Generation, of which he was, at least chronologically, a member. With his witty squint, almost militarily cropped mahogany hair, and curmudgeon's credo, he was more comfortably set in the manly certainties of his father's time, than his own.

T.J. McShane made a positive religion of conservatism. Never would he relinquish over $75.00 for a suit, and, as Doria often maliciously pointed out, it showed, oh boy did it show! Never would he dream of plunking down a week's salary on an imperial pair of Bally wingtips from some fine Fifth Avenue shop. No sir, yellow Nike running shoes would do him just fine for those special occasions, thank you very much. Besides, they had a certain piquant effect when paired with his Scotch plaid wool scarf, blocked in squares of fire engine-red that could knock your eye out!

And he'd continue to wear that grey flannel suit and Buddy Holly tie until they unravelled into threads, like the silk off an ear of Iowa corn.

As for McShane's temper, it might best be described as an Irish stew at a slow boil, reminiscent of Mr Fields, the landlord in the old Abbot & Costello comedies. The crabbed set of his shoulders gave one to understand that the proverbial wind was hardly ever at his back, and that, somehow, you were personally to blame. In sharp contrast, however, he was most gentle and soft of speech after his forays into his favourite pub.

Doria Sevenstars only just tolerated T.J., the best reporter on the New York staff, because he was of demonstrable value to her boss. But their history of personal animus went back a long way.

Due to his boss's tight schedule, it was McShane who had interviewed her, screened her really, half a decade ago in Florida, when, as a Welfare mother of two children, abandoned by her alcoholic husband, and dazzled by the rush of bad luck, Doria applied to Free's first newspaper for a much-needed job.

In those days, it wasn't easy to find work, especially for a former 'Miss Florida', who had no bankable skills whatsoever but a smattering of typing and the drive of desperation.

McShane had cast his cynical eye over her and scribbled something on a piece of lined yellow paper.

The upshot was: no way in hell.

Another applicant was already halfway through the door, when Doria flung herself onto McShane's cluttered desk. Furiously, she yanked her file folder out of the mess of papers. Scrawled in bombshell red ink, next to her name was the verdict: 'Princess Ticklefeather – too pretty.'

'What the hell does this mean?' she heard herself hissing.

McShane averted his ferrous eyes. Uh oh, an anti-discrimination suit. The libbers would be down on him like a ton of bricks. He shouldn't have been so careless. But really now, how could he hire this candy-ass chick with the milk chocolate eyes? She probably never saw a blue pencil in her life . . .

'For your information, I deserve this job. I know I can do it!' The words of her Uncle Shon-tee sang in her head. 'In the five hundred years of our people's brave struggle, *Chat-hos-tee,* my daughter, no Seminole warrior has ever surrendered.'

'Yeah, how?' he asked, arms crossed, unimpressed.

'I know because . . . I'm a woman who's raising two kids on her own.'

'So are millions of other women.'

Doria's mind raced. She had to say the right words to this balky little bulldog in order to get him to take her seriously. 'Yes, that's true,' she shot back in desperation, 'but I survived.' Survival, the art of her people . . . 'And I will go on surviving no matter how many smirking male bureaucrats try to bury me! And my name is Doria Sharpe Sevenstars. Not Princess Ticklefeather!'

She was shaken by a rage that had been wired up inside her for a long, long time. Rage at Rick Sevenstars for making her body sing, at America for making him doubt his manhood, at herself for loving him too much.

It was short-circuiting now, sparking out all over, and there was nothing she could do about it . . .

Oh God, no, she'd lost control! She'd botched it! He was going to kick her out of his office and Fleur needed a new pair of shoes, and she didn't know where she was going to scrape up money for this month's rent. The honky-tonk streets of Miami beckoned to her. That was the next step down . . .

'How many words a minute do you type?' McShane asked with quixotic interest. Actually, he had only just noticed that, when angry, Doria rose up like a carving of polished teakwood to a handsome height. If a man kissed her, he imagined, her soft, mauve lips would seem twice as large, twice as yielding. He wondered if those fiercely intelligent eyes would ever go gentle – even in love. Doria was speechless.

'You have a hearing problem too?' he said dryly. 'I asked about your typing speed. Which I hope is half as good as your talking speed.'

'One hundred words a minute,' she lied giddily, 'and counting.'

He nodded. Without another word, he buzzed Josh in the next room. 'I'm sending someone to see you.' He jerked his thumb towards the inner office. 'Madam Sevenstars, go right on in. That performance was well worth it.'

Doria had only a split-second in which to compose herself. She need not have worried. With the uncanny sense Josh Free had for the fanatical creative spirit (what had reasonable people ever accomplished?), he recognized her immediately as one of his own. On a hunch that she would not be restricted to secretarial duties for long, he gave her a political piece to edit. When she was done, he skimmed the think column of words, and, apparently liking what he saw, explained that she would have to relocate. To New York, New York. Doria stared. She'd come in as one of the disinherited – she'd go out as part of an empire! The dazzling alteration in circumstances made her head spin, but somehow she gave him to understand that she'd be happy to relocate. To New York. Or Hoboken. Or Timbuktu . . .

Their association had lasted these five blissful years, during which time she'd come to love Joshua Free and to loathe the cocky T.J. McShane with an equally unbalanced passion.

'I hear the Salvation Army got in a new load of boots today. Why don't you check it out, T.J.?' Doria needled impassively, her white teeth glittering in the copper face.

'Nope, tonight I thought I'd read the next chapter of *The Last of the Mohicans*. Want to join me?'

Her smile tightened a notch. 'No thank you. Not that I wouldn't leap at spending a whole evening with you. It's just that I have more exciting things to do – like cleaning my oven.'

T.J. grinned broadly at this, revealing the lecherous gap between his two front teeth. 'What a sweet thing to say! It's obvious the woman adores me.'

'Hah!' Doria snickered. 'It's obvious that your brain is legally dead . . .'

'What the hell is going on out there?' Josh sounded like he was eating nails.

Doria went pale, unable to cope with Josh's displeasure, which she was usually clever enough to keep at bay.

T.J. had a different reaction.

Now what that man needed, T.J. observed for the hundredth time, was a woman. Not one of those stilt-legged glamour girls, their souls imprinted with dollar signs and designer labels, oh there were plenty of them for rich and restless Joshua Free, but a real till-death-do-us-part kind of woman, with full hips and a full heart. Someone to sink his life into. It would turn him on to a world beyond the office walls. And get him off T.J.'s aching back.

Somehow it had never occurred to T.J. that Doria Sevenstars might be that woman. True, she was matrix rock, rich and dense. But she would weigh down the soul, stick in the throat, like too-heavy fruitcake. Besides, he couldn't imagine not having the Princess for himself, to taunt and hassle and harry at will. They belonged to each other in enmity: they were wed in orneriness. Her beautiful face hid the most cussed stubborn spirit he'd ever run into – maybe one even more stubborn than his own. That, in itself was a source of endless fascination for T.J. McShane.

'T.J.! Get your skinny ass in here!'

McShane blew Doria a mocking kiss as he headed into Free's office, her pretty scowl being the last thing he saw before he was sucked into the whirlwind of Josh's brutal energy.

CHAPTER TWO

The imposing grey stone edifice of Graff-Lowell Clinic sat in a sprawling green park off York Avenue where river breezes and the smell of freedom incongruously blew.

Cerretti had taken the woman there because, in his neat mind, quality belonged with quality. Satisfied he'd left her in capable hands, he went on his way.

After extensive testing and two days of bedrest, the patient had been diagnosed as an amnesiac with severe symptoms. Then, in a stroke of good fortune, Dr Alfred Beckstein, internationally renowned for his groundbreaking work in the treatment of this disorder, agreed to assume her case.

'She's in Room 217,' the day nurse told the slight, silver-bearded man with the distinct foreign accent and the dark, expressive eyes of a rabbinical scholar.

Dr Beckstein nodded and set off down the long, softly lit corridor to the corner room. The only survivor of World War II among his German-Jewish family, he'd been lucky enough to get out of Germany, before the Nazi web tightened, on a cargo ship bound for Africa. From thence, he'd come to America.

Because of the enormity of the evil he'd seen, the inexpressibility of his personal experience, Dr Beckstein had been forced to search far afield for the keys to unlock the human mind. Thus, his reputation for controversial therapies – and for boundless mercy.

As he was a man tempered by the sorrows of his age, his patients seemed to recognize his kinship to them – and to derive comfort from the unshakeable rock of his strength and compassion. Cerretti had indeed done well. One day, the woman would thank his anonymous kindness in bringing her to Dr Beckstein – and new life. But for now, at least, she seemed as unconscious of the hand holding her up from the pit – as she was of the pit itself.

They had told him she was found wandering in a fugue state, a victim of severe hysterical amnesia that had left her without memory, even of such basic things as the taste of apples.

Beckstein slowly opened the door to 217. He felt at such times as though he were entering another world on special visa, the unique world of a human psyche, with its own laws, its own gods. Over the years, he'd trained himself not to anticipate what he would find there. It was folly, even blasphemy, to try.

Sitting against the sun that streamed through her window, she was a figure out of a dream. His gaze went straight to her languid hands, resting in her lap like flightless butterflies on a bed of flowers; after that to her face, smooth and enigmatic as a child's. With her slim waist and drooping neck, she had the satin glow of a nineteenth century ballerina. He felt as though he were regarding her through a jeweller's loupe.

Troubled by the cascade of sunlight, Dr Beckstein closed his eyes.

He put out a hand to steady himself against the white-washed wall. Only gradually did he become aware that the woman behind whom the sunlight rained had that look of vulnerability and puzzlement at the cruelty of the world, as though she expected better at their hands. She had that air, how well he knew it, of youthful tragedy, to be later unfolded like a dark bloom.

He must save her from that flowering. Somehow he promised himself fiercely, he would save her . . .

In the constant company of pain, she did not even notice him, could not tell whether she had lived or died, the world had so little in it that was familiar to her. She suspected she must be alive, though, because the women in white with their big, scrubbed faces kept shoving metal trays at her, heaped high with hot-steamed foods smelling of earth that made her want to retch. If they urged her to eat, she mustn't be dead, must she? Still, how stupid of them to imagine they could keep her anchored to this strange white place with bits of bone and shards of green, if she really decided to leave. She could feel herself growing lighter, incorporeal, with every passing hour: It was her secret. Soon she could just rise out of the window, with the other forms of light, and escape to the world beyond pain.

At times she thought the tumult in her head was a good thing. It gave her focus. Otherwise, it was just too hard to pinpoint boundaries, as ceilings, walls and floor merged and solid objects flew through space before her eyes. Worst of all was when other people went slanting by, their voices yapping at her from across great, dizzying voids. Sometimes she tried to answer. Mostly, she did not. Maybe they thought she was rude, but it was important for her to be still and to wait for the signal she knew would come. If only she could shake the queasy feeling that when the message was finally given, she might not recognize it after all . . .

She drew a painful breath.

Had it always felt like this, to be alive, as though she were trapped beneath the sea and had to hold her breath to survive? Yet where would she go if the air were the vast ocean that pressed upon her lungs and made her head scream? She was caught, oh God, she was caught beneath the sea . . .

Dr Beckstein could feel the terror that impaled his patient like a butterfly upon a pin. Her hands fluttered in her lap as though she would speak through them. Her deep-set violet eyes were haunted as if she were questioning why she'd been punished, as if she suspected that merely to be alive were to offend.

Dr Beckstein warily approached his new patient. If he were to know her secrets, he must walk lightfooted across her soul.

Kindly, he held out a tray of food which had been left on her night table. The nurses had said that she'd refused to touch solid food since her arrival at Graff-Lowell.

The woman stared over at the tray, then away.

Dr Beckstein laid it aside again, and settling across from her at the sunny window, sat in tacit communion with her. Somehow he understood this was what was required of him, as though a mysterious exchange of energies must take place, and he must become like her to know her.

As night fell and darkness came over the room like a woman's mood, altering its texture and shape with shadow, he began to see that he'd been privileged to stay with her, permitted to taste her suffering, and for the first time in many long years, to look into the face of his own.

At last, after a week of their silent ritual – the putting aside of the proffered food (some of which she ate after Dr Beckstein left, as if to reward him), sitting together in the quiet room, in acceptance, the patient overjoyed the healer by reaching out . . .

'You are kind,' she said one grey, blurred day much like every other winter day. 'You don't have to be kind.'

'Don't I?' the doctor asked, strangely moved by the sound of her voice, so profoundly sad like a soul lost at sea.

'No. No one does.'

He didn't want to push her too far, but he had to know certain facts of her inner being. 'What do you look at all day?'

'Myself.'

'And who is that?'

'No one. Everyone. Sometimes I think I'm the luckiest person in the world, because I've been given a second chance. I can be anyone I want to be, take a whole new stance in my life.' Suddenly, she began to weep.

He resisted an urge to touch her. 'Then why are you crying?'

'Because I'm so lucky.'

Dr Beckstein was pleased. Emotion. It was a good sign. The ice around her senses, her memory, was cracking away. Now their work could begin.

She smiled sideways at him, as though she knew what he was thinking. Dr Beckstein suspected it was really because she was afraid, and needed a friend.

So their talks continued, painstakingly, day by day. For him, it was a labour of love.

For her, it was a limitless well of fears. All that darkness inside her head, oh God, would it never end . . .

There was one recurring dream, or was it an imperfect memory, of a sun-haired young man. She couldn't make out his face, but he would rear up, incandescent, from a darkness tense with strange and wonderful melody. Barely touching her, he would grace her face, her hair, her breasts with fingers light as air, and her blood would grow so hot, so heavy in her veins, that she must fall to the ground at his feet. Dropping to his knees, he would press her to his bright chest, and the scent of wildflowers in the darkness would grow so thick she could hardly breathe through it. Then she would behold herself – and be amazed.

For the flowers would be gushing up crazily from her eyes, her mouth, her marrow. Long, heavy racemes of Japanese red, like chains, on saffron yellow garlands of baby-soft daisies, latticing her breast, twirling about her slender limbs. She was a live green spring garden and he must pluck the blooms from her to make room for more and then more . . .

At this point in the dream, the weird music darkened in timbre to the blast of a winter storm. The woman appeared with her damning eyes, melding with the storm into one awesome entity, blowing the cold, hard wind that swept the Bright One from his lover's bed.

Every night, he waited for her on the other side of the sky, across a misty chasm, and beckoned her to cross.

Terrified, she would set foot on the ropey, swinging bridge as the storm, in wild voices of tympani and flute, went shrieking through the air around her.

In the end, the dreams had her pitching backward into a violet abyss that stretched down forever. Dear God, how she would scream and scream, but the real horror was, no sound would come out of her mouth, no one would ever hear, not even the Bright One who still held out his loving arms . . .

As the dream faded, she would hear a voice clearly saying, 'Tell me the name that is written on your heart.'

Fearful again, she glanced at the chair opposite, where the man with the beard would sit. Dr Beckstein, yes. He was the only light in the great cloud of her days. If only she could reach back – touch the darkness – remember . . . Instead, the trembling would come upon her, the nightmares.

When she was first taken to the hospital, she didn't trust anyone, not even him. But then she did trust him. It was his steady hands, and the way he had of looking her straight in the eye. The others never did that, the big nurses in their heavy-soled shoes, the pious doctors who tried to bleach out their clinical smell with expensive hand-milled soaps. No, they all looked away, embarrassed at her pain.

She wondered if Dr Beckstein, too, was lost.

If when he held out his arms, he too touched the darkness.

Perhaps the two of them shared a secret only they could bear . . .

CHAPTER THREE

Outside, liveried chauffeurs, slim and upright in waiting Mercedes. Inside, red leather, silver urns and horsey prints.

It was New York's elite '21 Club', where the host of the upstairs dining room had just seated newspaper mogul, Joshua Free, at the very best corner table. Free was lunching at 'Jack & Charlie's' with his crony of fifteen years, T.J. McShane, not so much for his love of the cuisine, as for the perverse delight he took in the ongoing feud between the restaurant staff and the cantankerous young reporter.

McShane invariably ordered a beer, brewed as close to home as possible if only imported were on tap, while Josh would ask for 'Khisu,' a trendy Korean mineral water at $4.50 a glass, to clear the palate for a wildly expensive Lafite-Rothschild, if only to have the supreme pleasure of hearing McShane mutter darkly against 'fancypants frog swill' within earshot of the haughty sommelier.

T.J. was thus his boss's answer to every high-priced pretension of the New York scene. As such, he was indispensable to Josh Free's mental hygiene. Homely as an overstuffed dinner of corned beef and Guinness, McShane could sniff out highfalutin foppery at thirty paces, and like a loyal watchdog, kept Josh's life relatively nonsense-free. As a direct consequence, he was permitted to say things to his boss that would earn most employees the boot.

'So, why pretend you're here for lunch?' T.J. was grumbling. 'You never actually put anything in your mouth, but your foot. You're too busy chewing on that damned phone!' He waved in disgust at the black telephone squatting on their table. Free had just conducted a high-level conversation with the distinguished Senior Senator from New York, and the Ambassador of Lebanon, during which McShane had consumed his own as well as Free's lunch of steak tartare and petits pois while he eavesdropped shamelessly. His saggy features seemed to slip even further down his face. Free was the man who knew everyone, but never let anyone know, or care, for him. 'Can't the world live without you for two bloody hours? What are you, the Pope?'

'No, he likes Lutece.' Josh humorously motioned him to be quiet. 'By the way, you gave it a good try with the "Jane Doe" story. Too bad they didn't let you up to see her.'

The phone jangled again. This time it was Nicole on the line. Josh's blue-green eyes deepened a shade.

'Yes, you were right, I am lunching at "21" today.' He spoke calmly enough, but McShane could see the tension already settling into his face, as it invariably did whenever Josh got anywhere near his ex-wife. It seemed he was still looking to fix blame for their divorce on some outside force, because it hurt too much not to. But everytime Nicole mentioned her new life, the home, the children, Josh Free looked like a man whose heart was breaking, again. She only reminded him of what he was missing, would always miss . . .

The corners of T.J.'s mouth dipped down. Nicole's call was good for at least a week of terror in the newsroom. Her visit, whenever it struck, would be good for another week more.

With the hated phone finally whisked away, Josh turned his formidable attention on T.J., his Celtic god of perversity. Nothing impressed, nothing pleased McShane, who went the way of contrariety in all things. Once, when Josh was holding forth on the scenic glories of Nova Scotia, McShane had shrugged and commented, 'Beauty, hah! I've seen enough beauty to last me a lifetime.'

Josh never tired of telling this tale on his disputatious friend. But that was the key word: 'friend'. T.J. was an unimpeachable friend to Josh Free.

Josh sipped his wine thoughtfully. He'd have to make it up to T.J. for this wasted lunch hour. Maybe front-row seats for the Rangers. T.J. loved anything you needed a helmet for . . .

Just then, the waiter bustled over to their table, self-importantly, bearing a chilled split of Taittinger's champagne. 'With the lady's compliments.' He bobbed his head at the glamorous party across the room. As Josh swivelled in his seat, a fabulous face from the glossy pages of Harpers pouted at him. That was all it took. Flashing an apologetic grin at McShane, Free rose and presented himself, like the arch Southern gentleman he was, at her flowering table.

Left now to his own devices. McShane ordered another lonely beer, built a matchstick pyramid on the tabletop, and exchanged dirty looks with the head waiter. Only then did he leave, knowing full well that when Josh got back to the office that afternoon, a measure of the tension in his body, at least, would have been melted cleanly away in the arms of Miss Debutante, while he, with all the aggravation the man had handed him, would probably come down with a peptic ulcer . . . or two.

Wasn't that always the way?

Her neat white room, 217, had become the hub of the universe for Dr Beckstein, her small ceramic lamp the miniature sun lighting his way. Never before had Alfred Beckstein been so profoundly in love with a case, as through the encamped winter days, he delved into the patient's psyche, excavating for the sunken door that would open up on to the labyrinth of her past.

Who was the shrill woman and 'The Bright One', who, night after night, drew the young woman into his arms? And why hadn't his patient's family yet found a way to reclaim such a precious member? The girl's remnants of memory were highly erotic and charged with fear, a fact which only added to her soft mystery.

She must have come from hell into his care . . .

The doctor's comfortable office, dressed in tradition, was filled with shifting shadows that memorable morning, as a rainstorm shook the trees outside his twentieth-floor window. His green-shaded desk lamp threw the only illumination in the book-lined room. His patients seemed to like it that way; it was always somehow easier to talk in semi-darkness. An untouched tray of Viennese coffee in a white porcelain pot lay on a side table, the one soft, domestic touch in the otherwise Spartan setting.

She had come in to see him with an unquiet air that day, as though she'd sensed his excitement about this particular session.

'How are you today?' he'd asked, motioning her to sit on the chair beside his desk.

'I didn't sleep well last night.' She was looking out the rain-washed windows.

'The dreams again?'

'Yes?'

'Did you do what I told you? Did you stand your ground and question the characters in the dream about who they were and what they wanted from you?'

She shook her head. 'I was too afraid.' Her hands twisted in her lap.

'That's all right,' Dr Beckstein soothed. 'That's all right. You'll try it again another night.'

'And what about the tunes?'

That had been something new. Every once in a while, she'd said, these little melodies went churning around in her head. She didn't know where they came from, but was happy for the companionship.

'Yes, they're coming more often now. They're so lovely and sad – I wish I knew where I'd learned them!'

'Will you hum one for me now? Perhaps I can tell you the name of the song.'

'I'm sorry,' she said, 'but they go out of my head as soon as they come in . . . I can't remember.'

'All right.'

In his attempt to get in touch with her repressed memories, he had even tried hypnosis during a previous session. But the patient in 217 had been a poor and resistant subject, refusing to accept his suggestions, some evidence, at least, of a stronger will than the doctor had credited.

But then, in reading a new commentary on the work of Carl Jung, he'd come across the use of the Tarot deck as a trigger for the subconscious.

34

The young clerk at Brentano's on Fifth Avenue had stared when he'd purchased the colourful Marseilles fortune-telling deck. Dr Beckstein had brought them to their session today, sensing the thrill of a breakthrough in the air.

'Some coffee?' he offered, to put her at ease.

'No, thank you.'

'Then we'll just get to work, shall we?'

He took the box out of his desk drawer and opened it.

He had decided to approach it like a game.

After smiling at her, he spread out the twenty-two major cards on his desk, from the wise 'Fool' to the window on eternity that is 'The World'.

She seemed surprised at first, then leaned out of her chair and began to look over his shoulder with great interest. The cards pulsed with a mysterious life of their own.

'All right now,' he said in an even voice, 'I want you to look at these cards which represent different rites of passage in our lives. Some of these pictures, I realize, seem frivolous, others forbidding. But all of them are extremely ancient, powerful symbols that every human being holds in his or her own mind.'

She was quiet now, intent on viewing every card.

'Now,' the doctor sat back in his chair. 'Without thinking too much, pick up the card or cards that most appeal to you, that most speak to you.'

She hesitated. 'I feel silly.'

'It's good to feel silly once in a while. It's liberating to play and imagine. Go on.'

The patient's hand hovered over the cards, then almost immediately, she picked up the card called 'The Lovers' which pictures a handsome young man who seems to be torn between a mature looking woman and a beautiful young maiden.

'Good.' 'The Lovers', Dr Beckstein knew, had to do with a romantic triangle, or the choice a young man must make between two women he loves. It was a situation which could only be solved by a leap of intuition.

Next, she tapped her fingernail on 'The Empress',

which suggests the feminine principle, and, according to Jungian research, a voracious mother figure (perhaps the mother was one of the women in the romantic triangle of 'The Lovers'.)

'There's something about this one . . .' the patient said.

'Yes?' Dr Beckstein edged forward in his chair, as the rain pattered against the window.

'I can't explain it. I'm attracted to it, and repelled at the same time.'

'Yes. I see.' Very interesting. The literature on the subject mentioned that whenever our lives are blocked into rigid dichotamies, the 'Empress' inside oneself must be called upon to heal us with, of all things, womanly love.

Dr Beckstein paused. 'Anything else?'

She stared for a long moment with her faraway eyes and, sighing, set her fingers down on the most bestial and to Dr Beckstein, the most fascinating card in the deck. 'The Devil', with his leathery wings and claws.

'I don't know why I chose that one. I think it's horrible.'

'That's all right. Think of it as the Dark Angel. We all have a Dark Angel.'

Dr Beckstein studied the woman for a moment. Yes, even this lovely creature had a dark side, with which she must struggle. Her choice of 'The Devil' betrayed her terror, as well as a fascination with the dual nature of the Self.

With these clues in hand, Dr Beckstein began to see that what had appeared to be weakness in his patient's psyche was actually a species of strength. He had observed that even though she was eating more of late, she never seemed to gain weight, but instead was fading, marking each morning by how much lighter she had grown during the night. Her skin, she'd said, felt brittle and thin as eggshells. Her hair was a dull lustre of antique gold in the lamplight. All her energy seemed focused, the muscles of her lovely face tense and drawn in a concentration of labour which seemed to deplete her physically: the labour of willed forgetting. As the English poet, Matthew Arnold said, 'We forget because we must/And not because we will.'

Elated by these revelations. Dr Beckstein smiled at his patient, who asked if she could go back to her room now, she was so tired.

For the first time, she had taken breakfast with the other patients in the spacious dining room with the butter-coloured walls. How good it felt to be out of her airless chamber, to mix with living people again! Lately, her world was too full of ghosts and whispers.

For a special treat they were having fresh, hulled strawberries, imported from California. She crushed the sweet fruit with the tip of her tongue, and let the juice fill her mouth with cool delight.

There was something else to make her happy today.

Today, there would be a session with Dr Beckstein.

Almost as if to please him, she was starting to remember impersonal, non-threatening facts – historical dates, mathematical formulae, the residue of a college education. She had also betrayed, much to her own surprise, a knowledge of fluent Italian.

She could see the tall, marble-faced Reverend Mother at Latin lessons. 'The ablative of "agricola", Signorina . . .?' By what name did she call her? She stole envious looks at the diners around her. All these lucky people had names . . . she strained to see her own. But no, it was still blurred, a window after heavy rain. Her mind would hold out the promise of a complete memory – then snatch it away like a teasing boy on a picnic in May.

Piangi, piangi, madonna trista. Ma più nulla. Non lo rammento.

If only she could picture a letter addressed to her, a doorbell with a nameplate, the hundred different ways one is summoned by family, friends, official strangers. None of it yielded any hope.

She set down her spoon, suddenly taken over by a desperate thought. What if she weren't meant to remember? Ever. Maybe that was her punishment for great personal sinfulness (she must have done something very bad – the woman in the dreams cursed her and the

'Bright One' taken away) – or for the original fault: the sin of being alive.

Never to know if somewhere there were a parent, husband or child, a best friend or colleague waiting for her, hurting for her because she had left them without word! It was a daily torment, to think she might be giving intolerable pain to someone she once loved. And not to know if anyone loved *her* at all. Oh, not to be loved . . .

The pain in her head flared again. She held her hands to her temples and swayed rhythmically. The nurse hurried over. Luckily, Dr Beckstein was scheduled to see this one today. It seemed that only he could comfort his patient. No one understood quite why . . .

She herself knew why, as the dull-eyed nurse led her back to her room to wait for Dr Beckstein. It was as if he too had left behind a precious friend – and would never be free to love again.

It was all right that they were taking her out of the dining room. Because now she had all this time to herself, to prepare for his coming through that door . . .

She had begun to look forward to his visits, primping her lovely, silken hair, softly rolled at the sides, knitted into a chignon at the back; wheedling lipstick from the night nurses so that she could redden her pretty lips; wearing her sky-blue crepe de chine dress bought on a shopping tour with one of the paramedics. No wonder the others had begun to comment on how she perked up at his presence and how the formidable Dr Beckstein softened at a glance from the mysterious patient in 217.

Doria Sevenstar's typewriter clattered to a halt.

Quickly, she hooded it with the black vinyl cover, then flipped open a compact, checked hair and make-up and smoothed the day's kinks out of her tomato-red knit sheath. Her bronze cheekbones gleamed above the high-notched collar.

She wanted to look especially fine tonight.

Down below her window, the snow-dusted city was gearing up for a gala night at the pitch of the winter season. Long, black limousines, like submarine creatures behind aquarium glass, wended their way to museum openings, theatrical debuts, and that rare dinner party where the conversation was even better than the cuisine. Department stores dangled their lures of tinsel and red velvet ribbon. Homebound workers bought chestnuts on icy street corners to warm the hands as much as the stomach, while shoppers pored over the holiday windows and planned their celebrations.

Doria ran over her own plans for the night's festivities. The children, the *chee,* would come: seven-year-old Fleur, *Im-pock-pock-ee,* 'The Flower,' escorted by her elder brother, Benjamin, twelve. They would all go to see the new Spielberg movie and then the birthday boy would choose a restaurant for their dinner. With a twinge of amusement, Doria suspected it would either be McDonald's or Blimpie's, as Ben was at the age when anything more elaborate than red meat and white bread slapped together was considered sissy stuff.

At five-fifteen, on the dot, the children arrived in a burst of day-glo jackets and wind-brightened faces.

She gathered them to her. Her daughter, sinking into her belly, rubbing the soft, raven-wing's hair against her mother's cheek. Her son pulling away too soon, embarrassed at his own pleasure at being so fiercely loved.

They were full of pleasant babble about the schoolday. Ben had been named quarterback for the school team. Fleur's gold-brushed painting of maize was nailed up in Art Class.

Then, as Doria had secretly, fervently wished, Josh was drawn from his inner sanctum by the lilt of the children's voices.

As usual, Doria gave no hint of the fires that burned her, lest she risk the destruction of their professional relationship.

It hadn't always been that way with Doria, though.

There had been a time when she had hazarded everything on her passion for a tall, dreamy husband who drank too much when the work on the truck farms and cattle ranches dried up. She might have stayed with Rick Sevenstars forever, if only for those nights under the

39

shadows of wild oak and magnolia, when he held her in his strong arms and spoke to her about the running pickerel and the Chief of Snakes, the strong magic of the *wil-lis-waw*, and the campfire blaze in the weird marshes where the alligator bayed and the plume birds danced in the silvery cypress of the Seminole 'Flower Land'.

But when the children came, the mother in her took over from the passionate lover, and for their sakes, she could no longer tolerate the bitter weakness of the man she loved. By matriarchal tribal law, which teaches respect for women and will even raise up the wisest to 'sachem', the children belong to the mother. The desperate loneliness belonged to her as well.

Even before Rick Sevenstars, the warmth of family, so important to her tribe, had vanished from her life. Mother had been the first of the Shon-tee women to break with Indian ways. She'd stopped celebrating the Green Corn Ceremony, spoke only English, cut the bonds to clan and custom when she married Frederick Sharpe, a white man, who ran a small dry goods store in St Augustine. Pining for her people, she had wasted away in a few years' time, leaving little Doria to her father's care. A patient, pious man with a permanent look of dismay on his lean face, he had raised her to the best of his widower's ability. Then, when Doria was seventeen, he had remarried, a white woman this time, and moved to San Diego. He had never even seen his two grandchildren. Doria had always suspected it was she of whom he had been so secretly ashamed.

With the gentle touch of a much smaller man, Josh brushed back Fleur's midnight hair, and, although it was not her day, gifted her with a pastel tin of the Georgian fruits – a jumble of papaya, slices of coconut, sunny apricots, dates, and raisins – that she loved. Fleur received it as though it were a box of jewels.

'So you're a football player now.' With the air of mystery grownups like to assume on children's birthdays, Josh held a foil-wrapped package high behind his back. 'Well then, you're going to need this.'

Benjamin also accepted his gift with dignity.

Inside the package was a professional-looking green-and-white football helmet, autographed by Richard Todd himself. 'Thanks, Mr Free. I mean, this is like, awesome.'

Josh beamed over their heads at Doria Sevenstars.

Face to face with her fantasy, she panicked. Once she had followed a strange man down four city blocks simply because he wore the same elusive aftershave as Free – lime, orange peel, pimiento and leaf oil of the bay tree. If he ever touched her in passion, she feared her heart would go pop like a firecracker, her knees would turn to spumoni . . .

Reckless with love, she took the plunge. 'Would you like to come with us for a movie and dinner, Josh?'

'Oh my darling,' Josh swept down on her, picking her up from under the arm pits, lifting her high in the air with his smoothly rippling arms. 'I want to share junk-food dinners with you every night of the week. I want to sit beside you at the movies for the rest of my life. Don't you know I love you, you little fool?'

Her heels kicked at the sky with wanton joy. 'I always dreamed you'd say that, one day . . .'

The children's eyes glowed like the citrines she'd seen in Harry Winston's window.

They'd have a daddy . . .

By the time Doria crashed down from her daydream, Josh was already swinging on the bristling grey beaver coat that made him look like some grand barbarian king.

'Oh, hey, a movie and dinner with you guys sounds a lot better than the night I have ahead of me. But I'm afraid I'm due for drinks and a bull session with the Mayor, and I already cancelled out once before.' Fondly, he ruffled Fleur's hair. 'See you tomorrow, Doria.' The next thing she knew he was out the door, beyond her reach . . .

Doria's ego sank. She peered at the hours in Toyland stretching ahead of her, suddenly daunted by the prospect of cold burgers and hot Video games. Why fool herself? That man would never see her as anything more than the indispensable Ms Sevenstars.

Doria was so busy nursing her misery, she hadn't noticed that, like an ill wind, T.J. McShane had blown in from the corridor, and that he and her Benjamin were presently engaged in a lively discussion of field goals and penetration zones, while Fleur climbed on to his denim knee and pretended to understand it all.

Doria felt herself coming down with a snit. Well, actually, why should she mind the intrusion? At this point, the children's tastes ran the whole gamut from Ronald McDonald to KISS. T.J. McShane, she thought with some malicious satisfaction, surely fit in somewhere between.

She was not prepared, however, for the next turn of events . . .

'Why don't you come with us, Mr McShane?' her son asked innocently. 'We're gonna have a real bitchin' time.'

'Ben!' Doria shot a warning glance at Fleur, who, happily oblivious, was fussing with the lid of the dried-fruit tin. Doria didn't know for whom she felt more humiliated: herself or the children. What if T.J. thought she were some poor Miss Lonelyhearts, coaching her son to scrounge dates for his mother? Her heart melted as she looked down at her Ben. What if McShane, flinty, squinty, hardnosed McShane, felt pity for her fatherless boy! That, above all, she couldn't bear. Not pity. Not from, oh God, T.J. McShane . . .

'It's time to go, children. Or we'll be late for the movie,' she called brightly, shepherding them out of the office as fast as she could manage.

'Hey, hold on there!'

For perhaps the first time, Doria detected a touch of confusion, a misplaced step in her adversary, who actually seemed to have gone pale right down to the freckles. She pivoted on her heel, arrested by the intriguing sound of this new voice.

'You didn't ask me if I wanted to go, Princess.' The old, cool mockery seemed to vie with another, warmer note in his brown eyes.

'Well, it's Ben's birthday,' her voice was as thin as her patience. 'He gets to make the choices tonight.'

T.J. winced. 'Thanks a lot. In other words, if they can stomach me, you can too,' he said under his breath so that only she could hear.

'Read my lips,' she retorted, wishing, for once, that he, and not Josh, were just a figment of her imagination.

The hard glint returned. He set his houndstooth cap at a jaunty angle atop his head. 'So be it,' he taunted, 'Princess.'

Flanked by the traitors in goosedown, he strutted out, bluffing to their rapt delight, about the time he whopped Ali at arm wrestling.

Doria switched out the overhead track lights.

It was going to be a long, dark night.

CHAPTER FOUR

The night was a cobalt-crystal globe, brimming over with moonlight. Along the park outside Graff-Lowell, a stark row of lamps illumined a glisten of white, crosshatched by the wave of tree branches, like an ink and wash sketch. Although the thick nape of snowfall muted all sound, there could occasionally be heard the distant pop of a car door as Christmas Eve celebrants stepped ankle-deep into the unploughed city streets.

How sad for the children, the night nurse thought, moving from the window and seating herself at the old warhorse of a grand piano. To be found in such a place on such a night! There should be tempting boxes piled high under a giant evergreen tree, young friends to warm their hearts, family to care . . .

But these were the children of misfortune, the ones left behind. Some of them were very beautiful indeed, with their blank eyes and smooth faces, as if life hadn't yet marked their bodies with the sign of her profound disfavour. Still, at night, they howled like the river wind, and their ward smelled of disinfectant and despair.

She played the opening chords of 'Jingle Bells', her fingertips heavy with pity on the keys. It was the least she could do for the poor little things. The children seemed to be cheered by the music, even if some of them didn't sing along. The notes, scratchy as old tin, bounced off the walls in the high-ceilinged rumpus room, hung round with crayoned drawings of bad dreams and broken promises.

Nurse Rader was so absorbed by the fingers that wouldn't fall right, it was some time before she noticed that her garland of children had been joined by the amnesia patient with the haunting eyes.

The woman hovered close by the piano, head bowed low, as though apologetic for having inlaid her sorrows against those of the children.

The youngsters stopped singing. They became fitful and fell to bickering among themselves. They twirled their hair about their fingers and worked their mouths like hungry, newborn birds. One of them wept.

The nurse abruptly lifted her balky fingers from the keyboard. The music trailed off.

'Would you like to play something, dear?' she asked in a soothing voice. 'Is that why you're here?'

When the patient nodded, the nurse immediately made way for the young woman to approach the piano.

As she floated down to the bench, her soft blue dress billowed out like the corolla of a cornflower.

Then, with tears sliding down her cheeks, she poised her hands over the keys and began to play a simple air. It was 'Michelle'. She played it solemnly, like a hymn. She played it well. She played it again and again, until the children, already excited by her strange behaviour were moved to protest.

'Make her stop,' wailed the girl with the hollow face.

'Another song. Do another song.'

The nurse lowered her strong hands on to the patient's shoulders. 'That's all right, dear.'

The young woman immediately froze. The light went out in her face.

Once the nurse had walked her safely back to her room, she rushed to call Dr Beckstein.

'Come quickly,' she had said when his wife put him on the line. 'Something is happening with the new amnesia case!'

The doctor brought a sharp wedge of cold with him into her hothouse room . . . tomb . . . womb, sometimes she got the words mixed up . . .

When he saw her in the chair by the window, the cornflower blue dress flowing about her legs, he became excited as a boy. He fingered the spray of white violets, impulsively bought and secreted in his coat pocket, on the way to the hospital that holiday eve. Knowing how much she liked pretty things, this lady with sad eyes the colour of *Wasser*, wild plums of his childhood, he'd thought they might calm her. 'The nurse tells me you were playing a song. Why did you keep playing that particular tune?'

She tilted her head and Dr Beckstein was reminded of camellia petals on a stalk bent back by the wind. She did not seem to know what to answer him, although she was quite eager to please.

'Who is Michelle? An old doll? A childhood friend? Think back, imagine the face of this "Michelle" . . .'

But at the repeated sound of the name, she became deeply agitated, and Dr Beckstein concluded it must be something more than this. Perhaps once she was herself 'Michelle', a dainty melody of a name. Enchanting. He would call her 'Michelle'.

He settled back into his chair, waiting for her to break the silence.

'Thank you for coming,' she said at last, and he was astounded by the rage of tenderness that swept over him. Like a magician under the lights, he pulled out the tiny curl of white violets, and proferred them to 'Michelle'. The years fell away. He was young and strong again. 'For you.' It was then the spell was shattered, for both of them, as she shrank back from the blooms with an expression of profound disgust on her beautiful face.

'Death and decay. These are pretty dead things. Make her take them away!'

'Yes, yes.' Thrown into confusion, he rang for Nurse Rader. 'Will you dispose of these, Nurse?' he asked gruffly when she came in.

Nan Rader met his eyes in understanding. 'I should have told you before, Doctor, this patient will not water the plants in the ward or tolerate any cut flowers in her room. She seems to have a special horror of growing things.'

'They are diseased,' Michelle spoke again, 'with mortality. They are already dead when they are born.' Her skin was the colour of blue ashes; her hands shook; she panted for breath. 'Have to get out . . . can't breathe with them in here . . .' Pale, she rose from her chair.

At that moment, with this sight of his patient's terrible fragility and need, Dr Beckstein snapped forever out of his living dream. Pity and shame burned in his heart for having made her more than what she was, out of his own weakness.

He stayed with her, in the darkened room, until her breath came easy, her colour flooded back, and Dr Beckstein knew he'd been forgiven.

The night sky had deepened from royal blue to pitch black by the time Dr Beckstein emerged from Graff-Lowell's wooded park to the busy street below. Already the crisp pathway of snow had been trampled into liquorice-tinted slush. A freezing, steady rain sliced down over the holiday city, as he set his steps towards home.

CHAPTER FIVE

At first, Doria called it coincidence and then plain bad luck that T.J. McShane would just happen to drop by her office whenever the kids were coming to meet her after work, or that Saturday morning would find him in front of her Chelsea apartment house with a fistful of Mylar balloons, or a Chinese dragon kite to fly.

But when such incidents began to pile up that holiday season like slush in a Manhattan gutter, she had to suspect a puckish will behind it.

What could she do? The man she'd specialized in hating had been smitten by her son and daughter. Even worse, if the light in their faces when he came slouching into view were any accurate indication, they'd fallen hopelessly in love with him.

Could there have been a switch back there in the hospital nursery? Were these really her children?

Slyly, patiently, Doria had tried to cajole the youngsters out of their strange affections, seizing every opportunity to heap scorn on McShane's cartoonish couture, the goofy yellow shoes, the moth-eaten scarf, the West Point cut. In turn, they staunchly defended him, proclaiming him 'fun to look at', 'tubular', and 'a really cool guy'.

In vain did Doria fill their weekend and school's-out schedules with a whirligig of activities – circuses, children's theatre, movie matinees, reasoning that, in the way of most fickle young minds, her offspring would soon enough consign McShane to the scrapheap of last year's toys.

Instead, they only begged all the louder for McShane's fulsome company, or, in the rare event of his absence from their circle, speculate endlessly on what T.J. would have thought of this clown's performance, that brontosaurus' pea brain, etc. For Doria, it was a comic nightmare by Disney.

As if this weren't enough to unnerve her, she had caught herself responding to a quirky warmth in the man. God help her if she'd been brought low enough to sort of like him, the way she sort of liked cold showers in heatless winter, or French cheese so mouldy it ran off her plate.

Matters were faring no better on the office scene, for ex-wife Nicole's Yuletide visit to New York with her toddling family had left Josh Free in a foul mood indeed. He hadn't even asked Doria, resplendent in gold tissue, for a dance at the company Christmas party at Bond Street, a yearly embrace of which Doria dreamed months in advance. Now she'd have to wait for the earth to roll around the sun all over again, before she could get into a good clinch with the man she loved.

In gloomy retrospect, it was T.J. who had seemed to turn up everywhere that godawful night. He'd bought new shoe laces for the occasion and kept giving her lemon-sucking smiles, his attempts, she supposed at Dickensian bonhomie, as a special holiday treat. Heartlessly, she had condemned him, if only for not being Joshua Free . . .

In a fit of female pique, she had stormed out of the light-flashing disco with a creep of a political correspondent who took her to the Mudd Club, got crashingly drunk and knocked out the punkster lead guitarist, leaving Doria to see her date safely home, so unmanoeuverable had his alcohol-numbed limbs become.

The festivities had ended at last in a frozen dawn, with Doria limping home to the New Year, two hundred dollars the poorer – between the Club bill, the cab ride, the babysitter – if immeasurably richer in New York City wisdom.

There she stood at the entrance to her building, a veritable font of female woes, with one open-toed shoe a puddle of ice, a gold-leaf earring gone forever, and the bedraggled coif of a newborn beagle. What the new doorman made of her she could only guess . . .

No doubt about it, Doria Sevenstars had touched bottom. From her location far below sea level, upwards was the only possible way to go. Mildly cheered by cliche, she let herself into her sleeping apartment.

Never be more sober than your date, she told herself wearily as she finally slipped her shivering body between the cold sheets.

Never introduce your kids to an Irishman in silly shoes.

And never, never, she flicked off the three-way night-table lamp in staccato punctuation, fall in love with a man . . . called . . . Free . . .

It always seemed to be snowing that winter – a slow, grey spin of cotton gauze, as the colours, scents, and sounds of the world were packed away until April and Michelle's small room became a quiet isle hemmed in by fogs and frost.

There was silence everywhere. She came to think of it as a tangible medium, white and thick as the snow that piled up against her window like milk poured from a bottle, or God's grace tipped into the pure container of the soul, as pictured in her first-grade catechism.

Silence caked up on doors and along precise corridors. It dusted nurses' shoes and settled into the bones. For this, her bitter season, it cushioned Michelle from the shock of other people, from too much inquisitive light. It cooled her burning head and healed the places inside where her heart was rent.

Besides Dr Beckstein, the only ones that talked sense were the trees – a thin file of poplars marching down to the open city beneath her window. If she were very still, she could hear them speak to her of yesterday . . .

Then, unexpectedly one morning, the cut-out square of window in Michelle's lonely room grew brighter, the glass pane warmer to the touch. It was spring again.

The very next day, the clouds softened to the texture of whipped cream. The air turned silky in the garden. The hard white shell of winter finally cracked and a green world rose up between the shards, old and new at once. Like the other patients with one foot in this world and one in the world of dream, Michelle grew restless. Her pale skin glowed, her breasts felt tender and full. The snug white room seemed to shrink to walnut size and

50

her spirit beat against the walls like celestial wings. It was time to leave silence behind . . .

At her special request, Dr Beckstein began to accompany his patient on strolls around the city. Most of the time they ended up in Fort Tryon Park, at the Cloisters of the Metropolitan Museum.

Then something curious had happened on their last visit to the Cloisters. They had just emerged from the pleasant galleries lightly scented with orange trees, into the open-air walks of the herb garden high above the Hudson, when all at once, she had begun to tremble.

The doctor watched her closely, thinking at first she might have been upset by the profusion of plants. On the other hand, she had almost conquered her phobia. It was only certain kinds of cut flowers which disturbed her any longer. He suspected then that some object in the herb garden – the brick wall, perhaps, or the slow flow of blue river beyond – had set off bad memories.

How wrong he was . . .

Like jewels from a slipcase, the gorgeous images had come tumbling into her mind so fast she barely had time to capture them for her friend . . .

All had been order, peace, ancient tradition, and lone pleasures in the quattrocento convent school nestled in the Tuscan countryside. As if in a dream, she saw herself as a wide-eyed young girl, motoring up the steep hillside for the first time, looking down in awe at the gold-brushed city of Florence spread out below.

She'd arrived there by way of the generosity of Mama's anonymous 'friend', a person she herself had never seen, who liked to send gifts of money on her birthdays and every Christmas. Gifts that one could start substantial bank accounts with, gifts that were so generous a poor girl with no father could attend a rich girl's school. Who was her benefactor? Mama never liked to say. There were so many things Mama never told her, as if to talk were to be weak a fault her mother abhorred. Why, her daughter wondered, had she never married, when she was so achingly beautiful that men stopped in the streets to look at her. Who was the man who had fathered her child, and

51

how come he wasn't here with his family, when they so obviously needed him? And why, when her mother looked at her sometimes, did she have a frown on her face that pierced her through the heart?

Mama's beauty was like a knife that cut her, the day she'd told her daughter that she was going to be sent away to a school in Florence.

'You'll be with me for the summer after graduation,' she'd said, unpinning the billowing white sheet from the clothesline, as she leaned from the window. The daughter stood very still, holding the large straw laundry basket, listening.

'Then you'll leave for Italy.' The line squeaked in the pulley as her mother reeled in the clothes like family banners. Her auburn hair smelled sweet as strawberries, her daughter's favourite fruit. It shone with flashes of gold in the sun.

A lot of words came out of her that day, words she didn't know she had in her, emotional, pleading words, words of love for her mother.

'You'll learn how to be a Christian lady,' Mama had said matter-of-factly at her daughter's protests about leaving her friends, the old neighbourhood, herself. 'Just like the Blessed Virgin. When you come back, I'll hold my head up high and show them all that people without money don't have to live without class.' She snapped off the wooden clothespins and let her freshly laundered white slip float down into the basket her daughter still held. 'Do you understand?'

She nodded, even though she didn't. She'd cried the whole night before she'd left on the plane.

But ah, the austere voluptuousness of drinking cold milk from earthenware bowls! The long trestle table where their simple breakfasts were laid! The fresh-baked bread! The orange slices that glowed on the plate! Never could she have imagined how well the convent life would suit her, how years later amid the bustle of career and city lights, she would long for its quiet splendours.

She'd had a small, whitewashed room overlooking a court, where she slept on snowy, starched sheets, wrapped tight as a drum, and pressed with the precision folds of the nun's white habits.

How she had loved the regularity of bells calling one to prayer, to the Angelus! Morning Mass meant the coolness of marble on the knees, the sweet splash of holy water, the worn leather missal with one red satin marker. There was a white dove once, she remembered excitedly, that flew into the clerestory during matins, trembling for a moment in the sifting dust motes that streamed through the stained-glass window of the Sacred Heart. She had been especially devoted to the Sacred Heart, all pierced with cruel arrows, a pulsation of suffering as vast and boundless as space itself. Being young and believing herself invulnerable, the taste of martyrdom was sweet on her tongue.

Arrested by these golden visions, she had stopped to lean against one of the stone columns spaced along the brick-walled garden. In her bright red dress, she flickered like a Paschal flame.

'Go on,' Dr Beckstein urged, charmed by some of her reminiscences, and disturbed by others. She was obviously laden with guilt: a block to remembrance.

She stared at him blankly. 'But I don't recall any more. It was just . . .'

'Yes . . .?'

'So beautiful. I had a beautiful life.'

'You can again.'

She brushed away a wisp of hair, the shade of the Florentine sunlight. 'Yes. Thank you for saying that, doctor.'

'Would you like to stay here or walk some more?'

'I think I'd like to walk.'

He took her arm and together they crossed the hushed Medieval galleries and descended the stone stairway that led out to the sun-dappled paths of the riverside park.

Although Michelle still did not recall what part she had played in the past, she was full of plans for the future: for getting an apartment, a job, a new identity. She chatted on companionably.

'What is it you would like to do now?' the physician asked when she'd grown quiet. 'Ah, look, a robin,' he pointed his ebony-handled walking stick.

'Something in the arts,' Michelle replied promptly, without thinking.

'Are you trained for any one in particular?' In this way, he hoped to trick her subconscious into revelation . . .

'No, I don't know.' She moved away in confusion. 'Just dreaming.'

'Are you sure?' Dr Beckstein pressed. 'What made you say that?'

But Michelle seemed unwilling to discuss the subject any further. She stooped to pluck a dandelion and blew the downy grey puff into the teeth of the brisk river wind.

'I know some influential people. I can secure a job for you,' he offered.

Her eyes were soft lilac upon him. 'Dr Beckstein, my dear friend, you've already done too much. You've given me this Park, the spring . . . all the world again. But now I feel . . .' She hesitated, reaching for the right words, careful not to bruise him. 'I feel I've got to do this myself. It's important that I make my own way. Do you understand?'

He nodded with satisfaction. 'Perfectly. And what's more, I think it's a wise choice. For whatever reason, you've been given the task of reinventing yourself. You might as well start now.'

Looking at her, he was reminded of those exquisite French liqueurs, Poire Williams, the ones which are made by allowing a branch of fruit on a living tree to grow inside a glass bottle.

He remembered that the liqueurs thus produced were not of the highest quality. A good tree, like a good woman, needs no such protection, he concluded, but must grow as it will, in freedom.

'Shall we go? You seem a little tired.'

She nodded 'yes'. Arm in arm, they made their way to the doctor's black Mercedes-Benz.

Minutes later, they arrived at the Clinic, just in time for lunch.

Will she be strong enough to choose life?

Dr Beckstein stripped off his thin gold glasses and settled back into the driver's seat.

His active part in the case was over.

Of course, he would encourage her to call on him, whenever she felt the need, but Michelle was well enough to re-enter the world on her own.

He glanced over at her with affection. It would not be easy for her – to begin with, there were basic survival skills of which she knew nothing.

And then there was her 'repression' of self. It was important that she be very careful from now on. He would tell her that. Others would do with her as even he, a professional, had been tempted to do: make of her an ideal image, for she seemed to embody the romantic longings of men. They would not see her for the flesh-and-blood woman she was. She had become that most dangerous of mortal creatures, a living symbol, the unconscious Eve of Eden, before the curse of self-knowledge.

Jung had been right when he'd said that emptiness was woman's secret. What did men know of the infinite night, the eternal pit, the vast silver barrenness of the moon? These were woman's domain.

The amnesia – (was it a form of self-sacrifice in which she was protecting someone from a memory she considered unspeakable?) – would only make it easier for men to create her as they went along.

She smiled at him, as he came round to open the car door.

Poor child.

She would have to be vigilant if she were ever to find true love. _

The summer bore down on the city with the hard intensity of a fever, leaving Park Avenue an urban shimmer in the morning sun.

Lucky for her, she had dressed in tropical linen today, quite a contrast to the pricey fox coat she'd been wearing when they first found her wandering the streets. Now it was an obscene extravagance for a woman without a name, without a place, and had been buried in cold storage with the rest of her identity. She supposed she'd never wear it again.

A wilted copy of the *Times* Employment Section tucked under her arm, Michelle crossed the intersection against the red light, uncaring. Once again, the wilderness of grey towers looming up around her reminded Michelle of the play cities she built on her nursery floor, the kind of milk-carton structures that all looked alike, and, even to a child's eye, stiffly uninhabited. Ah, what she wouldn't give to belong to one of those towers now, to ride high into the blue empyrean on its air-cooled elevators, straight to a desk with a brass nameplate and a small, set place in the scheme of things.

'What do you do?' they would ask her, not even bothering to glance up from busy stacks of paperwork, clutching a live telephone in their powerful hands.

'Michelle Smith' had decided to tell them she wanted a receptionist's position. That seemed modest enough. She'd had to invent some tall tale about being out of the job market since her marriage, it made things easier, and gave the faded glamour of the Barbizon Hotel as her address. She'd had to sell off the last of her diamonds to pay for lodging there.

Fastidiously, she'd taken a typing course and now she could pluck out letters on a typewriter with enough speed to get by.

She made 'a nice appearance' too, or so the personnel people said. 'That would be a plus.'

Then why did the managers and executives, desperate for office help, overlook her every time?

What in God's name did they mistrust in her? Did they sense the shadow of another woman hanging behind?

Maybe they saw in her their own unhealed wounds . . .

As again and again, the doors of the city were slammed in her face, she had come to think of it less as punishment for her sins, than as a challenge to find out the terrible reasons. Hadn't Dr Beckstein advised her to embrace her loneliness like a lover? Only by lying in its empty arms, would she be able to find herself.

For as of now, Michelle Smith was nothing but a slap-dash personality, a patchwork of characters out of books she'd read, TV talk show guests, fancied reminiscence.

She took to inventing whole families for herself, to populate her empty past . . . That pretty girl waiting in line at the bank, the one with the yellow hair and the long legs, that could be her little sister. They would have shared their teenage years together, trading little bits of their young dreams, giggling over boyfriends and crying over spilt milk.

The distinguished elderly gentleman, flagging a cab on Fifth Avenue. An important executive, an uncle who took time out from his busy schedule to send her flowers on college graduation day, with a note attached: 'To the next President of the United States.'

She secretly suspected that the peerless Katherine Hepburn was her maiden aunt . . . What a handicap it was to lack a name! She imagined her emptiness had a sound which other people could hear and stand clear of, like a beggar's cry.

To understand the continued rejection, she tried to picture herself in a camera's cold view, and, like most people, failed at the feat of objectivity. Yet she felt somehow that, for the rest of her life, she would be carrying around an eerie notion of her former self like a snapshot that didn't take.

She may have had a new Social Security card, a new identity, but what would prevent her from making the same mistakes all over again, when she had no memory of the steps that had brought her to this desolation? Was error written in the blood, so that we are doomed to set up our problems over and over again, until we get them right, like some failing language student repeating words she doesn't understand?

Michelle started across the street.

When she was about halfway there, the heat-softened pavement stuck fast to her high heels and she walked right out of one pump. She tiptoed back over the hot tar to retrieve it. What misery! What an evil end – to melt down in the sun and become a permanent part of Park Avenue and Sixtieth Street! The Tomb of the Unknown Job-seeker . . .

Slithering off her pale green linen jacket, she slung it over one arm. June already, and she was no closer to having her apartment, a job, some friends to call her own.

At the corner, Michelle gave in to the murky city heat, and sought refuge in an air-conditioned coffee shop. Perched at the crowded counter, she ordered a tall iced tea and shuffled through the index cards on which were neatly typed the appointments her personnel agency had set up that morning. None of them had even remotely panned out. Sipping her tepid drink, she stuffed the hated cards into the Sweet'n'Low bowl.

'And what's more his prints come out like mudpies!' cried a woman in the booth behind her.

A male voice sounded in pleading cadences.

'He needs me in the Gallery?' the first voice rose petulantly. 'He needs a lobotomy, that's what he needs! Writing on the floor like a maniac. Spilling his damned homemade yoghurt all over my desk. The day's work ruined. And it was *strawberry* yoghurt. I'm allergic to *strawberry* stinking yoghurt!'

'Now wait a minute, Claire . . .'

'No, I'm sorry. I was hired to be a receptionist – not a zookeeper! This is it. This is the limit. I quit!'

The young woman flounced out of the coffee shop, her ears still smoking, while her mortified companion sank slowly into his seat.

No one could have been more surprised than Michelle when she placed one narrow, white-strapped shoe in front of the other, and found herself at the strange man's table. 'My name is Michelle Smith,' she talked quickly. Failure had taught her well. 'I couldn't help overhearing . . .'

'No, I'm sure. Neither could the entire East Side.' He was thirtyish and balding fast, with a round face and a lemon-coloured handkerchief folded like an Origami butterfly into his jacket pocket.

'I'm looking for a job,' she began again.

'So who isn't?'

Michelle ignored the sceptical tone. 'That young woman just quit. Is it possible that I might fill the position?'

'Possible, but not plausible.' He patted his forehead with the saffron cloth.

Her face fell. She slid to the edge of the booth. 'I'm sorry to have bothered you . . .'

'Hey, wait a minute.' His small black eyes went shiny as Sicilian olives. He'd had An Idea. 'Do you eat red meat?'

'I beg your pardon?'

He shook his head, dubious again. 'Oh, I just don't know, honey. You look like the breakable type to me.' He flung down a few coins as a tip, and rose from the booth.'

'I'm sorry.'

Blinking as he emerged into the harsh June sunlight, he again dabbed at his brow with the handkerchief. Michelle flew after him.

'Does this have to do with restauranting?' she asked, coming up behind the man, whom she now saw was well over six feet.

He dangled his unconstructed *cafe au lait* jacket over his shoulder as he eyed her up and down. 'You again? You remind me of my last boyfriend. Look, darling, you don't know what you're asking.'

'What is the job?' Michelle persisted.

He seemed impressed, in spite of himself. 'Okay, it's a sort of go-for in a photographic gallery. Could you do that?'

'Why not?'

'Why not? That's what they all say. Well, I'll tell you. The money's modest to begin with. And the working conditions are on the weird side . . .' Then: 'Oh what the hell! Come on, dearie, there's nothing to fear but fear itself!'

They walked for three bustling blocks uptown, at which point the man led her up to a neat red-brick townhouse on Madison Avenue. Michelle had just enough time to read the name etched in a brass plate on the door – BARTOK GALLERY, Maximilian P. Bartok, Manager – before stepping into its dim, chic depths.

Spaced along the cool, cream-coloured walls were over-

59

sized black-and-white glossies of Manhattan Island. A hopeful Michelle noticed that the receptionist's desk fronting the entrance was conspicuously untenanted. Wasting no time, the nattily dressed man, who had since identified himself as Alexander Bartok, cousin and assistant to Maxim, steered her through a short corridor to an office in the back.

Lolling at a desk directly opposite was a young woman with a mess of red confetti for hair and a make-up job that looked like an explosion in a pastry shop.

She ogled openly.

'Wait here,' Alex directed in his harried way, before disappearing into the gold-knobbed office.

Michelle pitched a smile at the girl.

Her immediate response was to bury the flaming head in the heap of neglected file folders on her desk. A minute later, Alex Bartok reappeared, beads of sweat popping on his brow. 'You can go in. If you dare. Good luck!'

Once inside, Michelle felt as though she'd come upon an underground grotto.

The entire room, which was cavernous in size and had a panoramic window flowing like a sheet of water down its main wall, was washed in earthen colours. The pool of carpet, suede-covered walls and ceiling, furniture and accessories – all were geological shades like stalactite stain, burnt calcium and lichen green. Michelle half expected the wall-to-wall carpet to splash and bubble beneath her feet, her body sucked up to the knees.

To add to this odd design effect, there were eerie noises – wiry underwater squeaks, clicks and buzzes – which Michelle finally identified as whale songs, emanating from a burled stereo speaker set high above the room like the symbolic crown in Olivier's classic film of *Richard III*.

Most extraordinary of all was the long, distinguished old man in pinstripes who was hanging upside down, like a fruit bat, in his gravity boots. As Michelle stood and watched in stunned silence, he spoke to her thus: 'Natural and pure. Everything in here is natural and pure. Light, decor, food, exercise. I insist on it!'

Michelle fixed on the pink rosette of his mouth, which,

of course, she was observing from an odd angle, and spoke to it.

'My name is Michelle Smith. I'm here for the receptionist's job.'

'Have a cup of my homemade yoghurt. It's blueberry today.' He waved airily towards a small freezer in the corner of the room.

'No thank you. Now about that job . . .'

'Do you smoke?'

'No.'

'Do you hunt seals?'

'No, I . . .'

'Is three hundred dollars a week all right?'

'Yes, but . . .'

'Well, there you have it,' he boomed jovially. 'But remember, Miss Smith, man was not meant to walk upright. Nor woman either.'

'No, Mr Bartok.' She stood uncertainly.

'That will be all.'

Michelle went out from the office in a daze.

Cousin Alexander was waiting. 'I see it went well. You never know with him.'

'He is a touch eccentric, isn't he?' she observed with some discretion.

Alexander Bartok snorted. 'A touch. But don't let Cousin Maxim fool you. He's brilliant at his job. Besides,' he added in a soothing tone, 'he travels a lot and is rarely, if ever, here.'

Michelle walked over to the receptionist's desk and ran her hand lovingly over its polished pinewood surface. This time the other secretary sent up a tentative smile like a weather balloon.

'Will this be mine?'

Alex gave a nod. 'You can start tomorrow. Gallery doors open at ten a.m. sharp. But you'll have to be in by nine-thirty.' Humour glimmered in the full moon of his face. 'Don't you want to know why?'

'I'm afraid to ask.'

'Aerobics,' he said flatly. 'Mr Bartok personally conducts the classes and expects all his employees to come.

61

That means you and Ginger there.'

'Mr Bartok,' Michelle laughed for the first time in months, her heart floating light and fancy-free. 'I wouldn't miss it for the world.'

It was heaven on Fifty-first Street. If the *New York Times* employment section had failed her – its real estate section had brought Michelle a home. The warm sunshine on her face when she rose to the peace of her East Side apartment. The spare elegance of the meals she prepared for herself, with one perfect eggplant, raspberries for dessert, perhaps a tea rose on the table. Simple gifts, but it seemed she could not get enough of this new life, as greedy for detail as any child questing on hands and knees. All in all, the fresh air of independence was a heady brew, and Michelle could feel herself growing tall and strong on the diet, shoulders rubbing up against the blue vault of the sky.

In those early days of her freedom, Michelle's letters to Dr Beckstein had see-sawed between elation and despondency. Might not the world be taken from her again?

Thus, even as she quietly blazed in the big city setting of her new career, she trembled within, knowing she was at heart a sham, a hollow woman with no family, no love, no wealth of years to fall back on.

All she knew of her past was a nameless guilt. And she knew she was guilty because she had been deprived of the comfort of love.

For her, there were no hushed midnight calls, no sweet obsession with the touch of one man, no morning kisses to start the day. She felt sick with longing, but knew that, because of her lost experience, love was full of dangers for her.

She might have looked like a woman, but inside she was again a young girl. 'The maiden', Dr Beckstein called her in German, susceptible to male fantasy and control, as she had no clear image of who she was.

For the moment, at least, she'd found a ready escape in her work.

Gradually, as the summer months gave way to the crisp blaze of autumn, Michelle mastered her daily chores which turned out to be anything but routine. The chiaroscuro world of photography began to spring alive for her. She spent long hours in dusty library halls, took weekend courses in SoHo studios, consumed every publication on the young art she could get her hands on.

Her pleasure in small things communicated itself to all who met her, and she soon became a favourite at the Bartok Gallery. Even the unpredictable Maximilian Bartok trusted her artistic judgment, and during those rare periods when he was in *grand tenue* at the Gallery, he would strive doubly hard to concoct new dishes involving seaweed, royal jelly and other exotic edibles for her special delectation. The old man, said the grapevine, believed Michelle Smith had an eye for quality.

Which was why Alex Bartok had taken her aside the afternoon Helmut Rigel was in with his impressive portfolio.

'I know he's gorgeous, darling, those decadent green eyes and that scar, have mercy. But if I were you, I'd keep him at arm's length. I mean, Maxim is always telling me to get rid of him, but he's utterly brilliant you see. Did those award-winning photos of L.A. street gangs. He's one of those innovators who never makes a penny. Like when he had his models pose with bag ladies and won advertising medals for the fur company, but didn't sell any coats. He's hopeless, darling, and really not for you.'

Michelle nodded pleasantly, not understanding a word of his harangue.

She was too busy watching the controversial young photographer, lean and lithe in a black turtleneck and jeans, fold his arms, prop one foot against Max's spotless, cream-coloured wall, and stare at her without blinking, exactly like a great cat.

He had a patrician nose and a long, elegant slash of a mouth in his narrow face. His hair was a thick shock of auburn, sheared smooth above the ears, and he had a habit of holding his elbow and slanting one hand up like a flag, with a smoking Turkish cigarette pinched between his fingertips. Most intriguing of all, there was the thrill of a thin white scar glowing on one high-boned cheek. Michelle had already fallen in love with that scar, a sketch of tragedy. Panther-slim, Helmut Rigel was a man who moved with a dangerous, erotic poetry. In this way, he could move easily into a woman's heart. (Now what was the date of that Reardon show?)

A metallic whir suddenly brought her gaze up from the work on her desk, straight into the glassy eye of a camera lens. Never before had one of the photographers seen fit to photograph her. She was aghast.

Even more so, as he did it rather insolently, as though she were there for the taking, her privacy violated without the ghost of a thought.

'Please stop.' Unconsciously, she crossed her arms over her breasts.

'Why please?' She noticed he did not lower the lens from his target.

'Ah, good.' He went down on one knee, pointing the camera like a gun. 'You are too pretty, too blonde. I like this distasteful look, more interesting.'

Time and again, Michelle tried her best to ignore him and get back to her work, but she couldn't manage to do it, with his intense presence a mere few inches away, the eyes like green pools stirred by the finger of God.

'You have lovely, pale hands,' he observed. 'You play the piano?'

She shook her head. 'No, I . . .'

'Umm, and look at that nice tongue . . .' He had a trace of a German accent.

Michelle shot up from behind her desk. 'Please . . . I have work to do.'

She walked uncomfortably to the filing cabinets, and pulled out one drawer. It slammed shut again. The young man with the pale scar had kicked it closed with his foot. He stood frowning down at her, his eyes a cloudy green and distracted with visions.

'You don't belong here, a common worker. With your white beauty, you were made to inspire art, like the courtesans of Greece and the hostesses of the French salons. A modern odalisque . . .'

Michelle was transfixed, listening . . .

'I am having a showing of my work tonight.' A small,

printed card fluttered down to her. 'This is the address. I will see you there.'

Michelle watched him go out in rapt fascination, which was why a worried Alex Bartok had again offered his words of advice, knowing it was already too late.

There were a million good reasons to take up the invitation.

After all, why shouldn't she begin to live like a normal woman again? She'd done battle with her desires long enough. Feeling righteous, Michelle had the cab stop at the SoHo loft on Spring Street, where Helmut Rigel's work was being shown.

The air was so warm and damp that the material of her royal blue blouse with the surplice collar stuck to her back as she climbed the stairs of the musty hallway. Every so often, she looked nervously over her shoulder. Was she very early? No one else seemed to have arrived yet.

Uneasy, she knocked at the door.

Helmut opened it himself. 'Come in.'

Under the high ceiling of the loft apartment, there was barely a stick of furniture. The rough walls were painted red. On the right was a ten-foot-square cubicle that Michelle figured as a dark room. To the left was a huge, custom-made platform bed carved out of solid white oak, spread with a thick Indian coverlet, black figured in gold. Unwashed dishes were piled in the dingy porcelain of the sink, and long-empty wine bottles encrusted with the wax of spent candles littered the floor around the legs of the plain wooden table.

'This is your apartment,' she said.

'How clever of you.' Helmut motioned towards the dark room. 'And this is my studio, where art is made – the only art you'll ever see at Bartok Brothers.'

'You are very good.' Michelle hung back at the doorway, neither in nor out of the loft.

Her instincts told her to turn tail and run.

She took a step forward.

'You are committed now.' His face was almost classically handsome when he smiled, an elusive smile.

'Yes.'

'A glass of wine?'

'All right.'

Michelle cast around for a chair. Finding none, she perched on the edge of the bed, her long legs tucked under her.

He handed her a brimming glass, and reclined against the pillow with his hands folded behind his head.

As he did not bother to make conversation, Michelle sat there awkwardly, not knowing what to do with her hands or her legs, or even her lips which seemed to be locked in a nervous little smile.

Helmut reached out and trailed his finger down her spine. 'You're perspiring.'

Michelle blushed.

'It is sexy. Water is always sexy.' He was kneeling directly behind her now, blowing into her ear, softly, nuzzling her neck.

The warmth was now a red hot glow that spread all over her body in seconds flat. She was taking deep breaths and then she was lying across the bed with Helmut over her, doing delicious, indescribable things to her with his bruised mouth and artist's fingers.

'I knew,' he said between licks, 'that you would let me make love to you when you let me take your picture. Photography is the only honest art. Painters and sculptors lie routinely, but one can not dissemble with a photograph. One can not hide in it, either. The eyes will always speak the truth. As yours did.'

'What did they say?' she breathed in great deep rhythms, as Helmut pushed her whispery white silk skirt up her parting thighs, and found his way into her.

'They said: "I am alone and afraid. Love me"'

And so he did, so that she was neither lonely, nor, any longer, afraid.

'Tell me something,' Rigel said, his eyes deep green and dangerous in his pale face, 'did you ever think that your Gallery might burn down to the ground one day in a beautiful burst of orange and pale red? What a fabulous photograph that would make, hmm?'

'Are you threatening me?' Alex Bartok didn't blink. He set down Helmut's photographs on the desk before him.

'Not at all. Not at all. Merely making an observation. Artists do it all the time, and as you've told me over and over, I am an artist, ergo, I can not sell.'

'I'm sorry.' Alex looked away in a dismissal. 'These are brilliant. But I can't use them on The Man of Action exhibit. You're too unorthodox in your treatment, too disturbing. You wouldn't fit into the concept.'

'You are all such mice!' Helmut spoke softly. 'So terrified of the new! I have contempt for you all with your glossy galleries and empty souls.'

'Yes, we know that . . .' Alex replied tiredly. 'And now, if you will excuse me . . .'

Helmut laid his palms down on either side of the white oak desk. 'No, I do not excuse you! You at least have taste, Bartok, although you do your best to deny it! Give me a chance, show the art world that Alexander Bartok has some balls . . .!'

Outside the office, Michelle worked on, oblivious of the argument.

When Helmut emerged, he had a tight smile on his face.

'Another blow for the philistines,' he said at her query. He kissed her full on the mouth. 'I'll see you for lunch.'

His lean, black-shirted figure was out the door before she could speak again.

All that fall and winter, Michelle divided her time happily between the Gallery and Helmut's Spartan loft.

He called her his Muse and made love to her for hours on end. Michelle thought maybe she had found the key to her woman's soul in the photographer's hands.

In return, she cooked for him, and kept his loft in order, adding touches of comfort and colour from her own beloved apartment, which something told her she should hang on to, just in case love ended as abruptly as it had begun . . .

On weeknights, when he wasn't working, he took her

on subway rides to places she'd never heard of – like Sunset Park in Brooklyn, where incredible renovations were taking place in turn-of-the-century brownstones, and bought her cheap dinners at Cuban-Chinese restaurants on seamy Eighth Avenue.

On weekends, it then fell to her to provide the pot luck meals around which his druggy friends plotted artistic anarchy and other magnificent obsessions.

Michelle didn't even hear them half the time – as long as Helmut told her that, for him, taking her kiss was like stealing the fire of the gods, that his work had never been so ravishingly sensuous, almost female, and emotionally profound, she was content.

Every so often, Alex Bartok would cluck over her and inquire after her health, which seemed radiant. That was the extent of it. He knew these things had to run their courses . . .

She'd rushed home breathless one night, her good news wrapped up inside her like a surprise package.

'Helmut, I've been promoted to Director of Contemporary Photography. Mr Bartok said, and I quote, "out of sheer talent and yeoman work". End quote. Isn't it wonderful!' She laughed gaily, kissing him on the lips.

His hands were in his back pockets and he was scowling at a print he'd just made and clipped on to a board on the wall.

'That is charming, Michelle. I am happy for you.' And with that, he'd gone back into his dark room.

It was around that time when Helmut started coming in later and later, drunk and distant, and more silent than ever.

On one such night, he came upon Michelle studying his newest batch of photographs – a series on deaf mutes.

They hadn't made love for days, and the air was filled with unshed tension.

'Helmut, I've been thinking about this series, about why the Bartoks didn't want it in their last exhibit. It's not because they're imitative of Arbus. It's the way you photographed them, they're not sympathetic at all, like her subjects were. There's no emotion . . .'

Helmut went white. His hands shook as he pulled the photos out of her grasp, and tore them to pieces before her eyes.

'I see,' he bit off the words, 'this is what the expert thinks, is it? Michelle Smith, the photographic genius who has never even taken a picture with her brownie camera! Well, this is what I think of your expert opinion . . .' He pitched the pieces up into the air, and they drifted to the floor slowly like a storm of black and white snow . . .

'Helmut . . .' The man had spent months on the prints in this series. Her heart broke. She was to blame for this sickening waste. 'I love your work, you know that. I just thought I might be able to help you.'

'You don't help me!' She had never seen him so furious. He looked now like the stranger that he was . . . 'You hinder me. You and your soft, womanly, man-strangling love . . .'

He'd quit the apartment in a rage, leaving Michelle alone in that huge, hedonist's bed, to weep and wonder why . . .

The next time she'd come to see him, there were photographs of an exquisite Oriental girl hanging on the rough red walls. She looked about sixteen.

The tourmaline eyes burned into her. 'She is beautiful, isn't she?' Helmut asked coldbloodedly. 'I am very excited by this face, the face of an angel who seduces men . . .' He was already inventing another woman.

But I am your Muse. I am the one who taught you that art is just another expression of love . . .

Helmut turned his back to her, poring over the photos.

Michelle could see there was no use for her here anymore. She had not been content in the role he'd created for her. She had dared to have her own ambitions, her own sense of truth. As a result, she no longer registered on the screen of those far-seeing eyes, would never again appear in his sepia visions.

In silence, she packed her few things and left the studio loft where she'd fallen in love, never to return.

She had no one to blame but herself. Dr Beckstein had warned that men would tend to see in her whatever they wanted to see. From now on she'd have to fight for her real self to break through: that must be her lifelong task.

Since the love of men was locked away in her past – she'd take to brusqueness and efficiency, like many of her sisters, too afraid to yield up her softer side. She must take care. She would not be moulded like cheap clay, annealed in male fantasies, glazed with their selfish desires. She would fight the tyranny of false lovers, like Helmut Rigel.

She would fight to stay out of a dream.

PART II

JOSHUA

CHAPTER SIX

Great pots of miniature white orchids pended from the high ceiling of the Bartok Gallery, frothed over the cleared desks and covered every available inch of the bleached hardwood floor and thick Chinese rugs.

In the centre of the room, a jumbo-size buffet table laid with a snowy lace cloth offered up a panoply of tiny, tender vegetables: eggplants, radishes, celery; smoked sturgeon artfully arranged on silver platters; and hundreds upon hundreds of succulent oysters on the half-shell, all displayed on a glittery bed of ice-like cut diamonds from Neptune's private store. A Flemish still life of tempting fruits glowed on yet another tray.

Outside, the limos lined up for blocks. Flash bulbs popped like fireworks on the Bicentennial.

It was the gala opening night of the Men of Action Exhibit by highly acclaimed photographer, Allon Reardon, and despite the cold drizzle tonight, the brownstone gallery scintillated with luminaries: Egon von Furstenberg, Arlene Dahl, Diana Vreeland, Halston, even His Bleached-out Eminence, Andy Warhol, had turned up to view the master's latest efforts and to be exclusively and exhaustively photographed doing it.

Michelle Smith had worn bare black that evening, her white-gold hair held high and back by silken bands, her shoes dark and narrow, pitched so tall she almost seemed to be on point. Deftly, she moved through the sequined and tuxedoed throng, praising here, nodding agreement there, expertly peddling the most expensive portraits in the overwrought world of art.

'Michelle.' Alexander Bartok touched her arm. Always a natty dresser, tonight he sported impeccable black evening dress, a file of diamond studs lighting up his shirtfront. His bald head poked up straight and shiney, an egg in the white cup of his collar, below which a black satin bow tie flared out stiffly as his professional smile.

'It's going marvellously, just marvellously!' he spoke *sotto voce*, nodding over her head at some famous faces across the room. 'Reardon is in peak form tonight!' He motioned to a far corner where the celebrated photographer reigned over a brilliant circle of East Coast elite. 'We're particularly pleased with the way you've handled this debut. I'm happy to tell you that there will be a bonus in your pay cheque next week. And I don't mean an extra ration of lemon yogurt!' He gave her a parting wink as he waded off into the shallows of celebrity.

Michelle glowed down to her toes. It had all been worth it, the cold meals in cardboard cartons, the late, late nights, the photographer's tantrums.

Taking a turn around the Gallery, she indulged a sudden urge to review her handiwork. More than one critical pundit had called the hanging of the photos 'sheer perfection'. It had been a special treat to see her 'name' in print . . .

Moving from one to the other, Michelle studied the series of photographs dealing with politicians, businessmen, scientists, worldbeaters of every stripe, spaced along the Gallery walls.

Like a victim of black magic, she was drawn to the spot directly in front of Number Eight, the one photo out of the lot which had exerted a personal fascination from its mounting, a few short days before. (Had it only been a few days?)

It depicted a rugged man in dungarees and a workshirt against a background of African mud huts, hunkering down in the midst of a circle of shy, smiling children. Behind him, crates of food, paid for out of his own pocket, it is said, are being unloaded and distributed to the beleaguered villagers.

With the party booming at her back, she ran the fingers

of one hand over the raised, gilded nameplate. Joshua Free, it gleamed, tycoon and globe-trotting crusader. She flipped through the catalogue with quiet interest . . .

'Joshua Free – a man who moves in the mainstream of historical change, a self-made millionaire by age thirty, whose journal the Los Angeles *Guild-Examiner* is already a serious rival to the popular LA *Times*.

'Coming from the owner of a fabulously successful string of newspapers throughout the Southern and Western United States, Free's loan of capital and personal promise of expertise went a far way in persuading the Chicago Tribune Syndicate to keep the embattled N.Y. *Daily News* alive.' She moved down a few paragraphs.

'What makes Josh Free so special to readers of his journals is that he is, above all, a man of proven principle who never fails to put his money where his mouth is.'

In recent months alone, Michelle had heard on the TV news, Free had personally sponsored a fact-finding mission to Latin America where he championed the cause of refugees caught in border crossfire, as well as financing an airlift of millions of dollars worth of food to Somalia and other famine-stricken African nations.

'The name "Joshua Free",' the unblushing valentine ended with a rhetorical flourish, 'is a rare emblem of honesty and activism in American political journalism, and no photographic tribute to the great public men of our century would be complete without him.'

Well, well. Josh Free's ears must be burning. Michelle folded the catalogue. Now if only he could walk on water . . .

She stared up at Free, wondering. Was it all media hype . . . or something more real?

One thing was for sure, he'd got himself a public relations man worth his weight in oil.

As the cork popped on yet another magnum of imported champagne (the Brothers Bartok had spared no expense; Reardon was their chief moneymaker), Michelle was sorry to note that her mind was once again running more on Free's private relations . . .

What were they all about?

The thirty-five year old magnate, a denizen of magazine covers from *People* to *Newsweek* and back again, did have a few obvious attractions that might suggest an answer. Heroic height. The shoulders of a god. A noble head of blue-black hair, trained no doubt, to tumble over his marble brow in just the right, romantic spot. His conceit must be stifling. She fanned herself with her hand.

In fact, Michelle Smith was secretly taken with the man's very breadth and substance.

There was nothing mediocre about his features, each one was aggressively individual, purely itself. From what people gossiped (the Reardon photos were in the signature black and white) he commanded his men and compelled his women with a pair of daunting salt-blue eyes. His jaw had a blunt, squared-off shape that lent the impression of intellectual charisma and moral integrity. His mouth was what could only be called a generous curve. His head rose majestically from between the powerful set of shoulders like an eagle from a rock. When he laughed, he would roar, like a pirate king.

Michelle could tell from these physiognomic clues that Free was not a man who wasted himself on fools or foolish causes, but a doer, who breathed purpose, fostered strength. He would take his own counsel, and keep his emotional sources hidden. Being sensitive to secrets, she liked that last quality best.

What, she'd begun to fantasize freely, *would it be like to kiss that mouth? To feel the marine tongue rise to hers. How well would he love her, this man of power . . .?*

'Yum, yum.' In the clinch of a hot-red-and-white striped minidress with barber pole stockings to match, Ginger, the Gallery secretary, shimmied up beside Michelle. As she spoke animatedly, the pinned-in cone of Ginger's hennaed hair swayed like a fez atop her head. Her breath smelled of bubblegum and brandy, the breath of a precocious child.

Irritated beyond all reason, Michelle took in the girl's outlandish costume. She'd already run out of patience with Ginger's stubborn infatuation for the handsome tycoon, which had caught fire the day his photos went up,

74

and tonight, was rising to adolescent conflagration. Especially as the nineteen-year-old.had the most appalling taste in men and spent entire lunch hours sobbing on Michelle's shoulder about one tight-jeaned heartbreaker after another – rock singers, bartenders, hunks met jogging in the Park – who promised from the first to do her wrong, and, to no one's surprise, did. Something to do with blood circulation, pre-shrunk denim, and the male heart, Michelle suspected.

At least she'd learned her own lesson in one go-round with Helmut Rigel.

'Now he looks like the kind of man I could really get into . . .'

Michelle blushed as though she'd been caught at a blue movie. 'He looks just like what he is – a social-climbing Southern cracker. Rude. Crude. And unbelievably . . .'

'Sexy,' Ginger grinned.

Michelle didn't turn a hair. 'I was going to say "conceited", unbelievably conceited.'

'Who cares?'

'I do.' Michelle, who had her dander up, was not averse to overstating her case, although she was careful to leave Helmut's name out of it. 'I know that type, Ginger, The Smug and Superior Male. Just look at those eyes – he's madly in love with himself. How could he have anything left for a woman?' She went for the devastating phrase, the one that would hit on Ginger's working girl nerve . . .

'And I bet he's a bitch to work for!' she cried when she'd finally got hold of it.

'He is,' drawled a julep-flavoured voice behind her. 'They love it.'

Michelle became conscious that something terribly important was about to happen to her. She swivelled to face it squarely, as Ginger's eyes pooled round with surprise. The last thing Michelle remembered thinking before her world changed forever, was that, in her narrow striped mini, the little redhead resembled nothing so much as a candycane waiting to be licked . . .

Courage leaped from every pore. Decision reigned behind the eyes: a jolt of stark, sea-beaten blue, set deep in a world-wise, angular face. He had the arrogant stance and steely stare of a conqueror.

'Hi, I'm Josh Free.' He swept Michelle with his Caribbean-coloured gaze, his face all stark angles and sea light, his skin a sailor's deep bronze.

'How nice for you.' Michelle wouldn't be taken in by the trick of his beauty. 'Didn't your mother ever tell you not to eavesdrop? You might hear some unflattering opinions.'

'I've heard them. Other people's opinions don't mean cowcakes to me, Miss . . .?' He made a move towards her and she caught a whiff of a bracing lime-based cologne, with subtle undertones of West Indian breezes and pirate stores hidden beneath warm sands . . .

As for Josh Free, he'd noticed the willowy blonde as soon as he'd set foot in the Gallery tonight.

It would be hard not to. In her softly draped black dress, her shoulders, arms and throat gave off the dull sheen of crushed Oriental pearls. How brilliant to wear black! To glow like a summer morning long ago . . .

It may be that in every man's life there comes one perfect morning, one perfect day of youth that will reverberate in him till his dying breath, urge him on to a lifelong quest for something he cannot even describe, unless it be in terms of a woman.

For Josh, it had come at dawn, his fifteenth summer at Uncle Louie's overgrown country place on the outskirts of St Petersburg, Florida.

The light was different that morning. Josh had been filled with a strange sweetness, a restlessness that brought him out of his tumbled bed to the window. A wreath of moths fluttered against the sinking moon, and except for the crickets' cry, the earth seemed to be holding its breath, like Josh, in expectation of some sudden outbreak of the divine.

Barefoot, he had crawled out to the paint-chipped window ledge, and, grabbing on to an overhanging arm of the old pear tree, stepped into the crook of two swaybacked branches. The late summer pears glowed mysteriously as he reached out and plucked one.

Never before, never since, did he hold such marvellous nectar on his tongue. The fruit melted down like sugar in his mouth with each crisp, cooling bite, and for a few solitary hours, Josh knew ecstasy and wonder in the arms of the old tree.

Afterwards, he had climbed back through the window and gone down for a hearty breakfast of hotcakes and pork patties as though nothing out of the ordinary had occurred.

But he was changed, and he knew it.

Odd, to think about that now. After so many years.

Something about this blonde and beautiful woman had brought it all back to him tonight . . .

How sorely she reminded him of everything that had gone wrong with his personal life – or lack of it – since Nicole divorced him five years ago!

If only he could be happy with satisfying his prodigious appetites, which was easy enough for a media star to manage. But casual affairs only deepened his sense of emptiness. Maybe it was because his father had been a preacher down in Tampa while he was growing up. That had ruined mere pleasure for him, nipped hedonism in the bud.

Uncomfortably for him, Josh had grown up a moral man, so that he was careful never knowingly to hurt an exiting lover, but was always kind, allowing her to believe she was the one with the eminent good sense to break it off.

It wasn't difficult for him to do it that way. He genuinely loved women, always had – if not one in particular, then Woman in the general sense. The warm, scented place in the bed where they'd lain, the moon-clocked rhythms of their bodies, the wonderful swings of their minds. On some instinctive level, he loved the mystery and magic of women, although to date no single one among them seemed able to cut through to the core, profoundly move him, restore him to himself. He longed for the night of the chrysalis, the metamorphosis into lover, and that longing drove him to seek the wonder of what he believed he'd never find.

Now, after five years of bed-hopping, he was thoroughly weary of the whole, smiling game.

His usual way out of the cycle, the technique holding sway for the last six months, had been to fling himself into his work with such hard intensity, that he lost track of the hour, the day, his own gnawing sense of unease, inevitably becoming so drained that he came to feel, if not peace, then nothing, nothing at all.

For him, work was the best narcotic.

Nicole had said it was his only love.

He realized now she was right. But he had been too naive to see it then. Nicole, the ex-*Vogue* model, had three kids, a mansion and a swimming pool in Palm Beach now. She sent him photographs of herself with second husband, Ralph, her erstwhile divorce lawyer, growing fat and rosy over barbecued ribs. Very happy they were too. She still looked Josh up whenever she was in New York and he sent baby presents, each time, little spoons made out of beaten silver, and ceramic dishes with scenes from Beatrix Potter painted all over them. He never once forgot a birthday. The twins called him 'Uncle Josh', if little Paul was too young to do anything else but spit up on him, Joshua Free even loved that intimate gift.

But every time he left them to fly home, his heart twisted inside him and he'd wonder whether the young maverick who had sailed around the world, alone, at twenty and built a journalistic empire out of a two-bit job as a Florida real estate salesman, was nothing but a goddamn fool.

Then again, he wasn't enough of a fool to overlook this woman in the Gallery with the pretty hands, and the violet eyes. He could swear she perfumed the air whenever she moved those hands, that delicate head.

And damn it, he even liked her nerve! He was too much the Southerner not to be captured by the mist of vulnerability that clung about her, and too much the man not to be intrigued by her obvious talent (he had been told of her role in the exhibit) and the disturbing glow of sensuality of which she didn't even seem to be aware. She was a beauty undiscovered, which made her all the more alluring to a passionate adventurer like Joshua Free.

'I've been around too long to pay much mind to other people's ideas,' he said evenly, 'especially when they talk like damn fools.'

As she took stock of the man who had rudely leapt from a black-and-white plaque on the wall into over six infuriating feet of living colour, Michelle promised herself she would not be moved – even though her job might well be in jeopardy if one of the stars of the exhibit should run her down to the Brothers Bartok. 'I've always heard,' she said all ice, 'that in America we have free speech.'

'Hey, now,' he said in his soft Southern charm of a voice, 'I think it's real quaint of you to believe that, Miss . . .?' he tried again.

'I'm Ginger Lake,' the young redhead stepped between Josh Free and her glaring co-worker. 'And, like wow, I'm a big fan of yours. I think your portrait is the best one in the whole exhibit! Very . . .' she pinched her plucked brows together, with the exertion of thought, 'lifelike!'

He turned to her with candid, if tolerant amusement, as though she were a toddler who'd dribbled banana-fudge ice cream down her best party dress or made a rude noise in company.

'Pleased to meet you, Ginger. It's not often that a country boy like myself gets to hear such open praise – or otherwise,' he shot a galvanizing glance at Michelle, 'for the way he looks, but I'm not even sure I'm responsible for it. Mr Reardon is a genius and I suspect any simulation of life in the portrait is entirely due to his skill with a lens.'

'Excuse me.' Refusing to be fixed there by his cool, cobalt eye, filleted by his down-home wit, Michelle took this chance to steal away.

Hurriedly, she made first her farewells to the artist and his friends, and then her apologies to a puzzled Alexander Bartok. Pleading exhaustion, she threw on her sensible cloth coat and beat a hasty retreat through the paths of celebrity, out into the damp night air.

Well, good for Ginger Lake, née Gloria Lefkowitz of New Rochelle, she thought, hunkering down into her roomy red coat and stepping up to the kerb where the taxi had just whooshed, splattering her all over with puddled rain. She'd finally met 'that kind of man'.

Michelle simultaneously wished them great joy and good riddance, for Mr Free in the flesh was every bit as intense as he was on celluloid. The very air around him hummed with crude energy and his hawkish blue-green eyes dug deep into her heart. He was no respecter of secrets, she could see that now, but stood the enemy of shadow, the archangel of home truths. Being such a mystery to herself, she could never feel comfortable with a man like that. No, Josh Free was not what you'd call a comfortable man. More likely, he was another Helmut Rigel.

Trailing a plume of white vapour in the rain, the cab zoomed off for the safety of home where she dreamt all night of fortune and men's eyes, the very pitch and colour of Caribe seas . . .

CHAPTER SEVEN

The damp morning after the Reardon show, Michelle convinced herself it wasn't anything like common envy that prompted her to corner Ginger Lake at the bubbling coffee pot.

'Well, what happened? Did Josh Free ask you out?' She gave elaborate attention to the stirring of the coffee in her cup. To her surprise, Ginger shook her bright head and the grenadine hair fanned out in permed waves of annoyance.

'Ask me out?' the girl said, recklessly cutting out a large, diet-smashing slab of Danish pastry for herself, and wrapping it in a napkin. 'All he wanted to know about me was *you*. He kept bothering me until I gave him your name and then he squeezed your phone number out of me too. I mean like, really.' She sucked the sugar from one finger while eyeing Michelle, top to toe, with fresh appraisal. 'Maybe he's into, you know, like blondes.' She examined a barb of her hair.

'Ginger, it doesn't really matter what he's into if I'm not into him.' Michelle went back to her desk, a brisk dismissal of the whole subject in the woodblock-tattoo of her high heels. Busily, she thumbed through a sheaf of receipts from last night's record sales.

Ginger sidled over, alternating currents of doubt and hope playing over her kewpie-doll face, like neon on a sign. 'You're not?' she asked, and the pastry crumbs gilding the corners of her mouth lent her, for an instant, a piquant innocence.

'No, I'm not.'

Michelle squirmed. It was wrong to tell a lie to a child. Even to a tall, precocious one like Ginger Lake. 'He's just the sort of man to break your heart, and lose the pieces.' *Didn't Ginger have a mother?* . . .

'Oh, right.' Ginger wandered off to the Mr Coffee

81

coffee-maker, tilted the pot and carried a flamingo-pink mug of steaming brew to her desk. It had the word 'Foxy' handpainted on it in big gold letters.

Michelle breathed easier. Some things are better left unsaid, especially when she herself had no idea how she really felt about Josh Free. Meeting him had been a bit like tasting avocado for the first time (at least she thought it had been her first time). She wasn't sure if she liked it – but wouldn't mind just one more bite . . .

A full ten minutes passed in silence before Ginger bore down on Michelle's desk like a pinball inside a tilted machine. She shook out her hair ferociously. 'No, I don't care . . . The fastest speed ever recorded would be between the time Josh Free asked me to dinner and the time I showed up at his apartment with my houseplants and a year's supply of sexy underwear!'

'I'll be sure to tell him.'

'You do that!'

Michelle sighed. She was beginning to regret ever having met Free. Some men were just too hot to handle, even in fantasyland. He had the kind of eyes that would glitter in the dark. She was a little afraid of him. It was thrilling . . .

Meanwhile, Ginger eyed the clock on the wall, wondering whether His call would come before lunchtime and whether she herself could manage to take it – without Michelle Smith ever knowing what heaven she'd missed.

With the sixth sense of the unrequited lover, Doria Sevenstars knew that a major change in Josh's world had occurred sometime between five p.m. last night and ten a.m. this morning.

First of all, there was the new Rolodex card, neatly printed 'M. Smith'. She tried envisioning a dentist named 'Murray', with a big chromium yellow Cadillac, and fingers that tasted like mint. But it didn't soothe her. There was something ineffably feminine about that 'M.' . . . '*M*other, *M*adonna . . . *M*istress'.

Then too, there was the furtive manner with which he'd slipped her the file card, as though he were implicating her in some clandestine scheme.

What's more, he'd had his hair cut that very day.

Some men, to celebrate a promotion or boost their sagging egoes would purchase expensive sports cars or Havana cigars, or sail off on a grand tour. Joshua Free had his hair cut. His thick curling midnight hair that Doria wanted to plait in and out of her fingers and tug at in love.

Towards the end of the work day, he had repaired to his gleaming private bathroom, steamed and showered his body, brushed his hair till it crackled like flame, switched shirts and changed ties. When he came forth, his skin was rubbed fresh and glowing pink and tender for love.

Seconds later, a surreptitious pass by his desk revealed he had also dabbed on a few precious drops of the oil he'd brought back from India, a pungent ichor of Asia and mystery, till this curious day left uncorked in its tiny flask.

Doria crossed and uncrossed her legs, wriggling with envy. Never had she seen him so ardent, so humble . . . so unsure, except in her own desperate fantasies.

The meticulous care he had given his body put her uneasily in mind of a bridegroom on his wedding day.

What was happening to him?

In agony, she'd seen the red light blink on his personal extension, as several times that morning he'd picked up the phone, only to let it drop, with a heavy thud, before the call was completed.

M. Smith?

Fervently, she wished he could complete the call. So that then she could pick up and hear the voice of her rival.

Or, with godly intercession, that of Murray the Dentist.

At five o'clock, dusk was already settling over Manhattan Island like a giant grey flannel blanket from L.L. Bean.

Her last appointment over, Michelle Smith leaned back with a soft groan. She'd been waiting all day to do this . . .

With a flick of her toes, two giddy high heels went sprawling out on to the carpet. Next, she rubbed the sore muscles on either side of her neck with both soothing thumbs.

'G'night, ladies.' Alexander Bartok eased on his snappy grey fedora, and, heaving a package wrapped in brown paper under his arm, pushed out of the fan-lighted door. After a decent interval, Ginger snapped shut her compact, dropped it into the thin red envelope bag, that had once been an alligator. Wriggling her fingers at Michelle, she was about to follow the boss out, when the phone buzzed softly.

She picked it up, none too eagerly, with a roll of her black-pencilled eyes.

'Bartok Gallery. Who's calling, pleez?'

Her shoulders stiffened. Then she turned, with a decided pout, to Michelle. 'Well, gag me with a spoon,' she said aggressively. 'It's for you.' She didn't even wait for Michelle's response, but quit the Gallery in a huff.

Michelle put her ear to the receiver, curious. 'Hello?'

'Miss Smith? This is Josh Free. We met at the Reardon Show last night.'

The rebel accents conjured up the man. Improper. Intense. Intimidating. 'Mr Bartok has already left for the day. But if you would like to leave a message . . .?'

A fourth quality, impatience, seeped into his voice. 'This isn't a business call, Miss Smith. As you damn well know.'

'What else can it be?'

'Now look here. I admit we didn't get on all that well last night. But that doesn't mean anything. Sometimes I'd rather have an exciting enemy than a dull friend.'

'Have you considered what I'd rather have?' She realized then that her bare heel, with a will of its own, was dancing nervously on the floor.

'That's just what I wanted to discuss over drinks,' he said smoothly, 'at Windows on the World. All right? Oh, and by the way, I think I might like to buy the Reardon portrait.'

Now there was no way out. A rich, influential client wanted her to dine. How could she refuse?

Minutes later, bundled into the back of a cab, she was speeding crosstown, dreading the moment they would meet again.

What a softhead! To say 'yes', when a man like Josh Free could only mean trouble for a woman like Michelle Smith. What had made her do it?

Naked curiosity, came the likely answer. She just wanted to see what kind of jive he'd use to dance her away from that first dismal impression, what jaded techniques he would try to get her into his penthouse bed, ringed round, most probably, by gigantic blow-ups of himself in sundry heroic poses, open-shirted, chest hairs flashing, sleeves in a gallant roll-up, as he ministers to a grateful, slobbering world. Mr Wonderful.

She lied to herself in this pleasant fashion until she was actually sitting across from him in a dining room atop the World Trade Centre, when the delirium of city lights was strung out below them like some brilliant newborn galaxy, and the champagne began to sing inside her head like a thousand crystal-throated birds of paradise.

To be fair, the preceding ninety-second elevator ride, that carried on nonstop, and shot patrons to the one hundred and seventh floor like some expensive drug in a hypodermic, had not been conducive to a clear head. Nor was the dizzy energy of the marble and bronze cavern into which she finally emerged.

Still shaky, she'd crossed under the mirrored canopy of the bar and continued on through a Pac Man maze of marble tunnels, inset with faceted glass and photomurals – until she reached the guardian at the gate, toiling over his Great Book of Names. Hungry mendicants whispered among themselves, and attended his every utterance.

She, however, had only to signify that she was with Mr Free to be whisked instantly to a V.I.P. table on the terraced floor.

The handsome room ran to cool curves, carpeted in brisk, brick red and rounded off with sand-hued banquettes. Well-dressed diners relaxed in chairs of cane and wood, amid brass railings, studded columns and spotlit white walls.

From every table could be seen lofty Manhattan vistas of distant spires, encrusted with white, yellow and blue lights like so many precious gems. A swirl of stars spilled on to the sky's bijouterie, to complete the fabulous picture.

Back on earth, the wine list boasted over a hundred vintages, all ready to be enjoyed. The table sparkled, with a loaf of French bread in a silver bowl, curls of cold butter on a china tray and lustrous crystal.

And presiding over it all was the figure of Josh Free, stark and brilliant in his immaculate grey Valentino suit, pale as smoke, his snub-collared white shirt, his lean silk tie of Japanese Red. A silver watch fob glinted magisterially on the soft weave of his wool waistcoat as he sat, relaxed and easy in his powerful body. All animal grace and sensual fire, he watched her move with those imperial turquoise eyes. She felt honoured to be so intensely seen, and then hopeful, as though his deep focus might make her more real to herself.

He stood politely and drew up her chair. Civet, coconut and spice – a dark scent of the Raj beat at his pulsepoints and spread warmly on the air around them.

He said he had ordered for her.

First, a sweet saute of white raisins and livers in crisp, hot pastry. An earthy baby aubergine, grilled with soy sauce and a tang of ginger. And then a punctiliously roasted pigeon, accompanied by a thick prune sauce. The Dom Perignon came iced in a tall silver bucket while their tulip glasses were invisibly refilled, like Beauty's in the old tale.

'You are impressed?' The royal blue eyes narrowed.

Michelle felt her shoulders burn naked under her dress. 'Not at all.' Her hand shook as she lifted the thin stalk of the champagne flute. She was being tested.

'Good for you. My ex-wife was very impressed.'

He was circling her, taking her scent, poised at the entrance of her heart. Strongly compelled by the double-charm of his looks, the curl of his voice, to come forth and love him, she had a crazy impulse to bolt from the table, from the skytop restaurant. But she couldn't move.

'You're not a native New Yorker, are you?' he probed.

Smiling like a madonna, she said, 'The view is as spectacular as I'd heard.'

'Yes. The backdrop becomes you.' A Baroque pearl against velvet, he thought. A painful beauty. What does she hide? 'I think I'm picking up the karma of an only child. *I* was an only child . . . of a Baptist preacher.'

'As to the Reardon . . .' she went on evasively, even as her head spun with the lilt of good wine.

'I'll buy it.' Lightly, he brushed this small business away.

They dined in uneasy silence for a while as he studied her closely, more and more certain that he was seeing only the crude outlines of a woman, not the woman herself.

'Do you regret having come tonight?' he asked, finally, resolving then and there not to let her know how her beauty worked on him.

'I haven't decided why you wanted me to.'

'Isn't that obvious?' He didn't smile. She noticed he seldom did. 'To sleep with you.'

'No, that's not it. You can sleep with a lot of women.'

He seemed pleased. 'You're right.'

'Then why?'

'Don't disappoint me, Michelle.'

She felt herself dollying into his electric-blue eyes, dazzled by the power he already had to wound her. Insanity – when they'd only just met, when she'd resolved to stand guard against all men who might overtake her and her secrets.

Their dessert came, an airy citrus mousse with paper-thin slices of lemon floating on top. She curved her spoon into the white froth.

'I think you're here because you want to know me,' she said simply, sensing that she was right, and that, again, he would be pleased.

'Yes.'

'There's more.'

He nodded.

You want me to know you, she thought, startled to be able to read him so clearly. She would have to throw him off.

'Are you really a philanthropist – or would power-monger be a better word for it?' she asked, suddenly cold.

'Neither.' He frowned. She was slipping away. Maybe he should just let her go. 'I do what I do because I have to. Like an oak tree or a racehorse. I don't try to get anything out of it, but the doing. Do you understand?'

'I understand . . . Josh.' In spite of herself, she felt her body opening up to him. The personal interest of such a man was the headiest of wines and Michelle Smith could not resist one sip of it, then another, and another. It had been so long since she had been loved a little.

Still, her pleasure in Free was overshadowed by her fear of telling him that she was an amnesiac, a freak, half a woman.

She must break it off now, before it was too late.

Before he asked her to meet him the very next night.

Before she could say 'yes'.

Overpowered by her fears, Michelle declined his inevitable invitation, pleading a prior date which both of them knew did not exist.

The look on his face would stay with her for a long, long time.

CHAPTER EIGHT

T.J. McShane crouched over his favourite bar stool and swigged down a mug of warm beer.

At first, he'd thought it was only for the kids – the allure of chocolate moustaches, the feel of a soft, small hand beating within his palm, the thrill of a touchdown scored in the lucky jersey he'd given young Ben Sevenstars, athlete extraordinaire!

As the summer days melted down, though, T.J. realized that Doria was inextricable from her children, wound in the psychic sinew, stitched into the heart. He couldn't love them without loving her too, she of the high-rigged ass, the caramel bosom – the hair, black and heavy as that of an Old Testament Queen.

He waved at the bartender. The heavy-moving man with the scar carved on his chin spoke gently. 'Yeah?'

'Hey, Ron, you ever been in love with a woman and two children?'

He shook his head, daintily. 'Who? Me? Nah.'

T.J. pushed his empty mug across the counter. 'Again.'

The beer foamed into the round-handled glass. T.J. studied it intently, as though an answer might be written in its murky depths. But no answer was forthcoming.

She just kept swimming around and around in his head like the angelfish the children had once put into the bathtub. He wished he could somehow pull the plug . . .

His temples pounded. Damn, it was bad enough that he'd forfeit his freedom for the splendour of ebony eyes, for Doria's thighs, but did he have to have his sinuses blocked too? It was too much for one man to bear . . .

Worse. It was getting worse. Recently, he had seen the gravity of his condition when the Suzanne Somers look-alike in the secretarial pool had invited him over for a drink at her place – and he had, incredibly, declined, because he'd promised to drive Fleur to her ballet lessons!

He could just hear his old man hooting away, calling him 'fool'. But then Himself had scoffed at everything, with the exception of James Joyce and the Internal Revenue Service.

Anyway, he *was* a pixilated fool to fall in love with a crazy broad of a doe-eyed Native American, who couldn't spend two minutes at a time in his presence without getting a lethal migraine.

The whole idea was terrifying to him.

He washed it all down with another warm beer.

He would soon forget her, Josh decided brashly, as he stood at his office window overlooking the bright commotion of the metropolis below. He would forgo her. If not today, then tomorrow, or the day after that. By now he could win his battles with great desire.

Since last night's disappointment, he had been re-playing the notes of her voice in his head, remembering her body's perfect *danse*. But it was an empty exercise. This woman's soul was shuttered and barred to him, the quadrants of her mind remote as any undiscovered star. It would be a waste of time to want her; that he continued to do so was more a tribute to his animal stubbornness than to her soft, bewildering beauty.

For once, he had walked through the day's business, unfired by the electric charge of the newsroom. Even T.J. had found it prudent to ask if Nicole had called, and the wonderful, tough Ms Sevenstars had brought him coffee – foul, cold and syrupy, but an unliberated act of charity, just the same. Josh Free wasn't used to the charity of his friends. He wasn't sure he liked it.

Impetuously, he grabbed his oyster-white cashmere scarf, and, whipping his coat over one arm, was crossing Thirty-Fourth Street before it dawned on him that for a man with no particular place to go he'd left work way too early on this still, clear Friday night in November. Well, he might as well get into playing hookey . . .

Slackening his pace a bit, he looked up at the autumn sky that slanted over the basilica of Manhattan lights like a ceiling of polished blue stone. It was a moving sight, but, as usual, for Josh Free, there were too many other people taking the air for him to fully enjoy it. A prowler, he preferred the empty bar, the lonely hour when the city rubbed up against him like a smokey-eyed woman who's stayed the night, and whispered only to him . . .

It hadn't even occurred to him where his steps were bent until he saw the brass nameplate screwed into the brownstone facade, and his attention was drawn upward to the high windows, mellow with lamplight. All at once, his mood, the night, made sense.

Inside, the others were just finishing their work.

She glanced over at him, startled, then lowered her flower-coloured eyes.

'The photographer who shot me . . . I'm here for his number. I want to commission some work . . .' Now that he was here, it was all he could think to say.

'Oh. Well, just a minute.' She looked up the number on a Rolodex, scribbled it down and handed the index card to him. 'We could have done this over the phone, you know.' The voice was coolly professional.

'Yes, of course. But I was in the neighbourhood.'

Michelle's colleagues discreetly looked away. Last-minute papers were filed. Coats were slipped on. Lights were switched off.

Then, they were alone, in a dimmed photographer's gallery, where the shadows of things were displayed on the walls as if they were real.

'I've given you the telephone number.' She moved calmly from behind her desk, but as she passed him he caught her hard by the arm.

'Damn it, woman,' he said. 'What the hell are you hiding?'

Her breath caught in her throat. 'I don't know what you're talking about. Just because I refused to go out with you tonight doesn't mean there's some deep, dark secret behind it. See how the male ego plays tricks on us . . .'

'No, oh no, that's too easy. I know you're attracted to me, Michelle. I can tell by the way your breath quickens when I come near you,' his lips were close to her hair, 'and the wild scent you give off when I touch you, like rose petals crushed between my fingers.' He brushed her cheek with the back of his hand, half roughly. The cheek suffused with warm colour.

'Let me go.'

'And I know another thing too.' His searching eyes frightened her. 'There is no other man in your life, hasn't been for some time. You weren't going anywhere tonight, were you?'

She canted her head, as if from a blow.

'Were you?' he demanded.

'No, I wasn't! Now why don't you go . . .?' She could feel the fragile structure of her new life sway beneath her feet, the hull about to crack under the weight of his demands . . .

Josh prowled the Gallery floor, both hands thrust deep into the pockets of his fur coat, the sea-washed eyes cruel and chafing. 'Why is it, I've been asking myself, she knows all the vital statistics of my life, from the catalogue, from gossip, from what I volunteered – my boyhood in Florida, the preacher father, the failed marriage – and I know next to nothing about her? She never talks about family, where she came from, who, in God's name, she is.'

Michelle knew she should offer him some harmless fable, but her tongue was stopped up. As in her worst dreams, she couldn't speak in her own defence.

'Prison, maybe. A criminal flight,' he went on ruthlessly. 'But you're not agile enough a liar to live like that for long.'

His words bit deep into her heart. Was this the man she had wanted to make love to her?

'Shyness?' The questions kept coming. 'Well, yes, I must admit I was almost convinced of that. But now I see you're not shy at all. You're terrified.'

She pushed back her hair with a sharp, nervous jab. 'What are you talking about?' She'd been right. He was a bully. He took pleasure in her dissection.

'Tell me the truth now.' He reared up before her like a judgement. 'You don't have any family, do you?'

Michelle could see the potter's wheel spinning towards her, the lathe, the knife, the chisel drawing near. 'I don't know.'

'And where are you from?'

'I don't know . . .' It was a whisper, a supplication. Leave me to the wind, to the ashes, to the hollow house.

'And who are you, "Michelle Smith", if that is your name, who in hell are you?'

The Gallery melted into a wavering field of weird greenish lights, the trap door of the world yawned open beneath her heels, and she was in free-fall again, somersaulting through the void, her arms flaring out stiffly like those of a drowning woman. 'I . . . don't . . . know.'

It was then he caught her to him, in the ebb of one passion, the flow of another. 'It's all right,' he soothed, 'I had to do that. I wanted to help you. It's all right,' he spoke into her parted mouth, not knowing half of what he whispered to her in the Gallery that night, or even if he meant it, only that he must still the sharp flutter of the heart against his chest, bend the bright head to his cheek, and beg again and again, for her forgiveness.

She asked to be taken home, and then she wept, and then she told him her story . . . about Dr Beckstein and the terror of touching the darkness.

It took courage at first, for she believed no man would want a shadow woman without a past, but it was a relief to pour out her dram of mystery to someone, anyone.

She spoke to him of loneliness, quietly, in the back seat of a cab, its windows clouded like an old man's eyes. He held her hand the whole time, and that, and the dimness, helped. The free-fall stopped.

She believed when he left her that night she would never see him again, not understanding that she had attracted the powerful tyranny of his interest. Josh Free, who felt he had nothing but a past, was wholly taken up by the miracle of a fresh start, the chain of memory and regret struck off by one resounding blow of fate, and Michelle Smith seemed to him a prodigy of guiltlessness – innocent and erotic at once.

But there would be time enough to tell her about these curious new sensations of his (God, he already missed her), when she was ready to hear them.

One arm upraised to flag a taxi, he stood at the kerb, only marginally aware of the midtown bustle surrounding him.

An older yellow cab detached itself from the winding string of traffic and drove up.

'Sutton Place,' Josh directed the driver as he stepped in.

Later, he might think of passion.

Would there be a later? Should there be? Why get tangled up in the mess, he who had always shunned the heat and din of other people's lives?

And yet, she filled him with a rare joy, a sweet nostalgia he couldn't name. Like the moon in eclipse, she drew his eyes upward.

He traced a circle on the frosted window with his fingernail, and peered out the rapidly closing peephole at the glittering city that no longer satisfied since she'd come into his world, floating free of the past, since he'd learned from her that yesterday's truths can vanish in the blink of an eye, and that today's full measure of life was all that really mattered.

How splendid and dangerous to be one such as she! Michelle Smith was what we all are at birth – innocent, at the mercy of those who know the world better than we – of those who claim to love us.

A woman at the mercy of love.

He was intrigued.

'So . . . what do you think is going on?' Doria inquired, taking care not to lift her cloudy eyes from the mounting hill of memos she'd managed to ignore all morning.

'I don't have the slightest idea.' T.J. scratched his head. Like the sad spider plant at the window, the Princess looked in need of a good pruning today. 'I tried to pry it out of him over a beer, but you know Josh. Tight as a tomb!'

'I have reason to suspect,' Doria said faintly, 'it's a woman.' As fantasy, Murray the Dentist just didn't work.

'Oh, you female types think everything revolves around you!'

Doria let the hot flash of annoyance pass. 'I heard him talking to her. It's serious.'

'Yeah?'

Doria hitched her shoulders.

94

Their speculations were interrupted when Josh came rumbling through the office like an armoured tank, growled an incoherent greeting, and disappeared into his room, letting the door slam behind him.

T.J. screwed up his face. 'That is not happy.'

'He's impossible,' Doria threw up her hands in misery. 'Last Friday he left work *before five o'clock*!'

T.J. whistled. 'Male menopause?'

'Won't you ever grow up?' she hissed.

He frowned down at the floor, hands in his pockets, the red scarf blazing around his neck. 'You got it. How about dinner tonight,' he asked, suddenly soft.

'The kids are away on a field trip,' she yelled over the electric buzz of the pencil sharpener.

'I know,' he shouted back.

'What?'

'I said "I know"!'

The grinding ceased. 'You mean . . . just me and you . . . for dinner?' Her yellow fascia of No. 2 pencils clattered to the floor.

'Is there a law against it?' T.J. scowled, as they simultaneously bobbed down to pick them up, and rammed into each other's heads . . . 'Jesus H . . .'

'Oww!' Doria shot up, rubbing the sore spot on her crown. 'Why don't you watch where you're going, Nijinsky?'

T.J.'s face went scarlet as his muffler. 'Hey, give me a break, you're no twinkletoes yourself!'

'Get out of here!' Doria waved her arms as though she were shooing away a large, dumb farm animal. 'Get out!'

'My pleasure!' T.J. retorted, giving his scarf end a self-righteous tug. 'And your spider plant looks like hell!'

'Why you little . . .' she cried. 'You can shove your dinner up . . .'

But, a member of a wise and witty race, T.J. had already slid out the office door.

The flowers were delivered to the Gallery swathed in paper cones, twirled into nosegays, fizzing out of tall wicker baskets. Tongues of flame from bright, Brazilian

95

jungles. Tender purple shoots of the cool forest glens. Painted carnations and tea roses fresh as rain. The square, white cards always bore the same message: 'I'm sorry I made you cry . . . Josh.'

On the third day of this perfumed deluge, she phoned him.

'I'm the one who should apologize,' were her first quiet words. 'I shouldn't have tried to dodge you.'

'You did what you had to.'

'Do you still want to see me?'

'Do you want me to?'

She sighed. 'I think so. You're sort of implicated in my life now, a magical transference in the word. You see, you know my story.'

'Stop feeling so guilty about it! You've got a chance to start again. That's more than most people can say.'

'If only I could be like most people . . . with in-law and lower back problems. I'd love a bland, unexceptional life.'

'Your life's not so bad.' Sometimes he would go hard on her, if she needed it. A way of being together, a blueprint for love unfurled itself before him. 'You're making good money. You have an interesting career. You're beautiful . . .' He remembered the curve of her neck, the ivory hands. Desire rushed through him. 'I want to see you,' he said under his breath. 'Now.'

'I can't leave work.'

'Tonight then.'

She hesitated. 'All right.' She wanted to see him too, in the way one yearns to see a fever reach its peak. Because she'd run a fever of the heart ever since that night in the Gallery – as she alternately damned herself for letting Free stray too close, and then, regretted bitterly it had not been close enough.

Anticipation of the glittering prize he held out to her – an end to her loneliness – was almost more than she could bear.

'I'll pick you up at seven at the Gallery.'

'That's fine.'

'Goodbye, then, Michelle.'

'Goodbye, Josh.'

Troubled, Josh clicked down the phone. Even now, in hot pursuit of her, he was at war about the woman. With barely concealed excitement he asked Doria to pick up tickets to an Itzhak Perlman concert at Carnegie Hall. At least he and Michelle wouldn't have to talk much tonight. He could just watch her, luxuriate in being near her, bathe in her glow.

There would be time after all for that voluptuous vertigo of new passion, that plunge into her dark, vibrant depths . . . time to learn how she must be loved.

That magical night, the bright lights of the concert hall dim.

The conductor taps his baton. The orchestra begins to play.

In her rose-and-white scarf chemise, Michelle seems elated, her eyes sparkle. She strains forward in her seat like a young child, as though she can't get enough beauty, as though she will breathe the music through her skin, a new plant scenting water.

Josh leans over. 'Which instrument do you like the most?' he asks her on a hunch.

She makes a gesture with her remarkable hands, a bowing motion. 'The violin.'

'Why is that?'

'I'm not sure. Maybe because it has such a human shape, a human voice . . .'

In turn, he nods, filing away this information for future use.

Then she turns back to the concert, enraptured, as Itzhak Perlman fills the auditorium with a sound of men and angels.

For Josh Free, it is not enough to watch the woman beside him. He yearns to make her comfortable enough to love him. But he knows it will take time and patience to peel away the layers, and that the possible rewards will be great. For her, this one time, he must try to be patient, to give her room.

Once, when the music had especially moved her, she inadvertently brushed against his shoulder. She fluttered a second, and then settled, permitting herself to rest lightly along his side.

The perfumed warmth that rose from her body left him dizzy with longing.

After the concert, over dinner at the romantic River Cafe on the water, he asked her if Michelle Smith were her real name.

Done up like the dining room of an elegant yacht, the Cafe glowed with pink-shaded table lamps which cast a flattering light on the celebrity patrons scattered about the darkened room. Beyond the window, the Brooklyn Bridge twinkled, intricate as a constellation of stars. A dreamy Michelle broke the petals off a stalk in their vase. 'No, it's not my name. Does that matter to you, Josh?'

He reached for her hand. It burned where he touched her. 'I'd like to be able to say it doesn't.'

'Don't you ever lie?'

'Only to myself.'

'You're the first person I've told any of this to, besides Dr Beckstein,' she confessed with sad, downcast eyes, realizing with a pang, that not even Helmut had known of her shrouded memory. He'd been too in love with his fantasy of her to care . . . 'I'm not even sure why I did it. Maybe I wanted to scare you away – before you got too close.'

His eyes were cool blue stones. 'I may as well tell you now, I am not a patient man by nature. But I am stubborn as sin and you'll see I don't let go – once my journalistic instincts are aroused. Whoever Michelle Smith really is, I'll do anything I can to help find her. I promise you that much.'

Michelle watched him closely, wanting so much to believe, to be saved.

All these months, amnesia had meant having to walk a tightrope blindfolded – unable to see where she'd come from, or where she was going to.

To have someone to guide her across now would be a wonderful thing . . .

The possibility of connecting with another human being again – of not being so nakedly alone – almost took her breath away, almost obscured the fact that Josh Free hadn't yet offered her the protection of his love. A part of him still stood aloof from her, examining, turning her this way and that like a chunk of flawed crystal, whose radiant intricacies would, sooner or later, give way to logic.

Nonetheless, looking into his clear, fierce, mariner's eyes, she knew that what he'd said was absolutely true.

She had made a friend.

She went out from the restaurant, rejoicing in the gift.

CHAPTER NINE

Michelle fumbled at the belt of her pearl-white Oriental robe, embroidered with scarlet dragons. Who could be beating at her door this early on a Saturday morning?

She spoke into the intercom. 'Yes?'

'It's Josh.'

She buzzed him up, in a romantic turmoil. Smoothing the gold bell of her upswept hair, she waited at the door.

Seconds later, looking ruggedly handsome and ready for action in his chocolate bomber jacket and faded Levi's, he strode into her sunny studio, holding out a rented violin and an unknown piece of sheet music like the Magi's gift. Vivaldi. *The Four Seasons*. Something Michelle had said the other night, her ecstasy at the theatre, had given him an idea. So when he passed this music place on Broadway and Forty-third, he'd stopped in and bought . . .

'How about a cup of coffee?' Michelle had laughed her silvery laugh, thinking he was playing with her. 'I can't read this chickenscrawl, Josh. I'm just a lowly assistant to an art dealer.'

With all his official and personal efforts to discover Michelle's identity being thwarted at every turn, Josh's frustration finally boiled over. 'God damn it! I came all the way up here with this cockamamie violin. The least you can do is try it!'

'You are serious . . .'

'Yes, I'm serious!' His face darkened with anger.

Hastily, Michelle sank down at the edge of her sofa, newly covered in a flower-sprigged Laura Ashley chintz, and thumbed open the sheet music to the first page. It was the 'Winter' section of the piece. Helplessly, she appealed to him. 'What next?'

He spun around a Conran kitchen chair moulded in plastic like a lump of white Turkish Delight, and plunked down on it, legs akimbo. 'Pick it up, woman. Pick it up and play!'

With a sense of the surreal, she lifted the violin to her shoulder, trying to remember how the master Perlman had done it the other night.

The bow did fit neatly into her hand. The smell of the varnished wood beneath her chin seemed to Michelle the world's finest perfume. Her eyelids closed, her lips parted as though she would kiss.

Inwardly, Josh cheered her on. *Goddamn, she's going to do it!*

She touched the bow to the violin.

The most grating cacophony either of them had ever been unfortunate enough to hear, issued from her instrument.

Michelle's eyes flew open. It was almost as though the instrument had singed her skin, the way she fanned out her arms and dropped the violin to the sofa cushions.

She rounded on Josh with fire in her mouth.

'Are you happy now? Have your precious journalistic instincts been satisfied?' Hidden in her anger was the fear that as soon as Josh got to the bottom of her story, he would lose all interest in 'Michelle Smith', that he was more enchanted by her mystery than by her essence.

Isn't that what Dr Beckstein had warned her against?

'What in the hell are you talking about?' Josh bellowed, coming to his feet and unsettling the chair. 'Here I'm trying to help you . . .'

'Maybe I don't need your help. Maybe I don't want it!'

'Michelle . . .' Stung by the truth of her accusation, he didn't go on. Face it, he had been treating her more like some brain-teaser that would yield to his almighty male efforts, than as a woman of feeling. 'Okay. I guess I pushed too far.' Then, because it was hard for him to be wrong, even for her sweet sake, he added, 'But why can't you trust me a little?'

She turned from him to tinker at the kitchen counter, while he watched the crimson dragons leap across her graceful back.

'It's just that I don't want to break again, to start the

free-fall. This time I might never snap out of it. You've got to be more careful with me, Josh Free.'

He felt in the bone that she was right.

What he didn't know was that Michelle grieved because she was, against all her rules, falling foolishly in love.

'I'm sorry,' was all he said.

He left her then because he hated her and he wanted her and she didn't want him, because she was heartbreakingly beautiful and had stood at the window of his dreams, her hair a rain of silk, her long white hands a hieroglyphic of passion across his bare chest. In this way, he had begun to love her bitterly, without balance, the way he had always wished to love.

In a rout of disappointment and desire, he'd walked the Saturday streets, ending up at his chic health club, where he'd taken a sauna, and then emerged, steaming, to plunge his body into the sparkling iciness of a cold tub. It was as though he were trying to awaken himself from the atmosphere of dream she had woven around him, to drive out one extreme sensation with another. In vain, he reached for the right charm, the countermand to passion. He hoped it was not too late.

Home again in his Sutton Place penthouse high above the city lights, where the cool shimmer of mirrored screens, tall Japanese urns and steel floors gave the urbane precision he favoured in all things, Josh Free saw that it most probably, wonderfully was.

For weeks, the violin lay untouched on the table.

It was the first thing Michelle saw in the morning; she could sense it, alive and glowing in the wood, throughout the night.

More than once, she pleaded with Josh to come and take it away, but somehow he never got around to doing it, and somehow, she was secretly pleased that he hadn't.

How good it had felt to hold the instrument close to her body, like a beloved infant!

For one unbearable moment, it had almost seemed as though she could actually play it. If she were able to empty her mind of all preconceptions and misgivings, if

102

she were to pick up the strings once more and try again . . . might she not find some clue to the woman hiding inside her, just as Josh intended?

She switched on the arc lamp, casting a warm circle around herself. Outside, a light, chill rain pattered against the window. The mantel clock under the bell jar chimed seven times.

Michelle tucked the white robe about her legs. Then, shy as a new lover, she stretched out her hands, and ran them over the smooth, honey-coloured wood. Her fingers tingled with the odd sensation that she had stroked a living thing. The bow vibrated in her palm. The strings seemed to wait for her touch.

She studied the Vivaldi piece for a moment, the black notes dancing rhythmically across the page, like figures painted on an Egyptian urn.

To the hammering of her pulse, she began to play.

The pure, clear beauty of the violin stunned her.

Instinct flowed in her strokes.

She was a musician, a classical musician.

Head whirling, she leaned into the music, every muscle, every sinew at the service of Vivaldi's icy blasts of sound.

She felt stretched to breaking, plucked apart by her fingers' own frenetic motions. And then, she was the instrument, the music issued from her, luminous, clear and bright.

As the bow flew in her hand, she wanted to stop, because there was pain in the extraordinary pleasure, but she couldn't do it all at once. Frantically, she wound down the piece, her face chalky with the strain, her arms and neck aching with the unaccustomed exertion.

Then the room blackened. She fell back against the pillows.

But not before the window of memory yawned open, and scenes of her past life began to stream in like chill winter sunlight . . .

It was Friday night. She peered out of the musician's pit at the jewel-box glitter of the first stage-left box seat.

Yes, oh yes, he was there again, just as he had been every other night that wondrous week, the handsome, artfully attired man with hair like a helmet of Florentine gold, a charm of a man with an aristocrat's cheekbones and skin with the downy blond softness of a petted boy. Gazing down from his box he looked the way she imagined her father would have looked, if only he'd stayed with his little family. Calm, distinguished, sure that everything was right in his world because he willed it that way, because he alone held a birthright to happiness.

She imagined the bright-haired man must love music too, and the notion lent a special enchantment to the night. She was touching him with her music, affording him intimate pleasure, even though she was just an anonymous hand plucking at a violin.

Between the anticipation of performance and the young man's superordinary presence, the excitement burned brightly in her face.

With his special fondness for the young musician, the first violinist was concerned. 'Are you feeling all right? You look flushed.'

Favouring gentleness in men, she rewarded him with a smile. 'I'm fine, Gregor, really.'

She was herself a blonde of the palest hue, a shy, slim woman with quicksilver eyes pointed like a gypsy dancer's and it was common for first-time acquaintances to mistake her fragile appearance for weakness. But on second glance, she had all the symptoms of strength – managing her chequebook as handily as other people's lives. Her stranded, angry mother had seen to that much, although she hadn't been entirely able to root out her daughter's sense of responsibility for others.

As a music student, she had always been the kind one, the one who listened well. Sometimes her friends called her 'Sister Dear'. Now, years later, she was a promising violinist at the start of a brilliant composing career. This was no time for other people and their tangled lives. It took a while but she had come to see that a woman's first responsibility was to get her own life in order. Only then could she guide others, gently, to do the same.

The house lights went down. The conductor ascended the podium, lifted his baton. La Boheme began and once again, she was lost in the wonder of her music. Afterwards, there would be a drink with the first violinist, a late supper, early bed, alone. A placid life, far removed from the exalted romantic dramas played out behind the Metropolitans' golden curtain.

But tonight is different.

Tonight, after the performance, there is a shining black limousine waiting for her at the stage door. Seated inside is the magnificent blond man.

She would always remember his hand resting on the car door, a hand long and white as a young sea bird. She had never seen such beautiful fingers. She couldn't tear her eyes away.

'Will you join me for dinner tonight? I'm a stranger here in New York.'

Simple words, but to her they were words to set music to.

How clever of him to phrase it just like that: he, the stranger; she, the one to give service. Still, she hung back in a shy rapture. Up till now, the major cycles of her life had been so finely tuned, so carefully orchestrated. This wild impulse to love, this listing towards an unknown force was new and wonderful and frightening too.

'Please . . .' He held open the car door, one hand gracefully outstretched to receive her.

As if from another world, she heard Gregor's voice, calling her back. 'Where are you going? What about our drink?'

She half-turned her head, as though she would speak if she could, but the young man had folded his fingers over hers. An erotic shock ran through her and she stumbled against his side. As he led her into the Rolls, she had the distinct feeling she had crossed over an ancient, invisible boundary to a rare and beautiful place – a place where men were magnificent golden animals with hands burning white as God's pure grace. She knew then she would be this man's lover. The dream had begun.

It was close inside the car. He sat too near her, their knees not quite touching through the expensive fabric of his suit.

105

It took a moment for her to realize he was talking to her, very close to her ear, with a sound like the drone of a hot summer's day on the campagna.

'I'm glad you accepted my invitation. It would have been a lonely night for me.'

The sleek limousine rolled silently through the evening rush, as he spoke to her. 'You see, I'm from out of town, here on business. I have a late night meeting and no one to spend the time between with.'

'I'm from out of town myself,' *she sounded breathless.* 'I came here only a few years ago for my music studies.'

'You are very good.' *He had the remote, flawless face of a Medici.* 'I was watching you.'

'And I was watching you.'

'What did you see?'

'Myself,' *she would have said if she'd had the courage, if it didn't sound so extraordinary to her.* 'I saw myself.' *Instead, she described a businessman in his early thirties, with sensitive hands and a civilized manner, the kind of man her mother had bred her to marry and make use of.*

Through the years that wounded woman had nursed her young daughter with equal parts of love and bitterness. Now she would extract from the girl the burden of her dreams – great wealth, status, independence from men.

As she'd told her daughter often enough, it hadn't been easy for a woman alone, raising a child on the salary of a department store clerk. To get along, she'd moonlighted as a hat check girl in a fancy seafood restaurant with a bubbling lobster tank and a wine list, as long as her arm, encased in red leather. Sitting in her shadowy cloakroom, she watched the slow-moving lobsters scuttle along the bottom of the tank, on their nightly way to oblivion. From her first evening on the job, she'd refused to prepare a shellfish meal at home.

Life with mother was full of quirky moments like that. Her sensitive daughter could never be sure what mood would be holding sway, or how she could best protect herself if it wasn't a good one . . .

Like that one time in winter when it had snowed all the day before and an exuberant six-year-old, she had clutched her mother's hand tightly as they trudged through the deep fall.

Underneath her coat, Mama wore her daughter's favourite dress, the white one with the big coral buttons set all the way down the front, like little suns. To make her happiness complete, the little girl's red rubber boots left perfect round impressions in the snow.

That morning the sky had been very blue, too intensely blue for it to be an accurate memory, while all around her the world was melting. Water slid like chandelier lustres from cherry trees, alders and maples; water gushed glittery as diamonds in the gutters.

Surging with an unnameable joy, Emma had needed to run through the snowy field of the streets, the red boots beating against the whiteness. It was too late when she threw a laughing glance over her shoulder – and caught her mother's unguarded look of pure disdain.

The sun went out of the day, of a young child's life. In her moment of distraction, she ran smack into a winter-coated gentleman, toppled down, and rolled over and over into a high bank of snow.

'Are you all right, little girl?'

Her cheeks pinked against the cold wetness; as she swallowed some snow like a sea brine that stung all the way down to her toes.

What had she done wrong? Why did Mama hate her so?

The elderly man bent to help her up; she gasped for breath like a failing swimmer. 'Is this your little girl?' He tipped his grey felt hat at her mother who had come up alongside them, swinging her patent leather bag aggressively. Men always made some sort of salute to Mama's beauty.

'Yes. Thank you. I'll take care of this.'

The kind old man flashed a smile with lots of gold teeth in it. 'You should watch where you're going, Sissy. You could get hurt.'

She didn't answer. She was too busy watching her mother's face, sharp-edged and unfamiliar against the crazy blue tilt of the sky.

When the man had moved off, Mama fixed her with a cold stare. 'Don't ever do that again,' was all she said.

But it was enough. From then on, the child became stealthy and timid about her joys, and her love for her mother was never again unmixed with a nameless fear. If in death – she'd only been fifty-five at the time – her small, fierce presence had gone from her daughter's life, the lessons still lingered, a trace mineral in the blood. Tonight, they would be tested as never before.

With its love seats and walls of flame-coloured velvet, Orsini's on Fifty-Sixth Street gave off a sensuous darkness. A luxury of crystal chandeliers sent what light there was eddying into intimate corners where lovers dined, while in the background a tape of 'Una Furtiva Lagrima' played. She, the musician, could not have been thinking very clearly, for she seemed to know all the words, but found the melody hard to place.

She sat slender and cool beside him, like a marble nymph. Her exotic dish of rice, veal marrow, saffron and wine lay untouched on the table before her, as Michael described how, sitting in the twilit theatre, he had first noticed her exquisite hands playing over the violin. He had become fascinated, he said, smiling with the easy grace of man who was born to be served by women.

'Looking at you,' there was a note of wonder in his tone, the same wonder she had known when he'd touched her for the first time, 'is like staring into a mirror.' He seemed uncertain. 'I know that sounds strange. I don't usually talk like this. Must be the wine . . .'

'No, not strange at all,' she said in a low voice. 'I feel the same way.' Had she spoken too soon, opened herself up too easily?

It didn't matter anymore . . . She wanted to bear him gifts of herself, had no desire to hold back. So she talked about what was closest to her: the transcendance of making music, the strictness of her upbringing, the insuperable fact of Michael's beautiful face, his gentle manner, so striking in an American man.

Being young, she accepted all her own mythologies as truth. The look of callowness on his perfect face as he listened did not alarm her. The easiness of his smile,

108

beguiled her all the more. After all, Michael was her dream man. One did not question a dream.

'Dessert?' the waiter asked.

'Just the bill, please.' Michael leaned towards her. He rustled like money. 'Would you like to take a carriage ride, like a real tourist?'

Having lived frugally, as young musicians must, she was enthralled. 'Yes, I would like that very much.'

'I can see you're a traditionalist, like me.'

'In many ways.'

'Good. Then that's what we'll do.'

When he reached for her arm to guide her from the table, the cuff of his dark blue suit slipped back, and she noticed the fine, thin bones of his wrist, the tender blond hairs along his arm. This image filled her with such a fierce protectiveness, she wanted to gather him to her, rock him against all harm . . .

They rode in shy silence to the edge of Central Park by the brightly lit Plaza Hotel, where the chauffeur let them out. Nearby, a horsedrawn carriage with a fiery red leather interior and two blazing rear lamps, waited. The driver tipped his tall hat to them as they stepped in.

'Just drive around the Park,' Michael told him, slipping a large bill into his hand. 'I'll let you know when to stop.'

The gentle sea motion of the carriage, the clip-clop of the horse's hooves along the lamplit path, lulled her to drowsiness. She leaned her head against Michael's shoulder and looked up at the stars. The stars! Most of the time, in the city, one forgot they were even up there. With a burst of gratitude she realized that Michael had made them manifest, opened the sky for her, and poured out the stars like diamonds, over their heads.

His lips were cool against the burning of her skin. He laid kisses along her neck like a string of Oriental pearls.

She gasped for breath. Her silk chemise rode up her thighs as she reached out to him. Her flanks in his steady hands, he pulled her against his taut body.

In that brief span of seconds, she lost all sense of place and proportion.

For the first time in her life, a time that comes to all women who love, she surrendered completely to instinct. The feel of him on her hands seemed inevitable, the scent of his skin, like a sacred incense, the tidal pull between them too powerful not to be obeyed.

'Love me, Michael,' she whispered, *willing him never to let her return to the way she'd been, cut off from these new worlds of passion, unregenerate and unhumbled by love.*

She let herself be moulded to his body like a second skin, an energy aura. She wanted him inside her, like a heartbeat, like a song.

Before this, she had only drowsed her life away with her little dreams of music and her quiet bed. Michael had changed all that now, Michael and his angel's hands, and his blessed, blessed love . . .

Then abruptly, maddeningly, he released her.

Her blow caught him on the side of the face, before she was even aware of her anger. With equal passion, he captured her fingers and pressed them to his lips. 'I want to love you. I will. But it's got to be right, when I say.' He signalled to the driver. 'I'm taking you home.'

It was as though the stars had gone out. She couldn't bear to look him in the face, having turned him away with her greed and her grasping . . .

'You're very quiet,' he said, when they'd finally rolled to a halt before the Plaza Hotel and he was handing her down from the carriage.

'I've already said too much.' She wished she had the power to erase the memory of what had happened that night, and begin again, this time with a proper happy ending.

'I come from an old family,' Michael offered by way of explanation. 'I don't trust anything that happens too fast.'

They both got into the Rolls. While the yellow bars from passing headlights rolled across the dim interior, she spent the trip preparing herself for the moment when he would say 'goodbye', she never knowing what they could have been together, he leaving her an imperfect woman, for she felt in her heart that only this man could teach her what it was to truly love.

'That's all right,' she said when they'd reached the garishly lit lobby of her building on East Seventeenth Street. 'You don't have to come all the way up.'

He frowned. 'But I want to.'

She could tell Michael had ways of doing things, unvarying, methodical, beautiful ways which taken together gave the impression of a moral code. In reality, they were just grace notes, aimless brilliancies in a life without pain. They rode up in an empty elevator, not speaking a word.

The dull metal doors slid open. The couple walked down the hall to the corner apartment where she clicked the key into the lock.

'Good night, Michael.'

He laid a restraining hand on her arm. 'Wait a minute . . . Don't you want to see me again?' His crown of fair, baby-fine hair made him seem very young, very lost.

'I didn't think you wanted to see me.'

With unexpected tenderness, he tipped her face up to the light, and pressed his mouth on hers. 'Does that answer your question?' he asked, when they'd finally broken away in wonder. 'I'll call you tomorrow night.'

'I'll be waiting.'

Caught between emotions, she watched him as he disappeared into the elevator.

Should she have called him back?

On the one hand, the unhurried care he was taking with her made her feel cherished and unique. On the other, she needed him to love her as she'd never needed anything before. She wanted more from this man than from any man before.

She looked down, astonished to see that her hands were trembling.

Maybe it was better Michael had left her early tonight, after all. Things were going much too fast – and she was breathless with first love.

CHAPTER TEN

The fresh-cut blossoms began to arrive at eight o'clock the next morning, some with the dew still on them, until her small apartment was giving off the sultry scent of a rich man's hothouse.

Michael must have plundered an entire forest for her!

She went about stroking the petals, burying her face in their fragrances, thrilled by the casual extravagance of his gesture, when for years she had measured pennies with an artist's starved good taste.

That evening, she was almost too excited to go to the performance of Boheme.

Lingering before her pierglass, she dressed with extra care in her most bewitching black satin dress, an antique from a SoHo shop, for which luxury she had once saved for over half a year.

Gaily, she attached a white rose to her hair, which flowed like water down her back. What was it a white rose meant in the language of flowers? She smiled as she remembered: a worthiness to be loved. To be loved!

Out on the street, the autumn air was biting on her skin. She crushed the tan cloth coat against her slenderness, her long hair blowing like delicate leaves in the wind. When she arrived at the packed theatre, and descended into the orchestra pit, her colleagues watched, and wondered what made her glow so from within.

The picture of a lady, she sat elegantly straight in her chair, brushing her fingertips over the folds of her black dress, prolonging the instant before she would lift her gaze to the seat where he would be, all glittering-eyed and impassioned with love for her. This was a new, intense pleasure to be savoured: the anticipation of a man's full focus, of his eyes running upon her like a caress, of her body yearning towards him beneath her thin dress. It was unbearably erotic to wait for that one perfect moment, that shock of recognition. 'He wants me . . .' Her breast rose and fell, shallowly.

Gregor nodded his customary greeting. The musicians readied their instruments . . . men in chiaroscuro, women in sweeping black dresses, their dark flow broken only by the pale curves of their calves and the delicate Chinese arch of their feet.

At last, when the maestro ascended the podium, she decided it was time. With a deep, physical excitement, she raised her gentian eyes to Michael's seat over the red velvet bank of the Golden Horseshoe.

But with the first bars of Puccini's most romantic opera, she came upon a stranger sitting in Michael's place.

Disappointment flowed through her like electricity. She hated that well-fed usurper with the dark precious moustache, hated the whole painted sea of audience, hated herself most of all for being so easily fooled . . .

She glowered into the light of her music stand. Anger tingling in the nerves of her fingers, her fierce emotion communicated itself to the strings of her violin, and they cried out shrilly under her hand. When Gregor raised his bushy eyebrows at her, she coloured to a deep musk rose, like a madder dye seeping into damask.

Arias were bravoed, preludes played, curtains rung down. Somehow, she got through the performance, comforting herself with thoughts of her brilliant career. To be an acolyte of Music, a high priestess of Art, that was her aim. There was no room in a great artist's life for personal sentiment . . .

Her knees trembled under the delicate black dress. She didn't believe a word of it anymore.

The minute the curtain fell on that night's interminable performance, she rushed up from the pit in tears.

Gregor chased after her on the stairway that led to the stage door. 'What is the matter with you tonight?' he called out. 'What were those notes you were playing! God knows Puccini never wrote them!'

'I know, I know, Gregor. Please. I'm sorry.' She stopped in mid-flight.

'What is wrong?' he asked, more softly. 'Are you in some kind of trouble?'

Members of the opera chorus went swishing by in their wide costumes, parting for them on the stairs like a stream in the path of a boulder.

She shook her head, firmly. 'Nothing is wrong.'

'Would you like to talk about it over a drink?'

It hurt to refuse her friend, but the last thing she wanted was to go out tonight among the lovers. It would just point up her loss.

'Gregor, I'm sorry. I'm tired tonight. Maybe Saturday?'

'Yes, if you would like that.' He tried to cover his disappointment.

She touched his hand. 'You're always there when I need you.'

The old musician seemed moved. 'To me, you are an important part of the music we make here. Someday you will be a great artist.'

'I've always believed that someday I will.' And she wouldn't let Michael or any other man tamper with the dream that burned at her core.

'All right then. I will let you go in this odd mood that you're in.'

He walked her to the crowded stage door exit.

Just as Gregor was about to turn back to the pit where, in his haste to catch up with her, he had left his violin, a liveried chauffeur came up and handed her a vellum envelope.

It was a message from Michael. 'Had to leave on business. How about dinner tonight?'

Hardly daring to believe her good fortune, she flung her arms about the bemused first violinist, knowing she was being childish and irrational, knowing that her Michael could vanish tomorrow.

'Where? How?' In the throes of a wild happiness, she questioned the chauffeur. 'If he's out of town . . .?'

'This way, Miss.'

Questions were written all over Gregor's face.

She declined to answer them.

114

With an apologetic parting glance at her friend, she ducked into the limo. It glided out of the sharp-edged Manhattan night into Queens and on to bustling Kennedy Airport.

She rapped on the glass partition with her knuckles. 'The airport? Why here?'

'Those were my instructions. There's a jet waiting,' he said crisply through an intercom.

Luxuriating against the soft cushions, she threw back her wild honey hair. The generosity of Michael's company was overwhelming! What an expense account he must have – and such a young man too! A ripple of pleasure ran through her to think that the hard-nosed corporate world had already recognized what an exceptional person Michael was.

'This is the man I've been waiting for,' she told herself over and over to make it real. 'He's here at last. I'm going to meet him now in a private jet, and he's going to take me, God knows where, to heaven maybe.'

While the chauffeur sought the right terminal he explained that Michael was in Miami, closing an important deal and that, if she wished, she was to join him there for dinner.

'But I haven't any clothes,' she protested, giddily, 'no luggage . . .'

'My employer will provide whatever you need,' came the terse reply.

As she had done, the night she met Michael, she fell into the fantasy with the ease of a born dreamer. People never bothered about petty details like suitcases and itineraries in fairy tales. Why should she?

The chauffeur saw to it that, in a happy daze and clutching her violin case to her chest, she had safely boarded the Lear jet, whose silvery wings arched in the darkness of the runway like Jacob's angel.

To her further astonishment, she was the sole passenger on the flight. There was a polite pilot, co-pilot and hovering hostess to see to her every whim, and that was all.

From then on, nothing seemed quite real, as the aircraft rolled along the runway and launched itself into space.

They served her caviar in a silver dish and a hundred dollar bottle of Taittinger champagne. She licked her fingers like a greedy child, and drank too much wine, her head spinning crazily with the aeroplane through the clouds. All the while, the Brandenburg Concertos rippled out of her headphones, and she could see them take shape in her mind's eye, a celestial intaglio, a golden tree with its roots in the skies. She felt drunken and decadent and marvellously high as she opened her black case, took out the violin and played along with the recording.

The hostess stopped in the passageway nearby to listen. Never had she been so moved by the pure splendour of sound, the splendour of emotion running high and free.

Two hours later, it seemed just a snap, the jet touched down in tropical Miami. The air in the cabin grew sultry. She hooked her coat over one arm and tucked her violin case under the other. Then she shook hands with the crew, the four of them smiling as though they had shared a good joke together.

Michael stood waiting for her in the V.I.P. lounge. A brilliant dash of white linen suit, soft felt fedora, and angel-blue shirt. She thought of him then as a cob, a male swan, with his finely moulded head, and elongated frame, rising above his fellows with a heartbreaking grace.

Her heart played arrhythmic percussion in her chest when he saw and smiled at her.

'There you are,' he said easily, as though she had come from just around the corner to be with him, instead of clear across the wild blue skies. 'Good trip?'

'Oh God, yes.'

'You had the best pilot on the East Coast. We stole him away from American for outrageous sums.'

They strolled towards the lounge exit.

As she walked by his side, she found it hard to keep up her end of the conversation, so much was she enjoying the muscular sway of his body under those creamily expensive garments. She remembered how surprisingly lightweight he'd felt in her arms. At that moment, she knew she would bear him gladly in her heart, for the rest of her days.

'I thought you might like to stretch your legs before we go

116

on to Key West,' he was saying in his reasonable voice, when she was feeling anything but reasonable.

'Key West?' She held on to the exotic sound of it.

'Yes. Didn't Lincoln tell you?'

'Well no, he didn't.'

'I'm sorry.' He lifted his fair eyebrows. 'It's all been arranged. We're flying down tonight to our beach house. You'll love the beach house.'

She didn't get a chance to respond as little explosions of happiness went off inside her.

'How about a champagne and caviar break first? I know a fabulous restaurant not too far from here.'

'I already had caviar and,' she slurred her words, 'lotsa champagne. On the plane. Wasn't there a song about that – the champagne on the plane . . .?'

'You are funny. There's no limit on pleasure here! I mean, it's not like deer season or something. You're allowed to have as much cods roe and grapejuice as your heart desires!'

'Uh, Michael.' She reached out for his arm as the room seemed to heave up around her. 'I think my heart has just stopped desiring.'

'In that case, how does a cup of coffee sound?' He grinned at her, perfectly handsome at her arm.

'Fine. And could we just have it here at the airport?'

'Whatever you want.'

Her relief showed and made him laugh.

They shouldered through the seething glass and metal cauldron of the airline terminal, and camped out at a coffee shop counter where two Rastas in dreadlocks were showing lots of teeth and arguing about music.

She spoke dreamily to the blond man beside her, as she hunched over the vaporous mug that was supposed to bring her feet back to the ground. 'I must say your company is very generous.'

'My company?'

'You know. The jet, the caviar, the works, divine! They must think the world of you, Michael.'

He seemed charmed by her words. 'Oh yes, that they do.'

*She drained her mug of strong black coffee and reques-
ted a second cup. She imagined it was muscular enough to
stand alone, without the mug. In her ear, the ocean roar of
alcohol dulled to a soft buzz.*

*Three cups of coffee later, Michael consulted the thin
gold line of his Cartier watch and suggested they move on.*

*Arm in arm, they went out to the V.I.P. lounge and
through the tunnel, on to their waiting jet. The humid night
air caused the tendrils of her fair hair to cling to her neck
and curl about her forehead like a gilded wreath. But
Michael was pina-colada cool in his white linen suit, his
back set straight and firm as the mast of a Newport sloop.*

*She sat with her hand in his throughout the short flight. It
felt welcome there, congruent to love.*

'What are you thinking?' he asked softly.

*'I'm thinking that none of this is real. That I'm going to
open my eyes and find that I'm still in the pit, mooning over
Puccini's score and the Maestro is going to scowl at me,
jabbing his baton and calling me a dreamer. You must be
someone I made up out of the clouds we're flying through
right now . . .'*

*He caressed the curve of her cheek. 'Oh I'm real. But I'm
not so sure about you.'*

*She sighed with contentment. Workaday reality far be-
hind. The topics flowering ahead. Something mysterious
and splendid waiting at the edge of the ocean for Michael
and herself.*

*In what seemed like minutes after they'd boarded, the jet
made a smooth landing in Key West, the piratical paradise
basking in the Southern sun at the tip of the continent.*

*Like most places on the edge of the world, Provincetown
in Cape Cod, Montauk on Long Island, there was freedom
blowing in the fresh breezes that churned in off the coast,
individual choice sparkling in the gem-coloured waters,
cleft blue for the Gulf of Mexico, green for the Atlantic. No
pedigrees held sway here among the candy-coloured stucco
and billowing sails. No old fortunes, no family names. Just
bare, bronzed men and women and the big sun they worshipped at the end of every day on Mallory Dock, as it
dipped itself red-hot into the cool lap of the seas. With its*

118

chequered history and dubious ancestry, Key West was the ideal place to invent oneself daily, preferably as fancifully as possible.

Not that there was any lack of sophistication here. As Michael was soon to show her, there were restaurants to rival any in Manhattan – from haute cuisine to antique opulence. But as always in Key West, there was a choice with a chasm in between. You might wile away an evening in the fashionable purlieus of Pier House . . . or vibrate to funky jazz and Margaritas under the parachute canopies of Sloppy Joe's, Papa Hemingway's favourite dive. One day, you could spend an afternoon touring the wealth of art galleries, and the next swigging beer on the beach. Either way, you were encouraged by the very spirit of the 'Cayo Hueso', to please your own damn self – because everybody else was having too much fun to care.

With the first draught of Key West air, she could feel herself working loose from under her feminine reserve, the tight spring of city nerves uncoiled. Her temples throbbed with the heavy fragrance of hibiscus and lemon verbena swirling in the breeze. The balmy temperature made her want to curl up in Michael's arms and sleep forever . . .

As they tooled along the highway hugging the shore, Michael drove with the top down on his white Mercedes convertible, so that the wind that always rolled in from the ocean, whipped her hair behind her, and stung her cheeks till she gasped.

The car wheels grated on the gravel drive when they at last turned into the beach house. Michael switched off the ignition, and suddenly all was quiet and the clicks of cicadas. Michael sat back, grinning.

She stared. The 'beach house', ablaze with bronze light, was a Spanish-style mini-mansion with a roof of red tiles and a file of arching windows, the whole embowered in a lush grove of orange trees.

The masonry, the low retaining walls, the exterior stairs, the guest house all showed superb workmanship. It was obvious the stones had been imaginatively selected before they were hand-worked into rainbow-coloured mosaics in brick red, pale green, banana yellow and white. The fountain-splashed gardens looked wet and seductive and one whole side of the terraced stone house was entirely festooned with ivy.

In the back, framed by a weeping cypress tree, a pond-like pool had been set, a sphere of lapis lazuli. Beyond, the surf roared into the darkness, stretching out to the ends of the universe . . .

A round-faced woman greeted them at the high-arched door. She wore a breezy blue-checked dress and looked comfortable in the house.

'This is Mrs Fellows,' Michael introduced her with pride. 'She's a native of Key West. She's everything here – cook, housekeeper, wardrobe supplier to my guests. We couldn't live without this lady.'

Mrs Fellows smiled. 'I'm so pleased to meet you.'

She smiled back, shyly.

'This way.'

She followed the woman's broad back into the house through the domed, brick-lined entryway.

The interior was a wash of pure white slashed with dark wooden ceiling beams. Only a Navajo wall hanging relieved the austerity of white with a sunburst weave. The front hall opened on to a loggia and its burnished wood floor, black leather couch, abstract charcoal, and brass pots brimming with a fuzz of sea grape and oleander.

Further on, a staircase and balcony led to the eight airy second-floor bedrooms, each of which gave way to a slate-tiled verandah. Here, she was delightfully reminded of the Tuscan farmhouses she had visited with the nuns, buildings cool as vanilla ice cream, their olive trees and gardens a green shimmer under the noonday sun.

'Michael, when you said, "beach house" I pictured a weekend hole in the wall, with electric lights. I never expected this!'

'May you always be so pleasantly surprised. Come on, I want to show you something.' He took her by the arm and, walking her in front of him, propelled her into the country kitchen, which sported a chequerboard floor, blue-and-white Dutch tiles and a gourmet's dream of copper pans and cooking utensils hanging in row after gleaming row above them.

'You're treading on sacred ground right now: this is where the best key lime pie in the state is made. With real key limes. No one knows Mrs Fellows' recipe. Once upon a time, the wife of a visiting businessman offered to trade her yacht for it. Mrs Fellows refused.' His hazel eyes twinkled.

The young musician was beginning to see that Michael's company could work any wonder.

'I happen to have two pieces of pie in the pantry . . . if you're interested,' the housekeeper drawled, just this side of coyness.

'What do you say?' Michael asked. 'You're the guest. Shall we have dessert before dinner?'

'By all means,' she said gamely. None of this was real anyway.

'Shall I lay the table in the garden?' Mrs Fellows was already bustling about, shovelling fresh-ground coffee beans into her spotless ceramic pot.

'No. I think we'll take it right here in the kitchen. That'll be fun for a change.'

And that was how she began her first night in the Garden of Eden, at a rough-pine kitchen table, wolfing down a lighter-than-air, improbably green American version of ambrosia called key lime pie with a man she was almost certainly going to love forever.

The next morning, after an extravagant evening of dining and dancing all over the unsleeping town, she awoke to the shrill cries of the gulls, gliding and looping in the blue world outside her window.

Her high-ceilinged bedroom, done up in blonde woods and white wicker, thrilled with sunlight. She could smell the clean ocean air beyond her slatted French doors.

In a spell of delight, she walked barefoot over the sunny wood floors to the redwood closet, intending to belt a robe over the cappuccino satin and lace teddy that had been laid out on her bed when she and Michael tripped in at four in the morning.

The sight that greeted her left her giddy with female pleasure. Neatly hung on fragrant cedar hangers were a Pasha's ransom in the latest Parisian fashions. The collection reflected the musical leitmotif of the day: creamy crepe

121

dresses with the nipped-in shape of a violin, geometric bicolour creations like upside-down guitars. Jackets with harp-shaped lapels and blouses with piano-hammer-shaped sleeves.

In a lighter vein, there was an assortment of swimsuits, Bermuda shorts, designer jeans, particoloured tee shirts, skinny gold sandals and spikey black evening heels of glitter and style. Each labelled item had been meticulously folded and stacked along the side and top shelves. All in her size! Deciding quickly, she chose a pair of khaki camp shorts and a billowy white-cotton sailor blouse. Then she clicked open the doors leading to the verandah, where she was treated to salt breezes, confectionary clouds, low-flying gulls in a peerless blue gouache – and Michael waving up at her from his green-and-white striped lounge chair.

His physique was trim and tight in spotless white tennis shorts and open-throated royal blue tee shirt that showed off his golden chest. His blond hair looked soft, shiny and clean as though it had been dried in the sun.

'Come on down, Sleeping Beauty. It's almost noon.'

'Oh no!'

'There's still some breakfast here, if you hurry.'

'I'll be right there.'

She all but flew down the long flight of stairs and out on to the cypress-shaded garden patio, with its terracotta tiles and wrought-iron furniture. The table was laid with a roseblush cloth; a silver coffee service gleamed upon it.

Settling across from her, Michael whisked away the napkin that covered a straw basket of hot baked croissants. A soft breeze rippled the tablecloth, as he offered her a dishful of creamy butter rosettes and a plate piled high with gem-cut pineapples, strawberries, papaya and mangoes.

'There's an incredible quiche lorraine, if you're still hungry. Mrs Fellows made it this morning.'

'Hey, I'm game. Must be the sea air.'

Michael sat back in his seat, watching her eat with gusto. 'It never fails to amaze me how sylphs like yourself often have the appetite of a stevedore!'

'You don't understand, Michael,' she countered, laugh-

ing. 'I had a performance last night. I have to keep up my strength!' *She buttered a second croissant.*

'Oh, I see.' *The gold flecks danced in his warm hazel eyes.* 'As good an excuse for gluttony as ever I've heard. It's one of the Seven Deadly Sins, you know.'

'One of the nicest, I think. I've always felt that we all had to choose one and specialize in it, do it up big. I like the sin I've chosen. It's got a lot of style.'

'Of you they'll say: "she ate not wisely, but too well",' *he teased.*

She sat back in her chair, hands resting on the arms, and parted her lips in a smile. 'Not the worst epitaph surely.'

He leaned forward intently. 'In my eyes, nothing you do is without charm. You are the most completely beautiful woman I've ever met. Even with jam on your face.'

'Pardon me . . .' *She fluttered the napkin against her lips.*

'Just kidding, beautiful.' *He paused.* 'You're making me too happy. Sometimes I wonder if we haven't dreamed each other up after all.'

With her elbows propped against the tabletop, she folded her long hands and rested her chin upon them. 'Does it matter, Michael, even if we did?'

He stared out towards the wrinkle of turquoise sea, as the cypress waved its leaves in the gentle breeze like a woman unbinding her long hair, and the palm trees clacked their fronds against the hot blue sky. 'Hey, that's too deep for me. I'm not a very curious man. I don't ever examine what life brings. For me everything has been – I don't know – as clear as the reef waters out there. I guess everything always will be.'

'You know, Michael that's exactly what I thought when I first saw you in the Opera House, how easy you are with life, how, if the peach falls from the tree, it will fall into your hand, how if you loved a woman . . .'

'She would love me . . .?'

She met his questioning eyes. 'Yes.'

Without another word, he scraped back his seat and rose to his feet. In the next moment, he was standing behind her chair, his hands burning into her shoulders, his lips nectarous upon hers.

123

Her head arched back against the firm muscles of his stomach, as desire rayed through her body, leaving her weak and helpless with hunger for him. For more . . .

'I'm making you a gazpacho for lunch and some fresh-baked bread if that'll . . .' Mrs Fellows suddenly appearing on the patio, turned beet red.

Michael straightened up and shaded his eyes from the sun. He swung his head in her direction. 'That will be fine. Thank you, Mrs Fellows.'

The woman made a bee-line for her kitchen sanctuary.

'I think we've scandalized the poor woman.'

'On the contrary. We've made her day.'

Michael watched her, thoughtfully, giving her time to want him again.

'Why don't we go for a swim,' he suggested. 'The sun is already getting hot.'

'That's a good idea.' She supposed Michael's 'ways' would not allow for lovemaking in the afternoon, while the beloved housekeeper went banging among the pots downstairs, and turning red about the ears at every pagan thump of the bedstead. 'An inspired idea.'

'That's because I have you for inspiration.' He'd love to taste her sweet pomegranate lips. 'Good enough. I'll meet you at the pool in five minutes.'

Upstairs again in her bedroom, she opted for a white maillot with a scarlet hibiscus stroked down one sinuous side. With nervous fingers, she pinned her hair into a sleek chignon.

Michael was already cutting cleanly through the water when she came to sit by the edge of the pool, her shapely legs dangling over the side.

With this moment to herself, she admired the ripple of Michael's shoulder muscles, the elegant line of his blades, the strong strokes that carried him swiftly through the blue water.

The sun was hot on her back. She lowered herself into the sparkling depths where the water was warm and silky against her skin, then began to glide across the pool.

Just then, the glass doors of the kitchen slid open and Mrs Fellows re-appeared. 'I'm leaving now,' she proclaimed in a high, proper voice. 'The whipped cream in the yellow bowl is for the pecan pie,' she added primly, as though only certain appetites could be legitimately satisfied on a fine sunny afternoon.

Michael waved breezily from the pool, giving her to understand that she was free to leave for the day.

The glass doors shut with a disapproving snap.

They were alone, and intensely aware of each other across the water.

As if they'd each heard a silent signal, they'd begun to swim towards the shimmering disk of sun in the centre of the pool. When they'd drawn close enough, he reached out his arms and she grabbed hold of his hands, and suddenly, they were a warm tangle of limbs, the water swirling softly around their bodies like a bolt of blue satin.

She moaned, first when he found her soft lips and fastened his mouth there, as though he would draw the very breath from her. Then again, when he stood in the shallow water, and, placing his hands on either side of her hips, raised up her whole body. Her long legs closed possessively around his back.

His avid touch was everywhere, testing the contours of neck and belly. The maillot lapped down, like an unfurling flower, over her breasts, and she felt the sun kiss them – or was it Michael's hot mouth? And then it was gliding over the smooth tilt of her abdomen and down the curve of her legs.

The dual sensation of Michael's deep, deliberate caresses and the motion of the water set her shivering. 'Ah, Michael . . .'

The sound of her soft voice seemed to excite him even more . . .

His hands played over her tapering flanks, the strands of his blond hair beaded with water brilliant as jewels. It seemed he was invading every hollow, every space of her with his agile tongue and fingers . . .

When they could no longer bear the savage hunger possessing their bodies, they reared against one another in the water. He found her burning centre and they rocked towards ecstasy.

Then he took her into his arms and carried her from the pool, water streaming from his bright hair.

Laying her down upon the sun-warmed grass of the orange-scented grove, he reclined beside her.

She couldn't tell where she was or how she had come to be there, only that she was giving light from a source deep within, a secret place that had never before been without shadow.

He raised himself on one elbow. 'This was your first time.'

'Yes.' She wasn't sure if she had actually spoken or just dreamed that she had.

'You're an extraordinary woman.'

She smiled as he pressed another kiss upon her open mouth.

'You look like Eve, all tangled up in the grass like that, your hair unbound, and smiling like the devil . . .'

And then the heat came upon him again. He rested his weight upon her, his arms filled with desire, curling about her neck, and she wanted it always to be like that, the two of them, naked under the sky, loving to the rhythm of the ocean, souls rooted to each other as the earth to the trees.

Oh, Michael, she said over and over, like a prayer, like a psalm, oh, Michael, my golden-eyed love, my brother, my own, never take your heart from me.

CHAPTER ELEVEN

The yacht beat into the wind, its mainsail lifted like an aeroplane's wing against the azure stretches of the sky.

Michael and the three young crewman of the 'Patrice' moved swiftly on their sneakered feet, while going about the business of the seventy foot sailboat.

Standing at the prow, she looked out into the turquoise line of the horizon, as though the truth of things could be discerned in vapour and blue foam.

The wind whipped her hair straight behind her neck like liquid flame. Days of sunbathing on the yacht had left her skin a tawny gold. Nights of lovemaking had illumined her eyes and rounded out the hollows in her heart. She had never before been so proud of her body, or felt so free in her woman's soul. And all because of a man called Michael who had loved her music and made her into an instrument of his love.

He came up behind her. She could smell the salt sea on his skin and in his hair. She closed her eyes to receive the drug of his caresses.

'What are you dreaming about up here, all alone?' he asked.

'You.'

'That's only right. I am the captain of this ship.'

And what a ship it was . . . the opulent staterooms with circular, gold-canopied beds like something Diane de Poitiers might have used to entertain her King, marble fixtures of the 'head', the galley stocked with vichysoisse and iced lobster tails, not to mention a wine cellar any French bistro in the Michelin guide would be proud to possess.

'Michael, I'm afraid I'm getting spoiled with all this wantonness and luxury. It may be too rich for my poor girl's blood.'

'Nonsense. You were born for luxury.' He nuzzled her

ear. 'And for wantonness.' He propped himself against the cabin wall. 'What about tomorrow's performance? Have you decided?'

'I have.' It was wrong, she knew it, putting a man before her music, but there was nothing else to do. She couldn't let this time in paradise end . . . 'I'm going to call in sick.'

'You are so beautiful.' He kissed the tender crown of her head. 'I've got to get back to the crew. We'll have lunch in fifteen minutes, okay?'

'Okay.' The sun slipped behind a cloud as he moved quickly away. She turned back to the sea.

Just exactly what was it she was trying to do? She who had worked all her life to get to New York and the lustre of the Metropolitan?

It seemed there had always been music in her head. She didn't know precisely when it started. Probably before words.

She'd sung with her mother's recordings of Caruso and Pons from the earliest age, as soon as she could talk, really. She'd composed ditties on the school piano, and scored the little musicals about daisies and talking bears that the fifth grade put on in Spring. On her tenth birthday, her mother's gift of a second-hand violin had changed her life.

The instrument had become at once companion – and teacher. Never again had she been lonely when mother's moods had shut her out. Her destiny became something honed and brilliant and special.

Of course, she'd had no money to start with big important music schools, when the moment came to choose one. The scholarship had been a godsend. Composing became her mountain, her heavenly light. Her compositions were just now starting to sound like something fit for a concert stage, so this was the time to take the world of classical music by its well-brushed lapels, to burn like a star. Instead, she was turning her back on every wish she'd ever devised, for a man she didn't even know . . . couldn't ever predict. Wasn't there some biblical sin connected with burying one's talents?

Oh but the loving, the loving . . . Her heart quickened at the thought of his embrace in the garden, amid the sultry perfume of the lemon verbena, the liquid brilliance of the *lime tree's trailing blossoms . . . Oh, she didn't know how much longer she could hold back from Michael . . .*

Still, if he had his time-honoured ways, she did too, when it came to loving. After all, she was her mother's daughter and it was just too easy for her to be swept away by the attentions of an ordinary man with the glitter of wealth to make him shine. She wanted to be certain that it was Michael she cared for and not his company privileges.

Once, when she had declined a rich, world-famous tenor's invitation to his Venetian palazzo for some Lucullan pleasures, she had managed to contract the flu and stay home from work until his guest engagement was over. This timely malady had saved her the embarrassment of watching his spoiled, full-moon face, engorged with anger, glowering down at her from the eerie blackness of the rehearsal stage every day. In that case, at least, the principle of caution had served her well. She prayed it would still do the job.

Michael was back with two blushing glasses of Campari and soda. He smiled at her.

With the sun in her eyes, she smiled back, a novice in love.

The putt-putt of the shrimp boats ploughing back to port; the slap and suck of the ocean waves against the piers; the cry of a night-flying bird; the cradle-rock of the moored yacht: impressions of a night spent alone on the sea.

Locked together on their circle of bed, they had kicked off the gold-threaded coverlet. It lay in a froth at their feet.

She called his name.

Stretched out beside her, gilded by the light of the over-head lamp, Michael taught her the luxury of skin on skin, the velvet of his tongue, the fire of his hand, while she moved and sighed in her lover's arms, imprinted by his passion, the book of his dreams.

'Why don't you just tell them you can't make it?' He was furious with her, speeding down the coastal highway, his foot heavy on the accelerator. The lights twinkled from small craft along the shore, like a holiday at sea.

'I told you, Michael. If I don't get back to New York in time for my performance tomorrow, I'll lose my job with the Opera. Please try to understand, I've worked for this position all my life. I can't throw it all away now just for . . .'

'Just for what, goddamnit! Why don't you say it? Just for me.' For an instant his face looked petulant and unpleasable.

She ran her hand through her streaming hair. 'Michael, calm down! And don't go so fast!' She wasn't ready for the dark side of his personality, having convinced herself with callow and typical generosity that he didn't have one.

'Don't I mean anything to you?' His accusing eyes fastened on the curving road ahead. 'Haven't these last few days meant anything?'

'Of course they have . . . How can you even ask such a thing?' Blasphemy. If only he knew how close she felt to him, how totally at her lover's disposal. But he mustn't be told. Not yet. For her protection, and his – if in the end she would choose to leave him for the music.

With a sudden swerve, Michael turned into the sandy crook of the deserted beach. He switched off the ignition, got out of the car and went around to open her door.

She glanced up at him, puzzled.

'Let's walk.'

She swung out of the white Mercedes convertible. As they walked, she stopped to slip off her sandals. The moist sand felt good pushing up between her toes. Meanwhile, Michael stared straight ahead, his body charged with tension.

As it was a full moon night, the empty beach was warm with yellow light. She eased her arm through his, but his muscles were hard and unyielding.

They went on for a while in silence.

'My God, you're cold,' he said with bitterness.

The tide splashed up against her legs, and whirled away.

'You really don't care that you're leaving tomorrow, do you?'

'You don't know what you're talking about, Michael.'

'Then why must I be the one to say it? Why must I explain? Damn it, can't you tell that I love you!'

'Michael, don't . . .'

He paced in the sand. 'I've gone over and over this in my mind. Sometimes when you were sleeping beside me, I would watch you through the whole night, trying to see what you are, trying to understand you. Half the time, on the boat, when you were sunbathing and you thought I was working on the rigging, I was standing off somewhere looking at you, trying to decide if you and I were for real or not. And now I know the answer. You were right when you said it doesn't matter if I've dreamed you up. The fact is, it would be unbearable to live without you. I can't let you go. Tomorrow. Or ever.'

Be careful, a voice inside her said, you're going to lose him, the man you love . . . 'Michael, listen. I have a talent and a promise to keep. And being your mistress won't fulfil that promise. I saw what that kind of life did to my mother. It made her bitter, and closed her heart to happiness. I don't want that for myself, Michael. I can't waste my life on you or any other romantic hero. And if you love me, you won't ask me to.'

'Mistress?' He took her hard by the shoulders. 'I never intended you to be my mistress! I want to marry you.'

She stared up past him at the full yellow moon, not wanting to see his eyes. 'Marriage was never part of my plan, Michael.'

'You're afraid.'

'No.'

'You think you're going to disappear if you marry me. You think no woman can exist in the shadow of a man . . .'

'It's true.'

'You're wrong,' he said softly, urgently. 'Believe me, you're wrong. I don't get into deep reasons or heavy trips about love, but I do know that I must have you in my life, that I'll never be whole if I let you go now. If you'll only be honest with yourself, you'll realize that it's the same way for you. We belong together.'

131

She wanted to laugh at him, to walk away free and clear, but she couldn't. His faith had moved her: she'd begun to trust his passion.

'This is crazy. I have only till tomorrow to decide . . .'

'That's the way it is with love,' Michael said. 'Like a free-fall, a leap into space. When you come tumbling down you might break into a million pieces. Or then again, you might never have to come down.'

She lifted her gaze to the moon again, suddenly afraid to look down . . .

It rained all through the night and into the dawn, so that Michelle awoke the next morning to the sound of raindrops splattering against the windowpane with the hiss of an open flame.

Immediately, she tried to conjure up the man who had held her, loved her. She knew hers had been no ordinary dream, that he was a presence real enough to call her back to a vanished life . . .

Why had she left him to come here? She reasoned it could only have been she who deliberately had forsaken that sun-swept Eden for New York City. She could not conceive of a power outside herself that could separate them, a fission of the heart. How it pained her to think she might even be a married woman, once loved in ways she'd forgotten, in ways every woman should be loved.

What had she done to deserve this kind of loss?

Her hand shook as she dialled Josh's home number.

One ring, two rings, three . . . she felt she would be lost, spin off into space if she didn't connect with him, right here, right now . . .

On the fourth ring, he answered, sleepily. 'Who the hell is this? It's six o'clock in the morning.'

'Josh, I'm sorry, it's me,' the words tumbled out in a rush. 'Something's happened . . . I need you . . .'

'All right, slow down. What happened?'

'I played the violin. I played the Vivaldi. Beautifully. Like a real musician, Josh. And then I blacked out and I saw myself as I once was, in the other life I had . . .'

She could scarcely hold the phone steady in her hand. 'Josh, please come over. I don't want to be alone.'

'Try to relax. Have some breakfast. I'll be over as soon as I can.'

The phone clicked down, cutting them off.

In a daze, she wandered into the bathroom and splashed cold water over her face. She showered, and dressed in her jeans. Then she tried to force down the breakfast Josh had suggested, anything to take her mind off the beautiful dreams she had dreamed, to blot out the face of that unknown young woman in love with whom she now shared a body and a soul.

Then, blessedly, he was at her door, his stone-grey aquascutum darkened with rain, his eyes burning blue and steady as a flame. A pair of arms locked around her. 'It's good to cry.' He gave the permission.

She shook her head, pushing away. 'I did my crying at Graff-Lowell, when just being alive hurt so much I wanted to die. Now I only want answers.'

'All right.' Wasting no more time, he strode into the next room and sat down. 'Tell me about it.'

In the next hour, she recounted to him what she had seen – the young woman, the musical career, the idyll in the sun with a man whose name she couldn't even recall, a man who might be her husband. Crucial details melted away as she groped for them. She did not know what place in Florida had been the scene of her love affair, or to whom the summer house belonged.

'Was it a dream?' he asked when she'd finished.

'No, no, it was real! It was as though I were living it all over again.'

He could sense the great strain that remembrance had put upon her – the strain of walking between two worlds and feeling their gravitational pull like twin planets spinning apart in space. 'You won't let me comfort you. What is it I'm supposed to do?' he asked simply.

She hugged her arms to her body. 'I'm scared, Josh. There's something about that other life . . . I want you to keep me from going back.'

'That's the one thing I won't do.' He smoothed back her hair. 'You have to go back. Only then can you be free from whatever terrifies you. Only then can you stop running away.' Josh Free, once the independent, well knew the negative power of obsession, for Michelle was always with him now. 'I promise I'll get my research department working on your case. At least we've got something more solid to work with now.'

'Josh, I don't know. Maybe we should just forget it, stop poking around in the dark. It might be safer for me to move on . . .'

'Safer? Maybe. But you're forgetting one thing. That's you back there in the dark, or at least a part of you. Going on without her would be like tearing out your heart because it might break. There really is no choice, if you're ever going to stop shadow dancing.'

'I know you're right.' She leaned her forehead against his. 'But I'm still afraid.'

'Hell, people are afraid of themselves ninety-nine per cent of the time. You're right in vogue.' He filled himself with her scent. 'You know what else you are . . .?'

'No. What?' She frowned up at him.

'Exciting me . . .'

He half-expected her to draw away, but when she did not, he hooked his thumbs behind her ears and began to massage the sensitive spots, deeply.

He moved up the line of her jaw, pushed against her lips with his strong fingers. She felt his desire to learn her body, slowly, seriously. He was warm, very warm against her . . .

He bent his dark head to her mouth.

She turned her face away.

She could feel his energy draining from her, his passion, his strength . . .

'Josh, I didn't mean . . .'

'Shh. I asked for that. I don't blame you.' He picked up his raincoat and started for the door.

'Josh, wait.' She crossed to him. 'I don't want you to go.' She took him by the hand and raised it to her cheek.

'I must be crazy,' he exclaimed.

'Why?'

'Because I believe you.'

'Yes, believe me, Josh, believe in me.'

'I can tell you one thing,' he replied, casting down his coat over the back of a wingchair and catching her in his arms. 'Whoever you are, I think I'm falling in love with you.'

'Whoever I am, I'm falling in love with you.'

'In that case . . .' He pushed her by the shoulders towards the bedroom. 'Get your coat.'

'Why . . .?'

'You said you were a musician at the Metropolitan. Maybe if you walk in there and see familiar faces, it might trip off some more of those memories. Maybe someone will even be able to tell you who you were . . .'

'I don't know if I'm ready to know.'

He held up his palms. 'You'll never be ready as long as you let your fears get in the way.' He searched her face. 'And there's something else . . .'

She braced herself, being in love and in the dark.

'After all this, you're going to have to prove to me that you want me. And I'm not going to wait around forever for your friend, Michael, to go his merry way.

'So this is an act of good faith,' she said slowly, 'your coming with me to the Met.'

'That's one way of looking at it.'

'I'll get my coat,' she said, her heart beating faster.

PART III

MICHAEL

CHAPTER TWELVE

Doria's morning had been full of homely omens: the ceaseless grey Sunday rain, the leaking tap, the burnt toast, a cameo appearance of the spider who lived in her kitchen cabinet. Ben had a football game today.

When the sun finally popped outside of the clouds like one of Fleur's long lost balloons, Doria's mood had turned more sanguine. She waved goodbye to Ben in his full regalia, wearing the treasured jersey T.J. had given him, and drove off with Fleur to a birthday party in chi-chi Forest Hills.

Normally, she would not have missed one of Ben's games, but it was the only time she had to bribe the janitor up to fix the leak in the kitchen sink that was driving her family crazy.

The telephone call that afternoon still took her by surprise.

'Mrs Sevenstars?'

'Yes?'

'This is Coach Weems. I'm afraid there's been an accident. Your son, Ben . . .'

That was where she stopped hearing what Coach Weems said, racked by a maternal and conditional guilt: if only I hadn't let him go today, if only I'd been there, if only he weren't such an intense young man and I were a better mother . . .

'The ambulance took him to Lenox Hill Hospital . . .' The words were driven into her consciousness like nails in a plank.

'I'll be there,' she said dully, hanging up the phone.

She was already racing into the hospital lobby when it occurred to her that Fleur would be waiting at the birthday party in Queens, not knowing why her mother had never shown up. She hadn't brought the Saperstein's telephone number and remembered that it was unlisted!

Oh God, she didn't want two frightened children on her conscience today. But who could pick Fleur up and bring her to Ben's bedside? She had dialled the number before she even realized whose it was.

'Hello, Josh, this is Doria.'

The answering machine voice was instructing her to leave a message after the beep. Instead, she left unprintable directions for Josh then crashed the phone into its cradle. Damn him! He was probably playing kissy-face with that mystery woman of his. Who to call on a late Sunday afternoon . . .? And, oh Lord, what had happened to her beautiful Ben . . .!

The answer came to her in the unlikely form of a freckle-faced newspaperman in a vintage sixties pea jacket. 'It's okay,' T.J. said reassuringly. 'Just a mild concussion. The kid's going to be all right.'

'McShane, what are you doing here?'

'I go to all Ben's games. Not like some people I could mention.' He regarded her with bright sympathy. 'You look awful.'

'Thanks.' She started off for Ben's room.

McShane chased after her. 'Where's Fleur?'

'At a birthday party in the heart of Queens. She's expecting me to pick her up.'

'I'll go get her. What's the address?' he queried, as if it were the most natural thing in the world for him to do her a kindness, unasked.

She spun in her tracks. Of course, McShane would go! Why hadn't she thought of it before? She felt around the bottom of her purse and came up with a slip of notepaper. 'This is the address. It's somewhere on Queens Boulevard, whatever that is.'

'I'll find it.' He took it from her, and folded it into his wallet. 'Calm down, Princess. I told you. The doctor said Ben is all right.'

At that highly unusual moment, she had the wildest desire to kiss him.

Instead, she just turned on her heels and bore down on Ben's hospital room, where her brave, precocious son was already sitting up in bed, his pillows plumped, smiling at a pretty nurse with a definite wiggle in her walk.

The cab let Josh and Michelle off at Lincoln Centre Plaza where patrons of the arts thronged the area surrounding the fountain. Girls with long hair sunning themselves. Theatre parties in pearls and blue rinse. A street mime in a stovepipe hat.

Michelle seemed to hesitate before going into the Opera House.

Josh caught her by the hand. 'Hey.'

'For a moment there, I almost lost my nerve.'

'I know. Perfectly natural.'

'I'm all right now.'

'Good.'

They went in. The lobby was packed with opera-goers, the crowd particularly dense around the well-stocked bar. Above them, airy metal walkways were filling up with well-dressed promenaders.

'Wait here.'

Josh hurried to the ticket window. He came back brandishing two tickets for seats in the Golden Horseshoe. 'We were lucky. This party just cancelled minutes ago.'

'I wish I could be so sure. About the luck, I mean.'

At the sound of the first curtain bell, the now leisurely crowd would begin to surge towards the giant staircases flanking the lobby.

A lethargy came over her as soon as they entered the dim, velvet grotto of the Opera House. The usherette handed them a programme and swung an arm towards their row. For Michelle the whole scene had an hallucinatory edge as though she were walking in her sleep. Josh's hand plucked at her sleeve.

'What are you doing? Sit down, Michelle.'

139

She sank down in obedience, eyes closing on the sight of the Golden Curtain, the conductor's empty podium – her vision opening up on to the past . . .

The tympani echoed like distant thunder in the blue-lit cave of the orchestra pit. The black satin ties of the musicians gleamed against their stiff white shirtfronts. She wore a string of pearls like a warm caress upon her neck and in her hands was a violin, smooth as glass.

Somehow, the air was always soft in the pit, this pleasant balminess just part of the Metropolitan's magic . . .

Every night she liked to anticipate how the audience, like a fresh wind, exhaled excitement, and then its perfumed pleasure. It thrilled her to be part of that grand purring beast, the orchestra, with one quick mind and one proud voice. She was supremely at home here . . .

She lolled against the back of her seat, her forehead beaded with perspiration.

'Michelle?' Josh's worried face hovered above her. 'Are you all right?'

'Josh, you were right. I was here before. I played here,' she said, excited by the noise and scent of the theatre.

Josh rose decisively. 'Come on, let's go around to the stage door before the performance begins.'

When they got there, the young stage manager looked a question.

'I'm an old friend of the first violinist.' Josh flashed his press badge. 'Can I see him?'

'I'm afraid not.' He shook his head. 'He's preparing for the performance.'

Michelle swayed against Josh.

'Is the lady all right?'

'She'll be fine as soon as you let us through.' Josh bluffed it. 'We've come a long way to see him and we're not leaving until . . .'

'It's all right, Stan . . .' A grey, stooped man in evening clothes stood silhouetted in the stagedoor entrance.

'Mr Lvovich, these people say they know you.'

The old man gazed from one male face to another with a patient lack of comprehension. Then he saw her, half-obscured by the column of Josh's body.

'Emma? Emma Taylor? You're back . . .'

The next thing she knew she was in the stranger's arms. 'Gregor . . .' The name sprang to her lips. This man could tell her who she was, where she had been restore to her the life and love she had lost.

But, in the end, Gregor Lvovich could only reveal that she was Emma Taylor, a classical musician. 'You left,' he sounded hurt and puzzled, 'without even saying good-bye.'

'I have not been well,' she hurried to explain, pained by his sad look. 'I had amnesia. Do you remember the man I left with?' She held her breath, waiting for his answer, for her heart to be free of its shadow.

He paused to think. 'Some rich young patron of the Opera. We never met him. You never introduced us. It was all very sudden, not like you at all. But we heard,' he said regretfully, hesitant to let her go again, even in memory, 'that you married him.'

Emma was stunned. She shot an imploring look at Josh.

'That's something that still has to be proved,' he said, refusing to be bullied by rumour. He held out his hand in a dismissive gesture.

Startled, Gregor shook it.

'Thank you, sir,' Josh said. 'You've done Emma a service.'

She stepped forward to kiss Gregor Lvovich on the cheek. 'Yes, thank you.'

He captured her hand. 'But will you be coming back, Emma? You are a fine and gifted musician. Everyone thought so. It would be a great shame to waste so fine a talent!'

'I would like to come back some day, Gregor. But first I have to find Emma Taylor. It would be so easy to lose myself again in music. I remember how it was with me. Music was everything. It was enough.'

He kissed her hand with an air of quiet resignation, then he turned to Josh. 'I hope you know what you have here. Emma is – I don't know how to put it – more than herself. She gives light.'

'Maestro Levine is looking for you, Mr Lvovich,' the stage manager called over to him. 'He's waiting in his dressing room.'

'Goodbye, then.' The old man turned from Josh and Emma without looking back. For him, the music would have to be enough.

Josh's eyes were dark with concern for her. 'Oh baby, you look like you've seen a ghost.'

'I am a little shaky. I'm the ghost.'

'Would you like me to take you home?'

'No.'

'How about a drink in the lobby then?'

'I don't care.'

Josh took her arm and they re-entered the spacious, galleried room.

'Josh, wait,' Emma said suddenly, 'I think I'd just like to sit here for a moment.' It was all beginning to sink in . . . She was probably married. She would not be able to shrug off her past life like an old suit of clothes. There were infinite emotional complications.

Josh sat next to her on the red-carpeted staircase. 'You all right?'

'I don't know whether I should be happy or sad.'

He slipped an arm around her. 'Better?'

'Uh huh. How did you guess about the music?'

'Something in your eyes when you heard Perlman. The lights changed.'

'And when I first met you I had you pegged at an inch deep, a figment of your own imagination, slapped together with newsprint and tanning oil.'

'Wow. Hear that sound? It's my ego staggering.'

She looked directly at him. 'Oh, I have a hunch you can take it.'

'You're right. I can.'

'Why do you want to?'

'You've got a story I'd like to hear . . .'

'That sounds tame enough.'

'It's not.'

'Can I have that drink now?'

He rose and took her by the elbow. 'Come on.'

'I thought you were going to get it for me,' she protested.

'I am. There's a stiff drink and a shoulder to cry on at my place. If you're interested.'

'Thank you, Josh.'

'For what? I haven't done anything.'

'Your being here makes a difference.'

'I'd like to do more.'

For the entire cab ride to his luxury penthouse on Sutton Place, she sat quietly with him, knee to knee, her hand tight in his.

After a silent elevator ride, he ushered her in to the penthouse, where the cool glass and lacquered Orientalia of his sitting room seemd to soothe her. Josh stoked the marble fireplace to take the chill out of the air.

'Here, drink this.' He handed her a stiff shot of brandy.

Emma drained the glass, then held it out for a refill.

Again, he filled her glass with the rich old brandy.

Again, she drank it down. It seemed to relax her.

With his own drink in hand, Josh sat beside her on the black raw-silk sofa. 'Want to talk?'

'I don't know that it will do any good. If only I could remember Michael's full name – or even where we were in Florida. I feel so useless . . . such a burden!' She couldn't even bring herself to talk about the doubts that had cropped up at the Opera House. Michael had known she'd played at the Met, yet there were no inquiries about her. Could it be that they had parted in anger . . . or worse? Could it be he didn't want her back at all?

'Just relax. It will come to you. Here.' He had her lean her head against his shoulder, and for, once, she did not resist. He played with the bright, golden strands of her cascading hair. Then, somehow, his fingers came to rest gently on either side of her soft mouth. He looked down at her with a clarity and strength of emotion he had never felt for a woman before. 'I'm going to kiss you, Emma. Very softly. Very deeply. Now . . .'

143

Her body was dazzled. Slowly, enmeshed in this erotic new dream, she raised her arms to embrace him.

'Come to bed with me, Emma. I'm in love with you . . .'

She hung her head. 'Oh, my darling,' she whispered, 'you know I can't.'

'Michael again.'

She shifted up from the couch and moved to the lightly draped window. Folding her arms in front of her she stared down at the soft glitter of the night-time city, wondering if she would ever really belong there, anywhere . . . 'Michael loved me too . . .'

'Michael's gone.'

'Yes, but don't you understand, I'm not free to love you the way you deserve. I may be married to another man!'

He closed the space between them, drawn to stem her pain, if he could. 'Listen to me, Emma. I know all that. I'll take whatever you can give, go as far as you can, as slowly as you'd like.' His heart went out to her when he saw her fear and her struggle to overcome it. He was so proud of her strength.

'Why, Josh? Why would you do that for me?'

'Why! Because you're worth it.'

'And whatever I can give will always satisfy you?'

He held her face in his hands and looked into her eyes. 'Well, now, I didn't say that.' He began to kiss her again, a warm rain upon her brow, her eyelids, the curve of her throat. He longed to pull her down to the thick, scarlet-and-black Chinese rug where her garments would fall away, bright and easy as petals in the grass. But he held back.

'I want to let you see, Emma,' he spoke into her ear, then bit the lobe, 'that you excite me more than any woman I've ever known. God, I've waited a long time for this . . .'

She wanted to tell him that so had she . . . but the sensations he was unleashing inside her, the velvet explosions that went off everytime his body made contact with hers, left her speechless and yearning for more.

Open-mouthed, she rose to meet him, pulling him down on top of her. They toppled to the heavy silk pillows, and her skirt was riding up her thighs and she was turning on a

144

fiery wheel of pleasure, moaning under the rapturous heat of his touch.

But even as she opened herself to him, Josh knew he was in secret combat with another man for possession of her. It was Michael's hand stroking her to ecstasy, Michael's lips speaking low words of love: she tried to push his cruel beauty from her.

'Don't let me go,' she breathed, as Josh rocked into her, pouring out all the great energies of his soul, the rich store of his passion for so long held in check.

'Never . . .'

'Don't let me go . . .'

'Never, my love, never . . .'

There was no need for any more promises in the absolute light of the place to which they soared . . .

CHAPTER THIRTEEN

The table rambled the length of the cool, white conference room, and was littered with manila folders and cardboard cartons of murky looking coffee, while, ranged along the sides, the disciples of Joshua Free waited for the master to whip through the business of the day with his customary gale-wind force.

Except that today he wasn't whipping through at all. It was more like limping.

The morning had got off on the wrong foot when Josh had listened to his taped phone calls and reached a garbled message which suggested to him a challenging anatomical position. The crank caller, understandably, had left no name.

Then at the office, hungover from the emotional night before, distracted with love for Emma, Josh had found it impossible to concentrate on editorial minutiae. Here was a novel sensation for the newspaper mogul who'd once cared for nothing so much as a hard-won story or a promising lead.

He had barely set foot in the newsroom before sending his research department to toil over a list of names lifted from the deeds of expensive estates in Palm Beach, Boca Raton, Fort Lauderdale. It was a long shot, but maybe one of the names would trip off Emma's memory. He couldn't wait to show them to her, to earn one of those quiet smiles that burned through the clouds of his cynicism.

'Josh?' The political editor shot an exasperated look at T.J. 'What do you think?'

'What did you say, John?' Josh looked up from his reverie, a genial wolf at the head of his pack.

'I asked you if you wanted that story about the Church in Argentina on page three, or in the back of the night edition.'

'Sorry, John. My attention wandered. Leave it on three.' Josh set his palms on the table and got up out of his chair. 'People, I'm afraid I have some other business to attend to. Please go on without me.'

Doria blanched. T.J. lifted his eyebrows. The room began to buzz like an invaded hive of bees. It was unheard of for the newspaper tycoon to leave anything to chance – or worse, to subordinates, if he could help it.

In the centre of the storm, Josh felt peacefully detached from it all, the way he had when, as a boy, he'd been pumped with ether for a tonsillectomy at the hospital in Tampa. It had not been a totally unpleasant sensation, to float, without control, or care, on the shoulders of time.

Oblivious to the curiosity his announcement had aroused among the faithful, he headed straight for his office, admonishing Doria not to admit anyone short of God, or pester him with phone calls, 'Even if it's the goddamn president of Chase Manhattan,' which was saying a lot. Meanwhile, the daggers in her eyes bounced off his impervious back. She would never forgive him for being unavailable for Ben in his hour of need.

Barricaded in his glossy office, Josh dialled the console phone, anticipating the hard surge of pleasure he felt everytime he heard her voice the first time of the day . . .

'Hello?'

'Hello, Emma?' How he loved her name, her essence!

'Josh.'

'I hear a lot of hubbub over there. Did I catch you at a bad time?'

'Well, we're mounting a new show and the photo-grapher hasn't exactly been co-operative. He insists on having his two Russion Wolfhounds, Gogol and Pushkin, with him all the time and it's just pandemonium with whiskers around here today . . .'

'Sounds like fun.'

'Oh right! For a plugged nickel I'd feed the prints to the dogs for lunch, and tell the photographer once and for all just what a camera-toting, quiche-eating egotist I think he is!'

'Overworked?'

'Not really. Most of the time I love my job. It's just that days like this make you forget how good it can be. Sort of like an allergy to chocolate. Anyway, the worst is over.'

'I'm glad to hear it.' Josh doodled on his leatherbound pad from Gucci's by way of Doria. Lots of curves and soft, yielding shapes . . . 'How'd you like to get away from it all?'

'You mean, right now?'

'Uh huh. Live free! Take a chance!'

'Josh, maybe you can live free, but I'm just an employee of Alexander Bartok, Ltd.'

'Damn Bartok! Damn the Gallery! Come play hookey with me. I have this place in Saratoga, very quiet. We could be alone – and, girl, I'd sure like to have you alone for one whole day, without interruption. Then we could get in some serious loving . . .'

'But you've got a responsibility to the world press,' she teased, even as she warmed to the thought of a long, slow, delicious day in her lover's arms.

'The world can wait! As you just said, you're pretty much finished with this exhibit. And I suppose you have a few vacation days coming?'

'Yes, that's true but I was planning to spend them practising my violin and reading a few books on composition. I know I said I wasn't going to plunge right back into my music, for fear of losing myself again, but, Josh, it seems to be something I have no control over. The music just wants to come out. I've got to get it down on paper or out through sound waves, or something before I go mad with melody! Hm? What? Hold on.' Josh overheard the rumble of a male voice in the background. 'Sorry, Josh, the photographer says the little beasts are getting peckish and he wants to know if I have any caviar in the refigerator. I've got to go.'

He tried to keep his disappointment under control. 'Just a minute. I might have some news for you soon about the Florida house. Some lists of names.'

Tension crept into her voice, as it did whenever some ruin of her past hove into view. 'I see. Why don't I meet you tonight for a drink after work then? Since I'm not sure how long I'll be here, I'll pick you up.'

'Fine. I'll see you then. And Emma?'

'Yes?'

'I meant what I said the other day,' his voice was low and rich with feeling. 'I am in love with you.'

'Is that good or bad?'

'I don't know yet. I'll tell you when I get you to Saratoga and wake up with you in my arms.'

'G'bye, Josh.'

'Bye.'

He held the phone, warm against his ear, even after she'd gone.

So Josh's woman was deathly blonde and glacéed to perfection. Hah. She looked to Doria like a cleverly articulated doll from Switzerland . . . a creature reeking sweetly of dreams, bright in her blue cape, her hair a billow of saffron silk. Secretly, Doria envied her odour of innocence. This woman seemed to know nothing of night rain, the lonesome house, or the empty bed.

Doria hated her . . .

There was Josh turned in towards his blonde mistress like a saint in the grip of desert visions, his steep face smoothed to polished stone.

See him pouring from a gold-crested bottle of Mumm champagne, urging his friends to rejoice with him for choosing her, out of all the women in the world, to love . . . Emma . . . and never once did he notice the pulse fluttering in the hollow of Doria Sevenstars' throat, or the way her fingers worked on the Baccarat crystal in her hand.

But Tom Joad McShane did.

For T.J., it was the beginning of a pain the like of which he had never known before. Doria, his loose-limbed, crazy love, was pining for Josh Free. He could hardly make himself believe it.

And Emma, being Emma, heard the others' private little worlds shattering all around her. She felt as though she should apologize to the dark beauty who loved Josh Free, to the wounded doe eyes, as though she'd mortally wronged her. She wished too she could console the young

149

reporter, who tried hard to hide it with his jokes, but was suffering for what he had seen tonight . . . It had never before occurred to Emma that Josh might belong to others in love, that she could be a complication in another woman's life. This was not a role she especially wanted to play.

'Hey, if we're going to have dinner we'd better get going!' Josh bustled around them, the jovial, oblivious host. 'Will you join us?' he cocked his head at T.J. and Doria.

'The children . . .' Doria said faintly. 'I've got to get home.' How could she sit across the table from Josh and his mistress, watch their exchange of secret smiles, the pressure of his hand on her arm, without crying aloud her grief? She and Josh were well-matched, would love like lions in the sun! Of what use would this milk-faced mannequin be to Josh?

'T.J.?' Josh asked.

'Uh.' T.J. darted an anxious glance at Doria, who looked as though her seams had split. 'Sounds great, but prior engagement.' He forced out a grin.

'That's too bad.' Josh sounded jubilant, and it was painfully obvious to his friends that he wanted Emma Taylor all to himself. *The bigger they are,* T.J. thought . . .

'Good night, then,' Josh said. He ushered the woman out, T.J. bringing up the rear. Doria hung behind, busying herself at her desk.

When she was sure they'd gone, she sat stiffly behind her typewriter and began to jab out her resignation.

From now on, her daydreams would be full of scarlet beheadings and high hangings, quite public executions in which Josh Free figured as the doomed and handsome star.

Each time, when the words were not coolly stinging enough, did not convey the full weight of her disenchantment with Josh Free, she'd rip the paper from the machine, ball it up in her fist and lob it into the wastebasket. There was some comfort in this mechanical chore. But what, she fretted, would she do afterwards, how to face the lonely nights ahead . . . the years bereft of beautiful daydreams?

As her fingers stabbed out the corruscating letters, a cry of betrayal, her office door unexpectedly swung open. It was T.J. who stepped from behind and rested his lean, compact body against the door frame, arms crossed stonily upon his chest.

'Doria, I've called you a lot of things in the past,' he said. 'But until today, I never figured you for a bloody fool.'

Her dark head shot up, long hair flaring out like a cobra's hood. 'What the hell are you talking about?'

'You're upset about Josh's lady friend. You're a joke, Doria. A bad joke.'

'I'm not upset . . .'

'Oh no?' He stalked over to her desk. 'Then why did you just dump today's work in to the wastebasket, and file your cigarette butts in a manila envelope?'

She pushed open the folder indicated and sure enough, found a sad heap of grey ashes lying listlessly at the bottom. She snapped it shut again. 'It's none of your business what I do . . .'

'And what the hell is this?' T.J.'s milkmaid complexion was now a ruddy red, as he yanked the sheet of paper from the typewriter. The machine screeched a protest. 'Your resignation. Terrific. You've really got your head screwed on right, Sevenstars. You've got your priorities down to a "T"!' He seemed to be puffing out with the force of his indignation like the Superman balloon at the Thanksgiving Day Parade.

'Look at you, snuffling around like some lovesick alley cat, a grown woman, a mother! Face it Doria, Josh is gone . . .'

She leaned one palm upon the desk, and bared her teeth. Before she could curb herself, her other hand shot out in a stinging slap across his cheek. Caught off guard, T.J. staggered back, getting his head all snarled up on the monster spider plant swaying at the window. 'Ow! God damn it . . .'

Doria's mouth fell open. She ran around to the front of the desk. 'Oh, T.J., I didn't mean to. . .'

With the suddenness of a snakebite, T.J. delivered an answering blow to her cheek. In astonishment, she held her hand to her reddening face. Meanwhile, the tension seeping slowly out of his body, T.J. hitched his cocky

151

shoulders and straightened his tie. 'Ah, now I feel better,' he said with a wide, cherry pie smile. 'You've had that coming to you for a long time.'

Holding herself like a child, Doria rocked back against the desk. She would not cry in front of the grinning little monster. She would not break down and cry . . . She began to shake instead, her teeth chattering, her knees knocking together like castanets.

'Aw Jaysus, no Doria! None of that business now.'

'It's so unfair.' The tears were making hot salt tracks down her face. 'I gave so much to him. I took care of him all these years . . . He owes me more than this . . .'

'Stop it, Doria.' He cupped her by the shoulders and shook her more roughly than he realized. 'It's nothing but a fantasy. You're his employee, that's all. He doesn't know *you*. He doesn't care about Fleur and Ben and all the stupid, crazy things you do to yourself because of your stiff-backed female pride!'

'No!' She was shaking her head in denial, breaking away from him. 'I don't want to hear it!'

'Can't you see that he's in love with this woman?'

'There've been other women.'

'Not like this one.'

'What makes her so special?' she hurled back bitterly, wanting to hurt someone, anyone, in payment for the hurt so lightly inflicted on her.

'I don't know, there's something about her . . . tragic and unattainable. I think he loves her tragedy.' T.J. caught sight of the dark fire in her narrowing cat eyes and decided then and there not to pursue this line of discussion any further. 'Look, it doesn't matter what I say. The fact is Josh thinks she's special. Don't you see how he holds on to her as though she were the Holy Grail?' As with most modern men and their women, T.J. realized, Emma Taylor was Josh's religion. Just as Doria and the children were his own . . .

'You're wrong, you're wrong!'

'Wake up, Doria. Shrug off your little cloud of delusion. It's over. Finito. Stop giving all your energy to a fantasy, start living a real life, with a real lover . . .'

'I hate you!'

'So what else is new?'

'You've got no right to talk to me like this,' she accused. 'No damn right!'

'I've got every right, you airhead, I'm in love with you!' And with that painful revelation, he awkwardly, tenderly, flung his arms around her and his lips tasted of her tears . . .

Without thinking, she raised her leg daintily and brought her foot hard into his shin.

'Eejit!' he howled like his old father. 'Now what did you do that for?'

Doria slapped her hand over her mouth, not sure whether to laugh or to cry, while T.J., whiter even than the paper her resignation was written on, danced like a bantam cock on the balls of his feet. He curled an accusing finger in her face. 'You're a lunatic, you know that? A certifiable lunatic! This is butterfly net time! You're ready for a dark attic!'

'Why don't you just go away? Get out of my life!' she shouted at him, blindly.

T.J. went rigid with anger. It had finally dawned on him that being in love was a superhuman quality that the race hadn't got the knack of yet. It was time to bow out – while he still had all his working parts.

'You know,' he snapped around on his heels, 'getting away is just what I'm going to do!'

The door slammed in her face with a stark finality.

Doria stared numbly at the place where T.J. had been. She was too exhausted even to cry.

CHAPTER FOURTEEN

The lovers were set towards the dusk of a December evening, its blue light slowly sifting down over the skyscrapers that lined Sixth Avenue. The air outside the *Globe* building smelled like snow.

Josh held open the door of his silver Jaguar, watching Emma's suede jerkin and skirt, the colour of applejack, hug the parted motion of her backside as she bent into the sports car. From the look on his face, it was evident he approved.

'I liked your friends,' she told him innocently from out the window.

'Hmm?'

'I said I liked your friends.'

'They liked you,' he replied, coming round to the driver's side.

He slammed the door shut, then eased behind the wheel, while filling the front seat of the car with his Rajah's fragrance.

'Ready?'

'Ready for what? Where are we going? Why not take a cab?'

'You ask too many questions.' The key was already in the ignition, the clutch pulled, the motor humming.

He'd brought the overnight bag with the toiletries and a change of clothes that she left in his apartment 'just in case'.

Once she caught sight of the white tiles of the Lincoln Tunnel, it set in that they were not headed for the little cafe around the corner.

'Am I being hijacked?'

'Hard words. Let's say "conveyed to a pleasant place".'

'Against my will!' New York State flew by outside her window. 'There's a law against that kind of thing.'

His eyes sparkled like blue ice. 'I make my own laws.'

'Well, I don't! I'm not one of you powerful types.'

'But you are. That's the whole point. You just haven't recognized yourself yet.'

'No. I haven't even begun to do that . . .' She sounded tired.

'Huh uh. This weekend, I don't want you to fret about anything or anybody. I just want us to have a good old lascivious time. We deserve it.'

'You really believe that, don't you?'

'Of course.'

'Okay, what makes you think we deserve happiness, Josh? Why us?'

'Because we're strong enough to make it that way.'

That seemed to satisfy her. She eased back into the bucket seat. 'Now do I get to know where you're taking me?'

Josh made the turn-off to the New England Thruway.

'Saratoga. My house.'

'But that's about a four hour drive!'

'We're going to stop off in the Hudson River Valley at Deer Park Inn. You'll love it.' Josh's eyes flickered from the road ahead. 'And when we get to Deer Park, I'll give you a super massage that will make your body feel twenty years younger.'

'Hmm, sounds like a good deal. I think I might like being hijacked after all.'

He smiled at her in the mirror. 'Do you like *me*, after all?'

'Yes. But not for the reasons you might expect.'

After checking the computer on the walnut-veneered console, Josh turned the wheel hand over hand, and they exited from the highway. 'How do you mean?'

'Oh, I suppose most women would be attracted to your good looks, your money, your power?'

'Now don't tell me I've wasted my whole life chasing after the standard glittering prizes – and you aren't the least bit turned on,' he interrupted.

'Once I would have been turned on by all those things,' she said, thinking of the harsh lessons her mother had tried to teach her. 'But the reason I'm with you, that I

155

must be with you, is that I feel you can see into me, maybe even know me better than I know myself. In a way, you look at things a lot like a woman, deeply, the real things that most men are too busy for, and end up missing all through their lives.'

'I'm going to take that as a compliment.'

'It is a compliment,' she replied, amazed that he could think of it any other way. 'What about me? Why are you with me?'

'To be honest, Emma, sometimes I just don't know. You're too independent, prematurely so.'

She looked hurt in the mirror.

Sensitive to her moods as any first lover, he put a comforting hand on her shoulder. 'Take it easy. I said "sometimes". It's so hard to think straight when you're sitting right here next to me. I suppose the answer is: I'm here because I need to love you, and to do it well. I've never worked so much before with a woman. It's not an easy thing for me. I don't feel very safe.'

So Josh was frightened too! It was good of him, kind to let her know she was not alone. Feeling closer to him than ever before, she gave a pressure on his hand.

A quarter of an hour later, directly after climbing a small blue ridge, the Jaguar glided into the well-lit front yard of the old Inn.

'Well, here we are.' Josh switched off the ignition.

They moved away from the parked car. The wind was cold and cutting as it soared up from the dark valley below. Josh waved with his hand.

'You can't see it now but the Hudson's a steep drop down there, about a couple of hundred yards.'

'I like the sound of the wind here, Josh – I almost said "song". It seems to have a different pitch when it gets anywhere near water.'

They walked up to the neat privet hedge that limned the sprawling white eighteenth century villa with its myriad green awnings and glassy duck pond. As the two of them crunched along the gravel path, an ancient sycamore tree by the tavern gate bent in the wind. Josh dropped his arm around Emma's shoulders. 'Cold?'

156

She shook her head. 'Not at all. I've never felt so warm.'

A burst of heated air welcomed them into the brilliantly lighted foyer. The lobby walls were papered with a period floral garland design in eggshell and wild plum. Violet crewel-work wingchairs stood close by the baronial stone fireplace and the adjacent hallway was rich with cherry-wood antiques. Everywhere was the patina of pewter and the effulgence of brass objects. Grapevine wreaths of starfruit, lady apples, cherries and kumquats lifted from a Della Robbia print, hung from the walls, with a twirl of pine and huckleberry leaves tied by a huge red gingham bow strung gaily in between. The whole place seemed to be celebrating some eternal, country holiday.

Josh waved Emma towards the reservation desk. 'Come on, I want you to meet Mrs Fulham.'

He hit the bell on the solid pinewood table and within seconds, a woman in her seventies came out of the back room. Although there was a trace of heaviness in her step, all thoughts of age were swept away by the enthusiasm of her smile.

'Josh! I was beginning to think you wouldn't make it tonight. It's good to see you, real good!' She stood straight and firm as a girl of twenty in her soft heather-coloured wool dress. The pink furze of her hair fanned out from her head like cherub's wings, and behind the glass rectangles of her silver pince nez, she had eyes the colour of faded blue gingham. Emma noticed that on each of her arthriti-cally curved fingers, she wore a magical copper ring. She shook Josh's hand warmly with those ravaged fingers.

'And this is Emma Taylor, Louise. I wanted you to meet her.'

Emma stepped forward with a friendly smile. 'It's beautiful here! You must be very proud.'

A romantic, Mrs Fulham took her by the hand. 'One thing about Josh,' she said in her cracked Yankee voice, 'he sure enough knows a good thing when he sees it.'

The elderly woman moved out from behind the knotty-pine desk. 'Come along, I'll show you the room myself. It's the one Ed and I used the first night we stayed

157

here, and has an authentic nineteenth century Quaker
wedding quilt. We always called it the "Honeymoon
Suite" because of that quilt.' She led the way up the
stairs. 'Ed passed on last year,' she said over her shoulder. 'The funeral was grand though, wasn't it, so full of
flowers and so many friends! Now that he's gone, I just
can't get excited about the spring season coming on like I
used to . . .'

'Ed Fulham was the kindest man I ever met. And the
worst poker player ever to sit down to a game of stud!
It's too bad you didn't get a chance to know him,
Emma,' Josh said for the old woman's sake.

'Kind? Oh Lord, yes,' Mrs Fulham repeated as she
helped herself up the maplewood stairs by means of the
elaborately curved banister. 'Kind as could be. But no
man's fool.'

They had reached the first-floor landing, which was
littered with handwoven white oak baskets bearing a
golden fuzz of dried wildflowers. Blue-and-white-check
bags of herbal sachet rested on the deep rectangle of the
windowseat, beneath a billow of curtain in honey satin,
swept back with a flourish. Mrs Fulham stopped to re-
arrange one of the sachet bags, before proceeding to a
door at the end of the first floor hallway.

She fitted the long key into the lock, and the door
swung open to reveal a richly detailed bandbox of a
room, wrapped in a rose-and-cream-ribboned wallpaper
and boasting a magnificent eighteenth century silver gilt
bed, piled high with quilted pillows and other lacy in-
dulgences in the form of neckrolls and hearts, butterflies
and bolsters. Dominating one wall was a breathtaking
mantelpiece of imported white Italian marble beneath
which a wine-dark fire surged and snapped like the
Aegean sea.

Josh set down his overnight bag, while taking stock of
their good fortune.

'You'll be able to see the River from here tomorrow
morning. A real pretty view,' Mrs Fulham explained, as
she went about busily plumping the pillows and rolling
down the sheets.

Two foil-wrapped cubes of a locally dipped caramel creme rested at the foot of the bed. Josh popped one into his mouth.

'Hungry?' their hostess asked.

'What do you think?' Josh replied, smiling.

She nodded. 'I'll have the Chef send up some lobster thermidor and wild pecan rice. How does a Pouilly Fumé sound?'

'Just right.'

'Uh huh. You can dine by candlelight. That's what Ed and I did the first night. Had no electricity then. Just this broken-down old house, each other – and a foolish notion that we could make it all work out.' She raised the back of her hand to her eye. 'It did, you know. For fifty-one years it worked out just fine.'

'It did at that,' Josh said kindly, realizing she was talking about her marriage and not the Inn. 'Thank you, Louise. The room is perfect.'

As soon as the door closed behind the old lady, Josh went over to Emma, and, lifting the heavy, honey-coloured hair from off her neck, laid a kiss there.

'You're a nice man, Josh Free.'

'Oh, no. And I thought I'd kept it hidden.'

'Did you really come all the way up here for Mr Fulham's funeral?'

'Of course I did. Ed and Louise Fulham are like the folks I knew in my boyhood, only with different accents. Salt of the earth, my father used to call them.'

'Yes, I think that's why I feel so at home here. It's good that you brought me.'

'Well, you may not know it yet but I happen to be particular about the people and places I love. I kind of like to bring them all together, get them to know each other.'

'It's worked with me! I love Mrs Fulham and I think this place is wonderful.'

'You should see it when it snows. Currier and Ives time.'

'Maybe it will snow tonight. The temperatures are supposed to dip way down.'

'Not in here.' He began to rub her shoulders with the balls of his hands. 'I predict it's going to be absolutely torrid in here.'

True to Josh's prediction, the frigid river wind did howl and seek among the rafters of the old Inn that night, but Joshua and Emma were warmed by the fire and feather bed of their princely room, where they dined off silver trays on a sultanic seafood meal and two superb bottles of Pouilly Fumé.

For dessert, there were hot vanilla *pots de creme*, which Emma spooned into Josh's mouth with the dense silver ladle wrapped in a napkin of handmade French lace. Reclining on the Shaker hearthrug, he passed her kisses in between mouthfuls.

'Umm, I don't know which are sweeter.' With his blue shirt half-unbuttoned, arms crossed behind his tousled head, he looked like some great tawny cat stretched out by the spitting fire. 'I'll have to taste them both again, just to be sure . . .'

Afterwards, buried under the heavy antique quilt, in the silver-gilt bed that once belonged to the perfumed mistress of a Union general, they loved one another again and again, only giving in to sleep, under protest, at sunrise.

Later on that miraculous day, she awoke to his kisses.

'Good morning, you.'

As she snuggled against his sleep-warmed body, he stirred against her buttocks.

'You're arousing me like that,' Josh said gruffly. 'Maybe you'd better move off if you want to go back to sleep.'

In answer, she turned and licked at his lips with her tongue.

'In that case, I'll go put the "Do Not Disturb" sign on the door or Louise will have our breakfast rolling in to a Sousa march. She's a morning person.'

Unwilling to let him go, even for an instant, Emma kept her hand hard on his back as he leapt up from the thickly piled bed, a magnificent male animal at the height of his powers, tall and naked in the clear morning light.

160

Josh threw on his monogrammed robe and set out the sign.

'Hell, it's cold out here.' He jumped back under the bedcovers.

'I'll keep you warm,' Emma promised. How quickly one became accustomed to happiness, as though one deserved it implicitly, just for being alive! Of course, it would all burn off and blow away one day, like every other fine thing in her life, leaving her with nothing but the distillate of yet another dream.

But until then, she would let Josh love her, because he was extraordinary at it, because he made her, for a time, forget that she was lost and incomplete, and always would be, no matter how many Josh Frees there were to sweeten the truth and delude her.

This time, their lovemaking was unhurried and intricate in the warm cave of the bedcovers, filled up with the sweet moistness of a garden after rain.

Afterwards, they showered together, then bundled up warmly for a brisk turn around the grounds. Emma, slim and glowing in an orchid down jacket, pewter grey corduroy jeans and dramatic suede boots laced up to her thighs; Josh handsomely wrapped in his majestic plaid wool coat of navy, green and gold, with a smart pair of oxblood gloves and an Irish tweed hat, the latter birthday compliments of T.J. McShane, to finish off the outfit.

They admired each other from across the room.

'I like the way you dress,' Emma said with decisiveness. 'Kind of unexpected – but very grand.'

'I guess I take some getting used to . . .'

'Not much,' she said lovingly, 'not very much at all.'

'It's good to hear you say that.' He had just motioned her to go before him when a scratching went up at the door.

'Who could that be?'

'Well, I just bet it's an old friend of mine, Ralph Waldo Emerson by name.' And sure enough, when he held open the door, a splendid sun-coated Irish setter sprang into the room. Josh hunkered down to ruffle the animal's silky ears. 'Hello, boy!'

Quivering with excitement, the dog lapped at Josh's face with his pink crepe-paper tongue.

'Yes, that's a good boy!'

Emma remarked that the animal was trailing a lead.

'That means Mrs Fulham wants me to take him for a walk,' Josh explained. 'Do you mind?'

'Not at all. He's beautiful.'

'So are you.' He took the lead in his red-gloved hand. 'Shall we go?'

'We shall indeed.'

Then, they were bounding down the stairs after Emerson, with scarcely enough time to wave at the pinkish blur of Mrs Fulham's head bobbing up at them from behind the reservations desk like a strawberry in a parfait.

Outside the Inn, it was clear and brilliant as an upstate winter morning can be. The sharp river wind brought a rejuvenating tingle to their bodies, a refreshment to their urban souls. Emma could now see the white swan arch his neck over the glassy pond like a porcelain figure in a China cabinet, the pair of ring-necked geese honking their argument on the bank like two grey clerics on a Sunday afternoon.

The regal Emerson sniffed and scratched at patches of the sere yellow grass, his flyaway coat rippling in the wind. He leaped joyously in the air.

'Come this way, Emma,' Josh called. 'I want you to see the river from up here. It's the perfect day for it.'

They made their way to the back garden of the house, and along the shaded woodland paths which sloped down steeply to a fringe of flexing pine trees. Above them a bluejay squawked noisily.

Emma slid part of the way down, with Josh and Emerson in the lead. When they'd come to the pine trees, Josh pointed upwards. 'See through those branches? That ridge of smoke-blue? That's the Hudson.'

Emma could just make out the silvery span of a bridge, and the chugging barges that criss-crossed the waters beneath it. Standing there with the sun on her face and Josh strong and loving beside her, she felt her spirit could just fly right up out of her, across the River, clear and free of all cares . . .

'God, but I love this place!'

'I love you.' Emerson was curled, a red ball of silk, at their feet, his sides panting in an allegro rhythm. 'Do you know that since we've been here together, I haven't given a damn about the city desk? That's a first. Here, look at this. Ask me what a "deadline" is.'

'Okay, what's a "deadline"?'

'I don't know.'

She laughed, knowing what he'd said was true. Never before had Josh Free turned his back on his career for a woman. But it was love, not ambition, that possessed him now, deepened him, chastened him. Like Emma Taylor, he was kicking over the traces of his old life in pursuit of something infinitely richer, something he couldn't even define.

She slipped her arm around his waist.

'You know, Emma,' he began, 'I always thought love was about *getting* something – good times, a scratch for the itch, the envy of other men. Now I see it's not that at all. It's got to do with having to give, more and more, until it starts to hurt, until you can't see straight for caring about that other person, the one outside yourself – the one who is yourself.' He smiled down at her. 'But I guess you know all about that. You're a woman.'

Emma was moved by his words. 'What I love most about you, Josh, is that you're not afraid to look into your own soul. I think that's what men most want to do – and what they most fear. Dr Beckstein was so wise. He tried to tell me that I would reflect men's inner selves, their secret desires. At first, they'd be drawn to me, but then they'd be repelled by the part of themselves they'd seen in me.'

Josh rested his hand on her bright hair. 'You can stop right there. I'm not going anywhere.' *But maybe she was the one preparing to go, running backwards to the arms of her past. To lose her now to Michael, to a dream, would be unthinkable.* Josh tried – but failed to imagine his life without Emma, and knew then he was helpless before her

163

frailty. She was one of those women who come over a man like fate. Now only fate would set him free.

'Shall we settle the bill with Mrs Fulham?' he asked. 'It's getting late and we still have a way to go.'

'All right.' Emma started back up the grassy slope, arms crossed behind her. 'Josh . . .' she called, deep in thought.

'Hmm?'

'Do you think Michael dreams about me?'

He felt a spike drive into his heart. The tops of the pine trees darkened as a cloud passed over the bright winter sun.

He pretended not to hear, bolting up the hillside with Emerson running beside him.

She called to him again, struggling to keep up. 'Josh, wait!' In a blur of awkward motion, she tumbled to the ground, thrusting her hands out before her to break the fall.

With a pang of remorse, Josh turned back. He went down on one knee before her. 'Emma, I'm sorry . . .'

Watching them with his soft eyes, Emerson paddled a velvet paw against Emma's shoulder.

'I'm all right.' She seemed incapable of looking squarely into Josh's face.

'Here, let me help you.'

'I said it's all right.' She came to her feet, waiting for him to speak. Then, frustrated, she broke through the wall of silence. 'Why are you so angry at me?'

'Oh come on, this is silly. I'm not angry.'

'The truth, Josh.'

'I refuse to get into this. Look, I didn't make you fall . . .'

'Don't you understand, I'm still falling!'

He softened. 'And you need me to catch you, is that it?'

'Yes.'

'Don't worry. I will.'

'For how long?'

'I don't know. Don't ask me those things.'

She rumpled Emerson's silky ear, and he pushed his cold nose into her hand. 'Well, at least Emerson likes me.'

'Hey, I like you. It's just new to me, that's all, this "you come first" trip. You're not the only one who's going through changes, Emma.'

'I know.' She squeezed his hand through the woollen glove. 'Why don't we start back?'

'Yeah.' Josh tugged on the slack lead and the three of them made their way up the hill to the porticoed white mansion, where new guests were arriving in shiny foreign cars.

Josh showed her into the foyer. 'Why don't you go on upstairs and freshen up? I'll take care of the bill, and then we can hit the road.'

She pulled off her gloves and blew on her hands. 'I'll see you later.'

'Umm.' Emerson was heading for the registration desk, with Josh one step behind.

She glanced back at him once from the white pine staircase, her tall, powerful saviour, dwarfing the other guests, like a man of myth.

Why was it, Emma wondered, that the woman must always be the stronger?

CHAPTER FIFTEEN

At high noon, armed with two whopping jars of Mrs
Fulham's gardenia-scented apple jelly, a surprise picnic
lunch because 'they'd missed breakfast', consisting of a
mellow English Stilton, sweet butter, crusty bread, wal-
nuts and a full-bodied red wine, plus an open invitation to
return to Deer Park Inn 'whenever you've got a hanker-
ing', Josh and Emma finally took to the road.

Gradually, the shadows of the morning burned off as
they drove full speed ahead into the colouring-book disc
of the sun. Along the way, they swigged the wine from the
bottle, told bad jokes, and sang golden oldies with the
stereo. Josh even opened the sun roof for a brief time,
until the wind got too strong and Emma begged for relief.

Two hours later, they reached Saratoga, watering hole
of the old New York rich; and Josh's high house on a hill,
a mansion which turned out to be a hundred years old and
built entirely of solid red brick. The caretaker had kept it
in mint condition.

With a fitting sense of pride, Josh pushed open the twin
carved-wood front doors. The house had never been so
important to him as it was now – because now, its stately
beauty, its breath of bygone grace, was a gift to Emma.

In turn, she was fully conscious of the honour he'd
shown her by bringing her to his beautiful home, and
made sure to exclaim over such serendipities as the re-
stored fanlight gracing the carved doors and, the many-
lustred Baccarat chandelier culled from the summer cottage of a Vanderbilt estate and now lighting up Josh's
spacious front hall.

'I want to see the upstairs . . .'

'Go on,' Josh said, grinning.

At the staircase, she had to catch herself on the newel
post.

'Emma . . .?'

166

'The staircase . . .' She was white. 'It reminded me of another house I was in once . . . I think I can see . . . no, no, it's fading now. I can't seem to remember.'

Josh could feel himself sinking in the quicksand of her need, losing his grip on the slippery coils of her past life. He hated telling Emma to remember an affair which could only spell disaster for him. But he knew as only a man who loves can know, that he must do what he could to aid her rediscovery of self.

'Emma, you must try! This is what we've been waiting for. Don't let it slip away.'

For his sake, she reached upward, against the press of darkness. She felt the strength of Josh's belief, the steadiness of his love fill her. It let her go out to the truth – or what portion of the truth she'd allow herself to see . . .

Michael's seventy-five year old family mansion, a Neo-Palladian with a file of long, light-filled windows, resided in the exclusive suburb of Boston called Chestnut Hills. Of a cold, unwelcoming beauty, it could be approached by way of a green serpentine path that rambled through its landscaped grounds.

As soon as Emma saw it, she realized that the mad money Michael had been spending so freely was nothing less than his own. At her repeated queries, he had finally admitted that he was indeed the Chairman of the Board and majority shareholder in Boston Trust Group, in addition to being the scion of a very old, very wealthy family line. The Lear Jet and Key West beachhouse were, incredibly, counted among his personal properties.

'Why didn't you tell me?' Emma demanded in confusion, as the Mercedes rolled into the sweeping driveway.

'I told you I'm a suspicious man by nature. Wealth like mine teaches you not to trust anyone. I had to be sure of you.'

'And are you, Michael?'

'Yes, of course. Completely.'

She was beginning to regret coming here, to his father's home. How stupid to have believed that their love was enough to protect her! She'd already sacrificed her career –

*what more would she be asked to give by these people who
loved Michael, before they accepted her for their son?*

'Will your parents like me?'

Michael frowned out the car window at the familiar
garden vista. The topiary cones of yew. The blazing beds in
regimental scarlet and gold. 'My parents don't "like" anyone. They rule people. It's what they do best. I think it's
something handed down in the genes.'

Emma's anxious expression prompted him to take her
hand. 'That's why I wanted to marry you first in Key West.
Present them with a fait accompli. That's how I deal with
them best. But you seemed to want it this way, and I respect
your beliefs, Emma. I don't ever want to do violence to
what you believe.'

Suddenly afraid, Emma held on to his hand as they
turned up the drive. In the dizzy discovery of their new
love, she had not understood how fragile, how exclusive it
all was. The world did not love with them, or want to share
in their joy. They were alone. And in danger.

Patrice touched her fingertips to the pulpy, darkening
leaves of the Cychnoches orchids. Her favourites, and they
were in decline. She'd have to move them to a stronger
light.

Oh yes, she liked these airplants, with their firm flowers,
their aerial roots seeking out the high nook of a jungle
branch, the anchor of a tall forest tree. They seemed like
wonderful, showy acrobats, creatures of the upper regions,
never needing to climb down to the dust of the earth.

Patrice sighed. What a morning! The telegram, Michael
had a fiancée, and now the greenhouse was filled with sun
and swelteringly hot. She cooled herself with a palm fan
Michael had brought her from the Keys. See how he was
always thinking of her, making his beau gestes.

Dear Michael. Her only son. Her raison d'être. Her
reward.

No need to worry. She had weathered the boy's ro-
mances before. Although he had yet to broach the subject
of marriage with any of those nameless, faceless, forgett-
able little girls, pretty in a hapless young way, he had gone

168

so far as to introduce them into the family circle on various holidays home. Good form, always. She smiled, confident she had taught him well.

Patrice moved on to the Cymbidium. Extravagant blooms, but cold-blooded. They thrived on the moist, sunless temperatures of the night. Like all her orchids, these were past prizewinners. She fully expected they would excel again.

An awful morning. With a worse afternoon to come, and there was so much more here to do, but the hot sun was now seeking her out among the flowering troughs. She pressed the dark flow of hair back from her forehead, where the skin seemed stretched to breaking over the spare, elegant bones of the skull. Her eyes began to burn . . .

Michael needed the comfort of his own peers, Patrice supposed, settling wearily in one of the British rattan chairs at the back of the greenhouse, to see him through family festivities. She closed her eyes, and held her fingertips to them. Soon if she were quiet, and very, very patient, the throbbing would go away . . .

To be sure, she'd never enjoyed similar family occasions when she was young. And he was so like her, her Michael, physically impeccable, and ruthless in his own understated way. They two had been accomplices from the time he was born – even before, she sometimes thought. He bound her husband to her as no vows, no threats ever could – because Philip had at least been wise enough to know that no other woman could have birthed such a flawless, reasonable son.

It was Patrice who had done it, through her will and her rage, she who had produced Michael to be her one perfect ally in an imperfect world. And he had responded brilliantly to her tending, had the vision to perceive his father's weakness, his mother's power. As a result, he had treated his father like the eternal boy he was, reversed roles effortlessly, with an assurance beyond his years.

Patiently, with infinite care, she had seen to it that Michael con the complete lore of his father's failings. Even better, while Michael's behaviour towards her husband had never once been lacking in the nuances of filial devotion (Michael may have been her son, but he was Philip's heir) the child knew the father in petty detail, and, as such, was a living, excruciating reproach, all the more effective because beloved by his victim.

Yes, she set her mind against the pain in her eyes, men were all too easy to control.

But Patrice respected women.

It had been women who had caused much of the grief in her life. Mysteries to themselves, they had the supernatural means to cause sorrow in others. Perhaps it was their expertise in suffering which gave them this power. Patrice never underestimated a female adversary.

It wasn't that she didn't want her son to marry, one day. If it made him happy at last, Patrice would permit him polygamy. But men were so often duped by unworthy loves, only imagined great passion in painted eyes.

Patrice had taken on the duty of exposing the other woman a long time ago. She would root out the motivations of this new girl, with the system she had perfected.

She glided up from her chair, with her clenched fist of a heart, looking forward to the challenge.

Michael's mother gazed up from the dancing spikes of her prize *Phalenopsis, only when Emma and her son were standing beside her in the close heat of the greenhouse.

To Emma, she looked like a woman who was an enemy to herself. There clung to her the bitter musk of memory, or then again, it might have been the flowers . . . Emma had never before realized the menace of orchids, their obscene pink tongues, the funereal perfection, the cloying, jungle rot smell . . .

But Emma wanted to love this woman, and the world she inhabited, to be loved by her!

Michael brushed his mother's pale cheek with his lips. 'Mother, this is Emma Taylor.'

The young woman offered her hand, hoping the touch of it wouldn't betray her feelings.

The hand held out to her in return was cool. 'My dear, we've heard so very little about all of this. Where has my sly son been keeping you?'

Emma flinched. It had been done subtly, expertly, but she'd been made to feel like a stranger, an intruder.

She wondered if inherited wealth always bred such fundamental unease in a woman. Patrice's lips were parted, she seemed slightly breathless in the heat, and Emma could tell that behind the illusion of light charm, Patrice feared she might be found out as one who hates her own sex. Even worse, Emma had already penetrated the woman's mask. They could never be friends now.

Patrice removed her thick gloves, carefully, as she did all things in her garden. 'Would you like some tea?'

'Something stronger, I think,' Michael suggested, 'for Emma.'

'Of course.' Two words. Yet with the social tone in which they were spoken, Emma had been put in the wrong.

She studied her rival. Michael's still handsome mother was severely tailored in muted tones of biscuit and mauve, so as to make Emma's raspberry cotton sheath stand out gaudy as a carnival queen's. What's more, the woman's voice was pitched so soft and low, one had to move closer in order to catch it, a trick of command. The heavy abundance of her hair, a shade of deep auburn and cut to the shoulder, was her only cosmetic indulgence.

Emma knew she would have to try to see Michael in his mother. It was the only way to keep from hating her back . . .

'Your father's in town today,' Patrice offered in her velvety voice as they accompanied her into the main house. 'I'm sure he will be devastated to have missed Elsa.'

'Oh don't worry, Father will have a chance to get to know Emma,' Michael replied, squeezing his lover's hand for courage. 'As I said in the telegram, Emma is going to be my wife.'

Patrice's smile never reached her eyes. 'How nice. We'll have a guestroom made up. It will be just like old times with, what was her name, Margot Cunningham. You know, Michael, I always did think you'd marry the beauteous Margot.' Patrice had linked her arm through Michael's and was chatting as they walked off. 'But all mothers are strangers to their son's hearts, aren't they, Ella?'

171

Emma's own heart broke.

From that first day on, Patrice insisted that Emma join her in the greenhouse among the poisonous blossoms, every morning at ten. As the weeks dragged on for Emma in that hot glass prison, the carnal perfume of the flowers became inextricably liked to Patrice's presence. With every swing of her soft, loose maiden's hair, more of the poison was let into the air, so that Emma would try to hold her breath until what she experienced as the daily violation of her privacy was at an end.

If Patrice was intrusive, Philip on the other hand, remained a chiselled figure in the distance, no more than a proper courtesy in Emma's life.

As for the equally charming Michael, he became increasingly attentive to his fiancée as the wedding date drew near. No wish for privacy was too extravagant, no whim of modesty too extreme to grant Emma, who preferred a quiet ceremony. Consequently, Patrice was overruled by the son when she spoke up for a sizeable gathering. Her generous offer of Great Grandmother's Edwardian gown was rejected by Michael out of hand because Emma had opted for a street-length ivory dress. And while Patrice wanted pheasant for the wedding feast, Emma wanted, and won, her less ambitious menu.

Nonetheless, the young musician knew she was only a ceremonial bride, superfluous and indulged by all. Even in his opposition to Patrice, Michael acted out a part for his parents, in an intricate, dynastic drama.

Was it any wonder then that at night, still awake in her bed, Emma could almost hear the scrape of metal on cement, as the last few bricks settled in at eye level, sealing her into fate, folding her into the walls of the old Neo-Palladian house, her lungs fluttering out a final protest under the unmarked stone.

Somehow there never seemed to be a chance to get in touch with the Boston musical set. Michael's plans for their precious time together never included concerts or plays anymore. In fact, most of their social life was now inscribed on their heirloom sheets, on their Shaker bed. A joyously in

172

love Emma could hardly protest. Especially as Patrice seemed to look the other way and discreetly left on weekend trips at superbly timed intervals.

Her only moments of privacy those days were the hours spent alone in her room, in the sole company of her violin. Eyes shut against all the world, she would touch, through the notes of music, the Emma who used to be, before love, the familiar Emma who was soon to vanish in an incense cloud of holy matrimony and suburban majesty.

Then Patrice complained of headaches, and naps interrupted.

Emma and her violin playing went underground, or, more precisely, into the attic, which was freezing in winter, sweltering in summer, and lonely in that vast house, all year long.

'Lovely,' Patrice exclaimed mildly over the eggshell-satin dress with the fashionably dropped waist. 'You look like a French doll. Turn around.'

Emma twirled, the smooth material pooling at her knees.

'Just lovely. But of course, Great Grandmother's gown is a nonpareil.'

Would Emma never hear the end of that wedding gown with its yellow-custard swathes of organza and Chantilly lace, studded with pearl nuggets like nutmeats in some overwrought Turkish dessert? A century's burden of family dreams hung upon those skirts. Emma could never wear that gown and breathe.

The girl slipped the simple dress clumsily over her head. She did not like being watched, exposed.

'Here, let me help you.' Rising, Patrice walked over to Emma who waited uncomfortably before the cheval glass. She brushed Emma's bare arm with her fingers and Emma thought how cold to the touch she was, like a statue in the park.

Patrice hung the dress on a padded black satin hanger, while Emma shrugged on her blue jeans and tee shirt. 'Thank you.'

'I noticed there were lots more wedding gifts on the hall table this morning, and you haven't even gone down to look at them. Aren't you feeling well today, Emma?'

173

'I'm fine, Patrice.' She still couldn't bring herself to say 'mother'.

'Then I think you should view them. And I hate to bring it up again, but I just can't understand why you haven't registered your silver and China patterns yet. You'll have such a hodge-podge at table, you'll never be able to entertain Michael's associates correctly.'

Emma bit her lip, drawing blood. Why couldn't they all just leave her in peace? Back in New York where she really wanted to be, her friends would just be sitting down to rehearsal. Gregor would be tuning his violin, handed down in his family from generation to generation, with that ecstasy of concentration he invariably had before he was about to play. When he'd done, he would tap her on the shoulder with his bow. 'Emma, the *cabaletta*. It dragged a little at the last performance. Once through, quickly . . .'

In the end, he would give a smile and a nod. 'Bravo. Emma, bravo!'

But she was no longer there to share the music with him. She'd given it all up to play mannequin for a woman with museum marble in place of a heart.

'Let's go down, shall we?' Patrice stood elegantly framed in the doorway. 'Philip and Michael will be joining us for lunch today.'

Emma tensed. 'But I made plans to go into Boston this afternoon. I thought I would drop in on a matinée concert, a friend of mine . . .'

'Emma, you wouldn't want to miss this last lunch with Michael before he goes off on his business trip, now would you?'

'No, no, of course not.' Another brick slid into place. Her time was not her own.

'Then come and join us. As soon as you change, that is.'

Emma could swear the woman trailed the venomous scent of orchids from the thickness of her hair. She would have to air her room before she slept in it tonight.

The door closed.

With grudging haste, Emma changed into a skirt and blouse and came down to the dining room where the family was quietly assembled.

In its burnished wood cabinet, the Cambridge-style grandfather clock ticked off the monotonous minutes while the maid went about serving hot shrimp bisque and pouring the Cabernet Blanc.

Holding court at either end of the rough-hewn trestle table made of Spanish Mission beams, Patrice and Philip seemed typically unaware of the others' presence, although Emma had come to know that some uncommon passion vibrated between them.

Michael smiled charmingly across at his fiancée, wondering why she had not touched a drop of the excellent soup.

Behind the shield of her hand, Emma yawned: the nocturnal dining room, with its carved boiserie and heavy plum taffeta drapes which seemed to muffle light and sound, never failed to put her to sleep. She stared into her plate, daydreaming about the Opera.

Patrice aimed a pointed glance at her husband, and, as if on cue, the weary and elegant man began to speak for her.

'Now that you two will be setting up housekeeping with us . . .'

'But that's never been decided,' Emma heard herself say in a broken child's voice. 'Michael and I like the city . . .' She looked to him, to her golden lover, for strength.

'But Emma,' he replied evenly, 'everyone just assumed you and I would move in here. The house is much too big for Mother and Father, they've been saying that for years. Besides, I love this house. It's where I grew up. There's no reason for me to leave.'

No reason but me, Emma thought. Love is his argument. If he loved me . . .

'You'll have the whole West wing to yourself,' Philip broke into her thoughts with his measured words, 'do your entertaining in complete privacy. The only thing we'll share is this dining room, oh and Cook and the others.' His job done, he raised his napkin to his lips in dismissal of the subject, like a lady with a fan.

'The house is magnificent, of course . . .' A feeling of panic swept over Emma, as bricks kept piling up around her, chinking in, one against the other . . . It wasn't fair.

175

They were all against her, a woman alone. Their emotional vocabulary, their ways of loving were foreign. She would never be one of them.

'Then it's settled.' Patrice's tone cut the thread of discussion. 'We are delighted for you, children. There's no finer house in New England.' She addressed her son.

'We'll have Jonathan Draper draw up an agreement, in which we'll have residence here as a life estate. But you – and Emma – will have the house deeded in your name.'

'Mother, that's too generous.' Michael was so grateful it was painful for Emma to watch.

'It's what your father and I want.' Whenever Patrice spoke to Michael her eyes were melting, as though he were her young lover, and not her son . . .

Emma felt trapped by this terrible generosity, by Michael's eternal minority as long as he was in his mother's hands. Because of her lover's weakness, hers would be a life among strangers.

'Nothing's too much to keep you comfortable and happy here.' Patrice raised her ruby flute in a toast. 'How could it be? I'm your mother.'

Emma mourned, for Michael, for Patrice . . . for the unwritten music that now would never be.

'I won't be gone that long.' Michael had a slight smile on his face, the smile he wore whenever she was near and sweet.

'I know.' She buried her head in his neck. 'It just seems so long, whenever you're away.'

They were standing by the gazebo in the back garden. It was sunset. His hair was pale and fine against the rose and orange wash of sky. She moved her hands down his tweed jacket. Her fingertips felt electric.

'Michael, do you think your parents like me?'

His handsome face held a look of puzzlement. 'Like you? What a silly thing to ask. They adore you.'

'How do you know that?' She rubbed her cheek against the harshness of his jacket. It was a chill evening and she was glad for the warmth of his embrace.

'They've said so. Many times. That's how I know.'

176

'How do they feel about the wedding?'

He held her at arm's length so that he could better see her face. 'What do you mean, darling?'

'Well, it was something of a surprise, our getting married I mean, and it might seem as though I came out of nowhere, and rode away with their son . . .'

He lifted her from the ground, with his arms locked around her waist, and twirled around with her until she laughed breathlessly. 'If anyone did any riding away with – I did! And I won't put you down until you promise to stop this foolish talk!'

'All right, all right!' she gasped, smiling down at him.

Her heels sank into the soft dirt, as he lowered her gently.

'I never knew you were such a bully!'

'I never knew you were such a worrier!' He looked suddenly sly. 'The problem with you is . . .' He backed her against the spreading cherry tree, lay his hands on either side of her face . . . '. . . is not enough of this.' He slid his tongue into her warm mouth and she seemed to liquefy against him.

Some time later, when they were sauntering back to the big house, arms linked behind their backs, he chided her again.

'Now this time, while I'm away, I want you to think nothing but happy thoughts . . . thoughts about Key lime pie and . . . a certain swimming pool in the sun – thoughts about you and me and the wonderful life we're going to have together. Will you promise to do that for me?'

'For you?' She cocked her head and rested it against his shoulder, briefly, fondly. 'For you . . . I would do anything.'

Michael nodded, expecting nothing less from the woman he loved.

The wedding took place in a false spring in March. There were five or six more weeks of sodden grey skies yet to come, despite the sunshine that day, and Emma sensed it. But nothing could have dimmed the radiance of her wedding day.

Under her wreath of baby's breath, she looked out on a crowd of strangers; Michael's colleagues, Patrice and Philip's well-heeled prep school friends. There had been too much shame burning in her to ask Gregor or any other of the New York musicians. After all, it was she who had abandoned them and her composing career. Well, this wedding marked the beginning of her new life, among new friends . . .

The flower-scented cavern of the greenhouse glittered before her. In the hush that precedes all rituals, the violinist struck up the Wedding March, an exquisite touch arranged by Patrice.

Wasn't it enough of a triumph to have the wedding set up in the greenhouse, amidst her malevolent plants?

A flashbulb popped and Emma started forward. Philip, who was giving her away, held her satin arm steady.

Very far away, at the end of the aisle that had been cleared, Michael proudly waited for her in his grey pin-stripe suit, looking somehow inevitable as though he were the archetype of all grooms, at all happy weddings. Her heart soared.

Then the brief ceremony was concluded with kisses in the air for the bride, handshakes for the groom. The best champagne flowed freely while Emma imagined the look on her mother's face as she would say 'You've done it, Emma. You've married a substantial man.'

She felt then as though her whole life had been a fated path down this aisle. Now that she'd come to the end of it, she hardly gave a thought to the broken plans, the music. There was only Michael, and his proud unquestioning love, flowing down to her through the years.

Her head rang with more congratulations. There was Michael kissing the tip of her nose. There she was, standing beside him, as she pressed the hands that kept coming. Every so often husband and wife would just look at each other, and smile.

'Would you care for an hors-d'ouevre?' The liveried waiter held a silver tray at his shoulder.

'No, thank you . . .' She was too excited to think about food . . .

'Of course you want to eat, Emma. I know you didn't touch your dinner last night and you had nothing at all this morning.' It was Patrice, swathed in ivory chiffon. 'Come sit by me, I'll bring you a plate,' she insisted.

How could Patrice have worn white, Emma asked herself with a pang, as though she were Michael's bride . . .? Oh, but a small price to pay for such a husband . . .

A light touch on her arm. Emma was guided to a folding chair tied round with white ribbons and there was peace and quiet for a moment as Patrice bent over the buffet table making selections for the bridal dish. A few minutes later, Patrice handed Emma a full plate. She sampled the delicacies as Patrice spoke softly to her.

'It's all right, Emma. You're not what I would have chosen for my son, but I see now that you really do love him.'

Emma stared at the woman with whom she was forever joined at the heart, in love with the same beautiful man. She saw her through a haze of utter happiness and could only feel benevolence and hope.

'We'll take care of him.' Patrice suddenly looked kind, if worn out by her love. 'You and I. You'll see, it will be all right.'

'Oh, there you are.' Philip came up in his dark suit, his hair a smooth, silver helmet, framing the blue-grey eyes. 'The photographer wants a picture of us together, Patrice.'

'Of course.' She rose from her seat with a rustle.

Emma watched as Michael posed in between his parents, Philip left slightly behind, Patrice luminous in her bridal-coloured gown, facing unconsciously, heavily to the left, towards her handsome son.

It was such an attractive portrait of the bridal party that it took her a minute to realize what was wrong with it.

She was not in the picture at all.

But then, startlingly, Michael broke from the frame of the living photograph, and hurried over to her.

'Darling, come on. I want this dance.'

He pulled her up by the hands – there was a gold band on one finger now – and she fit into his arms so smoothly, so effortlessly, as they circled the small dancing area to the

179

music of the trio they'd hired for this special day. They moved like honey together, everyone said so, and he whispered loving words into her ear, and she was so willing to hear them, cupped to receive them readily, and so very lucky to be loved like that, in a natural way, spontaneous as the flow of music, that any misgivings she'd momentarily had, were cast aside, and she felt happier than she'd ever dared to feel before.

CHAPTER SIXTEEN

Now that Emma was married to her son, Patrice seemed less interested in their little talks in the conservatory. Emma had more time to herself, and was beginning to have fun again. Above all, she loved being Michael's beautiful, young wife. It was a role she was born to play.

True to their word, Patrice and Philip had signed over the twenty bedroom mansion to Michael and his wife, shortly after the ceremony. Not content to stop there, they threw in a set of octagonal Venetian glasses with seventeenth century rose flutes, spectacular dishes of Portuguese and English vermeil, and a Louis Quinze cloth armchair built wide enough for the swath of a duchess.

As promised, Emma and Michael had the run of the spacious West Wing, along with its mirrored 'ballroom', long unused and just waiting to be filled with the shimmer of celebration. And since Michael's business interests called for occasional entertaining, Emma, as hostess, was expected to do just that.

If at first she had balked at such duties, her energies, deprived of their usual creative outlets, soon sought fulfilment in the rich woman's traditional arts of party-giving, fashion, and shopping, shopping, shopping.

From festivity to festivity, she became adept at concocting fantastic centrepieces for her table – articulated silver lobsters and sea shells on a cloth of floor-length moiré after a certain Dutch masterpiece of the seventeenth century, for example. Michael's guests were still talking, some uncharitably, about the night of her musical motif, when the gold-leaf menu was set up on a lyre-shaped musical stand and seraphic harpists sat weaving melody from every corner of the room. Emma didn't care about reviews. She needed the challenge.

Also, with the dinner parties came the need for good clothes.

Thus it was decided that an overpriced and dignified new

181

wardrobe would be created just for Emma by the finest couture houses in the world. For the first time in her experience, she had real jewellery with price tags from the likes of Harry Winston and Cartier, as her lifestyle began to resemble nothing so much as a pillaging of fancy caterers, Paris fashion houses and decorator salons.

In the early days of her marriage, the novelty of opulence served to carry her through the day. It was the nights that posed a problem.

Sometimes after a party, when the last candle had guttered in its Italian crystal cup, and the last Mercedes whooshed out of the long, sloping driveway, Emma would experience a curious hollowness in the pit of the stomach, her spirits pitched too high when the evening began, and now, fallen lower than ever before. At such times, Michael could never seem to understand her moods and above all else, Emma found this failure inexpressibly sad.

Her dreams were full of strange signs those days, cries from the heart, she called them. The hardwood body of her violin had shattered and cracked open. Inside was a human embryo, a golden child . . .

Once as she dreamt, she felt herself rise up from the bed, leaving the flesh-and-blood dreamer behind, so that the shadow figure then began to live life in her place. In vain, she struggled to raise herself by the elbows, to call out and warn the people who were, every one of them, fooled by the imposture. It was no use. Her limbs were numb, immobile. The shadow lived for her, ate her food, played in her bed. Years went by in which there was no Emma, but what the shadow let slip through its dark meshes . . .

After her own cries awakened her, it took half the night for Michael to convince her that none of it had been real.

For the next year of party-going and party-giving, all who saw the newlyweds went away thinking that husband and wife were fortunate in one another. And they were – Emma beggared by passion, Michael accepting her every sacrifice in the name of love.

When he was at home, they were always to be found

together, heads bent in some secret sweetness, arms linked like a magician's silver rings.

When he was away on business, Emma planned little surprises for his return – a jewel of an antiquarian book turned up in a Boston shop on a rainy afternoon, a basket of perfect pears left on his night table. Her life turned on his whims, had meaning only in his presence.

Their lovemaking was slow and serious, like a private religion they followed to the letter, and Emma claimed she was happy, although it was never clear to her, that year in Chestnut Hills, whether or not she spoke the truth.

With a rustle of black taffeta Patrice hurried into the library for a final spot check. This, because Christmas Eve was Michael's favourite holiday and she was bent on making the first Yuletide celebration since his marriage, a memorable one.

By the dinner hour, the three-storey house was filled with the smell of mulled cider simmering on a back burner, of the pine wreaths hung low on the windows under clouds of bronze-green and crimson ribbons, of bayberry candles twinkling along the rims of mantelpieces.

Patrice stood in the centre of the empty room, surveying her handiwork. She was pleased. Always a fire-warmed hideaway for tea and quiet conversation, tonight the library was touched by a majestic beauty, from the over-the-hearth panelling, lifted from a sand-coloured wall, circa 1690, to the cornices festooned with shaggy evergreen boughs wound in regal purple satin. For drama, huge butterfly bows, looped round with straw and gilt trumpets, soared in either high corner.

The windowseat played host to a dozen pots of blushing pink amaryllis from Patrice's own garden, and balanced upon the silvery blue American Primitive cane-bottomed chairs were stacks of foil-wrapped packages of every shape and size.

In one corner of the honest, hardwood floor, stood a drop-leaf table from the woods of Maine. Set up for a family buffet, it glimmered with transparent vases of paper-white narcissus, gold-threaded linen, and a pewter ladle in *a crystal punch bowl, which was filled to the brim with frothy New Orleans-style egg nog. Heaps of glowing apples, oranges and pears, smoked meats, savoury patés, cheeses and assorted nuts rounded out the feast.*

But the most dramatic touch of all was a floor-to- fifteen-foot-ceiling Christmas tree – a blazing green pyramid strung with cranberry-wooden beads and a spider web of white lights. Fanciful birds and Mexican straw dolls nested in its branches. Glass baubles and antique miniatures shivered like ice and snow against the dark weave of fir needles.

She had been right to supervise the decorating herself this year. Emma had no talent whatsoever for that sort of thing, no sense of tradition. It was pitiful what she had done to her rooms! Department store chic, Patrice called it. Outlandish. She didn't know how their friends all laughed at her behind her back. Poor girl, she tried so very hard . . .

'Merry Christmas.' Emma and Michael strolled into the room, their arms filled with bright packages.

Emma's Edwardian-style lace dress was of the most evanescent peach-pastel shade, something out of a pastry book, Michael had said, with meringue appliqué and buttercream piping. She had piled her hair high up on her beautifully modelled head and attached a fiery diamond clip to hold it back. Her eyes were violet brilliants.

The girl was attractive enough, Patrice conceded. If only she would do as she was told . . .

'Merry Christmas, Mother.' Michael, looking tall and trim in his chiselled evening clothes, bent over to give his mother a kiss.

She grazed him on the side of his mouth. 'Merry Christmas, son.'

With his hands in his trouser pockets, he looked around the room. 'It's just as I remember it from my boyhood. My mother's made a real Boston Christmas for us this year, Emma.'

'Yes, it's beautiful.' Emma never looked up from where she knelt on the floor, laying her gifts out under the tree. She would have to get through this night with the family, and then she and Michael could have their own, private Christmas . . .

Michael rubbed his hands together, briskly. 'Well, I'm having a drink. Would you like some egg nog, Emma?'

'All right.'

He ladled the heavily spiced egg nog into a cup, and handed it to Emma. 'Where's Father?' he asked, busy at the liquor cabinet.

'Your father's not coming down. He doesn't feel very well tonight,' Patrice replied.

'Not coming down . . . ?' Michael looked unhappy with his father's bad form, the break in tradition.

'Let it never be said, that unlike the esteemed Mr Ebenezer Scrooge, I was a man who did not keep Christmas well.' Philip in peerless black tie, threaded his way unsteadily into the library.

Emma caught a flare of whisky as he passed by.

In frosty silence, Patrice went over to the tree and fiddled with the ornaments.

'What's in there?' Philip motioned to the punchbowl.

'Egg nog,' his son answered.

'Oh no, I need the real stuff. I think I deserve it, don't you, Michael, for getting through another bloody year of wedded bliss . . .'

Patrice whitened.

'Father.' Michael shot a warning glance. Pouring two fingers of whisky, he held out the glass to him. 'Behave.'

'Thank you, son.' Philip took it. 'I just might do that. We don't want your new wife to think we aren't one big happy family here, do we? We wouldn't want her to guess the truth about this stewpot of hostilities, now would we?'

Michael's fist curled into an angry ball.

Fearing that he might actually strike his father, Emma stepped between them. 'Why don't we all sit down and open our presents?' She looked from one anguished face to another, wondering when they had all moved out of the ordinary world.

'Yes, why don't we?' Philip repeated. He took a seat by the fire, but he wasn't about to be silenced. 'Now that we're chatting, Emma,' he said familiarly, 'I'd like you to clear something up for me. Is it true what the servants say, that you're still a virgin? With Michael as a husband you could

185

be. Michael is his mother's son, not mine. He never was mine. She'd be the first to tell you that.'

'That's enough, Philip. No one is amused.' This from Patrice, pale and rigid as death, incongruously framed against the gay, lighted Christmas tree.

Philip seemed not to hear, his face flattened out with grief. He fixed Emma with his dead eyes. 'You know, it's a damn thing, being jealous of your own son. She made it that way. She's not like you and I, Emma. She doesn't bleed like you and I. No heart to pump it. She's an unnatural woman, Emma. If I were you, I'd get out of here before it's too late and she makes you into her creature too . . .'

Shaken, Emma reached behind her for Michael's hand. It was colder even than her own.

'I should have left you a long time ago,' Philip staggered up out of his chair and took a few wavering steps towards his wife. 'Either that or I should have killed you.'

The expression on Patrice's face gave Emma gooseflesh. It spoke of a loathing so intimate and desirous as to cross over the fine line of obsessive love. 'Go on upstairs, Philip. You've said enough for one night.'

'Did I hurt your feelings, darling? Here, let's kiss and make up under the mistletoe, like a proper husband and wife.'

He lurched forward roughly to embrace her, but Patrice stepped aside, and, unable to stop his momentum, he swatted the branches of the Christmas tree. A rain of crystal balls pinged on to the floor, shattering into hundreds of slivers like a pool of ice water.

'Now see what you've done! Go upstairs, Philip!'

He passed his hand over his eyes. 'I wish I could go. I wish I had the strength to go.'

'Go to bed, Philip.' Patrice's voice was thin ice.

'Yes.'

'To bed.'

'Yes.'

The library door clicked softly behind him.

Emma did not dare to articulate what she had seen and heard the night before, and the next morning, she and

186

Michael came down to a sombre Christmas. Outwardly, however, it was business as usual.

A roaring fire was lit, presents were distributed, an elaborate lunch served. No one said a word about either Philip or his absence on Christmas Day.

When all but his father's gifts had been opened, Michael presented Emma with a floor-length fantasy of a white-fox fur coat, so preternaturally soft that touching it was like running one's hand through a breeze. Heirloom diamonds, some as big as hazelnuts, had overflowed the pockets.

With vintage champagne, the newlyweds toasted one another across the glittering table.

Then Philip dutifully joined them, his hair a helmet of hammered silver, his blue eyes cool and untouched as a Prussian officer after battle. Only the hint of a shadow beneath his eyes betrayed the strain he was under.

After supper, they all retired to the library and settled around the fire as far from one another as possible, with the exception of Patrice who made a show of seating herself beside Emma, whether to please her son, or distract from her husband, Emma couldn't tell.

The woman chatted on pleasantly about her gifts, then began to question Emma about her own family.

'You speak of your mother often. Do you have a snapshot you could show me?

Emma was suspicious. 'Just one. My mother didn't like having her picture taken, some kind of superstition, I guess. I never found out who took this one.'

'If you don't mind, I would like to see it.'

'You would?' Emma moved up from her chair. 'I'll be right back.' She assumed Patrice wanted her out of the room for some reason.

The young woman heard the rise and fall of voices in the library as soon as the door snapped shut behind her. Were they taking the opportunity of her absence to speak about last night? She yearned for some detonation of truth that would set them all free. It was the silence that was so corrosive.

Upstairs in her biscuit-coloured room with the classical dadoes and plaster garlands, she took a satin-covered slip-case from off her closet shelf. Inside was memorabilia of her

187

early life – blackened high school ring, graduation auto-graph book, a wilted corsage of violets and a pack of dog-eared photographs.

She riffled through the pack until she came to a black-and-white still of her mother, cool and pretty in a frivolous summer dress and wide-brimmed straw hat that flopped over her eyes. In her right hand, she carried a slatted picnic basket and appeared to be laughing at the photographer as though he or she had just said something richly amusing.

Emma had always suspected it had been a 'he' behind the camera because of a certain flirtatious tilt of her mother's head. It was not a typical pose, which made the picture all the more tantalizing to her daughter, and spoke of that mythical time in our parents' lives in which we have no part.

She zipped shut the slipcase and left it lying on the white lace counterpane of her double bed.

When she was standing before the library doors, she tactfully paused for the family to finish their private business. Only then did she re-enter the room.

Tension boiled up around her like a sandstorm.

Philip, his back ramrod straight as though he were lashed against his chair, was boring into the fire. Patrice seemed to be re-arranging her face for Emma's benefit, as if some release of pure fury had begun a work of disintegration in the brief time her daughter-in-law had been absent from the room.

Michael jumped to his feet. 'Darling, what took you so long?'

Emma laughed to break the tension. 'I couldn't have been more than five minutes.'

'Was that all?' He drained his brandy snifter. 'What have you got there?'

'A picture of my mother. The only one I have, unfortunately.'

Patrice held out her hand.

Emma sat by Patrice, near the fire. 'I like this one because it's a happy picture, and mother didn't usually look happy.'

Patrice took the laminated square between her fingers and held it up to the firelight.

In the next moment, it was fluttering down into the hot lick of flames.

When Emma had started forward as though to retrieve it, Patrice had turned on her with a look of such forbidding contempt, that the startled daughter-in-law had hesitated just long enough for the photograph to catch fire, curl and blacken into ash.

Philip looked on, innocent of interest, as though he'd left the family long ago and could no longer be touched by them, but Michael, like Emma, had sensed that it had been deliberately done. 'Mother, why did you . . . ?'

'I'm sorry, Emma,' Patrice said in a flat voice. 'I must have been holding it too loosely.'

Emma's concern over her mother's photograph gave way to pity for the woman who had lost it. 'It's all right,' she responded quickly. 'It was only a piece of paper. I have my memories.'

'No, that was inexcusable. I asked to see the picture and then I . . . ' Her head bowed in an act of contrition. 'I'm afraid I must excuse myself for the rest of the evening. I have a terrible headache.' Stiffly, she rose from her seat. 'Will you come up now, Philip?'

'If you like.' With an exhaustion that struck deeper than muscle or bone, he moved up out of his chair, and waited for his wife to join him at the shadowy threshold of the room.

Lost in silence, the couple quit the library, and made their slow progress up the long, winding staircase.

Left to themselves, the young lovers stared at each other, uncertain of how to console . . .

In the deepening quiet of the room, the only sound to be heard was the hiss of the fire in the grate.

'My poor Emma,' Michael said at last, 'what kind of a Christmas have we given you?'

She came into his arms. 'We're here together. That's all I need to be happy.'

He kissed her shining hair. 'I feel I should apologize for my parents. Both of them. They've been acting almost as if something is coming to an end. I can't explain it. But I feel there's some kind of cycle about to climax. And it's going to affect you and me, Emma. That's what worries me. It's going to affect you and me.'

'Michael, nothing can hurt us. We're invulnerable. All

lovers are.'

'But there you're wrong, Emma. We're the most vulnerable of all.'

She laid her head against his chest. 'I don't believe that. But there is something . . .'

'Tell me, my darling.'

'Wouldn't it be better if we were to move from here, set up our own home?'

She could feel his whole body clench against the idea. 'I thought this was our home.'

'I just felt . . . with the new things we've discovered about your parents' relationship, we might be better off, more discreet, certainly, if we were to leave them to their privacy,' it came out in a clumsy spill of words.

'What new things?'

'Michael, your father's drinking . . .'

'What are you talking about? Everyone drinks.'

'Michael, I don't understand why you're denying what happened last night . . .' She trailed off when she saw her husband's blank expression, the shadow coming into his eyes. He did not want to see or hear. He especially didn't want her to. Because then he would have to change what could not be changed, behold his own father in all his terrible frailty . . .

'You shouldn't talk about things you don't know about.'

She could tell that he was tired, but that he would marshal his last bit of strength to fend her off. He would protect his family secrets, even from the woman he loved.

As she had done so many times before, Emma decided to let it go.

'You're right, Michael. I don't know why I even brought it up.' Her eyes rested on the box with the fur coat inside. 'Did I tell you how much I love my new coat? It's like warm snow. And I love you too.'

Michael's face shone with relief. 'Do you?'

'Of course.'

'Then let's be happy, Emma.'

'We are happy, Michael,' she said quizzically.

'Yes,' he sighed, holding her tightly to him. 'It's right for you to think so.'

CHAPTER SEVENTEEN

When Emma struggled up to consciousness, she was lying in an unfamiliar four-poster bed, with Josh hovering over her.

'You fainted,' he explained tersely. 'And then you slept. Here, drink this.' He handed her a chilled glass of freshly squeezed orange juice. 'For energy.'

'Thank you.' She sipped from the glass, then put it down on a table beside the bed.

'How do you feel this morning?'

'Fuzzy around the edges.'

'You look great.' He shrugged. 'What did you see down there?'

'We lived in Chestnut Hills, in a huge mansion with a winding staircase, like the one downstairs. That's what triggered the memory,' she added, exhilarated now that the pieces were finally coming together.

Josh sat on the side of the bed. He gave a whistle. 'You really got an eyeful this time, didn't you? Let's see, Chestnut Hills, that's in Boston, isn't it?'

'Yes, that's right.' Her eyes glowed. 'Oh Josh, let's go there! I think I would know the house if I saw it. I could find out who my husband was.'

'You married him then?'

'It looks that way.'

Josh's face fell; the mystery game had just stopped being fun. 'And I thought we were going to spend a luxurious weekend in bed . . . '

She took pity on him then, pulling him down to her, stroking his dark, tangled hair. 'We will, Josh, I promise. But first I have to go to Boston. I have to know. . .'

He looked unhappy. 'Do you realize that you might still be a married woman?'

'The word is "adulteress".'

'Hey, to hell with that! Who would hold you to it when you haven't been well? Anyway, by this time, it's likely you'd be divorced by reason of abandonment . . . or something.' Josh relaxed back against the pillows, spinning out the scenario that most pleased him.

'Do you think so?' The covers rustled as Emma sat bolt upright. 'How strange to have loved and lost my husband, without even knowing it. It's like something out of a dream, the way people weave in and out of my life.'

'And you in and out of theirs. Your husband must be frantic about your disappearance.' Troubled again, he sought her eyes as if he would impress there the superior claim of his love. 'I know I would be.'

'Josh, I'd love to be able to reassure you. I'd love to tell you that what's past is past, that Michael is no longer a part of me! But Josh, I can't honestly say it. I would be lying to you – the one thing I never, never want to do.'

She pushed off the covers. Turning on one hip, she came to her knees beside Josh on the bed. The satin ribbons on her dressing gown fluttered with the motion as she raised her hand and stroked his cheek.

'You've been so good for me, Josh.'

'But you don't love me, is that it? I'm just sort of a Dr Beckstein with balls to you, is that what you're saying?'

Emma clung to the silence which had so impressed Josh that night at Windows on the World. For to tell her lover about the crazy passion that welled up inside her whenever he was near, the deep love that sometimes obliterated all distinctions between his heart and hers, would be to expose him to pain and betrayal, to make cynical use of the most beautiful and fragile gift of this man's life. She couldn't do it – even if it meant she'd have to lose him.

What if she did find Michael again as she sensed in the psychic bone she would? What if she loved Michael again? What would she say to Josh then? No matter how deeply she loved him, she had loved Michael first, and must be prepared to sacrifice Josh.

'It's better for you if I don't love you,' she said quietly.

'Son of a bitch.' He slammed his fist into the wall behind the bed.

192

'Josh, don't . . . .'

'What do you want me to do, fall at your feet and sing anthems of praise?' He rolled off the bed. 'You're nothing but a self-serving tease, Emma, you know that? I'm tired of playing mind games with a high moral tone. I'm sick to death of it. Of us . . .'

He headed for the door, then half-turned. 'Luckily, I'm not even unpacked. We can start for home as soon as you're ready.'

'Josh . . .' She longed to run to him, to hold him fast, to communicate through the flesh the intensity of passion she couldn't frame in words.

What if he began to hate her? The idea burst in her head like a cannonball.

What if he left her?

She should tell him now, right away, that she needed him to need her, wanted him to stay angry enough to engage in her battles with the past.

But something unreasoned and unstoppable held her back.

It could have been love.

'All right,' was all she said. 'I'll be down in ten minutes.'

Taking place a scant ten minutes after their argument, breakfast was, at best, a sullen affair.

Resisting all Emma's attempts at civil conversation, Josh drank down cup after cup of his foul instant coffee with no milk, an extra penance, she guessed, for having lost control.

Gradually, she had given way to Josh's mood, and her forced chatter wound down like a child's mechanical toy.

Josh dumped the crumb-laden plates in the sink. He clattered at the stainless steel basin.

When Emma couldn't bear the separation anymore, she stole up behind him and laced her arms around his waist.

'Do you hate me a lot?'

One plate tinkled against another in the drainer.

'Do you want me to go away, Josh?'

He still didn't give an answer, but she could hear one forming in his mind and heart.

'Just say it, and I'll go. I'll never bother you again.'

'Liar.'

'What did you say?'

'I said you're a liar.' Up to the elbows in foam, and pinching her by the scruff of her neck like a boy with a kitten, he whirled so unexpectedly upon her that she lost her balance and toppled headlong into his soapy embrace.

'You're lying to me,' he kissed her between words, while she imagined his tongue leaving fiery marks all over her face and throat, 'you'll never get away from me. You're in me, a part of me. It's like some kind of madness churning in my blood . . .'

She yearned up to him. 'Oh, Josh, it wasn't supposed to happen this way!'

'It looks like it has to be this way, Emma, love . . .'

'Don't take me home, then.' She caught her breath, hating herself for saying it, needing to try him one more time.

Josh exhaled slowly. 'You want to go to Boston first?'

'Yes.'

'And you want me with you. Even though you know it will tear me apart, and I'll hate you for making me do it?'

'Yes.'

'Give me one good reason why I should.'

'I can't.'

The silence stretched out between them like a desert horizon. She could lose him now with her endless wanting . . .

'I must be crazy,' Josh said. 'Either that or I'm so much in love with you it's as good as being crazy. I'll take you to Boston.'

'Oh, Josh. I don't deserve you.'

'No, you don't.' He let her softness fill his arms.

Her skin against his was already slick from the soapy bath.

Her sheer blouse clung to the peaks of her breasts and tap water had made a dark vee down the front of Josh's denim shirt, so that, in the next dreamy moment, their easy move into the Roman bathroom with the sunken tub, tiled in gleaming rose and black, seemed to make perfect sense.

They watched each other undress, not saying a word, then lowered themselves into the whirling warm water.

Emma, her arms folded about Josh's waist, lay her cheek against his back, then nipped at the nape of his neck with the tips of her teeth.

A shiver seemed to run through him. He swung around, and, floating on his back, with his arms propped along the side of the inset tub, he pulled Emma into a sitting position on top of him. Her long hair trailed like stardust behind her in the water that massaged her body with steaming warm motion.

He closed his eyes, as she began her sensuous ride, up and down, faster and faster, a glide to Nirvana he wished would never have to end . . .

Their repeated lovemaking was rough, sweet, and eager – as if it were the first, or the last on the eve of parting.

The last reddish gold leaves of the season slid over her ankles as Emma walked out to the car that morning. Josh held open the door.

A dark cloud of blackbirds had settled in the treetops above them and their chatter was the last thing Emma heard before the rackety surge of the engine filled the milk-blue country air. They pulled out of the driveway and, rolling over the hilly suburban lanes, nosed back on to the New England Thruway, on the road to Boston.

With Saratoga behind, a silence bloomed inside Emma.

She held her head to the side, as if listening to it, her hair a swing of white gold in the corner of his eye.

God, all he wanted was for this journey to be over, and for Emma to be proved, once and for all, wholly his to love . . .

Emma shifted her weight from one scoop of her hips to the other. As the hours passed and signposts for Boston began to appear, she had played with the possibility of meeting up with Michael again . . . of ending her time with Josh.

Now she glanced over to where her lover sat, his hands heavy on the wheel.

'He's in pain,' she thought, ashamed, 'and I'm holding the knife.'

There was nothing to be done. Emma was too conscious of the wound she'd inflicted that morning to try to break through to Josh. She knew he would have to work it out for himself. She could not help him, just as he could not help her with their conflicted love.

'Hungry?' he asked, checking his black Porsche watch. 'It's noon.'

'A little.'

They stopped at a roadside inn where the sunny dining room had red-checked French bistro tablecloths and green Perrier bottles with wild flowers stuck inside them.

They ordered country omelettes and home fries and then Emma went on to the washroom to freshen up.

She pushed up the sleeves of her bulky black mohair sweater to wash her hands. When she reached up for the towel dispenser, she caught a glimpse of a face – it wasn't quite the face she knew to be her own – staring back from the mirror above the sink.

It startled Emma to see how much she had changed from last night to this moment, her features altered in some deep, instinctual way, as though the physical cells remembered what the conscious mind had forgotten.

It was almost as if, as she drew closer to the site of her former life, the last residue of Michelle, her feeling, her tone, was draining away, even as the pulse of Emma Taylor was growing stronger within her. She was, in some inexplicable way, becoming Emma.

She moistened a towel under the cold water tap, then held it to her forehead.

She must be calm, for Josh.

By the time she got back to the table, the omelettes had already been laid steaming at their places.

Josh picked up his fork. 'Looks passable.'

'Yes.'

'So dig in.'

196

Josh's appetite seemed to grow with the meal's progress. He kept ordering new courses, and was lingering over his third cup of espresso with a half-moon of lemon on the side, when Emma caught on to his game.

'You don't want to go, do you?'

'I'd be crazy if I did.'

'That's kind of childish, don't you think?'

'Very,' he said coolly. 'But then again, some of the best people I've known have been children. Come on.' He consulted the bill and threw down a couple of notes and some change on the tabletop.

Emma caught up with him outside the tree-shaded inn.

'Josh, I don't want to go on this way. I don't need you to be like this.'

'Oh, I'm very sorry. Emma doesn't want the truth. Well, that's too damn bad! Haven't you noticed yet that when it comes to love, we don't have too damn much to say about things, hmm? I didn't ask for you to be all tangled up in your mind and heart with some poor little rich boy, now did I? I don't "need" that, either, Emma.'

It took him a moment out of his anger, to realize that she was crying.

'What do you want me to say, Josh?' She wiped a hand under her eyes, her hair going back in the wind.

'Nothing. Just, let's go.'

He tramped over the browning lawn to the car, resting his hand on the door grip.

'It's just as hard for me, Josh. Harder.'

'I'll bet.'

The door swung ajar. 'Get in.'

She slid back against the leather seat in a turmoil because it was possible, quite possible that her man would never forgive her for asking him to want her less – and love her more.

Josh sped off in a roar of engine. He did not look at her, even once.

By the time they entered Boston, the late afternoon sky was marbled grey with clouds, the air heavy with unshed moisture.

Josh switched on the windscreen wipers as the glass

blurred like memory. The fall of water began modestly then swelled into dense sheets of rain that pelted the car roof with the sound of galloping horses.

'Do you think we should stop until this blows over?' Emma was temporizing.

'No.'

'Why not?'

'We're almost there.'

She was struck once again by the deterioration of his attitude towards her, since the outset of the trip. Like the first time, this sight of his begrudging hurt her deeply. A snapping of bonds, a swing away from love, a closure of the heart had begun, and she didn't know how to stop it.

With one hand on the wheel, Josh unfolded a colourful map that flowed over his knees. He glanced down. 'Let's see. Beacon should take us right into Chestnut Hills.' He bit off the words.

With a swish of tyres on the rainy tarmac, the Jaguar swept into a well-clipped, green-smelling enclave of rambling mansions and maple-shaded streets, all tagged with English country names.

Emma had the window moved down so that she could see better. The smell of the Atlantic rolled into the car and across the land.

'Anything look familiar?' Josh angled his face towards her, and she tried not to sink in the bright blue-green deeps of his eyes.

'Not yet.' Emma's hand gripped the arm rest. *Calm down. Nothing is going to happen that you and Josh can't handle* . . . But that was just it: Josh was retreating with every mile. She was going to be alone in this sad adventure . . .

They passed by the churning black reservoir, then on to Middlesex, Essex, Devon and Kingsbury Road. Up and down they motored, to Stone and Acacia Avenues, Clovelly and Old England Road. As they drove on, the tension billowed between the two lovers, and Emma found herself edging away from Josh, until she was squeezed up against the car door.

'Why don't we forget it?' she asked, too upset to explain herself. 'I think we've seen enough.'

'Oh no we haven't.' He squinted through the rain-smeared windscreen. 'Here's a block we've not tried. Old Orchard Road.' He read the signpost aloud.

That was when the funny sensation started up in the pit of her stomach, that left her heart fluttery and her hands like ice.

'Old Orchard,' she repeated, testing the name with her tongue.

They had come upon a hilly road crowned by a great white Neo-Georgian manor.

Emma's heart drummed a tattoo in her chest. Sweat glittered on her forehead.

'Josh.' Her arm flew out, and touched him on the sleeve.

'What is it, Emma?'

'Stop the car, Josh. That's the one.'

'Are you sure?'

'Yes, yes, stop the car!'

Almost before the vehicle had rolled to a complete halt, she pushed open the door and bounded onto the rain-washed pavement.

She stopped before the filigreed iron gate of the house. Tears pooled beneath her lashes.

Josh came up respectfully behind her. 'Don't you want to go in?'

The eyes she swung on him were frightened and he could feel her reaching down into deeper levels of strength.

'Not yet. I can't . . .' she said into his ear.

'All right.' Josh studied her, coolly, at this moment even more drawn to her mystery, her emptiness, than ever. She didn't even seem to be the woman he knew; some ecstasy of remembrance had taken her over. She was being transformed by the knowing, and he felt like a fool doomed to help her know, to cut her loose from their own love. 'But I'm going to find out, once and for all, the family name . . .'

He started up the brick pathway to the house, the cold fingers of rain dripping down his dark, slick hair into his jacket collar.

'No, Josh, please!'

The stricken voice stopped him in his tracks.

'I know the name.' Emma seemed to have just come awake, and to be trying to focus on him. 'But I can't face them right now. Please, give me a little more time.'

Immediately, he sensed her limbs were loosening, and he rushed to catch her under the breasts as her legs gave way and her head fell back against his heart.

'Emma, Emma, I'll do whatever you ask. I'll never hurt you, my Emma, my love.'

He somehow led her back to the car, her hair braided in wet gold streaks upon his jacket, her hand, slippery with rain, in his, where he held her close until she lay quiet and still.

'What did you see?' He flicked away a pearl from her eye.

She shook her head, hair drawn over her face like a veil.

'Don't you want to talk about it?'

'No. Not right now.'

She spread a blanket over herself in the backseat of the car and fell into a profound, exhausted sleep, while Josh made a promise driving in the rain that night, that nothing would ever make her afraid again.

When they arrived in New York the next afternoon, neither one would say goodbye.

She shook Josh to the core.

He loved her for making him feel so powerful, and hated her on the same account.

He didn't want to call her.

It was the first thing he did the next day.

The phone was engaged. She wasn't home. She hadn't even come into work, they said.

Josh scanned his memory for places that Emma frequented. Then he knew. The place Dr Beckstein had taken her. The Cloisters.

He found her in the Meditation Garden, where the withered pear tree was tacked to the wall like a crucifix.

'Emma?'

She was looking out towards the grey light of the Hudson, her hair tucked into a soft ivory lambswool beret. He could tell she had been crying.

'How did you know I'd be here? I was all set to go to work today and I ended up in this place . . .'

'I know you very well, Emma.'

'Oh God, no you don't!' the words seemed torn from her.

'Can you talk about what you remembered yesterday at the mansion?' He wanted to be gentle with her, couldn't understand why he had ever acted otherwise.

A sparkle of tears came into her eyes.

He raised his finger to wipe them away, as he had yesterday in the rain. The tendrils of her hair flew back in the brisk wind off the Hudson. Her full ice-blue skirts purled about her knees, as she shivered in the thin white jacket made of velvet.

'Let's go indoors,' Josh said.

'No.' The soft beret moved from side to side. 'It's better out here.'

'Fine.' Leaning forward, he steepled his hands on the stone wall. Without meeting her eyes, he spoke urgently. 'Tell me. No matter who you've been or what you've done, you know I will always love you, Emma. Nothing can change that.'

In silence, she held out her hand and gave a gentle pressure on his.

Then she quickly withdrew it, as though she had gone too far.

'Tell me what you remembered when you saw the house . . .'

CHAPTER EIGHTEEN

The art of making Michael happy kept Emma busy until spring.

Through it all Patrice would have Emma believe that the very grid of destiny could be plotted in a table setting, that salvation lay in the stacks of clean linen inside her closet. With her violin packed away so deep in the bowels of the house that even she didn't know where to look for it, Emma's world contracted to the scale of a prison cell paved with diamonds.

Whenever Michael was off expanding his financial empire, the Gardens delivered up family feeling like a lecture, punctually and with sharp Yankee rigour, so that Emma had no time to think seditious thoughts about the Metropolitan and her lost career.

And then Easter came with a rush of dogwood blossoms and garden parties under fluttering marquees . . .

Before the guests arrived, Emma was seeing to things with a swathe of long-necked calla lilies cradled in her arms.

The breeze blew her hair into a golden nimbus and the low-slung layers of yellow crepe de chine, so pale as to be almost white, billowed out like a Newport sail. A big, broad-brimmed straw hat, wound with a black grosgrain ribbon sat upon her head.

'I'm afraid we won't have enough champagne, Ma'am.' The white-gloved sommelier accosted her.

'Bring up another twenty-four,' Emma directed, without thought. Such decisions were made out of instinct now, out of boredom . . .

'Why don't you let me take those from you, dear?' Patrice Garden was breathtakingly gowned in a dove-coloured lace sheath.

'Oh.' Emma looked down absently at the flowers in her arms. 'I had forgotten all about them!'

202

'You were the picture of a Beauty Queen rushing about like that.'

Emma smiled, not knowing how to take the comment; Patrice thought beauty contests were vulgar.

It was the last time that day she would have leisure to think about it, for the guests began to arrive in long lines of antique Silver Shadows and sporty foreign beauties as shiny as new-minted dimes.

With Michael a polite figure in the background, she ran among her guests, flirting, charming, quaffing champagne, and seeing to it that all pleasurable needs were instantaneously fulfilled.

Once, as Emma brushed by, Michael captured her hand. 'Hey, don't I get any attention today?'

'Oh, Michael.' She whirled into his arms. 'Of course you do.'

He took either end of her broad straw hat into his hands and pulling them down over the sides of her face, gave her a quick kiss.

'That's so nobody will talk.'

'Let them talk,' Emma said dreamily. 'We're awfully wedded.'

'Are we going to tell Mother today?' he said into the shining coronet of her hair.

'As soon as there's a lull, Michael. I promise.'

'Good.'

'What are you two conspiring about?' Patrice left a circle of friends to join them. She swept back the bright hair from her son's brow.

'Now?' Michael nodded at Emma.

'Now,' she replied.

'What is this?' Patrice sipped her bubbling wine.

'We have something to tell you, Mother,' Michael said. 'Emma and I have decided to have a child.'

Patrice's face was very pale. 'Are you sure you've thought enough about this? You're both so young.'

'Mother, we've discussed every possible objection and we're set on it.'

Emma turned a look of surprise on her mother-in-law. 'We thought you would be pleased . . .'

203

'I am. I am. I'm delighted,' Patrice stumbled through the pat phrases. 'But, Emma, you are on the frail side. Bearing a child might ruin your health.'

'That's nonsense,' Michael snickered. 'That only happens in novels.'

'But think, Michael, children are such a burden and since you travel so much, most of it would fall on Emma.'

'You'll be here, Mother.'

'Yes, but . . .'

'I don't want to talk about it anymore,' Michael interjected. 'It's just a waste of time. Ah . . .' He lifted two glasses of champagne from a proffered tray. 'Here's some more wine. I think we should toast the mother-to-be, who, incidentally, did a bang-up job on this garden party.'

Patrice accepted a filled glass, but, Emma noticed, did not drink to the child.

These thousand different objections did not end here, but were continued right up to the day, a month later, when Michael and Emma glowingly announced that a baby was indeed on the way.

Emma, the temple of the miracle, worshipped at her own body, both because Michael wanted a 'traditional' child, and this was another way of pleasing him, and because now she would have a new purpose, a child all her own, to cherish and care for.

It was then Patrice Garden's behaviour took a strange turn, as she assumed a kind of nursemaid role, watching over Emma with an unhealthy passion, feeding her organic fruits and vegetables from her own garden.

At first, it was touching, the constant concern of the mother-in-law for the bearer of her first grandchild.

In the end, Patrice's care was exposed for what it truly was, a species of oppression. The mansion became a plush prison, and Patrice, Emma's soft-spoken jailer.

As Michael was seldom home those days, his wife was left to fend off Patrice's tender mercies on her own. Even if Michael were present, she knew from experience, he would only support his mother's course. Philip, in turn, was of no help whatsoever to Emma, involved as he was in his ever-

lasting bridge games, and long mornings on the putting green, respites from his own private pain, which, since that night in the library, had never been spoken of again.

In spite of all this, Emma was blooming. She walked with a spring in her step. The roses in her cheeks glowed. Her hair seemed more abundant and shining than ever. The new life within her was having an illuminating effect on the young mother-to-be.

One sleepy, rain-washed afternoon, Emma was standing with the interior decorator in the unfinished nursery.

'Shouldn't you be sitting down or something?' the designer asked.

'I'm fine.'

Dreamily, she ran her hand over the back of a white rocking chair by the many-paned window. Standing open, it let in the fresh, wet smell of earth and leaves.

'Do you want me to get your mother-in-law's opinion about the curtains?'

'No, no, that's all right.' Emma would rather drop in her tracks than call up that horrible, watching solicitude. 'We'll go with the tie-backs.'

The designer nodded, relieved to have the decision made. 'Dutch Cream?'

'Dutch Cream.' She let out a sigh. Here she was dissolving into pettiness, being eaten up by trivia, when once she'd given voice to giants, like Mahler and Mozart, when she'd held magic in her bow . . .

'That's a good choice, Mrs Garden.' He snapped shut his leatherbound notebook, and popped his felt-tipped pen into a shirt pocket. 'I'll be back next week with a swatch of the material.'

'Thanks, Roger.'

Scooping up his overcoat, he made for the door, pausing only long enough to peer into her face. 'You know,' he said, 'you really do look wonderful.'

'Thank you. I feel wonderful. See you next week then.'

'Bye.' With a waggle of his fingers, he was gone.

Easing back into the chair, she surveyed the cheerful white room. She placed her hands over her stomach and cooed softly to the child inside her, rocking from side to side, soothing them both. The amniocentesis had revealed the joy of a daughter. 'It's going to be all right, Michelle,' she whispered an ageless incantation against harm, 'everything is going to be all right.'

This was the point in the day when she'd begin to dread the evening ahead. Tonight, it would be early dinner with Patrice in the plush coffin of the dining room . . . both men away on business . . . a barrage of paranoid questions until she could finally escape into the blessed solitude of her room and think of the beautiful baby she was going to have.

Had she always felt like this on rainy days, as though she were sinking under a weight of dreams, losing her grip on the common sense of happiness? She seemed to remember there had been a way out, once. Through craft. Through her violin.

Her hands ached to touch its cool wooden body once more, her fingers to engage the bow in an easy motion of wire and muscle and sound. She needed biologically, intrinsically, to make music.

What had made her think she could stop? Whatever it was had been evil, against her nature. All at once, Emma felt afraid – for herself . . . for the unborn baby.

It seemed at that moment, with the dusk rolling into the room like a sea fog, and the strange ache in her heart, that this troubling sense of unease had dated from the instant she'd set aside her bow – as if it were her sacred duty to play and her punishment for not doing so, this house, this family, this oppressive love.

A sudden urgency took hold. Michael would have to be told of this. It wasn't fair for him to ask her to bury her talent when it was the only thing she had to give the world. With everything in her, she sensed that no good would come of turning her back on such a brilliant gift.

Only darkness.

Michael must be told, and Patrice, too.

If not tonight, then tomorrow, or as soon as she felt up to a fight.

Yes.

For the darkness had already come too near, and, in the silence, the whir of black wings . . .

Dinner at eight. The table was laid with its usual elegant abundance and Patrice had directed that a fire be kindled to take the chill out of the room.

She smiled patiently at Emma from across the table. 'Just we women tonight.'

'Right.' Devoid of appetite, Emma picked at her quail.

'The quail is much superior to last time, don't you think?'

'Yes.'

'Fresh wild game is so hard to get these days. You must never think of ordering from any shop that doesn't buy their birds from game farms where they've been allowed to range. Because they have a more varied diet, they have a better flavour than pen-raised birds.'

'The quail is very good.'

'Do you remember the quail from Canada we had on Thanksgiving?'

'Yes.'

'Now that was delectable, if matchstick eating. I almost didn't order that quail, because I generally like to go with the traditional goose on holidays. Especially as it's Michael's favourite meal. I remember how my mother always had ours decorated with kale, cranberries and nuts. A huge stuffed goose, roasting in its own juices . . .'

Out of duty, Emma made an attempt at conversation, when all she yearned for was the opportunity to burrow under the bedcovers, close her eyes, and fantasize about the child she carried. How they would play, how they would love . . . 'I finally decided on the Priscilla curtains today,' she said.

'Roger's a good decorator. Not a great one, mind you, but good. If you recall, I had suggested my own firm, Boston people . . .'

'Yes, but Michael and I felt that we would rather go with a non-traditionalist . . .' She spoke the words by rote. Patrice meddled. Emma parried. It was a little game they played that neither could win. Emma had been particularly hurt when she realized that Michael never even noticed it was going on.

'Why didn't you have some more soup when I suggested it, Emma? It would help build you up.'

'I didn't want any more soup.' The refusal would hardly come out. Tonight, she had no heart for the game.

Ignoring the reply, Patrice directed the servant to bring the leftover soup back from the kitchen and ladle more lobster bisque into a new bowl at Emma's place.

The steamy sea smell made Emma feel ill.

'I noticed,' Patrice went on, 'a pamphlet on breastfeeding lying on your night table. Why on earth are you reading that?'

A warning bell clanged in Emma's head. Another battle was about to break, and she wasn't ready for it, had no more energy to spare. Maybe she had been trying to do too much lately, between decorating the nursery and preparing a layette . . .

'I think breastfeeding is more natural. There are immunological advantages . . .' Emma's longing to lay down her head and sleep the next five months away was growing stronger with every pain in her belly.

'That may well be,' Patrice responded, 'but it's really not the thing for you to do. You'll be very sorry afterwards, Emma. Besides, I didn't breastfeed and Michael was, as you know, a perfectly healthy child.'

Every fibre in her being crying out for escape, Emma's gaze wandered and came to rest on a cut-glass decanter of Sauterne. Dr Lederer had warned against overdoing it with alcohol during pregnancy, but a glass with dinner 'may stimulate your appetite and relax your nerves.' It might be just the thing to get her through the night. She motioned to Marianne to fill her glass.

The woman hurried over and tipped the decanter.

'What are you doing?' Patrice's voice sliced through Emma's nerves like a razor on paper.

'I thought . . . a glass of wine . . .' If it weren't for Michael, she would have set Patrice straight a long time ago. Now it seemed too late . . .

'Wine? Absolutely not. Bad for the baby. You know that, Emma.'

'Pour the wine, Marianne,' Emma said.

Marianne set the decanter down in front of her, and took a step back.

With shaking hands, Emma spilled the water out of her tumbler. Grasping the decanter, she poured wine into the glass until it swirled over the sides and spattered the lace tablecloth. She tried to bring it to her lips, but her hand was trembling so, she had to set the glass down again.

'Stop it, Emma.' Patrice's face was tight. 'You aren't yourself.'

She rose from behind the table. 'Oh, but I am. For the first time in a long while I am . . .' That was when the roaring whirlpool sound began filling her ears with a hard vibration, the one that made her teeth ache and left her forehead an icy throb . . .

Something tightened and broke in her pelvis, like a plate shifting under the earth and a warm fluid trickled down her calf. She placed her hand over the curve of her belly, protectively.

'Ever since I've come to this house you've been working against me, taken everything from me. Well God knows it may be too late for me, but you're not going to get my baby!'

'Emma, stop it!'

'I'm trying to tell you . . .' The dizziness cleft her forehead like lightning. 'I'm trying . . .' She swayed forward, her hair a shining gold fringe, her hands pressed hard against the tabletop, her face a sickly white.

'Emma, you're not well . . .' The words seemed to float towards her packed in cotton.

'Leave me alone, just leave me alone!'

Emma stumbled from the room, unsure of how far or even whether her legs would carry her. Unsteadily, she aimed herself up the elaborate curved staircase on the way to her second-floor bedroom, her soft, waiting bed . . .

'Come back here,' Patrice called to her from a million miles away. 'You ungrateful, stupid woman . . .'

Dizzy, Emma looked down at her from mid-flight. 'Go away,' she moaned to herself.

'I've tried for Michael's sake, to do everything that was right for the two of you. I've denied my own impulses, my own sense of decency, all for your happiness. But that baby should never be born . . .'

Emma's whole universe was filled with a pain so intense she could only stare in wonder, gasping, groping for the handrail of the winding staircase. So this is horror, she thought . . .

'It was the photograph that made me sure . . .' As Patrice climbed the stairs, a whole side of her personality seemed to fall away, laying bare fierce and burning will to hate. 'Your mother was my husband's whore. You and Michael are . . .'

But her voice was clothed in darkness.

A foot missed the stair.

Two heartbeats seemed to stop at once, as the woman's words echoed like a gunshot.

CHAPTER NINETEEN

Emma floated above the bed around which the doctor, Patrice and Philip stood huddled, as if for warmth. A sweet peace filled her soul and light spiralled out of her eyes as she moved at will with the silvery currents of the air.

Up here there was no pain, no loss, no connection with the woman who lay upon the bed in a clench of agony, her womb spilled out like sacred wine from a chalice.

Emma wondered who that woman could be.

It was hard to remember, though, her feathery new body was too light for the burden of memory.

She watched with puzzlement as Patrice's face shattered and she called out a name.

'Poor Emma, the baby, the baby . . .'

CHAPTER TWENTY

In the end, even her eyes had betrayed her.

There was no definition, no fixity to the flyaway world. The room swam with objects and faces, disconnected densities of light and colour.

'She's up,' a voice wavered over her.

'She's trying to focus.'

The hand that sought hers was like a heavy rubber hose. Her nerves and body ached as though she had been beaten all over.

'Emma, you had a miscarriage. You lost the baby. But there will be others . . .'

She squeezed the world out of her eyes and held her hands to her ears. She had been frightened before, worse than this, when she had been running up the staircase. From whom had she been running?

'Emma, can you hear me?'

A pinpoint of light needled into her eyes. 'Let her rest now.'

'Yes, Doctor. But do you think she heard me?'

'She heard you. She's very weak, that's all. Let her rest.'

'I wish Michael were here.'

'He's due tomorrow, isn't he?'

'Yes.'

The room fell blessedly quiet. Behind the black wall, Emma realized that she was alone. They had all gone.

She opened her eyes. With fumbling eagerness, she reached down to where the mound of her stomach had been, warm and full of life.

But now there was no warmth, no life. She marvelled at the way it had shrunk. She was like a young girl again.

But then, remembering why, she held her beautiful hands over her face as though they were folded in prayer. The baby, oh the baby . . .

Sounds beat up from her that she had never heard before, sounds of grieving, ancient sounds, of a mother cheated of the fruit of her womb, her wound.

She wanted, quickly, to die.

She turned her face to the wall, but images kept circling in her mind, tormenting her into wakefulness.

From what had she been running on the staircase, before the baby . . .?

'YOUR MOTHER WAS MY HUSBAND'S WHORE. YOU AND MICHAEL ARE . . .'

Emma doubled over in the bed. She would rather die than remember anymore.

Patrice had said that she and Michael had committed the sin of incest.

Michael, her own half-brother.

Emma knew a small mercy, as the blackness came again.

She woke again to the whir of a waterfall in her head.

The bed creaked as she lifted herself from the mattress and set her feet on where she imagined the floor to be, just beyond her line of vision.

As the cold seeped up through her bare soles, and rose high into her body. She stood there in an ecstasy of self-hatred, knowing that she was poor and empty as the dead tree trunk in the back arbor. She wasn't sure why, but she ached to leave this place. It was a bad place. A place of death.

The nightgown was too thin. She would be cold.

She threw open the door to her closet and pulled out the first dress she came to.

Stepping into her boots, she neglected to put stockings on.

The fluffy white fur coat hung off a cedar hanger on the rim of the closet door. She arched on tiptoes to take it down. As she folded it over her arm, a red velvet casket fell out of the copious pocket.

She opened the case to the dazzle of diamonds.

How pretty they were. She decked herself in the matching clips, necklace and bracelets.

213

Then, sparkling, she moved, quiet as the passage from life to death, down the curved staircase of the old mansion, out the front door into the spinning white night.

'What do you mean, she's gone?' Philip blinked up from the haven of his morning newspaper.

'Just what I said,' Patrice seemed drained, a diminished woman. 'I went into her room this morning to check on her and she wasn't there. She must have left last night. Apparently, she took only her personal jewellery and the clothes on her back. Oh yes, the fur coat that Michael gave her for Christmas . . .' Her hands trembled as she pressed them to her thighs, as if ashamed of her own weakness.

Philip's eyes narrowed, 'Oh my dear wife, you have a lot to answer for.'

'What are you talking about?'

'You've been working on Emma for some time now, Patrice. Did you think I didn't know?'

'You must be drunk, Philip. You're starting to rave.'

'As a matter of fact, I'm sober as I can stand. What good is a daughter-in-law to you, Patrice? She'd only get in the way . . .'

'Be careful, Philip. You might say something you'll regret . . .'

'My whole life is regrettable. What's the difference, one regret more or less . . .? That's the freedom of total failure. But you wouldn't know about that, would you, my love? You never fail.' He set down his paper and rose, his hands in the pockets of his tweed jacket, casual in his long-nursed contempt. 'What can Patrice Garden do with a daughter-in-law, except envy her a husband . . .'

With superhuman control, Patrice resisted the bait. 'I don't want to argue with you when you're like this, Philip.'

'Where are you going?'

'To call the police.'

'Whatever for? Why not let her go? Then you can have Michael all to yourself. The way it's always been.'

'If you had been more of a man I wouldn't have needed my son for the job,' she hissed. 'Tell me, what kind of a husband have you been, Philip? Absentee, at best. I've had

214

all the burdens of marriage, with none of the privileges. No other woman would have stood for it. But because I've got principles, and character, our marriage has endured. I've made it endure.'

'Oh, bravo, Patrice.' He clapped his hands. 'You're the only woman I know who can make her sickness seem like a virtue.'

'You're the sick one.' She looked past his shoulder.

'We both are,' Philip needled, 'to keep up this sham of a marriage.'

'Then why don't you leave me?'

'No, no, that would be too easy. You see, I've got to stick close to you, Patrice. That's my punishment for ever thinking you were a woman in the first place. Lord, you're no woman, you're some kind of a devourer they don't have a name for yet. And that's your punishment. To have the knowledge every day, every night, every time you look at me that hatred lives under your roof, sleeps in your bed. And that you'll never be free of it, until they shovel the dirt over me.'

'That,' Patrice stopped only once in her progress to the door to say, 'will be a happy day.'

'For both of us,' Philip said to the empty room.

The strain, grime and fatigue of his all-night journey dragged on Michael's face and figure. He regarded his mother and father with a suspicion that was new and painful to him. Never before had the world taken from him. And now it had claimed both a wife and a child . . .

'But how could this happen? I left her in your hands. I thought you would take good care of her!'

'Michael, she slipped out at night when everyone was asleep.' Patrice spoke in soothing tones, as if to a child in the cradle.

Michael flung his Burberry over the back of a chair. There were lines in the smooth face that Patrice had never noticed before.

The parents had been dining when the son burst in on them, haggard and accusatory as a false messiah. Long resigned to his insignificance in the family circle, Philip laid his napkin on the table and got up from his chair.

215

'I'm due at the Club. I think I'll go now.'

'Yes, you go on, Philip. I'll handle this.' That from Patrice who hadn't taken her eyes off her son.

When Philip was out of earshot, Patrice laid her hand on Michael's arm, murmuring sweet names and childhood reassurances.

Michael winced, pulling away. 'Mother, don't you understand? Emma is gone.'

'Nothing will be helped by your becoming hysterical. You'll have to calm down before I talk to you.'

'Fine, fine.' He pressed his hands down on a chairback until the knuckles glowed white. 'What did the police think?'

Patrice's cold grey.eyes never flickered. 'I didn't call the police, after all.'

'What did you say?'

'I felt it would be better if we kept this private. Do you realize what this kind of thing would do to your chances for the governorship?'

'Somehow I'm finding this hard to believe. Are you telling me that for some vague dream of political power, you let the woman I love walk out of this house, and didn't even try to find her?'

'A mother has to do many things she doesn't want to – out of love, you understand.'

'No, I don't understand,' his voice boomed as he knocked the chair off its pins. 'I want Emma home, Mother. I want her back. In fact, I'm going out to look for her right now!' He turned his sullen back to her.

'Sit down, Michael,' she commanded. 'I have something to tell you.'

Michael hesitated, locked into a burning cycle of love and control that would never end while his mother lived. Finally, he picked up the fallen chair and sat back against it, his palms on his thighs. 'Go on.'

'You may not want to believe this,' Patrice spoke with care, 'because you're so deeply in love. But your wife left of her own accord.'

'You're right. I don't believe it.'

'Just listen! Emma left, not because she doesn't love you,

216

Michael. I am convinced that she does. It was because of something I told her, something I've kept buried inside me for a long, long time.'

'Don't play mind games with me, Mother. I'm too tired for games.'

'Michael, it's not a game. Soon after you were born, your father had an affair with another woman. I . . . saw her once. I followed them. It was the hardest thing I've ever had to do . . .'

Michael's expression softened. This was his mother. *'You don't have to tell me.'*

'I do. You'll see why soon enough.' She took a breath. *'This woman, Michael, was carrying your father's child. On Christmas Day, when Emma showed me that photograph of her mother, I realized that Emma was that child. Michael, you've married your half-sister.'*

A riot of emotions played across his face – disbelief, disgust, and finally, desolation. *'It can't be . . .'*

'I had to tell Emma, Michael. It was the only thing I could do . . . Please don't hate me, I don't think I could go on if you hated me.'

Michael's head bowed. Patrice prayed that he wasn't crying. He mustn't let her down the way Philip always had, in that weak male way.

'Do you hate me then, Michael?' she whispered.

'No, mother,' the sound of his voice was dry and coarse like the rustling of dead leaves. *'It was the right thing to do,'* he said mechanically, *'you always do the right thing.'*

'Yes.' Patrice crossed to her son and embraced him around the neck.

He grasped her hands with his. *'I had no idea. You should have told me before.'*

'Oh my darling, I wanted to.' She rained kisses on his forehead, she dug her fingers into his brow, smoothing away the sorrow and the pain. *'You don't know how many times. You were always my only comfort.'*

'And I was accusing you . . .' Michael felt a shock of guilt run through him.

She held her finger to his lips. *'Shh. That's nothing.*

That's forgotten. The important thing is that you understand what I've done for you.'

'I do, Mother. Emma's leaving was the cleanest and most merciful way to end the episode. But to think she would sacrifice herself like that, for me.'

'That's right, Michael. I knew you would come to see it was the only way. Once I explained. That was always the difference between you and your father and those like him. He could be bent and swayed by his emotions, in the most low and primitive way. You are a creature of logic and light. I love that about you.'

'I suppose I should file for abandonment and keep Emma's disappearance unpublicized.' For an instant, the businessman in Michael took over.

'Exactly.' Patrice was proud of her reach. *She could feel her son's resistance give way before her. 'It should be easy enough. Emma had already retired from her musical career, so you have only to tell mutual friends that you're having a trial separation and that Emma has gone away. Remember, if this matter isn't handled carefully, your aspirations to the statehouse will be shattered.'*

'Emma,' Michael said to himself, inconsolable. *'My only love, Emma . . .'*

But she was too far away to hear . . .

CHAPTER TWENTY-ONE

Changed now in its mood and lights, the Hudson looked choppy and cold. Josh had edged close enough to Emma, still leaning against the brick wall of the parapet, to see the toll that memory had taken. It was as if she had relived the actions and anguish of those last days all over again.

For the first time in his life, Josh felt the true helplessness of lovers. To bear her up from tragedy, to unyoke her from this desolation would have been supreme joy. Yet he could do nothing but stand by and watch her being crippled by the kind of losses that remain part of a woman forever. This was the price she must pay for having broken with time.

'"Michelle", was the name I had chosen for the baby . . .' Her voice was sweet and low as a lullabye.

'Oh Emma,' Josh said softly, imagining the golden-haired little girl who would never grow up. 'I'm so sorry. But maybe there will be others . . .'

'Yes, I remember Patrice telling me there could be. At least I have that to hold on to.'

She tipped up her face, chafed pink by the rough river wind. 'You know, Josh, maybe it's better for the child this way, if Michael and I are really of one blood. I have to think so, or I wouldn't be able to go on . . .' The tears flowed.

Cold comfort for my Emma . . . Josh hated not being unable to staunch the flow of her pain.

'I think I'd like to go inside now.'

They strolled into the Museum and sat on a wooden bench facing a blue fountain pool, where a circle of orange trees bloomed. 'So I'm Emma Garden,' she said, after a lengthy pause. 'Michael Garden's wife – and sister.'

'How do we know that, Emma?' He felt he must speak up now, strong and true, or lose her forever.

'But Patrice said . . .'

'Patrice could have been wrong.'

Emma shook out the folds of her dress as she shifted up from the bench. 'Josh, it's my duty to find Michael.'

'Hell, what about his duty?' Josh demanded more harshly than he'd intended. She was slipping away again, borne back on the tides of the past. 'Why didn't he find you? He's got enough money and connections.'

She moved away, hurt. 'I can't say. Maybe he didn't want to. Maybe Patrice persuaded him not to. Maybe he still loves me and suffers every day he's away from me. I don't know, Josh. Do you? Will you take the responsibility of saying that Michael Garden knows I'm his sister? Don't you think I owe him at least an explanation?'

He stood up opposite her, charged with a conviction that had been growing since he'd found her – more heart-breakingly beautiful than ever – alone in the garden. 'No, I don't, Emma. Right now I think your only responsibility is to yourself. Let your lawyer take care of Michael Garden.'

At a pressure of her hand, they moved as one out of the Cloisters, down the stone steps and on to the emerald spread of the lawn.

Emma spoke so gently he could hardly hear her. 'I never saw you afraid before.'

Josh stopped and pulled her to him. 'You're damn right I'm afraid! Because if Garden is your brother, you might eat yourself alive with guilt when you see him again. And if he isn't, you still might go running back to him out of some cockamamie idea of duty or loyalty or whatever goes on in that madly romantic head of yours. I don't want to lose you now to some fading dream. I want to marry you!' In a flash, the growing conviction had been made into words, and from there, forged into a future for himself and his lover. That was when the world shifted back into place for Josh Free, a world that smelled of freshly picked pears and glowed with morning sun . . .

Emma stared as though seeing him for the first time. 'After all that I've just told you – you're not afraid to complicate your life with a woman like me?'

'A woman like you!' He shook his head. 'I've been

220

looking all my life for "a woman like you"! Do you think I'm such a fool as to let you slip away now?'

'Josh, I just meant that . . .'

'And what do you mean "a woman like you"? Just what is it that you've done? What crime have you committed? Emma, in the last analysis, all you ever did was love. You *loved*, Emma. That's a gift, not a crime. Most people don't even know how to love as deeply as you do.'

'So maybe you picked the wrong man to give yourself to. If they shot all of us who ever loved the wrong person, the world population would be decimated by tomorrow morning. Anyway, the blame lies with Patrice Garden – and your own mother. If they hadn't kept their damned secrets you would never have got involved with Michael Garden in the first place!'

Touched by his militant love for her, Emma rested her head against his chest.

He lay one hand at the small of her back, protectively.

'Josh, I understand what you're saying and I love you even more for it. To think you can still want me – after all that I've been.'

He began to protest, but she held a finger up to his lips.

'Shh, it's my turn. You just have to accept that I must see Michael again. If I don't, there will always be something left undone. I'll never be at peace, never be sure of myself. Say you understand me, Josh!'

He buried his mouth in the shining mist of her hair. 'God, you're one beautiful, stubborn woman. Okay, okay, I accept the premise that you want to see Michael Garden to tie up loose ends. But promise me you won't contact him until we find out for sure if you're blood related. Things will come clearer to you once that question is finally answered.'

Emma gave a nod. 'All right. I promise to wait until we find out.'

'In that case,' Josh said, 'I'll get working on it right away.'

Emma ducked into the car, lost in thoughts no woman should ever have to bear. It was a situation for which only her nightmares could have prepared her . . .

How could she live with herself if she discovered she

221

had been part of an incestuous marriage?

On the other hand, if Michael were not her brother, she would, in good conscience, have to give the marriage another chance, no matter how great her passion for Josh Free, a man who seemed to love her more than she loved herself because he'd dared to embrace all of her, even the darkness . . .

She glanced over at Josh as he slid into the driver's seat. Perversely, she loved him even more, now that she might have to give him up.

He was a warrior, her Josh Free. For her sake, she knew, he would unearth the truth, even if he had to destroy his own hopes of happiness to do it.

A woman between two lives, she dangled by the barest thread over the abyss.

She felt herself sway in the breeze.

All the next day, blustery with a Northern wind, a storm gathering at the city gates, Josh Free felt as though his nerves had been sandblasted.

To his employees, he seemed fired out of his office, like a rocket from a silo, stirring up hot cauldrons of activity everywhere he went.

Doria Sevenstars had run her high heels into the ground trying to keep up with him, her yellow pencil pointed at his back like a dart, as he stalked the corridors of the *Globe,* dictating overdue memos and burning up old business at a mind-boggling rate.

T.J. shadowed behind them, like a priest with a condemned man, reciting a chronicle of the small disasters a daily newspaper is heir to. Josh put down these nuisances with his usual aplomb, but the sure satisfaction was missing.

Work had finally lost that magical quality of a healing for Josh Free.

He felt cut loose from all familiar moorings, operating on a margin of emotional risk and expectation that would have been impossible for him only a few short months before.

Emma Taylor tyrannized his thoughts; she played upon his heartstrings like the master violinist she was.

'Let it alone,' T.J. mumbled, sitting at the centre of the weak daylight in Josh's office. 'She's too far gone.'

By now, everyone at the *Globe* knew about Free's love quest. The medical records being checked in Boston, the newspaper files ransacked.

In the outer chamber, Doria's ears pricked up like those of a mountain lion smelling blood.

'I can't.' The freshening wind blew dirt-streaked clouds around the sky outside his high window. Josh waited for the fat splash of water on the glass, which came a split second later.

'Why not?' T.J.'s legs were stretched in front of him, crossed at the ankles.

'I love her.'

'So what?' T.J. knew what Josh's answer would be. But friendship had urged him on.

'Don't be an ass.'

A razor's edge of lightning shimmied through the sky. A riff of thunder followed in its wake.

The room was filling up with the chemical smell of city rain. Josh imagined the drops of acid eating away at the urban husk, while T.J. cursed his luck. He'd planned to ask Josh what he thought about his right-hand-man marrying Doria Sevenstars. He'd wanted Doria to know that Josh would gladly see her wed to T.J. McShane, forever and ever, Amen.

Now he'd have to wait, until this Emma Taylor business was over. The boss was the Great Stone Face whenever he was on a story. It was no use trying to chat him up about anything else.

In the meantime, Josh was busy watching the lights burn through the mist of rain in the office buildings opposite. His roast beef on rye, hold the mayo, lay before him, still wrapped tight in wax-paper chastity. The coffee had taken on a suspicious grey hue.

All Emma had told him was that her mother had been some man's mistress. It was Patrice who claimed that man was Philip Garden. Emma never knew who her actual father was. So what were the odds of fitting together the thirty-year old pieces to this sordid puzzle?

223

Anyway, if the Boston office didn't phone in soon with the information about Emma, Josh feared he might go mad.

The irony of it – one meagre gram of data – with his whole life hanging in the balance.

Josh went through a mental file of his best people in Boston – Sally Finn, with the ferret eyes and the non-stop mouth, Carter Hayworth, the proper Bostonian, Jake Kuhn, the old journeyman who never gave up a fight – and felt mildly encouraged.

Still, there was nothing like doing it yourself.

Doria buzzed.

He picked up. 'Yes?'

'Boston calling.' Her tone was accusing.

T.J. made as if to leave.

'Stay there.' Josh said. 'All right, Doria, put them on.'

'Hullo, Josh, it's Carter.' The voice had a boarding-school twang.

'Good for you, Carter. What did you dig up?'

'Pretty steamy stuff.'

He threw a glance at T.J. 'Shoot.'

'Wull,' Hayworth stretched out the vowel sounds unmercifully, 'the grapevine at the time was full of a scandalous case in which wife shot wild at straying husband. The details were all very hush-hush, but we kept at it till we got the name – one Patrice Garden. Anyway, she hit the mistress who was, are you following, carrying her lover's child.'

That must have been Emma, Josh's mind was racing . . .

The line crackled with static as the thunder rumbled down the sky again.

'. . . gunshot wound.' Josh heard Carter Hayworth say.

'What was that? Sorry, Carter, there was some electrical interference.'

'Oh, well I just said the hospital records confirm that the child was unfortunately aborted by the gunshot wound. The woman had another child though, a little girl, born out of wedlock from a previous affair. She was one year old at the time of the shooting.'

'Are you sure?'

'Positive. Sally followed up on the lead. She came away with the same story.'

Josh felt his heart snap. Michael Garden was not Emma's brother after all. She was. free to re-marry him. To leave . . .

'Josh, you still there?'

'Yes, sorry, Carter. You all did a good job. I appreciate it.'

'The hell you do. I had to leave off the election coverage for this flapdoodle. What's the big rush on it, anyway?'

'Huh? Oh, uh, nothing you have to concern yourself about. Well, again, thanks a lot. I owe you one. Tell Sally I send my love.'

'Darling Sal'll be glad to hear that. When are you flying out here again, anyway? It's been a while.'

'I don't know right now, Carter. Soon as I can.'

'Okay. I guess that's it then,' he said, feeling this to be an anti-climatic end to his labours.

'That's it. So long, Carter.'

'So long. Oh, wait, Josh.'

'What?' he asked, his impatience barely held in check.

'Tell that Irish bog-master that he owes me a beer.'

'Tell him yourself.' Josh was relieved to hand the phone to T.J. Then, he clapped his raincoat over his arm and shouldered out the door before T.J. could even object.

Doria broke the tip of her third pencil that day.

The brick box of the photo gallery was already emptied and dark by the time Josh arrived.

He found her, wind whipping up the pleats of her kelly-green skirt, at the corner of Lexington and Fiftieth Street, where she hopelessly competed for a cab.

Her face lit up when she picked him out from under the welter of black umbrellas bobbing up the pavement.

'Josh, what are you doing here!'

'Looking for you.' The sounds of the city during a rainstorm roared at their backs. Tyres brushing concrete, hordes of homebound footsteps, honks and beeps, the bacon-sizzle of rain falling to the streets.

'How's a drink sound?' He took her by the arm.

'A hot cup of coffe would sound even better right now.'

'Coffee it is.' He hoisted his giant black umbrella over

their heads, and held her arm tight under his own. A white woollen muffler was wound several times around his neck, accentuating the proud way he had of holding himself, and he seemed to her at that moment, pure and indestructible, plucking her from the midtown madness of rush-hour like a sky-eyed Lochinvar.

The raindrops pummelled the umbrella overhead as they ran across the avenue hand in hand.

When they reached J.B. Tipton's at Forty-Ninth and Second, Josh shook out his slick black hair like a puppy and cold drops of rain sprayed over her face.

'Hey!'

Collapsing the umbrella, he pushed open the door and they ducked inside, where the air was hung with blue smoke and the smell of wet cloth. The usual after-work crowd buzzed around the long bar, which was divided from the blonde wood tables by a gleaming brass rail. Secretaries with chipped nail polish and ever-hopeful faces, haggard businessmen barely able to bend the necessary elbow.

Josh steered Emma to the back and a table set squarely on a raised wood platform.

After they'd ordered a Scotch and soda and a coffee for Emma, she shed her hooded khaki raincoat.

She smiled at him above the small vase of flowers. 'It's good to see you.'

'It's only been a couple of hours . . .'

'I know. I still missed you.'

Josh realized this was not going to be easy – not that anything having to do with Emma ever was easy.

Their order came. Emma stirred the cream into her coffee dreamily.

'I spoke to Dr Beckstein today. He said that I had repressed my dark side and that was one reason for my amnesia. I felt guilty about so many things – the waste of talent, the child's death, my hatred for Patrice . . . the crime of loving Michael. In order to escape from that ugly side of me, I blotted it out completely.'

'That makes sense. No one can cut out an entire part of herself and not pay a heavy price.'

'But Dr Beckstein says I'm healing now, really healing.

And the proof of it is,' she looked radiant, 'a few weeks ago I finally finished a violin Concerto that I've been working on for a year. I didn't want to tell you about it until I was sure it was good. And Josh, it is! A small music publishing company is very keen on using it. The next step is to get an orchestra interested in my work!'

'I love to see you this way . . .' Right now, Josh was hoping he'd have at least one more chance to take her into his arms, to see those violet eyes blaze morning into his, to inhale the warm trace of her perfume on the jumbled bed clothes, still clinging to the place where they'd made love . . . before he released her to a life without him.

'Josh?' Her cup clinked down on the wooden tabletop.

'Hmm?'

'You're looking at me funny.'

'Sorry. A lot on my mind these days.'

A young man in a business suit, his tie loosened rakishly, brushed by their table. A ripple of laughter went up from the long, densely packed bar.

'So?' Emma asked. 'What's on your mind?'

'Oh, the usual.'

She reached her hand across the table, and curled her fingers over his. 'Your hands are always so warm.'

'It's from being stuck in so many pies.'

'You are an important man, aren't you?'

'Oh, yes, drastically.'

'Don't make fun. You're important to me.'

'That's what counts.' Should he tell her right here? Get it over with? Or nurture the lie . . .

Her eyes were all sparkly now.

'I seem to remember a proposal being made to me yesterday. Or was I just imagining . . .?' she flirted.

He held up his hand to flag the aproned waitress. 'Another Scotch here,' he replied to her query.

'Hey, Mister,' Emma said in a little while. 'You'd better answer that, or I'm going to start feeling pretty silly.'

'What was the question?'

'Josh, you're really spacey today!'

'I know. I'm sorry.'

227

'The question was: did you or did you not ask me to marry you yesterday?'

Josh shifted his weight in the chair, uncomfortably. 'I guess I did.' He took a long pull of his drink. The ice tinkled against the sides of the glass.

Her eyebrows rose quizzically. 'Don't sound so depressed.'

'Emma . . .?' Josh pressed forward across the table.

'Hmm?'

'I've got something to tell you.'

'Did you hear something about Michael and me?' she asked, slightly breathless now. 'Is that why you're acting so strange tonight?'

As he prepared to tell his woman that she was free to love another man, Josh flashed back to the powerful sweetness of the first time he met and was moved by her at the Gallery . . . the worlds of fire that opened up to him when he made love to her on their silver-gilt bed at the old Inn . . . the liberation of his deepest self into her keeping.

And there were fears, real fears of being free of her again, and the anger of a man running out of time . . .

In that instant he felt as though he stood on the crown of a great hill, a cool verdant valley spreading out below him. The vista of the sun spilling down to the trees got all tangled up with the image of the sun in Emma's hair that clear day by the Hudson. He knew then he could not live without her. Emma was the woman he loved and he was not willing to lose her – especially to some rich man's milkfed son who wouldn't even put up a fight to keep her . . .

'Josh? What did you hear?' Her words floated up to him on the hill.

'Hear? Did I say I heard anything? I just wanted to tell you that offer of marriage still stands.'

'But you do see I can't commit to anything until I know about Michael . . .?'

He nodded tiredly. 'The offer still stands. How about another coffee?'

It had been easy, this deception.

Since love had made him a liar, the others would be even easier . . .

PART IV

OUT OF A DREAM

CHAPTER TWENTY-TWO

For months on end, Josh Free went about his business like a man who hadn't betrayed his lover.

He called Emma three times a day just to tell her how much he loved her, and sent her little presents of perfect, exotic fruits, like persimmons and pomegranates, scratchy recordings by obscure maestros with Russian names, a silver bell, as though she had only to ring for his service.

At work, he was bluff and hearty, full of anecdotes at meetings. In society, he was the dream guest, single, sober and broodingly sensitive to women.

The weeks slid by like the leaves from the autumn trees below his penthouse terrace. The holidays passed again in a dazzle of gold foil and a storm of baker's sugar. Emma felt warmed by Josh's luminous attention. It was as though he had awakened one day inlaid with a new purpose, a power, a mission to cradle her life in joys. He encouraged her to take chances with her music, to go as far as she could with her composing gift, unjealously sending her off to Master Classes on weekends when they could have been together, and playing the widower to her endless practice sessions with a newly-formed, but exceedingly popular chamber orchestra.

She told herself it was only the cynical residue of her lonely days, that made her think Josh's talk too bright, his kindness too constant.

For what sin was he making amends?

Sensitive to guilt, she became still and patient around him, waiting for him to pour out his secrets.

When he did not, she became sad, as all lovers do in the face of their division.

For self-protection, she took refuge in her violin, all the while preparing to move back into the world of music. During their resumed sessions, Dr Beckstein challenged her to wholeness. Still Josh kept his silence.

Then it was New Year's Eve again and they were the social centrepiece of a gala affair at the Helmsley Palace suite of a celebrated Hungarian poet and his wealthy mistress.

Like fountains of light, a long line of polished chandeliers shimmered with liquid brilliance along the pure white ceiling of the entryway.

Emma had never seen quite so much designer satin, silk and velvet packed into one scented room. The men were charming and slightly fatigued. The women had small white teeth which they played like harmonia, in smiles. The mistress wore Lagerfeld gauntlet cuffs and heavy metal earrings that seemed to wear her down.

Emma came up to Josh, who, encircled by admirers, was brilliantly holding court.

He was galvanic tonight, sipping champagne and shedding charm. The circles under his eyes hardly showed in the holiday candlelight.

She wondered what was bothering him so deeply.

'Josh.' She plucked at his sleeve. 'It's almost midnight. Can we break away for a moment? I'd like to be alone with you.'

Nodding and smiling steadily, he eased out of the group of monied playboys and spa-running starlets.

'What is it, Emma?'

She took him by the hand. 'Can't we go where it's quieter?'

He seemed reluctant. 'Aren't you enjoying the party?' he shouted above the din.

'Yes, of course,' she shouted back. 'But I think I've had enough pressed duck and Drambuie to last me the whole year. I'd rather be with you.' The lake-blue taffeta rustled as she reached up to straighten his tie.

As always, when he was near her, he felt that yearning

230

to leap into her soul. The mystery of her wholeness burned like an aureole around her.

'It's midnight,' somebody yelled. 'Happy New Year!'

A half dozen clocks went off like a detonation throughout the suite, bonging them all into the revolution of time.

'Happy New Year, darling,' Emma kissed him lightly on the lips.

'Happy New Year, Emma.' Josh looked down at her, unsmiling, knowing that what he was about to do, might destroy them both. 'Michael Garden is not your brother.'

'What did you say?' she asked gaily.

He put his mouth close to her ear. 'I've known it for months now. Your mother's other child was killed. Michael is not your brother. You're free to go to him. Why don't you go?'

Not even waiting for her answer, he waded off into the throng.

At first she'd felt nothing but an overwhelming pang of relief.

Then her inner eyes came open and let in a wild confusion of shock and sorrow.

Michael Garden was her husband, legally, and by the laws of the heart.

For one paralysing moment, Emma hung there, blinded by old-fashioned thoughts of duty and responsibility. She must contact Michael Garden. She must see him again, resurrect their love.

But what about Josh . . . Josh . . .

She looked up just in time to catch sight of him edging out the double doors of the suite.

Only stopping to pick up her whispery fur, she inched her way through the partygoers, and chased him down to the lobby.

Outside, there was a light snowfall, and yellow balls of haze glowed around the streetlamps. Except for the doorman blowing puffs of smoke from the red 'o' of his mouth, the streets were deserted, as professional partygoers had contrived to make their sparkling entrances hours ago.

'Josh!'

His long legs were carrying him down the street below. Her high heels slipped and slid on the icy pavement.

'Josh, wait!'

He swung around, his face like stone. 'The chauffeur is shadowing you. He'll take you anywhere you want to go.' His words echoed down the quiet street.

'Why did you leave me like that?' she demanded angrily. 'What's wrong with you?'

'Don't make this harder for me, Emma.' Under the streetlamps, he looked like a stranger. 'I know you and your damned principles too well to think you're not going to go bolting off to Michael the first chance you get. Am I right?'

'Yes.'

'And you're going to try to forget me and whatever peace we had in one another's arms. Right?'

'Right, but . . .'

'Then it's over.' He resumed his brisk walk.

By gathering her voluminous skirts in one hand, she was able to keep after him part of the way, all the while watching the snow fall on to the inverted triangle of his navy-blue overcoat. But inevitably, as Josh intended, she'd begun to fall behind and finally had to stop, bewildered, cold and tired, in the middle of the snow-strewn streets, until he was swallowed up by the dampness and the blue fog of city lights ahead. The sleek, dark limo glided in her wake like a creature of the deeps. She signalled to the driver, in defeat. What was the use of following him in the car? He had shown her that he was finished with her, having come to the end of even his prodigious patience and resourcefulness. It would be a mockery of his feelings to pursue him any further tonight.

For his part, Josh knew the precise moment he'd left her behind, felt the shock of diminution. He could sense her going from him like a skein of blood, or a sapping of the life force.

That night, he cursed himself and Emma up and down the windy Manhattan streets until dawn.

Once the eternal boy in love, he'd become, since Emma, a man who loved.

Laughter filled his head: a damn fool's laughter at himself.

Because of that love, he would have to let her go free: Emma, the pear tree, and one perfect morning long ago . . .

The cuss words of Josh Free's best friend in high school rang in his ears.

It was all Emma's fault.

She should have been with him tonight, smart and smiling at his side, with those eyes like the stones in an Egyptian mask, more beautiful than any tequila-tinged sunrise on any New Year's bloody day.

One by one, his companions had dropped out, drunk under the table by the normally health-conscious Free. His all-night binge had left him brooding in this downtown bar on the first of the year, with an unclear world view and an urge to call everyone he'd ever met.

Now, standing in the cramped booth, feeding dimes into the telephone, Josh felt his spirits sag like the cheap gilt-paper decorations hanging limply from the ceiling. *Happy New Year,* they broadcast forced cheer. *Holiday Greetings*! they twinkled falsely.

As gruff, incredulous voices answered his ring, and profanities were exchanged vis a vis the time and aptness of the call, Josh fell deeper into his holiday depression. No one seemed to have the urge to talk to him. Of course, if he'd thought to identify himself, their reception might have been considerably warmer, but he wasn't thinking very well in that hot booth, with his hot head, oh damn you Emma, turn off those molten eyes . . .

When he was finally down to his last dime, and found himself dialling Nicole's chic exchange in California, he was filled with self-disgust, and hooking up the phone, swashed his way across the confetti-strewn floor, past the diehards who were still partying hardy at five o'clock this morning, in search of fresh air and a clear head.

The morning after the snow was windless and cold.

233

Above the highrises, purple and rose bars of sun were streaking the sky with iridescent light.

After a trek of ten blocks, with New Year's luck, Josh connected with the last free cab in the city, piloted by a morose and uncommunicative driver, which suited him just fine. He had only a fifteen minute ride in which to figure out why he was headed for his assistant's apartment . . .

Doria Sevenstars. He said the name aloud, smoothing back his fine black hair, and straightening his white tie. He'd always known in the back of his mind that she was in love with him. Now he polished off the evidence, kept in dry storage in the far corners of his ego. All the times he'd caught her studying him, when she thought he didn't see. The shy invitations. The way she had of thrusting out those empress's breasts whenever he walked by . . .

He dwelt on her many perfections as the cityscape flew by his taxi window beaded with ice, and the alcohol in his silver flask took effect.

The gift of silence! The superb grace of her body! The hidden dimensions of her passion!

He could hardly wait to tell her what glorious visions he'd seen of their bodies together, how masterfully he would fill her need.

Why hadn't he thought of it before?

The queenly Doria. He must have been blind not to see how she waited for him, in her bed, all these long years.

He had only to reach out his hand, and Emma and her haunting eyes would go away.

Doria would probably not even have answered the insistent downstairs buzzer at five-fifteen in the morning, if she hadn't only staggered in herself a mere half hour before.

Or if the children han't been packed off on a class trip in anticipation of her blow-out New Year's celebration at a funky loft party in the Village.

She tightened the terry cloth robe around her tired body.

'Who is it?' she asked the intercom in a sleepy voice.

'Josh,' the intercom seemed to say back.

'Josh who?' she yawned.

There was some static. 'Josh Free.'

Her eyes flew open. This wasn't one of her daydreams! She pressed her finger on the buzzer long enough for a shopping bag lady and a stray black cat to sneak in out of the cold, after Josh.

Doria was plumping up the red velvet pillow couch when Josh reached her apartment door and knocked.

She held it open.

He rose up in her doorway, blocking out the weak light of the common hallway.

'Doria.'

'Josh?'

Now that he was here, he didn't know what to do.

He hoped Doria did.

'Come in,' she said, 'I guess.'

He stepped inside, and shut the door, canting her weight against it for the eternity it took to compose herself.

'I hope I didn't wake you.' Idiot! he thought, of course you woke her. It's five-fifteen in the morning . . .

With its rich blue lights, her hair coursed down over the splendid breasts rising beneath her robe. Josh had never realised what a tall woman she was, how very elegant – even when caught by surprise in the middle of a crazy night like this . . .

'I thought you might like some company,' Josh tried.

Having rehearsed this delicious scene so many times in her head, she had a host of answers at her fingertips to help him along. 'New Year's can be a very lonely time.'

'It can.'

Even from where she was standing, she caught the flash of liquor. 'Would you like some coffee?'

'Good idea.'

Josh arranged himself on the pillow couch, which kept sliding out from under him, while Doria fidgeted at the sink, with the temperamental hot-water tap. For some weird reason, she felt like a stranger in her own kitchen. From the moment Josh Free had knocked on her door with love on his mind, everything in the world looked different, and was.

235

Oh, that's what he wanted all right. Love. She had suffered want too long, not to see the symptoms in him.

Her hand, with its sudden palsy, spilled the fresh-ground beans all over her formica countertop. She had to start again.

More than once, as she scrambled to complete the coffeemaking operation, she found herself straining to hear into the next room. He was terribly quiet. Oh, God, had he fallen asleep?

With growing impatience, she plugged in the electric percolator, and burst out into the living room with a trayful of chocolate-covered Ring-a-Lings, Fleur's favourite after-school treat, which was the only species of biscuit in the house at the moment.

Her smile and the tray of cakes hovered in the space above Josh's head. He stared at the Ring-a-Lings as though they were flying saucers.

'They're chocolate,' Doria coaxed, as if he were Ben. 'Have one.'

'No, thank you.' Josh was beginning to feel strange. The alcohol was burning off and his stint alone in the quiet living room had given him time to think things over. Maybe coming here was not such a good idea after all.

Doria set the tray down on the coffee table.

Coffee smells were beginning to drift seductively out of the kitchen.

She sat as close as possible to him on the couch, and his mind began to change again.

'Happy New Year, boss.'

'Happy New Year, Doria.' Her name was very soft on his lips. He wanted to be perfectly gentle with her because he felt so rough. He wanted to exhaust every erotic use of mouth and tongue, until she cried out with pleasure . . .

Her head brushed up shyly against his cheek and he turned to her. They began some light kissing, the tips of their tongues just touching, outside their mouths. Tasting, probing, he clasped her by her slim upper arms and pushed her against the pillow back.

'You make me feel so weak,' she murmured.

'You make me feel so strong.'

Josh took the two ends of the belt, and began to untie it. Slowly, he pushed aside the long robe, leaving her lovely body exposed to his view.

'Doria, you're exciting me. I don't know why I never came to you before . . .'

'Come to me now,' she gasped.

She bit his lip with her white teeth.

In wild excitement, Josh tasted his own blood, and he prepared to make a feast of her, to devour her. She would be more than a match for his appetites.

And then, suddenly, it went all wrong.

A crick in his neck, the bodies not fitted right, the intrusion of other names, other faces into the lovemaking.

She could feel him retreating from her, and everything in her cried out against the injustice.

'Doria, I'm sorry. I can't . . .'

Her eyes opened to the sea brilliance of his own, staring into her. 'But why? I know you want me.'

He lifted her chin. 'I want you all right.'

He moved off, chose a cigarette from his thin gold case, and lit up. 'But you're forgetting that you and I have been together for a long time. You and T.J., Flynn, Cruz and the others at the *Globe* – you're my goddamn family. And a man doesn't come sniffing around his family just because he's got the heebie-jeebies on New Year's Eve.'

Smoke curled upward from the tip of his cigarette. 'We do belong together, Doria, but in another way. We *are* part of the same world, but it's worlds away from what we're trying to do now. It would be a lie to say we're any more than that. And lest I come up smelling like roses, there's nothing noble about what I'm saying here. It's just that I seem to have lost my talent for lying to myself – and to women. At least, the women I respect.'

'Emma?' she asked, not looking at him.

'Yes, Emma's got a hand in this too. I can't seem to play musical partners the way I used to. Just doesn't work anymore.' He shrugged his shoulders. 'I'm truly sorry, Doria. And what's worse, I'm sober now.'

In the distance, Doria heard the tinkle of her fantasies being smashed to smithereens. 'Did you have to have an attack of morality just now?' she demanded, half-seriously. 'With me?'

'You can't be any sorrier than I am.' He leaned over to give her a perfunctory kiss on the mouth.

'Didn't we make a pair though?' she asked, feeling oddly relieved.

'Hell, we sure did. If we really got down to it, we would have set the sofa on fire!' Josh stabbed out his cigarette in the seashell ashtray.

'Come to think of it, I did smell something smoking before.'

They stared at each other and cried out simultaneously. 'The coffee!'

Together, they'd rushed into the kitchen, and sure enough, the defective wire on the percolator was shrouded in a rising cloud of black smoke. Josh, his hand wrapped in a dish towel, yanked it out of the wall socket. 'Doria, when you cook, you really cook!' he said, happy for the diversion.

Doria felt a tickle of laughter begin in the bottom of her throat, and work its way out.

Then Josh joined in and the two of them stood there in stitches, until the tears started in their eyes.

'Tell the truth. It was really the Ring-a-Lings that turned you off!' Doria panted.

'Well, they didn't help,' Josh teased.

'Next time, I'll try gingerbread men.'

'Good choice!'

When the laughter had ebbed, they waited uncertainly with bashful smiles.

'Well, I'm glad I dropped by tonight,' Josh said. 'It seems we had some things to straighten out. I know I haven't always been there for you, Doria, but I'm going to try to change that. From now on, it won't be the business that concerns me, but the people who make up the newspaper in the first place.

'Should be an interesting year.'

'Very.'

'In celebration I'll make us some *instant coffee*. How's that?'

'Sounds good.'

He wandered into the living room again and sat down, grinning to beat the band.

The telephone jangled on the end table.

'Could you get that, Josh?' Doria called from the other room. 'Probably some drunk with a wrong number.'

'Sure.' Josh picked it up. 'Hello?'

A lengthy pause ensued. Then, 'Who the hell are you?'

'Who the hell are *you*?' Josh was also about to ask the man if he knew what time it was, but the irony of the question was too heavy to deal with in light of his own activities earlier in the evening.

In any case, the caller had hung up, with a vicious thump.

'Who was it?' Doria came in with two red bistro mugs. She handed one to Josh.

'I don't know. He wouldn't say. Probably a drunk.'

'Probably.'

They sat side by side, sipping at their coffee companionably.

In their ten year association, Doria Sevenstars had never before been comfortable with Josh Free.

But now, strange lights no longer played about his head. The ultramarine jolt of his eyes had ceased to shake her soul. She felt again a wild relief, a lightening, as if some mischievous shadow had escaped back into the sky, leaving her in peace.

A half hour later, Josh left her with a chaste kiss at the door.

Gradually, as they had spoken man to woman, Doria had come to see that she had been carrying the burden of creating Josh Free, her Josh Free, all these wasted years. It had drained her energy and flattened her horizons which were populated by other men, men who would be happy to love her. Men like . . .

What a blind fool she'd been! How lucky she was to have caught her stupid mistake in time!

Was it in time?

Someone had tried to tip her off about this very thing, who was it now? She must be very tired not to remember.

As she cleared the coffee cups from the table, hooking a pinkie in each handle, Doria was beset by troubling images of none other than T.J. McShane: T.J. in his dumb cap and scruffy sneakers tumbling into her office like a marionette, at every flimsy excuse . . . T.J. as angel of mercy at Ben's hospital bedside . . . T.J. popping her one at the peak of frustration, in an excess of love . . .

T.J. loved her! That was what she'd been trying to remember all night, all these years. Doria's fingers let the cups slip to the floor.

Here was the man who would be proud and happy to love her . . . whom she would be proud and happy to love.

Lost in wonder, she stooped down to the carpet to pick up the beautiful cups.

CHAPTER TWENTY-THREE

Damn, damn, damn . . . Tom Joad McShane smashed the phone on to its cradle, and raked his fingers through his bristling head of hair so many times that it stood straight up like the wiry pelt of a terrier pup.

He left the loft's pink and grey high-tech kitchen for the gloom of the living area, where little knots of lingering guests sat in campfire circles around the red tips of their lighted joints.

'Have a drag,' offered an orange-bearded kid from Circulation.

'Nah, thanks.'

T.J. craned his head, trying to sift out the host and hostess from the ashes of the once-roaring New Year's Eve party.

Neither of them appeared to be there.

A few celebrants had nodded out by the fireplace, their heads resting heavy on over-stuffed Navajo print pillows. T.J. stole over to them and peered into their faces. Snores, and heavy breathing assaulted him. No hosts.

Even Miss Manners would surely let him off the hook if he took his leave now. He went into the bedroom where his coat would be buried under the hill of garments atop the king-size platform bed.

'Yes, there,' a woman's voice floated up from the floor on the far side of the bed.

T.J. scooped up his coat and hurried out of the room. He'd found the host.

On his way out of the loft, he caught the jade-green glint of a half empty champagne bottle. Maybe one more for the road.

He sat in a chair, with his coat spread over his legs and the bottle propped between his thighs, taking a swig now and again as he pondered the strange saga of McShane and Sevenstars.

They hadn't liked each other very much from the start. He didn't know how the hell he'd come to love her. Most eedjiotic thing he'd ever done.

Then too, she was always making him think there was some ray of hope, twinkling like the salt crystal around the rim of a Margherita glass. That wounded doe look would come into her eyes, and he would fall for her all over again.

Tonight, for instance, accompanied by the nerd from Promotion, she'd walked into the party looking like a damn empress, that provocative behind dancing in front of him like two cantaloupes bouncing in a paper bag.

He'd thought she would ignore him, since she'd never really forgiven him for bringing up that stuff about her and Josh. But lo and behold, tonight there was a reprieve! She'd left her nerd and spent most of the party dancing with T.J.

At the end of the night, when she was leaving, she'd gone all sentimental and kissed him for the New Year.

His head had bounced off the clouds (they were painted on the ceiling) on that one, which led him to phone her at home, to see if she'd got there safely. Like he was her old grandmother, or something. Maybe he was.

Because when she wanted a lover, she certainly didn't run to T.J. McShane. The nerd was there, instead. It was he who answered the phone – in Her Bedroom – while T.J. sat in a corner and stewed.

It was bad enough, watching Doria make a fool of herself over Josh Free. But to have a captoothed candy-pants from advertising on top of it, well, that was putting too much of a head on the beer.

Josh, of course, couldn't be fought. T.J. had realized long ago that Free wasn't a flesh-and-blood man to Doria, but some half-baked gingerbread she had cooked up at thirteen, and never let go of.

Maybe because Free was the kind of glamorous 'in' that Doria always wanted to be, he held a special fascination for the penniless girl who had become Miss Florida, and then, misused. Or maybe it was his ocean-bottom eyes.

242

Anyway, who the hell cared? He tipped back the bottle one last time, then let it down, with a defiant plunk, on a japanned table.

It was over! This was it! New Year – New Life. He was going to ask Josh for a transfer on Monday morning. He would fly to the farthest outpost of Free's printing empire, anywhere, so long as there were no reminders of Doria Sevenstars to make him mad.

True to his word, bags packed, hotel booked, and apartment speedily sub-leased, T.J. slapped his request for transfer into Josh's hand as soon as the boss walked in the door on Monday morning.

'What the hell is all this?' Josh grumbled, slamming the door to his office behind him for emphasis.

It had given T.J. a mean-spirited satisfaction to ignore Doria, presiding over her spotless desk, and stinking spider plant . . . making way straight into Josh's lair.

'Just what it says. I'm splitting. Taking off for parts unknown. I've been getting stale. Need some new places, fresh faces.'

'What are you, a travelogue?' Josh interrupted, irritably. He flung the sheet of paper down on his desk. 'What is it? You want more money? You can have it.'

'It's not the money.'

'Don't tell me you've been feeling neglected too! Look, I know this business with Emma has been distracting me. But that's all over now.'

'I'm not feeling neglected. Jeez, what do you take me for?'

The big leather chair creaked as Josh leaned back as far as it could go, his hands folded behind his neck. 'So, talk to me.'

'There's nothing to say. I want out. This is a big operation. Find me something far, far away. I promise you'll hear from me every Christmas with a nice Hallmark.'

Josh scratched his chin, in contemplation of the problem. Then he looked up slyly. 'It's a woman, isn't it? Come on, don't try to con me.'

'Anyone ever tell you you're a pain in the ass?'

'Once or twice.'

'Okay, it's a woman.'

'Anybody I know?'

'*Yes,* it's "anybody you know".' T.J. unwittingly darted a glance at the outer office.

A light switched on in Josh's face. He whistled sharply. 'Christ, it's Doria!'

'Why don't you use a bullhorn?'

Josh pounded his fist on the desktop. 'Doria. Can you beat that? God, I *have* been in wonderland!'

T.J. half-rose from his chair. 'Can I go now, Judge Hardy?'

'Sit down.'

T.J. fell back into his black-leather seat.

'You know, it's not entirely my fault that I didn't pick up on this before. You two do a great impersonation of mutual hatred.'

'I know. We even fooled ourselves.'

'Why stop now?'

T.J. smoothed the shiny material of his pant legs with both palms. 'Had enough. Last night – I don't know why I'm telling you any of this – last night she went home with some lover boy from promotion.'

'How do you know?'

'He answered the goddamned phone. Look, is this for *Sixty Minutes*?'

Propping his elbow on the huge desk, Josh cupped his face in his hand, and dabbled his fingers against his cheek. 'McShane, you're such an ass. That was no ad man. That was me.'

The air crackled menacingly between them. T.J.'s fists hardened into balls.

'You can get off the *Rocky III* act,' Josh told him with gruff amusement. 'Nothing happened.'

'What do you mean, "nothing happened"?' T.J.'s voice rose with his blood pressure.

'We chatted and had a cup of coffee. That's all. Doria's too good a friend to waste on a fling. Anyway, I'm still too tangled up in Emma to make any moves.'

'Glad to hear it.'

Josh came around to perch on the end of his desk. He folded his arms. 'Does she know?'

'Know what?' T.J.'s face crinkled in an expression of distaste. 'That I'm in love with her? She must, by now.'

'I agree. Or else she doesn't have the smarts I think she has. You and Doria Sevenstars . . .' Josh gazed up at the ceiling, as though answers to the imponderables were etched there. 'Takes some getting used to.'

'Hey, listen, I was thinking the Dallas office would be fine, or San Francisco.'

'T.J. . . .' In the succeeding moments, Josh hoisted his friend out of the chair, and propelled him by the shoulders to the door. 'Go out there and buy the biggest bloody diamond ring you can find on Forty-Second street and bring it back here and ask that woman to be your wife. Don't show your face until you do.'

'Huh?'

'Get the hell out of here!'

T.J. stood now on the other side of Josh's door, nose quivering against the wood, unsure of how he had arrived there.

'Can I do something for you?' Doria inquired with a shy awkwardness, new to them both.

'Yeah, you can tell His Eminence Gris, Joshua Free, that I don't take orders from him or any man else. And tell him, San Francisco's very nice this time of year!'

Doria's face set into a mask of puzzlement as T.J. swaggered out of the city room, and, unbeknownst to her, out of her life.

The morning passed slowly and painfully for Doria Sevenstars.

When T.J. didn't show up by lunchtime, she became worried, at which point a quick consultation with Josh sent her spinning out of the building, with his blessing, into the brilliant afternoon that belonged half to winter, half to spring. She caught a cab downtown, on a molasses crawl through midtown traffic.

Oh please, God, don't let him have gone yet . . .

She arrived out of breath at the steps of T.J.'s E. 11th St

brownstone apartment, just in time to see him loading up his rented Celica with tagged and tattered cloth luggage that Doria suspected Goodwill Industries must have paid him to take off their hands. His jeans and checked lumberjack shirt had long ago lost their storebought sheen, and now appeared to have been worn during a potato sack race in Central Park.

'T.J.!'

'Doria . . .' He looked shrunken in his misery, as though he had been deboned. 'You're just in time to see me off.'

'Where are you going?' she circled him warily.

Across the street, construction workers set up a metallic hammering. A little girl in a short red velvet coat walked by hand in hand with her East Side grandmother.

'I don't know. Probably San Francisco.' He slammed down the trunk in punctuation.

She moved into the pool of sunlight around him. 'Can I come?'

'What for?'

'You're hard.'

'So are you.'

'Not any more.'

With a cold grin, he leaned against the haunch of the Celica. 'How was Josh last night?'

She turned interesting colours. 'He was . . . Josh. I mean, the real Josh, not the one I made up in my head.'

'Oh?'

For the first time since their battle royal, he seemed to regard her with some respect. Still, she knew she had to work at it . . .

'Yes, he made me see that I've been in love with love, all these years. And you tried so hard to tell me, didn't you?'

She could see his shoulders relax.

'I did.'

'Well, I finally figured out that there was only one man who really cared if Fleur tore her tutu on the night of her ballet recital. Or if Ben's reading level went up two grades in six months . . .'

He was studying her face intently. 'Or if their mother gets herself loved the way she deserves to be?'

'Yes,' she said softly, 'that too.'

Her lips were very close to his. From across the street, a workman in a blue denim shirt hooted.

But then, in an unexpected move, T.J. picked up his rucksack from the pavement and hitched it over his shoulder. 'So long, Doria. It's been fun.'

'T.J.!' she cried, stunned. Then her eyes flashed a dark fire. 'You come back here!' On impulse, she grabbed the strap of the sack and pulled with all her might.

'Hey!'

The knapsack landed with a thump on the pavement. Not entirely zippered closed; it spilled out its contents, brushes, toilet articles, assorted books of an erotic nature, glass-framed pictures of Doria and the children, McDonald's burger wrappers of ancient vintage.

'Now look what you've done, you're a menace to society . . .!'

'Oh, I'm sorry, T.J. I didn't mean to . . .' She fell to her knees, intending to stuff back the mess of personal articles, but T.J. had got there before her and their heads collided with a noticeable clunk.

'Ouch!'

'Oww, Holy Christmas, Doria, not again . . .!'

Scrabbling on her hands and knees, while pedestrians picked their way curiously around her, Doria began to re-stuff T.J.'s bag. Irritably, he jerked his briefs from her hand. 'Can't you keep your nose out of anything?'

Doria giggled in embarrassment. 'I'm just trying to help.'

The construction workers were now collected in a regular lunchtime audience, while munching on man-size roast beef sandwiches and deli pickles and commenting on the lovers' antics as though it were a soap opera on TV.

As T.J. shot them murderous glances, Doria held up the last article, a crumpled paper bag. 'What's this?' She wrinkled her nose, opening the bag. Inside were white, unshelled pistachios. 'Umm, I love pistachios too.' She reached a hand in and lifted out a fistful, then noticed the glitter in her palm.

She held it up to the light, rainbows shooting down into her eyes. 'It's a ring.'

'No, it's a basketball hoop for midgets. Of course it's a ring. It's my grandmother's goddamn old country ring.'

'For whom?'

'Beats me.' T.J. scrambled to his feet with the parachute-silk bag.

He threw open the car door and lobbed the bag into the back seat.

'It's for me, isn't it?' Doria persisted.

'I did have some cockamamie idea about you and me and happy ever afterwards. But that's all tequila under the bridge.' He bounced into the driver's seat. 'So long, Princess.'

Doria popped her head through the open window. 'Yes, I will!' she cried desperately.

'You will what?' He turned the key in the ignition.

'I will marry you.'

'Who asked you?'

'You did. Just now. With the paper bag. And the ring.'

'God, are you weird?'

Stricken, Doria withdrew from the window. She jumped back, as the engine roared and the car pulled out of its space. The construction workers shouted their salty disapproval of T.J.'s behaviour, but to no avail. He was gone.

Doria's eyes stung with tears.

She came to a full stop in her mind.

T.J. was really gone.

CHAPTER TWENTY-FOUR

Like all wise women, Emma Taylor knew the power of silence. When Josh who was, out of pride, waiting for her to come to him, did not return her constant calls, she slipped quietly into the kind of solitude she had first learned at Graff-Lowell.

It wasn't that she expected forgiveness from Josh, or even felt that she deserved it. But she needed him – her best friend, her passionate, wonderful lover – to fathom the motives for her decision and generously give his blessing.

Once again, she was asking him to be better than he knew himself to be. It was the task women set themselves when they loved, a posing of questions, a raising of challenges. As far as she knew, no man had ever thanked his woman for the service, even though she may very well have stormed heaven's gates in his name.

And so, daily, Emma longed for the time when the wound she'd inflicted on Josh Free would knit and mend in memory.

As for the incessant ache in her own heart, that would be soothed by Michael's burning kiss, fade in the recreation of the paradise they'd once shared – whenever she'd find the courage to call him to her at last.

This was how Emma comforted herself, all through the long, grey, endless stretches of January, when Josh's place in her cold bed cried out to be filled and she would twist and turn in a spell of loneliness.

Her telegram to Michael Garden was wired on a blue Monday.

'*Dear Michael,*' it read, '*I want to come home. Love, Emma.*' Underneath was her New York address.

Michael's response came through on that brightest of Tuesdays. It had been cabled from Australia.

'*Dearest Emma: Will be arriving New York day after tomorrow to take you home. Your husband, Michael Garden.*'

First, Emma Taylor wept.

And then she waited. Michael was on his way, wholeness was at hand; loneliness at an end.

To fill in what seemed the gulf of time stretching between them – *she was far too excited to write* – Emma prepared her sunny little apartment for Michael. She feather dusted hard to reach places atop cabinets, and polished brass and pewter objects to a glare. She laundered linens and aired out all the closets, scented with sachets and satin-sheathed hangers. A two and a half foot loaf of braided bread rose in her oven and filled the rooms with its holy aroma. She hoped the Emma who was soon to emerge from Michael's memory would love the apartment, the adopted city – as much as Michelle Smith always had.

Through the rush of activity, Josh Free was a taboo subject, although at unguarded times, he would intrude upon her thoughts, with his swaggering blue eyes, damaging truths rolling off his tongue. She couldn't seem to banish him altogether. But she prayed with all her heart that, in the end, Michael Garden would.

And then, on the day she'd reached the bottom of the last closet to be cleaned, the one in her spare bedroom, she hit on the iron clasp of a cedar trunk she'd forgotten she even had. It was a relic of her mother's, belonging to another time, in Boston, long ago. Somehow Emma had never got around to looking through it.

Kneeling at the closet, she tightened the lime-green scarf holding back her hair. Might as well try for a clean sweep.

The chest made a scraping noise as Emma dragged it out into the early afternoon light. Sitting tailor fashion, she lifted the hasps and raised the lid. A scent of mothballs, cedar and lavender rose from its depths. A whiff of the past, clear and sad as the light on Boston Commons on a winter day.

'Mama . . .' Emma's eyes pooled with tears; she seemed to cry so easily these days.

Suddenly, she saw the black patent-leather pocket book with the metal clasp shaped like a miniature rose that Mama always swung by her side when they went shopping downtown . . . snapped it open. Inside, were a few neatly folded handkerchiefs with her mother's monogram, a wilted snapshot of herself, and a thin, gold-embroidered diary. It took her a moment to overcome an uneasy sense of eavesdropping. Then she journeyed through the pages, caught up in the life of a woman she'd only thought she'd known, the way we all think we know our parents . . .

'DECEMBER 23, 1951.' The entry caught Emma's eye because it was written in violet ink, in a violent hand.

I wish she had killed me. I wish she had killed us both – Philip and me. We deserved it. Not the baby. The baby was innocent. Patrice Garden is a murderess of a Holy Innocent.

Emma swayed back, clasping the diary to her chest. Poor mother, what she must have suffered to look at her like that, the day on the Commons, as if all life were poisoned, all joy suspect . . .

Emma opened to another leaf of the diary, where she came upon a name that resounded in her memory like a silver bell.

Andrew Fayette.

She searched for a face to go with the name.

A blond man with remote grey eyes and sea-cold fingers that touched your cheek in greeting. That was he.

'SEPTEMBER 7, 1956. *It's happened again, although I can hardly believe it. I've got a man, but I'm free of the happy-ever-after tripe that would usually come with him. Andrew Fayette is a merchant mariner blown into port by a happy wind, that can just as soon blow him out again. I don't care that he's twenty years my junior. I don't care that the landlord keeps giving me the fish eye downstairs. I don't care if Emma flinches when he touches her. I don't care. I don't care . . .*'

Emma felt cold; she read on to the final entry in the book.

'JANUARY 1, 1957. *Andrew's going back to sea and I sent him there . . .*'

251

Emma backed up to December of that year.

What she found there left her reeling with a new pain . . .

'DECEMBER 25, 1956. *Well, he ruined it. He asked me to marry him. How can I marry him, or anybody else for that matter? There is only one man I will ever love, and I can't have him so long as the wife-bitch is alive. Andrew is just another child to mother. For me, it will be Philip Garden or no one.*'

Even now afraid of her mother's angry eyes, Emma shut the book. She hugged herself, a perfectly still figure in the lengthening shadows of the day. A racket of steam went up from the radiator as the cold in the room deepened. The Gardens had ravaged her mother's life. She had almost let them destroy her own.

Could Michael bring her anything but shame and disillusionment, as his father had brought to her mother?

Huddled against the bed, her arms enfolding her body, she made herself believe that one could do battle with the past, and win, if love, the good soldier, only held fast and spoke true.

Thus, Michael's kisses would be her fate; one better even than Mama, with all her blinding rage against men, had ever dared to dream of.

Clutching Fleur by one hand, Doria bobbed up the metal slither of the Madison Square Garden escalator, while Ben planted himself squarely on an upper tread, his nose wrinkled against the odour that flew up like the smell of freshly turned earth from the warehouse of great beasts below. It was spring, and the circus was in town.

Fleur had especially loved the aerialists in their glittery pink tights, afloat in the rose-coloured sea of lights above the centre ring. The trapeze bars had swung slim, silver, and seductive, calling them on to fabulous flight. Too grownup in his Jordache jeans to go in for 'baby stuff', Ben had sneered at most of the 'Greatest Show on Earth'. That is until the lion-tamer, a proud, blond barbarian of a man, cracked the whip and Ben shot up in his seat like one of the great cats on its tense haunches.

Doria and the children dismounted one escalator and climbed on to the next, while, above them a long procession of families trailed molasses whiffs of popcorn, their eyes full of stars from staring too long into the white magic of circus lights.

The Sevenstars' tickets for today's event had been furnished by T.J. McShane. It was in the way of being his final legacy to them. All morning a glum Doria had been reflecting on their irksome provenance, and on the days that stretched ahead of her little family without the infuriating charm of T.J. McShane to brighten them. Damn! She'd had her chance at the gold ring. She'd blown it. If she'd had a thimbleful of sense, T.J. McShane would be where he belonged right now – at her side, annoying her to death, till death.

Fleur smiled stickily up at her, her mouth webbed pink with candyfloss.

If only she didn't throb with guilt about the children too. T.J. had been something special with them – took a child's love less for granted than most biological fathers she knew. Now Fleur and Ben must be deprived because of her blockheaded fantasy of hearts and flowers and Josh Free tied up in pink ribbons.

If only she had seen T.J. as he was – wonderfully flawed and funny and as fine a lover as Doria Sevenstars was ever liable to find in this urban cauldron of singles bars and lonelyhearts.

The trio moved on to the final descending tier.

Ben had asked, with that defiant look of his that never failed to wrench Doria's heart, why T.J. had mailed the tickets instead of bringing them himself.

At first, she'd been prepared to lie through her teeth. But she quickly saw it would be better all around if she were straight with the children.

'T.J.'s gone away for good. He didn't feel appreciated enough around here, I guess,' she'd said, staring down at the breakfast dishes.

'We 'preciate him,' Fleur had inserted here, innocently.

'Yes. We did,' Doria replied. 'He just didn't know it.'

Ben, a boy already abandoned by one father, had taken

253

T.J.'s flight much harder than his sister. He had been that close to trusting in him. Now, because he needed fathering so much, Ben would harden his heart against all male comers. Never again would he be taken in by a glib line, a goofy smile, and a good throwing arm.

Over the last few days, a cold, unboyish glint had come into his eye and Doria recoiled with worry over her son.

'Where would you like to go for lunch?' Doria asked. 'Burger King or Nathan's?'

Fleur waved her balloon at her mother. 'Nathan's!'

'Burger King,' Ben gave his sister a look.

'Hmm. We have a problem. I guess I'm going to have to break the tie. Unless, that is, someone would care to compromise?'

Hopefully, she glanced from one of her children to the other, but their young faces were set in the stubborn arrangements she knew from her own mirror.

'No, I didn't think so.'

The escalator touched down and they were swept along by the tide of people through the vast lobby and out the electronic glass-panelled doors.

'Well, maybe we should try something different. Something more fancy for a change . . .'

'Like Four Seasons,' Ben shot back.

'How do you know about Four Seasons?' Doria demanded in amusement.

'T.J. He said it was the biggest frog pond in town and he liked Clancy's Bar much better for good old liver and onions with a warm beer to wash it down . . .'

Doria smiled at the thought of T.J.'s heated culinary opinions. How she missed him . . . 'I wasn't thinking that fancy, Ben. No, there's a nice place in the East Fifties where you can try something called crepes. Would you like that? They have all different fillings . . .'

'Yuck,' Ben said.

'Ugh,' Fleur chimed in. 'What's wrong with a hot dog?'

'Because that's just what I'm afraid it's made of: hot *dog*,' Doria fired back.

The children whooped and Doria knew the sublime satisfaction of having made her children laugh, until she

254

discovered what it was they were whooping at, in the person of a slightly built, gap-toothed young man in a windbreaker, red muffler and scuffed sneakers who seemed to be doing a little war dance around her offspring.

They, in turn, leapt at him like a litter of hungry puppies.

'T.J.!'

'I decided to come back,' he said by way of explanation.

'I'm glad,' she responded by way of apology.

'I figured you'd be coming out just about now.'

'You figured right.' Doria felt the corners of her mouth stretch out alarmingly. She seemed to have no control over the smile that spread itself like a big, red clown's mouth all over her face.

They were passing a garden-variety luncheonette, when T.J. pressed a wad of bills into Ben's hand. 'Here, kid. Take Fleur inside and order your lunch – which will *not* be hot dogs,' he added sternly. 'Your Mum and I will be right in.'

Ben grinned, and catching Fleur by the hand, disappeared into the busy luncheonette. Meanwhile, a demure Doria stood off from the crowds on the pavement, and began a study of the restaurant's plate glass window which today proudly proclaimed the 'Slenderizing Special' on colourful posterboard. She hadn't yet dared to look at T.J., as though she were afraid too much scrutiny might send him up in a puff of fantasy smoke.

His hands dug deep into his baggy pockets. He ducked his head like a turtle into his collar. 'How was the circus?'

'Oh great. The circus was great.' Wistfully, Doria felt the love warmth sweeping over her, like the spotlights trained on the high-wire acrobats. She tended towards him, as though he were the cross-bar and she were about to leap. 'Thank you for the tickets.'

'My pleasure.' His eyes moved from side to side as he watched the mottle of pedestrians pass by.

'How was San Francisco?' By this time, Doria knew the poster by heart. '*Hambruger*,' it typed cheerfully, '*jellatin and cottage cheese*.'

'Lousy.'

'Why lousy?'

'You know why.'

Doria's elastic smile grew crazily. 'No. Why?'

He pulled a crumpled bag out of his pocket. 'Have a pistachio,' he offered, 'and die.'

She met his eyes. Then, Doria reached in her hand and lifted out a handful of nuts and a diamond engagement ring, all aflame.

'You were right the first time,' T.J. said. 'It *is* for you. If you want it.'

She slipped it on to her finger where it sat, solid and gold. 'It fits.'

'I smoke in my sleep,' T.J. confessed without cracking a smile.

'I'm too disorganized to steer trolleys in the supermarket,' Doria countered. 'I would rather sew up the buttonhole, than sew on a button.'

'I'm a bonafide sports freak. I drink too much. I have the temper of a pack rat before breakfast,' T.J. sounded almost proud.

'My moods can kill a cow. I'm stubborn as Richard Nixon,' Doria protested quickly. 'I think I snore.'

T.J. had her in his arms now. 'Hell, sounds like a perfect match. Marry me.'

She wrapped herself around his wiry body. 'Okay,' she spoke wise and meek in the face of a love she could touch. 'Just to show you. I will.'

CHAPTER TWENTY-FIVE

Emma checked her sleek blonde chignon in the foyer pier glass. She glowed brightly as though her flesh had been bathed in rose petals, pampered with velvet and pearl, impaled on light.

Michael had just called from the airport to say he'd be at her door in forty minutes.

A fluttering had gone up in her heart as soon as she'd heard his voice, gentle, full of sorrowful love. She was going to love this man all over again. She could feel it coming on like a contraction of birth.

Her love was being reborn.

A fine spray of rain tapped against her windows, but she could see the clouds lightening in the north. Overhead, a band of lemon-coloured light promised a clear late afternoon, clear enough to see herself in Michael Garden's eyes, as she had been, as she was meant to be: in love.

She had chosen a cashmere turtleneck sweater the colour of morning glories to wear over honey suede. Michael would later observe that, wound in these colours, she seemed lit from within.

After an interminable wait, the buzzer went off from downstairs.

It was Michael.

She pressed the button so hard that her thumb filled with blood.

Then he was at her door. A rap of knuckles.

The door swung open. He stood there, his gold hair tousled by the wind, straight and elegant, as she'd remembered in his impeccably fitted white French coat, looking like an ad for heaven.

Emma's nerves pulsed and sang with memories, like the strings of her violin.

She trembled under his hand.

'Emma, I've missed you so much . . .'

She collapsed against him, enfolded in his open coat as by the wings of a seraphim, her lips glued to his in a lingering kiss.

She was the first to break their embrace. 'But, Michael,' she said, 'I don't understand. Why didn't you try to find me before? All these months . . .'

'Believe me, I wanted to, Emma. But Mother convinced me that you had left of your own accord. You see, I thought then, as you did, that we were brother and sister. I thought you were making a noble sacrifice for me. Was I wrong? Was that a fatuous thing to believe?'

'No, not at all. You were right to believe that.' So Patrice had been the force behind their separation. How she must have rejoiced at Emma's fall from grace. How she must have gloated among the malignant plants . . . Emma set aside the hatred that burned her. She would deal with it another time. For now, Michael . . .

She sat beside him and told her story. For hours, they comforted one another for the long months apart, like lovers first discovering the miracle of their symmetry. He would, now and again, press into her hand with his fingers a message of love and support, when the very re-telling of her experience seemed to bring her too much pain.

When she was finished, he granted her the luxury of silence in which to hide. Only then did he speak of his own pain.

'I filed for abandonment, again on Mother's urging.' His gaze veered off. 'I got the divorce.'

She was so sorry for him, sorry and . . . angry.

'But I want to marry you again,' he said hastily. 'There's no question in my mind about that. This last year without you has been a nightmare.'

Emma stared at him in disbelief. So he had no questions . . . But she throbbed with questions! She recalled that night in the orchestra pit and her first highly coloured feelings about the beautiful Michael Garden. That he was a good man, well-meaning was sure – but with new sight, after her work with Dr Beckstein, after crushing loneliness, after Josh – Emma could now tell he was a man weakened by mother love, as well. What had Michael

Garden ever created? What had he ever achieved on his own power? For what had he ever suffered and fought?

Strange, how her memory had exaggerated the marvel of his presence. He was neither as tall as she had imagined, nor his beauty so gilded. There was something unfledged about him, as though the closer one came, the more indistinct his outlines. And why not? All his life, women had thought for him. Women maintained him. He would collapse without their sacrificial strength.

Emma felt him drag against her womanhood, and had to fight the impulse to lean away from his searching mouth.

'You do want to re-marry me, don't you, Emma?' Michael was asking, as though the possibility of her refusal had only just occurred to him.

To return to the prison in Chestnut Hills. To relinquish her violin. To become Mrs Michael Garden again.

Were Michael's soft, grey eyes and mellifluous touch worth such a terrible price?

And then there was Josh, the self-made man. He was so right for her, full of wonders and strong of heart! He knew her, he saw her as she was. His mature masculinity touched off a tonic chord in her soul that left her shimmering like a rainbow. They must be together . . .

Yet, how could Josh Free, above all a man of conscience, continue to love her if he knew how she'd turned her back on her deepest responsibilities, was too weak to seek out every dark corner of her past, and too cowardly to renew her great love?

She would no longer be a woman worthy of Joshua Free if she could treat Michael Garden like a stranger . . .

'You do want me, Emma? Or is it just that you'd like to stay in New York?' He gave a little shrug. 'We can arrange that. It will be hard but we can do it . . .' Michael was too elegant to ever fall over into a whine, but something in his voice disturbed the calm surface of Emma's memory. Then she had it. This was the voice he sometimes used to coax Patrice. No. Rather, it was Patrice's voice.

'Michael, I need time.' She eased up off the sofa, and busied herself rearranging the white peonies in a Chinese beanpot vase standing before the curtained window.

'Time for what?' His grey eyes shuttered. 'You either love me or you don't.'

'Michael, that's not fair! I've had to make a new life for myself, create an Emma out of whole cloth.'

He jumped up and stood behind her. 'Now you're talking like that psychiatric quack you told me about. Why must you make everything so complicated?' He spun her around by the shoulders, forcing her to face him. 'Can you look into my eyes and honestly tell me that you want me to walk out that door – and never come back?' His voice rang with unfamiliar passion.

'No. I can't say that . . .'

'Oh, Emma, I was so afraid I'd never find you again, hold you again . . .'

He covered her face with kisses, his hands lightly brushing her cheeks like butterfly wings.

Emma thrilled against his body, hating herself for the damned softness, the cursed malleability of womanhood.

'I need time, Michael,' she whispered as his hot mouth closed over her breast. 'Time.'

Doria meets her lover in the courthouse downtown at the sunniest curve of the morning.

She is wearing a grey satin jacket and slender matching skirt. A silver ornament swings delicately from her thick, upswept hair, and she cradles a proud bouquet of white roses against her arms, in the style of a beauty queen.

The two children are there, with shining, solemn faces, to give their mother away in marriage. Best man Joshua Free fingers the box with the gold ring that lies in his vest pocket. Rounding out the bridal party is Doria's old friend from the secretarial pool: she plays maid of honour. The Judge smiles. The party smiles. The only one who does not smile is T.J., the groom, standing stiffly in his rented black suit and wishing to hell he'd taken that extra last drink . . .

Afterwards, under the stained-glass ceiling of Maxwell's Plum, there is a crystal bowl of champagne punch, a chocolate wedding cake blooming with pink-sugar rosebuds, and around-the-clock festive toasts from the many well-wishers at the *Globe*.

In the Art Nouveau palace they've rented for the day, Josh Free gifts the happy couple with the use of his summer chateau in Barbados for their honeymoon. As a joke, he also presents his cavilling employee with a small basket of white truffles – about $100.00 worth. Doria Sharpe McShane is intrigued by the raw, thinly shaven delicacies from the Piedmont region of Italy, whose decadent aroma reminds her of something she can't very well discuss in front of the children. Delighted, T.J. sneers at Free's waste of good money.

The three friends repeatedly kiss and clap each other on the back in a tumult of good will, while Josh wonders where Emma is this morning, who Emma is this morning.

Then wonders why he even cares . . .

CHAPTER TWENTY-SIX

With Michael's miracle advent, Emma now had two totally
different men to choose between, two personae to go with
them. Defeated for the first time in his life at something
he'd really wanted to win, Josh didn't bother to call anymore. Supremely confident, Michael awaited her answer.

Once she'd been released from therapy, Emma Taylor
had promised herself total self-sufficiency. No more
crutches, even when they came in such beloved form as
Alfred Beckstein. Her occasional correspondence with
him didn't count for she only discussed the *fait accomplis*
of her experience, and did not appeal to the doctor for
magical directives on how to live.

Nevertheless, Emma was feeling enough at a loose end
to need a dose of something stronger in the way of counsel. It would ease the pain of freedom.

The call to Dr Beckstein, gave Emma the first peaceful
moment she'd had since the discovery that Michael
Garden was not her brother.

'Come tonight,' the old man had said. 'After hours. We
can talk.'

'Thank you, doctor.' She'd felt safer already.

He greeted her in the snug harbour of his book-lined
office at Graff-Lowell, as though she were a voyager come
home from the sea.

'You look well,' he said quietly, while peering over the
silver rims of his spectacles.

'And you.' She ran her fingers over the binding of a
huge black medical tome. This was the place of resurrec-
tion, the tomb from which she had sprung alive. She felt a
pang of compassion for the frightened, drifting woman she
had once been.

'Would you like some rum and cinnamon? I can heat it
on my hot plate,' he asked, rounding the other side of his
desk.

She smiled, remembering his sweet tooth. 'Yes, thank you. That would be very nice.'

He indicated the cocoa suede couch underneath the window with the fading light. She took a seat.

When the rum was heated the doctor handed her a transparent glass mug, swirling with steam. She cupped it in her palms. 'Smells heavenly.'

'Hot rum. Most comforting thing in the world.'

His swivel chair groaned under his weight. 'What have you decided, Emma?'

Her eyes looked startled, as though a light had been shone into them too suddenly.

'Oh, you thought I would make the decision for you.' His smile was kind, kinder than she had even remembered.

He shook his head. 'No. Not that I don't feel for you, Emma. How would any of us respond if life gave us a second chance. Whom would we choose to love? The answer might surprise us . . .'

Emma took a sip of her drink. Then her nervous fingers were at her mouth.

'Are you playing the violin again?'

'Yes.'

'You're sure you want to go back to music?'

'Yes.'

'Good. Very good. Because, Emma, by stepping from that path you lost touch with your reason for being. The psyche will not stand for that, so everything that came after was an elaborate way to get you back on course.'

'Do you mean because I married Michael and became what he wanted me to be, instead of what I need to be, it was necessary for me to start all over?'

'Exactly.'

'But the amnesia – it was because of the baby.'

'No, Emma. You had to get free of the divine images Michael had made for you to inhabit. Your mother-in-law's tyranny was beneficial. She forced you to act, to do battle for your true self, the one that is human and flawed . . and hidden.'

'And if I go back to Michael . . .?'

263

'If you go *backwards* to Michael, you will again be a goddess. With Josh, you will be a woman. That is the real choice you must make, Emma.'

'Dr Beckstein, I'm afraid that if I let Michael go from my life, I will never be whole . . .'

'If you don't, you will never be free.'

She bowed her head in thought, leaving the delicate nape of her neck exposed, like a Japanese mistress.

'This I can do for you, my dear girl,' Dr Beckstein said. 'I can ask your higher self a question. Now this question is for the real Emma,' he spoke with affection, 'so be truthful.' He waited for her answer.

'I'll try.'

'All right then, Emma. Tell me if you can: what is the name that is written on your heart?'

Her eyes grew brilliant, and pure. A peace passed over her like cooling water. She felt as though she'd just been awakened from another deep, long sleep. 'Thank you, Dr Beckstein. Now I know what I have to do – not for Emma, not for Michelle – but for me.'

The sky was aboil with clouds, the pavement giving off steam like a sauna, when Emma stepped out of a yellow cab on Fifth Avenue in front of the stylish Sherry-Netherland Hotel.

Upstairs in his gilded, palatial suite, Michael paced the floor, from time to time flicking his wrist to consult the gold wafer of his watch. He paused. Reflected in the long Louis XV mirror, was a man he did not recognize. It was shocking: the socketed eyes; the lean, ragged line of his figure. Michael Garden recoiled from the image of the golden boy brought low by love.

Then again, why should Emma want to cut him loose? The memory of what they'd shared was sealed inside them both. Surely, even the most flexible of women couldn't undo that seal . . .

Pouring himself a brandy, he felt for the packet of airline tickets in his vest pocket. Maybe he had been over-confident. Maybe she was actually happy in this passionate jumble of a city, with her artsy friends and burgeoning career. Maybe he'd go back to Boston alone.

He tried to remember how he had ever let her reach such a dangerous depth in him. He couldn't of course, because it hadn't been a conscious act. It had been as natural as the play of his muscles against hers, the fresh smell of her hair, the soft pressure of her breasts on his mouth. These things had been all that was necessary. These things – and his inbred conviction that every woman's love belonged to him.

He paused at the window, the brandy warm in his hand, gazing out to the damp, green Park and the shadows beyond, as though he might see her coming to him through the thickets of trees. He found himself straining to hear her footsteps, the quick, sharp breaths she took when she was excited by the greeting of her lover.

The brandy burned all the way down his throat, an added bitterness.

Emma's red wool coat whirled through the hotel door into the lobby where bored-looking women in black gloves and dresses of bizarre silhouette lounged under the chandeliers, and European businessmen sat, uncreased, in their Italian silks, their hair slicked back like dark marble. Constant trains of expensive luggage went rolling this way and that through the room, propelled by snappy-coated bellhops. From moment to moment, elevator doors slid open and clouds of pricey French colognes, the plunder of Grasse, were released into the air.

Emma rode up the scented elevators to Michael's suite.

On the way, she looked straight ahead, holding her head elegantly, her hands pale and still against the flame-red coat.

Even in this rich man's preserve, she excited comment. Obviously, a mistress on her way to a tryst. The sweet air of tragedy she gave off only made her more enticing. As always, she was a woman with the spaciousness of emotion to allow others in.

On the fourth floor, Emma disembarked and walked the hall to Michael's rooms. She didn't know how long she had stood there, her hand upraised, before she had the courage to knock.

265

Silhouetted in the fading light, Michael looked like a man whose parachute had just fallen open in time. 'Emma, darling . . . I've been waiting . . .'

'Hello, Michael.' Emma's voice as ever was musical, pleasing and low, the voice of a nun. 'I've been waiting too.'

He took her hand; his was cold. 'Come in.'

She hesitated only a heartbeat before she crossed the threshold and, smiling, entered Michael's world.

It was damned lonely without those two wild people around the place. Josh was beginning to regret having yielded T.J. and Doria three long weeks for a honeymoon trip, although he continued to love the idea of the children having so much fun at his seaside villa, as the ecstatic postcards with the flaming flamingoes proclaimed.

He approved copy for the first edition that day, discussed libel litigation with the newspaper's attorney, and did five laps around his health club pool before he was ready to face the unpleasant fact that he was going to have to forget Emma, once and for all, if he were to get on with any kind of life hereafter.

Following the first flurry of unreturned phone calls and scented blue notes ignored, Emma had given up. Now, damnably, Josh was even finding her silence seductive. It had got so bad that any attempts to date other women, long-limbed, beautiful, uncomplicated women, only seemed to open up whole new dimensions of emptiness in him. Going through the days without her was as frustrating as listening for a dance pulse that never came. The nights were even worse . . .

Josh read the first line of the lead story for the twentieth time without any of it registering: this called for emergency measures.

Josh's heart wasn't big enough for both of them.

Emma would have to go.

The copy swam before him in black and white waves.

At least, he'd had her loveliness for a brief time. A spectacular time. She'd been a wonderful gift on loan to him, for some unknown goodness he'd performed. Because of that gift, he now knew for certain what he'd always suspected – that a man has no business being without a woman he loves, that she is his Grail castle, without which he will never catch sight of his own soul.

What he'd seen in her eyes would have to sustain him through the empty years ahead . . .

Josh burst into the outer office where the gum-smacking temp with the perm that somehow reminded him of pumpkin pie (it was the soft, vegetable colour of the dye) watched him, with big eyes. He threw open the office door to the stuttering of electric typewriters. He walked on until he rounded a corner and came upon the plastic-walled citadel of his Political Editor.

'I want the front page completely redone,' Josh barked. 'It's too flat. We're not writing for Mr Rogers' neighbour-hood around here! This is New York City, home of Bella Abzug!'

'Huh?' The veteran editor with the blue pencil stuck behind his tufted ear, looked up in a stupor. They had just had the final copy approved minutes earlier.

The old ways, Josh decided with some satisfaction, were the best.

Toasting under the Caribbean sun, chic in their dark New York shades, Doria and T.J. McShane flattered them-selves that they had worked this love thing to the best advantage of all concerned.

Happily, they dribbled cocoa butter all over one another, and watched Fleur and Ben play tag in and out of the bubbling green-blue surf.

'Do you realize we haven't had a fight since we said "I do"?' Doria asked, taking a swig from her chilled Perrier bottle.

T.J. shaded his reddening face with one hand. His wife's pistachio-coloured bikini agreed with his highest aesthetic sense, as did the stolen kisses under the sun. All in all, he was one lucky son of a gun. 'That must be some kind of record.'

The tide pooled in and out with a roar, while the children's laughter floated up to their blanket from the sandy shore below.

'I have a theory that our bickering was due to unresolved sexual tension,' Doria observed, waving the squat green bottle at him. She was smart enough not to tell her husband what she and Josh used to do in her dreams.

'Oh yeah?' T.J. rolled over on his stomach in order to spread out the mottled pink colour his fair skin invariably assumed in place of a tan. 'I had a theory that it was due to your being a pig-headed broad.' He chuckled.

Doria pinched his shoulder.

'Oww! What was that for?' T.J. shot up, scrunching his blue fisherman's cap low over his forehead.

'Don't you ever call me a broad again!' Doria's face was flaming and it wasn't from the sun.

He held up his hand. 'Sorry, babe. I was just kidding.'

'No you weren't.' Doria folded her bronzed arms stubbornly. 'Ever since that first day I came looking for a job to feed my fatherless children, you thought I was a pushy piece of tail!'

'Uh huh, that's right. You were,' T.J., said lying back on the blanket and dangerously drowsy in the sun.

Doria reared up on her superb haunches. 'Why you little . . .!' She grabbed the first thing that came into her hand, which turned out to be Ben's used towel. Flicking it angrily at T.J.'s ducking head, she scattered grits of sand all over his tender skin.

'Stop it, Doria, stop it!'

'I had to be that way,' Doria defended herself, 'for the children! Do you think I liked playing a Valkyrie?'

T.J. was forced to come to his knees and seize her wrists, in order to stop the onslaught of sand. The newlyweds grappled passionately, their muscles rippling as though they were making love. In the fray, the bottle of suntan lotion was overturned and puddled in a brownish goo upon the blanket.

In the end, T.J. managed to straddle Doria, his knees crushed into the sand on either side of her thighs. 'Don't you know that I loved you for that, Doria? It wasn't unfeminine, or ugly to me. It was brave and very much

268

what a woman should do for the people she loves. I wish you'd stop being so damn defensive about everything! Especially with me. We're a team now, remember? We're on the same side. You'd better get that through your beautiful, thick head or we're going to have a hell of a rollercoaster ride ahead of us in this marriage!'

She quieted under his hands, her brown eyes blinking in bewilderment at the tears that welled up in them.

'Are you crying?' T.J. asked. 'What for?'

'I don't know,' she panted.

'Aw, no, aren't you happy, Doria? I thought you were happy.'

'Let me up. I feel kind of funny.'

He released his grip on her and she rose slowly to a sitting position, hugging her knees like a little girl on the playground.

'Funny? How?'

'You know, funny. Like when I was pregnant with Ben.'

A weighty pause ensued.

'Say that again,' T.J. enjoined.

'I went to the doctor the other day when we were souvenir-hunting in town. He confirmed what I already suspected. We're going to have a baby, T.J.'

The gap between his teeth seemed wider than ever. 'Wow. Wow,' he repeated, smacking the side of his head.

'Are you upset?' She gave a sidelong look through her long lashes.

'Upset? Why should I be upset?'

'I thought maybe it was too soon, you know. We've only been married a few weeks.'

'Doria, my loony sweetheart, you make me so damn happy I feel like I'm flying right alongside that sun up there!' He pointed his finger.

'I do?' Doria's face was lit from within.

'Yup.'

'Well, of course, I do.' Doria instantly grew more confident. 'You're a very lucky man, Tom Joad McShane. A ready-made family. An unparagoned bride. What more can you ask?'

269

'Beats me,' T.J. said, nuzzling her on the neck.

Just then all sixty wet, slippery inches of Fleur came flying into T.J.'s lap. 'Brr. I'm cold.'

T.J. wrapped a big towel around her. Ben loomed up, the sun outlining his boyish body.

His mother threw him a towel.

'Hey,' Ben cried mischievously, while blotting the sea water from his long, dark hair. 'Fleur wants to know what you guys were doing before.'

'What did it look like we were doing?' T.J. barked at him.

Fleur shot a quizzical glance at her mother who appeared to be unnaturally absorbed in the mopping up of the overturned suntan lotion. 'Sort of like . . . wrestling.'

'So, what's wrong with that? Between a man and a woman, there's an art to wrestling. A lot of good things can come out of wrestling. Understand?'

Fleur shook her head. 'Not really.'

'You will. Now shut up,' he said to Ben, 'and eat your sandwich.' T.J. flung a canvas bag the colour of the Italian flag at him. 'Wiseass kid,' he muttered irritably, but Ben could swear he was smiling.

CHAPTER TWENTY-SEVEN

Michael's world: coral velvet walls. Embassy halls. The whisper of silk and satins shifting against the skin. Lovemaking, breathless and rushed between Concorde flights. Caviar and complex social agreements. The subtle smell of money in the room. The magical parties. Permission not to think, to be heedless of anything but pleasure seized and value taken.

Michael's world: a mother with implacable eyes and cool hands. Orchids out of season. Drunken admissions of sin. Carte blanche for all expensive things – but self-knowledge.

It all came back to Emma as Michael Garden had drawn her into his richly appointed suite . . .

Laden with precious objets d'art, its antique furnishings were covered in cinnamon and vanilla silk moire. Ginger jar vases bloomed with tall bouquets of chrysanthemums and roses. A blue and gold Aubusson carpet sent colour and warmth flowing into the high-ceilinged room like a brilliant summer pool.

Emma feared drowning in that well of riches, sucked down into the depths of her former life with its all-consuming love.

Michael embraced her. 'You won't leave me ever again, will you, Emma?'

She hid her face in the fresh smell of his white cotton shirt, saying nothing.

'Things will be different this time, Emma, I promise you. We won't live in Chestnut Hill if you don't want to. We'll have our own home, just as you always planned. And we'll go back to the Keys. We were happy in the Keys . . . making love in the orange grove, dipping into the pool afterwards when Mrs Fellows isn't looking . . . You'd like that, wouldn't you, darling?' His voice had an edge of desperation. 'We'll have another baby.'

Still Emma was silent. She raised her hands to his tanned cheeks.

'You believe that I love you, don't you, Emma?' Michael asked.

'I do.'

Then there was no reason for this ache in his heart, this cold snap of fear.

He held her to him, suddenly without hope.

The old ways may have been the best – but they weren't working for Josh Free. It was useless to think he hadn't been changed by this last voyage into love.

During lunch at the 21 Club, he rang the Gallery.

No Emma Taylor. She'd taken the day off.

The phone buzzed hollowly in his hand, when he called her at home.

Finally, he tried Dr Beckstein.

His secretary connected them.

'Hello?' said the tired old man.

'Dr Beckstein? This is Josh Free, a friend of Emma Taylor's.'

'Yes, Mr Free,' the Doctor's voice lifted in interest.

'I've been trying to track her down. Do you happen to know where she is?'

'She just left my office a few minutes ago, I believe she's made up her mind.'

'If I may ask a stupid question . . . made up her mind about what?'

'Which man, which life to pursue.'

Josh paused.

'Care to give me a hint?' There was a backlash of irritation in his voice.

'Don't be angry, Mr Free. I am not your adversary, nor does my knowledge of Emma give me any special power over her decisions. I promise you, she will choose as freely as if she'd never met me.'

'Somehow I find that hard to believe.' Could he actually be jealous of the old man? Love had made him a fool.

'That's because *you* are still seeking power over her. A little free advice: you're going to have to distinguish be-

272

tween control and love, before you make your peace with her.'

'I love Emma,' Josh protested.

'Yes. But that doesn't offer either of you any protection. You will just have to be patient.' He sounded more businesslike. There was a rustling of papers. 'If I know Emma, she will be contacting you within the hour. I'm surprised she hasn't come yet.'

'Thank you, doctor.' Josh felt suddenly humbled by the older man's humility.

'By the way, Mr Garden is staying at the Sherry-Netherland Hotel, if you feel you must contact him for any reason.'

'Aren't you afraid I'll take a shot at him?'

'Not at all. Physical violence against Michael Garden would be a great waste of your energy.'

'You're right,' Josh admitted, with grudging admiration. 'I can see why Emma believed in you all along.'

'I believed in Emma,' Dr Beckstein said simply. 'In the end, that's all any of us ever need, one act of faith.'

Josh was reluctant to hang up on this man. Just talking to him brought him closer to Emma, as though she inhabited him in some mysterious way.

'I'll let you know what happens, Dr Beckstein.' Josh wanted to return his good faith.

'That will not be necessary.' The weary voice had come back. 'Whatever happens will be the right thing.'

'How do you know?'

'I know.'

'Thank you, Sir. I'm glad we had this chance to talk.'

'Good luck to you, Mr Free. And goodbye.'

'Goodbye.' Josh set the phone down, thoughtfully, feeling as though some powerful tributary of mental energy had been shut off to him.

Dr Beckstein had said Emma would be waiting for him, even now . . .

Josh didn't even stick around long enough for his elaborate lunch to arrive, but instead drank half a bottle of good wine, and took off for the office, in anticipation of Emma's arrival.

She hadn't shown up.

'No messages?' Josh quizzed the temp.

She shook out her hair, crinkled like spaghetti. 'Just the President of the City Council . . .'

'Tell her I'm out to lunch. Tell everybody I'm out to lunch until I get that message.'

'Yes, Mr Free.'

In the next hour, Josh plummeted dizzily from elation to despair. He refreshed himself with images of Emma in dire straits, called her every name in the book, and himself too, for trusting a shadow dancer and a broken-down old shrink. With every swing of the clockhand, it became more obvious to Josh that Emma had chosen Michael Garden and the padded cloister in Chestnut Hill. Well, she deserved it, Mamma's boy and all. He wished her eternal joy.

Then he got serious; he allowed himself to feel the awful loss of love. It softened his heart towards her, making him see that if the tug of the past was too much for the woman, he would have to forgive her that frailty as well.

Nevertheless, he ached to see her at least one more time before she flew off with Michael Garden into blue surburban skies.

The longing brought him to his feet.

His pride brought him back down again.

It was in this hectic state that Doria and T.J. found him.

The unfortunate prelude to their visit with Josh Free had them at odds with the bubble-popping temp who fixed them with her hoot owl stare and demanded to know who they thought they were?

'I'm Josh Free's grandfather,' T.J. growled. 'And this here,' he indicated Doria with a sweeping gesture, 'is his grandmother. We've just been married, thereby legitimizing two generations of the family line.'

The temp's face broke out in rainbow colours. 'I'm sorry. Mr Free said he didn't want to be disturbed.'

'It's too late.' T.J. imagined how the girl would look with a muzzle . . . 'Mr Free is already deeply disturbed.' So saying, he grabbed Doria's hand and butted into Josh's office.

'Hi!' They cried, flushed in the face, two great sunballs of energy. 'We're back.'

'No thanks to Betty Boop out there,' T.J. went on. 'And what's more, we're pregnant.'

Josh looked up from the laced temple of his hands. 'Where the hell have you two been?'

Doria threw her husband a look. 'We were on our honeymoon, Josh. The one you sent us on, remember?'

'Yes, well, don't make a habit of it.'

'We don't intend to.' A radiant Doria came in for a closer check. 'He's upset, T.J. We're gone for three weeks and he's an aged ruin when we get back.'

They sat on either edge of his desk, forming a protective phalanx.

'What's up, Josh?' T.J. asked humanely, having discovered, since his marriage, untapped sources of the fabled milk of kindness.

'Emma's chosen Michael Garden. She's with him right now.'

'And you're sitting here?'

'It's all over, T.J. Emma's made her choice and I respect her too much to imagine that I know better. Although what kind of life she's going to have with the little rich boy, I'll never figure out!'

At that, Mr and Mrs McShane both shared the expectation that Josh would explode up from his desk and pace the length of the room like a caged puma.

Instead, he sat there stockstill, a squarish block of bridled energy, a man in love with his own passivity.

'Well, go to her, Josh!' Doria burst out.

'Yeah, what have you got to lose?' T.J. put his arm around her supportively.

'Maybe that's what she's been waiting for, Josh. Some sign from you. Women do things like that.' Doria favoured her new husband with a loving look. 'They sort of dare you to love them.'

Josh stroked his chin. 'I *would* like to see her . . . one last time.'

'Do it,' T.J. urged, 'otherwise you'll always hate yourself.'

'Or Emma,' Doria added quietly.

Josh got up from behind his desk. A hopeful look surfaced in his eyes. 'Thanks for the meddling. I needed it.'

'Any time,' T.J. said.

'Of course.' Doria gave him a dazzling smile.

The newlyweds watched Josh don the heavy armour of his coat and set off for one last tilt at love.

The woman was blonde and beautiful. The man had the light-footed elegance of a dancer in a thirties movie, attired in his biscuit-coloured cashmere greatcoat and artfully dipped hat. The stylish young couple had just emerged from their hotel suite at two-thirty sharp, complete with Gucci luggage, and presumably, airline tickets to some fabulous spot on the Côte D'Azur.

Posed beneath the awning of the Sherry-Netherland, where the chic pair waited for the doorman to flag down a cab, they bent their heads together and spoke with earnest looks. Meanwhile, parked across the street from the lovers, Josh sat behind the wheel of his Jaguar and watched the pantomime that caused him so much pain.

When the cab pulled up alongside them, they got in.

Against his better judgement, Josh began to shadow their taxi as it nosed out of the kerb, reduced as he was to a bittersweet voyeurism in this final act of his love affair with Emma Taylor.

He could see the corona of Emma's hair, a float of gold dust, in the taxi's back window. Michael had his tailored arm around her shoulders, and still they were talking, easily, sweetly together. Josh begrudged every word, the hand that lingered, warm, on her back. He remembered the wondrous sensitivity of that back, the feel of it beneath his own hand.

Once they'd rolled on to the steel-ribbed pathway of the Fifty-Ninth Street Bridge, passing over the grey slate of water, Josh was positive that they were headed for Kennedy Airport. So his Emma was leaving on a jet plane with Michael Garden, without the bare courtesy of a goodbye to the man who had stood by her when all she had was a dream of herself, not even a name to give it substance.

Both hands gripping the wheel, he fought off the pain of this recognition.

A few seconds later, the skyline began to shrink. Green pool-table yards and low brick houses rose up on either side of the file of cars. They were in the outer borough of Queens. The taxi turned into the Pan Am airport lane, and Josh followed in its wake.

He parked only a few cars down from the beautiful couple, taking care not to emerge until they had vanished into the buzzing airport terminal, Emma's arm lodged comfortably in the crook of Michael's, as though it belonged there.

They melted into the baggage-check line, while Josh stood close by, watching.

When they'd finished with baggage claim, Emma and Michael proceeded to the airport lounge, peopled by handsome tennis pros, and chattering Club Med secretaries. They could have been any ordinary honeymoon couple, as tightly bound as the figures on a wedding cake.

Among other possibilities, Josh played with the idea of revealing himself to them, and demanding that Emma come back.

But like all good women, Emma Taylor had stripped him of his arrogance. He could only observe her from across the milling lounge, loving her too much.

Josh caught his breath as she inclined her head just so, the way he remembered from sunny mornings in bed, when she was about to say something funny, especially for him. He imagined she was going to do that now. But then the moment passed. It dawned on him that he would never hear her voice again. From now on, he would exist for her as Michael Garden had once done: a mere flickering of memory. Only this time there would be no Dr Beckstein, no idiotic newspaperman to recall her to past loves.

To think it was his instincts that had pushed her into Garden's arms! Why hadn't he just let it be?

How would Emma breathe, pent up in her suburban palace, cut off from the life's blood of her music? In the end, she would just have to find another way to escape the suffocation of that life. Who would be there to pick up the pieces then, he wondered, bitterly. Who would be the next man to heal her with his love?

A cough of static.

'Now boarding Flight 444 to Miami, Gate B,' the metallic voice eddied through the lounge.

Bags were collected. There was the scuffling of shoes on the hard floor as passengers queued up noisily for the flight.

In unison, Michael and Emma rose, their hands clasped in a taut weave of emotion.

Watching this, Josh felt a cry of protest lodge in his throat. He swallowed it down like gall.

'Goodbye, Emma,' he said very softly to himself, to a boy in a pear tree. 'Goodbye, my dearest love.'

Emma hung on to Michael like a drowning woman.

'Don't do this, Emma,' Michael spoke low into her ear, over and over again. 'Don't do it. I need you more than ever . . .'

She saw him through the soft focus of her tears, begging her to love him. She embraced him in an arc of emotion.

'It's time to go, Michael.'

'No . . .' The charm came unstuck. He grabbed at her.

Ashamed for him, she let her violet eyes swing to the ground. 'Goodbye, Michael.'

Remembering himself at the last, he pulled away, then reached down for his hand baggage. 'Goodbye, Emma.'

In the next moment, Michael Garden walked off, alone, and Emma Taylor was finally free.

CHAPTER TWENTY-EIGHT

Looking out of the thick plate-glass panels of the lounge, Emma stood perfectly still until Michael's plane had taken off in a whoosh of jet fuel.

With the lift of those wings, her past had flown into the blue sky, away, forever. She had freed the woman beating inside her, the woman who had wonderful mysterious music to give to the world, the woman who had foolishly lived in eclipse, all in the name of love.

Overwhelmed by private emotions in a public place, Emma tried to turn back the tears. She folded her arms, hugging her slouchy red coat. Oh God, she had her work cut out for her . . .

It wouldn't be easy getting Josh Free to trust her again after she'd almost thrown him over for a dream. If he'd give her the chance, she would spend the rest of her life making it up to him.

She had to see him. She had to know. Now. Before the fear of losing him became too great and she melted back into the anonymous grey city again, like the dream woman she used to be.

Then, she felt his warm hand on her hair. She turned . . .

Before he could say anything, she was in his sheltering arms.

'I thought I'd lost you,' Josh said huskily. 'I thought you had chosen Michael.'

'Didn't you know?' Emma spoke as though it were the most natural thing in the world for her lover to be standing there with his arms around her, as though she'd dreamed it a thousand times before, just that way. 'I love you.'

'Oh yes,' he said softly, 'I knew. But I didn't think you did.'

'You were wrong.'

Josh thought back to the extraordinary sequence of events that had brought his Emma back to him. At first, he'd been impressed by the unexpected power of his imagination. As if on cue, Michael Garden had exited stage left, while Emma, her sad, sweet smile floating after him, had stayed, beautifully, behind. Sweet delusion!

Now as her smile sparkled up at him, he realized it was no trick of the mind that had Emma Taylor walking back into his life.

The airport, the passengers, the roar of the jumbo jets outside the glass window – all of it vanished. There was only love, alive and glowing in one another's arms.

He kissed her hands, touched her face, her hair, joyously. 'Will you marry me now, Emma? Are you ready?'

She went cold. 'Is that why you've come?'

'I came to say goodbye.'

She only became fully conscious of what she was doing to him by watching the vivid alteration of Josh's face.

'I need time,' she told him, helplessly. 'I can't marry you now, Josh.'

'Emma, what are you saying?'

'Josh, listen, I want you in my life. God knows how I want you! But marriage . . . it's too great a sacrifice. I've just found Emma, Josh. Don't ask me to bury her again so soon.'

Josh seemed to retreat to a place inside of him.

In silence, they moved towards the exit doors. He only spoke again when they were at the exit. 'You might as well have gone with Garden,' he said grimly.

'That's not true!' She touched his arm. 'We'll be together.'

'Not the way I want.'

'It's what I need, right now.'

A quickening breeze met them at the airport entrance. Spring was a scent of green, a soft thrill in the air.

'I must be a glutton for punishment.' Josh shook his head. 'I keep letting you pull the net out from under me, while I do somersaults in the air. Why are you still playing with me, Emma? Do you hate men that much?'

280

'Not men. The power we women give to men.'

A breeze riffled the black hair curling over his forehead. He turned up his collar. 'And what am I supposed to do while you're finding yourself? Write a book about it? Join a religious cult? Go crazy?'

Emma seemed to look through him with her unearthly indigo eyes. 'Just love me, Josh. That will be enough.'

'I've tried that, Emma.'

'Try it some more.' She stepped out to the kerb, her hand floated up to flag a cab.

'Let me take you home at least.'

'No, it's better if I start doing things alone right now.'

She made a point not to pity him, standing there, openly hurting. She secured her cab and stepped in.

When she got up the nerve to look again, he was already gone.

The sky was afloat with chestnut-coloured clouds. A fine spring mist rose from the city like a spray of *eau de cologne,* while the soft sea sounds of traffic filled the late afternoon.

Any day now, the summer would snap open like a parasol in the green meadows of the Park, among the gnarled boughs of the trees. Emma's third life had begun.

In the last three months, she had put in for her old job at the Metropolitan, penned a piece for solo violin, chopped her golden hair to a fare-thee-well, and led Josh Free a merry dance across Manhattan.

She treated him, he claimed, with all the coy condescension due a visiting king who had neither the language, nor the situation well in hand.

During their times together, she forbade him to speak of marriage, or commitment of any kind. She wanted only gay suppers on the town, satin sheets in bed, a fine madness in his eye whenever he looked at her, as he often did, from his aisle seat across the Golden Horseshoe.

In the gentle drift to summer, she laughed aloud a great deal, showing the opal line of her teeth, and promising herself that this independent wheeling about in the greatest city on earth, was what she'd wanted all along.

'God, look at you! You're in love with your own reflection,' Josh burst out that balmy Saturday afternoon as they walked down stylish Fifth Avenue, and Emma had shopped for her own image in Tiffany's window. Lately, she was always doing that, in the mirrors of restaurant foyers, hotel lobbies, theatres. It was as though she could not get enough of herself.

Josh hated it, and said so. As long as she was in love with her own image, there was no room in her heart for him.

Emma knew this was true, and would be kinder to him, if she could. She also knew that, like all infatuations, this selfish one must run its course.

'I'm going away,' Emma revealed suddenly as they settled at the outdoor Café de la Paix, under the flapping red, white and blue awning. 'I thought I should tell you.'

Josh slapped down the menu. 'I suppose I should be grateful.' He looked back to the bill of fare.

'Don't you want to know where?' Her amethyst eyes clouded over. He was going to brood.

'Not particularly.'

The waiter sauntered over.

'Red Lillet for me, on the rocks. Emma?'

'White wine, please.'

The waiter took back the menus, and hurried off, scratching his pencil on a small white pad.

'I've had an offer from one of the best orchestras in London, Josh. First violinist. They want me to play my concerto at a major performance.

'You don't say.'

'And a teaching post at the Royal Institute of . . .'

'*Mazel tov*,' Josh cut in.

The drinks were served from a swooping tray. Josh sipped his, and watched the well-dressed crowds moving this way and that along the Avenue.

Emma did not touch her drink. 'You're angry.'

'No.'

'No?'

'No.'

His face was bland.

'So will you see me off at the airport?'

'If you like.'

The wind off the Avenue fluttered the blue-and-white checked tablecloths. 'And will you kiss me goodbye?'

'That's what you're doing to me, isn't it?'

'No, Josh. We can still see each other.'

'In our dreams?' he asked ironically.

She avoided his eyes.

He signalled for a refill. 'Don't bother to tell me. I know. It's what you have to do.' His voice went soft and intense. 'You're a fool, Emma. I've watched you for years now, and you still can't tell when you're happy. You seem to be missing that particular little gene. By the way, London is a lousy town to live in alone. It's damp in the winter, and there are no good American bars. I hope you hate it. I hope you wake up every morning, and kick yourself for leaving me.'

'I guess this hasn't been much fun for you.' She was studying him over the rim of her glass. 'My metamorphosis.'

'Oh, it's been a real treat. I just thrive on being turned inside out and upside down by a woman I can't stop wanting, no matter how many times she demonstrates her complete incapacity for sane, human behaviour. Playing the patsy is always an important role. It's what I wanted to be when I grew up.' He downed his drink and threw a few bills on the table. 'When are you leaving?'

She took a deep breath. 'Tomorrow. Nine o'clock.'

He didn't even blink. 'I'll pick you up at eight.'

The alarm clock's shrill raised Emma up from beneath her goose-down comforter the next morning. The window-panes were squares of mottled grey as the rain fell mono-tonously outside her new co-op. At the dismal sight, she curled back into the blankets, unequal to the tasks that lay ahead of her.

It felt like the day of an exam, or a stiff audition. Or even major surgery on a vital part.

When for the second time that morning she stubbed her big toe on her packed case, she remembered it was something even worse: a day for flight.

Vaguely, she showered.

A rush of orange juice would have to see her through the morning.

Wanting to impress her new employers, she chose a sexy straight skirt, of soft, unlined Italian napa. It had a kick pleat and was stunningly red. A boat-necked bronze tee shirt of silk *crepe de chine*, wooden bangles and red leather pumps helped pull the chic outfit together.

When she was dressed, she hoped she looked more confident than she actually felt.

After bidding farewell to her apartment, she waited in the lobby with her retinue of luggage, until Josh came for her.

Never once did she doubt he would. Love, she knew, had its ways, even at parting.

The silver Jag laced up to the kerb.

Josh received her inside without comment. As the doorman swung her bags into the back seat, and was paid for his pains, the rain popped on the pavement like hot buttered corn.

'Good morning,' Josh muttered, staring straight ahead at the streaming windscreen. The wipers sang in their rhythmic arc.

'Good morning.' She was pierced with an unreasoning irritation that he should be so prompt this morning. Almost as if he wanted her to leave . . .

Josh, fortified against the foul weather by his thick fisherman's sweater and wool slacks, looked fearless and self-sufficient, which depressed her even more.

'You're right on time,' Emma accused him.

'I told you I would be.'

She wanted to goad him to speech. She wanted to gore him to action. She wanted him to take her in his arms and lock her there for all eternity.

She felt for her tickets, deep in the pocket of the raincoat folded neatly on her arm, and held her tongue.

Josh somehow managed to find a parking space in the heavily trafficked lot. He hung a big-spoked umbrella over her head like a miniature pavilion and hefted her bag with one hand. 'Let's go.'

They walked in silence to the terminal, their heels dragging on the slick pavement.

All the while, Emma rehearsed farewell speeches.

The curtest ones seemed the best.

Or maybe none at all. Maybe she shouldn't leave at all . . .

They turned into the check-in area, as ever, filled with people.

Emma noticed then that Josh's eyes were the phosphorescent blue shade of shark-infested waters. His indifference to her going was pure pretence. She felt better, as she stepped into the Babel of the luggage line.

'This is where I leave you,' Josh said, abruptly, now looking strong and vulnerable at the same time.

'But you promised . . .'

'This is where I leave you.' He set down her bags in emphasis. His jaw line tightened obstinately. Women had no mercy . . .

Emma raised herself on tiptoe to kiss him. He swung his head, so that she brushed his cheek.

'Goodbye, then, Josh,' she said, stung.

'Goodbye, Emma. I hope you find what you're looking for in London.'

No, she wanted to cry, this isn't what it's supposed to feel like. Oh God, she wasn't certain about anything anymore. What good was her new position, the whole world for that matter, if Josh weren't there to share it with her . . .?

Her heart echoed hollowly with Josh's retreating footsteps.

The woman at the back of Emma prodded her with a finger. 'You're next.'

But Emma could only hear Josh's heavy goodbye, only see him going from her into the cold spring rain.

In the next moment, to the happy advantage of the people behind her, who could then move up a head, Emma swooped down for her bag, and peeled off from the queue.

She hurried out the electro-gliding doors.

'Josh?' She turned her head, first one way, then another, seeking out her love, as the cold raindrops pelted down.

'Josh!' Her voice was more desperate now.

As the jets roared overhead, the airport ran into a rain-washed blur.

She ran towards the parking lot, impeded by the binding leather of her skirt.

'Josh?'

He had closed his umbrella. He stood with his broad back against the wind.

Heedless of the cars that nosed around the lot snorting warm gusts of carbon monoxide and dotting the area with red lights, she threw down her bag and rushed up to him.

'Oh Josh, oh Josh, I was so afraid you had gone! I was afraid you had left me . . .'

She flew into his arms, half laughing, half weeping in the now driving rain.

'I leave you!' He grasped her by both lower cheeks with his hands, moulding the soft flesh as though he were a sculptor with a new kind of clay. His skin was slick with rain too, and the two of them shivered against one another.

'I surrender,' she laughed into his sweater. The cold drops of water stung her open lips, where he dropped avid if haphazard kisses.

'Like I did a long time ago . . .'

Her hair crinkled like gold foil in the rain. He moved his hand over her head, sensitively, possessively.

'Were you really going to let me go, Josh?' she asked in such a stricken voice that he let out a clap of laughter.

He shook his shaggy head in a spatter of raindrops. 'Don't you know me by now, woman? I would have found a way to get you back. We belong together, and there's nothing either of us can do about it. We might as well accept that now and make this a lot easier on both of us.'

'Josh, Josh, I want to marry you! I know now I can find Emma in loving you!' Joy lit up her face. 'Why didn't I see that before?'

'Because you'd rather make me crazy.'

'I did, didn't I? I'm sorry,' she said, smiling.

This only set off a new cascade of kisses. 'I think I'm going to have to do this periodically, to keep you in your place.'

Then, a sharp light came into his turquoise eyes like the cold green Atlantic waters into the Mexican Gulf, and he looked like the old, restless, passionate Joshua Free.

'Baby, I just decided we're going to take our honeymoon first.'

'Right now?'

'Why not! We're in the perfect place for it.'

Emma tossed her head and began to laugh. She knew that she'd made the right choice. Josh was life. Josh was light.

There was no other possible man for her.

'Okay, Josh, okay! But where will we go?'

'Someplace without newspapers.'

'Or photographic galleries!'

'Right.' Josh snapped his fingers. 'I know just the place. It's an island that hasn't been "discovered" yet. Surrounded by gem-green waters, lush with high palm trees and scented scarlet hibiscus. Set smack in the middle of the Caribbean. The perfect paradise.'

'What paradise is that?'

'It's called the Isle of Free,' he answered slyly, 'and you and I are heading there right now.' He took her by the shoulders and steered her back towards the crowded terminal.

'Whoa, wait!' Emma held her hands up against his chest. 'How do you know we can book a hotel room there?'

He wheeled about and hugged her. 'Umm, you smell so good.' He licked her lips. 'And you taste good. And you . . .'

'Josh!' Emma repeated, laughing again. 'How do you know?'

His eyes gleamed with mischief. 'I know my deliciously sexy wife-to-be because . . .

Emma's eyes came open.

She was alone. In bed.

In London.

The only thing that was real was the rain.

PART V

MORE LIGHT

CHAPTER TWENTY-NINE

'I know my deliciously sexy wife-to-be because . . .'

Emma opened her eyes.

It must be Monday. On Sunday nights she always seemed to dream about Josh at the airport, wafting her away to some paradise in the sun . . . And in that dream, she always had the blessed foresight to know she should turn back at the ticket queue, or be doomed to these disappointing dreams forever after . . .

The alarm hadn't pinged off yet. It was only six a.m. She didn't have to be down at the rehearsal hall until ten. Rolland wouldn't be here to pick her up till a half hour before.

She rolled back against her satin pillow, not even bothering to see how the day was unfolding beyond the white billow of her window curtains.

She knew.

It would be raining. It was always raining in London. Or else it was blowing, a picturesque and chilling fog around the venerable old streets.

Not that she didn't love her adopted city. It had done very well by her – accepting her as one of their musical own. There was her lovely flat in Montpelier Square. There were elegancies like the Floris scent shop on Jermyn St where her change was handed back to her on a mahogany plate lined in burgundy velvet. There was her soon-to-be performed opus at Covent Garden.

And then there was Sir Rolland Blake, world-famous conductor and her would-be paramour.

She had to admit, Sir Rolland had been a find. Artistic,

attentive, undemanding of either her time or her passions, he'd fitted neatly into her sophisticated European lifestyle. Over the last year, especially since rehearsals had begun in earnest, the two of them seemed to be drifting towards some kind of permanent bond, although without much fuss, either way. After the harrowing breakup with Michael Garden, the fiasco with Helmut Rigel, and the close call with Joshua Free, Emma welcomed the control she had when she wasn't especially in love.

Rolland was just perfect for a little communing over Beethoven, a light flirtation. She had yet to ask herself why she couldn't lie still under his hand, whenever their affair seemed to be listing towards the more serious.

If only these damn dreams would stop, she might have a little peace, a taste of happiness! She deserved it, if anyone did. After all, it hadn't been easy to prove herself to the cultured English audiences, or to those maestros of various countries who harboured prejudice against female musicians.

But she'd done it, with a dogged persistence that had surprised even herself.

In the meantime, her Concerto had been a great success.

Now after almost a year of dawn to dusk labour, *Cupid and Psyche,* was completed. And it was good. So good, in fact, that The Royal Festival Hall was opening its gala winter season with her first Choral Symphony.

With fierce pride, she looked over to the thick score on her night table. She'd bled into that music, the dark flow of her inner life. The myth of the archetypal maiden who undergoes the rituals of womanhood for the love of a god, seemed to arise from the deepest layers of her soul. In an inspired stroke, she'd asked the New Wave rock band, *Rebus,* to write the lyrics, so the Symphony should have an even wider appeal.

Emma sat up in bed, and rolled her fingers through the silky hair at her browline.

She might as well get up. There would be no more sleeping this morning.

There was never any sleeping after the Sunday night dream of Josh and the airport, and her dream self crying 'I surrender,' when the joy took root like a flower in her heart.

Sir Rolland Blake pursued the ideal of beauty in his art, as in his life.

Precision had no lesser meaning for the quietly passionate conductor who had once fired a recalcitrant oboeist during a production of *Die Valkyrie* in the Festspielhaus at Bayreuth, and then, cool as ever, resumed the performance.

Every morning before rehearsal of *Cupid & Psyche*, Sir Rolland showed up at Emma's flat in his immaculate Savile Row tweeds.

And, every morning, he proposed rough-and-tumble love for precisely one half hour before going down to the rehearsal hall, separately, as befits the composer and her famed conductor in a civilized British city.

Emma had thus far kept it down to kissing and light play.

'Give me that coda again,' he directed in the clipped tones that were once described by a disgruntled orchestra member as 'full of ground glass'.

When the orchestra had run through the troublesome section, Sir Rolland set down his baton. 'Your playing today has all the clarity and brilliance of a tallowy meat pie.' He levelled the royal blue crystals of his eyes at them.

The sole occupant of the front row in the otherwise empty auditorium, Emma nodded her agreement.

The orchestra played the coda again.

And again.

And once more for good measure, until Sir Rolland Blake felt in his perfectionist's heart that Emma Taylor's musical vision would be aptly translated by his army of men and one woman . . .

'Thank you, gentlemen . . . and madam.' Sir Rolland gave a slight suggestion of a bow, closed his scorebook with a *pfft* and descended the podium, an emblem of grace under pressure.

Emma rose to meet him, full of memories of the night she'd written that coda.

It had been just after she'd arrived in London. Friendless. Starving for news of home. Aching for Josh, until she thought she couldn't stand waking up another day without him . . .

Stubbornly, she'd locked herself in her chilly room, and to the accompaniment of the pipe organ of rising steam, had poured out the majesties of her woman's soul. It had been three o'clock in the morning when the coda floated into her inner ear and out on to the paper, crisscrossed with staffs and clefs and scribbled directions she only halfway believed anyone would ever need to follow.

'Why don't we lunch a little later? I'd like to talk to you about the Act I soprano air.' The maestro smoothed his pants into a perfect crease before sitting. 'Our dear Marya Varushnikov drags on it so desperately. She's afraid of the High C, you know, Emma. I can see her face taking on this sky blue colour every time she gets anywhere near it, and she begins to wheeze like an Alpine funicular an entire measure before.'

Emma gave him an amused look. 'I know what you mean. What do you suggest?'

He made a notation in his scorebook as he spoke. 'Aside from an oxygen tank onstage, I suggest we transpose a half-tone. That way, our sobbing soprano will have a psychological advantage, and we'll be spared the sight of that billowing face every night.'

Emma frowned. 'Down a half-tone. But it wasn't meant . . .'

'Emma, it's either that,' there was a thump as a scrim painted like the night sky was lowered by stagehands in jeans and turtlenecks, 'or we have Madame Varushnikov hauled up on espionage charges and deported some time before the world premiere of your piece.' He delivered this homily with a cool expression on his long, exquisite's face.

'All right, Rolland. We'll try it.'

'Good girl.' He gave her the ghost of a smile. 'You were lovely this morning. Quite lovely.'

Emma studied his hands, surprisingly small, if exceedingly refined for a man of his profession.

'Why can't we be more open about it, Rolland? I feel so prepubescent, sneaking around like this.'

'Unprofessional, Emma, darling.'

The stagelights blinked on and off as lighting technicians experimented with many-coloured gels.

'Shall we go?' He offered his small, correct hand. 'We have precisely one hour and forty-five minutes before the dress rehearsal begins this afternoon.'

No, Emma longed to say with a bright touch of rebellion, let's not. Let's ditch your armoured limo with the stuffed chauffeur and go out into the rain. Let's eat junk food with all the fixings instead of truffle soufflé, and wash it all down with gallons of Coca Cola, in lieu of your vintage claret precisely served at the bloody temperature of the bloody room!

'Yes,' she said with a sigh. 'Let's go.'

The Royal Festival Hall blazed with the excitement of an English-language Oratorio world première.

For a whole night before, Emma Taylor had devoted herself to meditative exercises aimed at serenity in the hour of challenge.

For an entire day before, Sir Rolland Blake had drilled the weary orchestra on Emma's composition, until their mouths and fingers played airs, over and over, in their sleep.

Understandably their lovemaking that morning had to be postponed . . .

In a haze of white chiffon that bared one shoulder, a diamond clip ashimmer in the moon glow of her hair, she could easily have portrayed the maiden who won the heart of Love.

Certainly, her hands, at least, were cold as a marble goddess' at curtain. After all, in the best tradition of dress rehearsals, theirs had been an unmitigated disaster. Cues missed. Tempo dragging. Madame Varushnikov with the seeds of a sore throat . . .

But in the end, Emma was driven down to the stage,

like a sailor to the sea, by thunderous waves of applause. In her pristine white gown, she'd bowed to the gala London crowd, with the joyful sounds of her woman's spirit still vibrating in the air around them.

She was happy at last.

Emma had shimmered in the dusk of the theatre, with an inscrutable light. The fire that sparked from her fingers as she played, had skimmed off the walls and shot Josh through the heart like an arrow of pure gold.

He remembered that she smelled like wild strawberries. In his dream, he licked the creaminess of her skin. Night after night, he would smother her in roses, give her a drink of spiced wine from his own mouth, draw her down to the ocean's edge where they would bask in warm, clear water, where her hair would fan out from her head like strands of Chinese silk. The fantasies were endless.

And that's all they were. Fantasies. Josh Free would never try to lure Emma Taylor down from the heights of her new life, or presume to cut short this creative spree. He loved her too much. So he'd come to London, incognito – just to see her, to hear her music which was most wonderful, strong and sweet and fresh as she'd always seemed to the man who loved her.

He'd closed his eyes to better hear the music – a waft of violins like the voices of women in love – and still he could see her in her ankle-sweeping white dress, as soft as a morning kiss.

She would never know he'd been here.

Tomorrow he would fly back home.

Tonight though, Emma, the music, were his own once more. In silence. In secret. As though he had no right to love.

In the next day's papers, the critics howled with delight.

'Emma Taylor's new oratorio, *Cupid & Psyche*, is a work of fearless beauty, sheer lyricism. The melodic intensity is a refreshing and welcome change from the electronic ditherings of latter years.'

'*Cupid & Psyche* . . . the workings of love among gods and women, the psychology of romance in a musical tongue.'

'Emma Taylor has a triumph! Her symphonic myth transposed to the subways and penthouses of New York City rings true in every bar. The New Wave rock group, *Rebus* has penned a stunning libretto, full of twentieth century power and rage.'

Even Marya Varushnikov reached her lowered 'High C'.

The composer had startled everyone at the opening night party by falling upon Sir Rolland Blake and kissing his mouth in plain view.

It was noted then that Maestro Blake seemed amused, as if to say, 'What can you expect – she's American,' although he looked not at all displeased.

If Josh could only have been here – Emma though so many times that hectic night, surrounded by a circle of admirers, receiving plaudits like roses tossed in the air – to tease her down to earth with his basic blue eyes, to bring her back up with one quiet nod, full of love and burning pride.

Unhappily, his gilt-edged invitation to the debut had been returned to her, unopened.

Sir Rolland's call came the next day, around noon, which was the time when Emma, with her champagne headache, was able to arouse herself sufficiently from bed to answer the phone that had been ringing off the hook all morning.

They'd been invited to play the Aldeburgh Festival in Suffolk. And when they'd come back from their provincial tour, an American debut in the Spring.

The Metropolitan Opera House in New York.

The Jackpot.

Emma was suddenly wide awake, her mind a clear crystal.

'Fantastic!' In the excitement she almost missed the next piece of news Sir Rolland had in store for her.

'Darling, it seems you had an eminent visitor in the box seat last night.'

'I did? Who, the Prince of Wales?' She was belting on her robe.

'No. It was Josh Free.'

She was silent, guarded. Then: 'How do you know?'

'He was recognized leaving the theatre by one of my American friends. Oh he was definitely there, darling.'

'Why are you telling me this, Rolland?' He knew the story of her affair with Josh. He wasn't supposed to talk about him like this.

'Just wanted to give you a chance to change things around, if you wish.'

Was he waiting for her to answer . . .? 'That's ridiculous,' she sounded more confident than she felt. 'I have no desire to change anything around.'

'It's good to hear you say that, Emma. Pick you up at the regular time?'

'Yes. See you.'

She clicked down the phone, sat at the edge of her bed, her head whirling.

So Josh had been there all along! As though she'd somehow called him to her, as though he'd known how much she wanted him there.

Yes, but *how* did she want him? She felt as though she'd been split down the middle. She loved him, she loved him not . . .

The sense of free fall, of losing control fluttered, ghostly, inside her. She couldn't tangle with the issue of Josh Free and his overbearing love right now. She was just beginning to fly on her own power. She couldn't have him pinning her wings back, dragging her down . . .

So here was one small detail of her great good fortune on which she hadn't counted.

The Metropolitan Opera House happened to be in New York.

Michelle Smith was in New York.

And Josh Free was in New York.

When she packed her bags, she resolved then and there, she would pack light.

After all, she'd be straight home to London in the fall . . .

CHAPTER THIRTY

The jungle was a dense green shimmer. Clouds of flies buzzed all the time, in the roads, over the faces of the 'missing'.

At the wheel of the jeep, Josh Free had shaded his own face from the bludgeon of the sun for which he had not been prepared. Here his clothes were always damp, and he never felt clean. The heat weighed down your lungs like stones, the sun tortured your eyes, as you rode along the dusty back roads in search of the camera's truth.

It had taken him a day to identify the smell that hung in the air.

It was death . . .

Josh had been the first of his fact-finding party to see the unidentified troops marching the nun out of her van, into the bushes.

He bounded up from the jeep.

'Stop,' he'd cried, 'American Press, American Press,' waving at the hand-held camera in his colleague's grip.

With the sick intimacy of violence, the soldier had lovingly aimed at the jeep with his Uzzi machine gun, implanted a black boot on either side of the narrow road, and sprayed bullets out of his stuttering weapon.

Josh's arm stopped one of the shells.

A red hot fragment of the sun lodged in his arm.

Pain splintered his consciousness into a million hot spiralling pieces, and he'd held up the earth with his hand as it fell on top of him, like the shovelled clods of a grave.

After Emma, Doria and T.J. who had religiously had Josh to dinner every Wednesday night in their cosy apartment, felt that Josh had become morose and more his heroic self, a persona in which he traditionally took refuge when things got too rough.

He'd begun to run his newspaper with a crusader's

dangerous fire. He was reckless, too reckless in his treatment of political hot potatoes in print, and his personal forays into the worlds's terrorist jungles.

'Stay at home a couple of nights a week,' T.J. told him over the stink of cigars, after one of Doria's interesting dinners. 'You don't personally have to hold up the world on your shoulders.'

A woman, Doria had been more to the point. 'Don't go to Santa Maria, Josh. They're killing people there.'

Josh had laughed it off, and lit up another cigar.

The next they heard of him, he was headlining his own paper, a martyr to his cause.

'We told him not to go,' T.J. kept muttering lovingly on their way home from the best hospital in town. 'We told him not to go . . . heroic fool!'

'I don't know, I thought he looked kind of dashing in his black-silk sling.' Although they'd both had a scare, Doria tried to joke T.J. out of it.

'Oh you . . . you think he's some kind of god . . .'

Doria raised her eyebrows. 'Still jealous?'

'Who me? Never.'

'I love you.' Doria planted a wet kiss behind his right ear.

'Me too. You think he'll be all right?'

'Of course. The doctor said he must have a tough hide, or else he wouldn't have survived that attack.'

'I guess it comes from chewing bullets all these years at the *Globe*.'

'Umm.' The taxi pulled into their block. 'What do you think, T.J., does Emma Taylor know about this?'

'Emma Taylor!' T.J. went into high dudgeon whenever the name was mentioned. Luckily, it was rarely mentioned. 'Emma Taylor is a fool too.'

'But maybe if she knew . . .'

'Forget it. That's all over with. Josh would never forgive you if you stuck your pretty nose in where it doesn't belong. Hey,' he exclaimed, 'what's that?'

'What?' Alarmed, Doria drew out a make-up mirror from her purse, and stared at her nose. 'Something on my face?'

'Uh huh. This.' He leaned over and gave her nose a swift kiss. 'That's what your nose is for, in case you'd forgotten.'

'I haven't forgotten.'

'Now no more Emma Taylor. You promise?'

'I promise.' She had her fingers crossed, as if T.J. didn't know.

Following her triumphal tour of the provinces, Emma returned, briefly, to London. She had already flown out of Heathrow on a nightflight to the States when Doria's letter reached the Royal Institute addressed to their former, now famous, violin instructor.

In New York, intensive work on the mounting of the Met's production of *Cupid* soaked up all of Emma's time and talents.

She had just enough leisure for rushed dinner conferences with Sir Rolland, who had been asked to guest-conduct, and little else in the way of social pleasures, or quiet reflection.

It was better that way. No memories of Josh imperilled her peace. No more confusing every broad-shouldered brigand of a man on the street with a certain lost love. And there was no time for that good cry she'd felt coming on, ever since her plane touched down in New York . . .

Only when the last bar of the last rehearsal had been played, could she sit back and reflect on the rising star that had led her back to the Met – this time as a triumphant composer.

For she felt she would be triumphant. She would take New York by the heart, as she had taken London before it.

Of course, there would be change again. She'd undergone it enough times to know its smell in the air, like snow about to fall on the city.

Fame. Artistic fulfilment. The greatest metropolis in the world spread out at her feet, its golden door flung open to her, the composer of a 'modern masterpiece' in song.

She had a right to be proud, having painstakingly, piece by piece, constructed an exemplary Emma Taylor, wanting, in this, her third lifetime, to be in perfect control. Thus she had succeeded splendidly in everything but love.

'What the hell is this?' T.J. ripped open the letter addressed to Emma Taylor, postmarked London. Upon skimming its contents, his flat face fell. 'Doria, get in here!'

She padded in from the bathroom with a moss green towel wound, turban-style, around her head. 'What did you say, T.J.? I had the water running.'

He thrust the letter under her nose. 'You promised me you wouldn't.'

She went purple. 'I know but I thought I could do some . . .'

'Okay.' His hands were on his hips, and he was dancing on his toes like a boxer. 'Okay, Doria, what else do you lie to me about?'

Her mouth dropped open. 'T.J.!'

'Come on, there must be other things . . .' He snapped the letter with his index finger.

'You've got your nerve! I've never lied to you, never!'

The boyish insecurities he'd tried so hard to keep under wraps were now spilling out all over. 'What really happened between you and Josh that night I called here, huh? Tell me the truth now, Doria.'

The look in Doria's expressive dark eyes passed visibly along the spectrum from hurt to fury. 'All right, that's it.' She bolted from the sunny living room, threw open the closet door, and grabbed T.J.'s overnight bag. Cramming it full of underwear and whatever else came into her trembling hand, she ran back to the living room and hurled it at the stomach of her astonished husband.

'Get out!'

'What?'

'I said get out of here!'

'But I live here.'

'Not anymore you don't!'

Doria stood behind the open door. 'If you don't go this minute I'm going to scream at the top of my lungs until the neighbours come up and lynch you . . .'

'Doria . . .' T.J. cast around the room as though appealing for outside help.

'Doria, what about the baby? The children?' His eyes gleamed with the certainty that this time-honoured argument would sway her. 'What will you tell them when they come home from school today?'

'I don't have to tell them anything.' T.J.'s brightness faded. 'They'll know. They'll know that you're the most pigheaded, insufferable little twit in the world and that no woman could be expected to put up with you for more than five minutes – much less a lifetime!'

'Doria, honeypot . . .' T.J. took a courageous step towards her.

'Don't come any closer, unless you want me to . . .' her eyes combed the room, 'dump this ashtray on your head!' She brandished the object menacingly in her right hand.

'See, I knew it, I knew I shouldn't have married a crazy woman! There's no air in the windmills of her mind, I said to myself. But no, I had to go and take the plunge, hoping against hope that for the sake of the children, you'd shape up, act sane for a change . . .'

'T.J., I'm warning you . . .'

Quivering with righteous indignation, T.J. clasped his roly-poly bag to his stomach and quit the apartment. He muttered blackly to himself all the way down to the street.

Alone, upstairs, Doria broke into belated tears.

'Josh!' Doria held open the door to her unkempt apartment. She hadn't had the heart for housecleaning, since T.J.'d gone. 'Come on in.'

'I hope you don't mind my dropping in like this.' Josh tried not to notice that Doria had two different shoes on, and that her lovely dark hair was tumbling out of its pins. Poor Doria. Things were worse than he'd ever suspected . . .

'No, not at all,' she said woodenly. 'We're . . . I'm always glad to see you.'

Josh stepped in, nursing his arm in the sling made out of silk. He looked around, slyly. 'Seems kind of quiet in here today.'

'Yes, well the children are out playing. The baby's asleep. Saturday morning, you know,' she replied, wilfully misunderstanding him.

'I meant T.J. He does kind of clutter up a place. When he's not around, it seems, I don't know . . . less alive.'

Doria busied herself collecting ashtrays.

'Any Ring-a-Lings?'

'For you. Anytime.' Doria cracked the flimsiest of smiles. She made for the kitchen, her stride showing a definite wobble, as her heels were of different heights.

She teetered back out with a plate of cellophane-wrapped Ring-a-Lings.

'Look, Doria, we're old friends,' Josh said while she searched for a place on her toy-cluttered coffee table to set down the tray. 'Can I be honest with you?'

Doria had finally given up and laid the tray on the carpeted floor.

'Doria!' Josh cried in a paroxysm of frustration. For a whole week now, his newspaper had resembled an armed camp. The tension between estranged husband and wife was so dense you could eat on it. If T.J. and Doria McShane didn't get back together soon, the *Globe* was going to come unglued.

'No.' Doria said, tightlipped. 'Coffee?' She had resumed her search for soiled ashtrays.

'Why are you doing this to T.J.?' Josh folded his muscular arms and rested against the back of the nubby-textured sofa.

'He needed to be taught a lesson, Josh, about trusting the people you love.'

'Fine, I can see that. But don't you think you've been a little bit hard on the man?'

Doria had run out of ashtrays. She commenced to pick up lint from her amber shag rug. 'Man? He was jealous, like a little boy.'

'Only because he's crazy in love with you, Doria. People in love don't act out of logic. They act out of a kind

302

of divinity. It can't be argued with or explained.' Gently, he stooped down to the carpet and raised her to her feet. 'Come on, I know you're suffering in there, why don't you tell him to come home?'

She shook her head, but Josh could see the sparkle of tears in her beautiful forest-brown eyes.

'He's got to learn . . .'

'Doria.' Josh held her chin steady with his thumb. 'Do yourself a favour. Call him.'

'Oh Josh!' Doria came into his arms. 'It's been so awful . . .'

'I know,' he soothed, 'I know.'

'Why do we do these things to ourselves . . .? I don't understand.'

'If I knew the answer to that . . .' He stopped short of what was on his mind, and in his heart.

'You'd be in London today . . .' Straightforward Doria finished it for him.

'I'm afraid so.'

She drew away from Josh so that she could look into his brimming eyes. 'Why don't you take a piece of your own advice? Make a phone call.'

He shrugged. 'I wish it were that simple, Doria. But if you recall, it was Emma who left me.' It was hard to say her name, as though she were a mountain he'd failed to climb.

A lull in the conversation gave Doria the chance to make a fool of herself. 'She didn't want to, Josh,' she told him oracularly.

He gave her a lingering look. 'What makes you say that?'

The brazen toss of her head, the brightening in her eye told him what he wanted to know. This was only a clumsy gesture of good faith. Doria didn't know Emma Taylor's mind anymore than he, or for that matter, Emma did – for all her dazzling womanhood.

'You're a good friend.' He looked grim. 'And now I'd better get going. I have some high policy to discuss on the tennis court.'

'Josh.' Doria held out a restraining hand. 'I don't even know where T.J. is.'

303

'You don't?' He seemed astonished. 'Doria, he's been crashing with me all this time. I thought you knew.'

'With you?' She looked at him blankly.

'Uh huh. Why the hell do you think I want you two back together so much?' A smile flickered in his handsome face. 'Can't stand having his sour puss the first thing I see every morning . . .'

Doria pursed her lips, thoughtfully. 'All right, tell him to come home.' She was all business now. 'On the condition that he never question me again on matters of faith and morals.'

'That's a tall order.' He zipped up his tan windbreaker.

'Those are my conditions,' she stated, a solid block of stoney will.

'I'll tell him. He'll be home for lunch,' he tossed this last piece of news over his shoulder.

When he was out of sight, Doria broke out in smiles.

Now if only she could get through to Josh about Emma Taylor . . .

CHAPTER THIRTY-ONE

In sweet anticipation of T.J.'s homecoming Doria had filed her nails, washed and brushed her lovely hair into two long ebony wings, and donned her best pair of designer jeans, topping it all off with the oversized man's white shirt that T.J. delighted in peeling of her body.

Then she sat, crosslegged and demure, in her sun-washed living room, waiting for her husband to come home and put things to rights.

An hour later, when he still hadn't come, nervous energy impelled her to grab her envelope purse, leave her baby with the neighbour and bolt out to the supermarket around the corner where she could lose herself in a phantasmagoria of foodstuffs. She soon felt a junk food fit coming on as she entered the store full of dazed Saturday morning marketers. Ring-a-Lings might do it. Or one of those Italian chocolate bars with the hazelnuts that give such a satisfying crunch under the grinders . . .

Stop it, Doria. You're compulsive. Get a hold of yourself.

With a will of its own, her shopping cart headed for the circus colours of the confectionery section. Just in the nick of time, she swerved off into fresh produce, where elderly women with plastic net shopping bags were bobbing up and down over the seas of fruits and vegetables, like lures in a fish pond.

Doria had intended to go straight to the sweet potatoes, but the aisles were so packed, she'd had to start all the way down at the fruit end.

A Seurat of blueberries, the colour of her black eyes. The red bumps of the apple bin. A pyramid of oranges, dyed to blaze like the sun.

Doria reached over to squeeze the fruit.

A hand clapped down on top of hers.

She spun around.

'I like tangerines a lot better.' It was T.J. in a plaid bowtie and lean, pegged jeans of retro fifties style.

'I don't.' Doria calmly went on squeezing the oranges.

Three tangerines went sailing into her shopping cart like a juggler's bright rubber balls. Nonchalantly, T.J. tossed one of them from behind his back.

'I said I like tangerines.'

Doria glared at him, but made no perceivable move to unburden the cart of the disputed fruit.

The wheels of the cart squeaked as Doria pushed on towards the sweet potatoes. T.J. kept up alongside.

'Josh said you wanted to see me,' he mumbled, his grey eyes hooded, like a hawk's.

'He did?'

'Yes, he did.'

Doria was fishing out and bagging the plumpest potatoes with gusto. 'He must have been mistaken.' Twisting the plastic bag like the neck of a chicken, she dropped it into her cart.

T.J. stood in her dust, as the cart rattled off. He shook with a sneeze or two out of sheer frustration.

By the time he'd collected his wits, Doria was turning into the artificially fragrant detergent and soaps aisle. She had nothing to buy there. It was just something to do until T.J. caught up with her again.

Delicately, she spun her cart wheels around a broken relish jar and its emerald contents.

T.J. accosted her at the bleaches.

'You didn't tell Josh you wanted to see me?' He was out of breath, and looking grim.

'Well,' replied Doria, poking her head into the depleted shelf, in search of her favourite brand, 'what if I did?'

'What if you did! What if you did!' Doria could tell without even looking back that wisps of steam would be curling out of his nostrils right about now. 'If you did, maybe we can save our marriage, our home! And if you didn't . . .' He pushed his hand down into her cart, and came up with the trio of tangerines. 'I'm going to take these tangerines and . . .'

'Well, I did.'

'What did you say?'

'Nothing. I didn't say anything.'

'I thought you said "you did".'

By now, isolated shoppers who happened to wander into the aisle, were eavesdropping shamelessly on their domestic dispute.

'Okay,' Doria said maddeningly, 'there's no need to beat a dead horse. I told Josh you could come home. On one condition.'

'Who are you to make conditions?' T.J. blurted.

Doria's eyes snapped. 'Goodbye, T.J.' She took firm hold of the bar on the front of the cart, like the helm of a ship.

'Wait, all right! On what condition?'

'On condition that you never doubt my honesty again,' Doria insisted primly.

'That's easy enough.' T.J. looked out from his sleepy eyes. 'What made you give me another chance?'

'Two reasons.' Doria ticked them off on her fingers as the cart glided to check-out. 'The children are sort of used to having you around . . .'

'Like their gerbils, right?' T.J. said in a grumpy voice.

'Right. And secondly . . .' Doria plopped her items down on the check-out counter as she spoke. They rode on the rubber raft to the waiting hands of the check-out girl. 'You do have a way of keeping the bed warm in winter.'

'That's it? Don't I keep something else warm?' He slid his arms around her waist.

Doria's nostrils flared. She felt warm as mink. 'Maybe.'

'You're a real heartbreaker, you know that, Doria Sevenstars McShane?'

She wriggled around in his arms. 'Yes, I know. Isn't it wonderful?'

Just then, T.J. gave a sneeze, the last gasp of his ten year frustration.

'God bless you!' Doria said.

'She already has . . .'

They kissed.

'That's ten forty-two,' the check-out girl said, bored.

They didn't even hear.

307

Splat! The ball sailed over the net at a killing angle.

The woman with long tan legs beneath her tennis white, bounded forward and whacked it with a man's tensile strength.

'Son of a . . . .!' With one arm still in a sling, Josh ran in for the ball careening towards him. He barely touched it with the tip of his expensive racket. 'You weren't supposed to get that!' he shouted across the court.

'Hah!' The woman threw back her head with a wild laugh, showing a dash of white in her bronzed face.

She spun crazily towards the net, in pursuit of the tennis ball. But she wasn't quite in time. 'Damn . . .' She let out a blue string of swear words.

'Game!' Josh called, triumphant.

'I want a rematch,' she said, a bad loser, intoxicated by competition.

Josh released her hand at the net. He folded his white towel around his neck. 'Whew,' he said, wiping the back of his hand across a forehead that glistened with sweat, 'you gave me quite a scare. I actually thought I was going to lose.'

'You almost did,' she said, without a shred of modesty.

'I know. I know.' He stopped to look at her superb form. Tall, gently muscular, blonde hair drawn back in a band, stripped for action on the court.

She was zipping her racket into its navy blue Adidas case.

'So, will you join my news team in Central America now?'

'I told you, I never do business with a man I haven't slept with. Too many unknown variables.'

They walked towards the showers together.

'That can be easily remedied.' His turquoise eyes gleamed like polished stone.

She drew him into the blue-tiled room and closed the door. 'I was hoping you'd say that.' Laying the clean, flat palm of her hand against his chest, she unbuttoned his shirt from the bottom up. 'That's what I like about private clubs. They're so private.'

'Here?' Josh asked, taken off guard.

'Here.' She trailed the blade of her tongue from the top of his breastbone to the navel. 'Then we'll talk.'

'That was the most refreshing shower I've ever had.' Freshly dressed in his stonewashed jeans and white tuxedo shirt, Josh met Annette outside the baths. 'What about the news team?'

'You do get down to business.'

He admired the way she moved in her trim khaki slacks and white China silk blouse that plunged down to her navel.

'So do you.'

'Umm, yes, but my business is so much more fun.'

They stood flagging a cab outside the Club.

'Tell me something, Josh.'

'Anything.'

'Are you married?'

'No.'

'In love?'

'No.' He'd hesitated only a fraction of a second, but she'd caught it.

'Who is she?'

'What are you talking about?'

'The woman you're in love with.'

'There is no woman.'

'But your eyes . . . when I asked you about her . . . they were like deep water. They changed . . .'

'A trick of the light.'

'Hmm.' She studied him, frankly. 'All right, I won't keep you in suspense any longer. I'll try it out. If I don't like it, I'll just fly home. No contracts.'

'It's a deal.'

'Fine.'

A checkered cab swerved up. Josh watched the swing of her long legs into the car. He rested his good arm on the rim of rolled-down window. 'When will I see you again?'

'I've been invited to a party for a concert premiere tonight, an old friend of mine is conducting.'

Josh blanched. 'Do we have to sit through an opera?'

'No,' she showed her teeth, 'of course not. But I do have to put in an appearance at the party. Old flame's sake and all.'

'What time shall I pick you up?'

'Seven.'

His hand pressed against his back, as he straightened up. 'I'll see you then.'

She blew a kiss through her fingers in the back of the cab, then promptly forgot him, till seven.

The New York music critics were in the house.

From where she sat, Emma could see their pens scratching across tiny white note pads.

'Oh God, please let them like it! Emma prayed. If inside, she was all opening-night turmoil, outside she looked tall and cool as a summer drink in her *creme de menthe* silk gown, one scoop of shoulder left tantalizingly bare. Her pale blonde hair, grown long again, was threaded with the sheerest net of pink freshwater pearls.

It had been left to Sir Rolland to coax the composer back to her seat after the first act intermission, so jittery was she about the reception of her work.

She needn't have been.

By the end of that interminable night, Emma Taylor was a bona fide star in the music firmament.

There she stood, in the grand ballroom of the Plaza Hotel, envied and adored and scintillating with fame at the centre of cultural New York. Celebrity yawned before her like Aladdin's glittering cave. She had only to reach out her hands and oh what felicities might be hers . . .

To the casual observer, Emma Taylor now rode on the top of the world. A rare talent, even bankable, beautiful beyond words and courted by the stellar names in contemporary classical music. What more could any woman ask . . .?

That no one knew her well enough to answer that question was the very crux of her pain.

The ballroom was flickering with hundreds of pink and green candles. A haze of spring flowers hung over the festively draped tables. Unknown, she looked down at her

310

drink, so that none of her many admirers could read the disappointment in her eyes. Pure sadness engulfed her like a song.

What did she really have? Where were the people who could have shared this evening's triumph with her?

Dr Beckstein would have been here if he could. But he was out of town with other responsibilities, other promises to keep.

And Gregor, dear Gregor was gone. He'd slipped away quietly one night while she was so busy conquering London. His heart, they'd said, had just stopped beating.

Now she would never forgive herself – for the waste of his friendship and the music they could have made.

A last regret cut even deeper . . .

So many times after a performance, when the applause had died down to a memory, Emma wondered how her life would have been if she'd stayed with Josh, worked harder to make love last.

Why was it that men could have it all – marriage, a brilliant career, children, while women were left to make a devastating choice?

Why was love synonomous with suffering in a woman's world?

'Emma, darling, congratulations!' Alexander Bartok pumped her hand up and down. 'We're all so proud of you!'

Emma shifted into the party mode, with facility. 'Thank you, Alex. You and your cousin were the first ones to believe in me when I came to New York. You gave me my first . . .' She paused in mid-phrase, distracted by the dramatic entrance of an athletic-looking woman in a black silk tuxedo with satin lapels and heavy geometric earrings of turquoise and beaten silver, that swayed when she walked. Her hair was a sleek yellow cap, lying close to the delicate skull and, casting into relief her exquisitely etched features . . . the long mouth, the aquiline nose, like the head on a gold medal.

Her deep, sensuous laugh rippled out of her chest, a diapason of female confidence.

'Annette Welles.' Alex looked envious. 'The highest

paid newscaster in the history of television. They say
she's close to being the richest woman in America too.
And the most ambitious.'

'She's very attractive.'

'In a gymnastic sort of way.' Alexander Bartok made
no attempt to hide his own curiosity and craned his
neck to see better. 'I wonder whom she's with tonight?
They say she only goes after the most fabulous men in
the world. It's a kind of hobby with her.'

Just then Sir Rolland Blake, a distinguished figure in
black and white, was receiving the woman's embraces
with his usual *sang froid.*

'Must be a friend of the conductor's,' Alex observed.
'Hey, I need a re-fill. Would you like . . .?' He tilted
his empty glass towards her.

'No thanks, Alex. You go ahead. I'll catch up later.'

'Good enough.' He pressed a kiss on the space above
her cheek. 'You've made it, Emma Taylor. You're at
the top. Be happy. You never know when it'll all go
. . . poof!' He threw up his hand.

Emma stared after him. After the personal losses
she'd suffered, that kind of reversal would have no
power to shock her.

When she turned back, none other than Annette
Welles was brushing by, with her boyish, leggy stride.
She gave off the scent of stellar success and boundless ambition. Is that my scent now too? Emma
wondered . . .

'Annette, wait. There's someone I want you to meet.'

The dark timbre of the voice electrified Emma. The
trip wire of her emotions went off with the touch of a
man's hand on her shoulder.

Josh . . . oh Josh . . .

She swung into his pirate's eyes, full of blue light.

'Congratulations.' He smiled at her.

'Thank you.' She smiled back at her Josh, with his
wound bound in silk, pitch dark as the day they'd parted. He must have seen her staring.

'I was in a country where they don't particularly like
journalists,' he explained.

312

To think he'd been hurt – without her even knowing about it!

She stormed at herself for a failure of love.

She felt ashamed.

She should have felt it happening inside, a break, a throb. Well, she was bleeding for him now.

Oh, Josh, smile for me again with those wicked, know-it-all eyes! Show me that cool macho edge, so urban, so sharp, so much camouflage for the loving man inside.

How did I even think of letting you go?

How can I tell you how much I need you back?

And now there was that intriguingly beautiful woman in men's clothes. Had Josh sought a new love as different from Emma Taylor as two women can be? She took some comfort in the thought: if he'd needed to do something like that, it meant he hadn't been able to uproot her memory from his heart. Yet.

Annette Welles stood at Josh's side, leaning against his shoulder with a proprietary aura.

'Whom do we have here?'

'This is Emma Taylor. The composer,' he added at her blank look. Since they hadn't even been to the performance, Josh had only just discovered the name of the guest of honour. It was strange coming to Emma from another woman's bed, the smell of her still on his skin . . .

'Oh.' Annette looked her up and down, and Emma felt herself being computed by a micro-chip mind. 'I like seeing women break through in fields that have been traditionally closed to them.'

'I understand you're something of a breakthrough yourself,' Emma replied, too brightly.

'Something of . . .' Annette was rapidly losing interest. It was men who held her attention, not other women. 'Well, you know I didn't have any lunch today. We were . . . shall we say, otherwise engaged.' She flirted with her eyes. 'That caviar looks possible, I think we'd better get over there before it's snorted up by all these starving artists. Come on, Josh.'

After only the slightest hesitation, Josh nodded his

313

head at Emma, then broke away, leaving his former lover startled to see how much he'd changed.

Oh, the old, inexhaustible energy still blazed within him, but it had been turned down, refined to a white glow. The air around him was dense now with frustrated longing – longing for what, for whom?

Jealousy gnawed. That woman, touching him with familiar hands, holding him, possessing him at night, as though he were hers, as though Emma hadn't burned through his soul like a flame . . .

Annette Welles was poring over the buffet table. 'There's that trick of the light again.' All of a sudden she looked like a journalist.

'You know,' Josh countered, still cool, 'you're beautiful when you're nosey.'

'You're sexy when you're in love.'

'Who's in love? You've got it wrong.'

'Have I?'

'Come back to my apartment tonight and I'll show you.'

Annette balanced her plate on the edge of the long table. 'Why wait till later? Show me now.'

'Excellent idea.' His eyes never wavered. She was insatiable.

Emma tried her best not to see the most highly paid woman in America, and the man she herself still wanted, needed, loved so much she'd fled across an ocean to escape him, leaving the party together, so obviously in love they couldn't even wait for the night to end, for their private time to come.

At great personal cost, she recalled what those private times with Josh Free had been like – the uplifting of the senses, a call to ecstasy, a home in one man's arms. Oh why had she let him go . . .?

'There you are, darling. I've just been telling Leonard about the Varushnikov, and he had the most amusing story about the original rehearsals for *Candide* . . .'

Emma was swept into the warm circle of their interest, by Sir Rolland's arm, his exuberance.

Obediently, Emma drifted away from the light that Josh

314

seemed to trail behind him, into another, harsher kind of light, the light of new celebrity.

After all, that was what she'd always wanted.

Wasn't it?

She had looked so fragile, so lost in that sea of glitter. His Emma . . .

He'd forgotten how those violet eyes opened up like a morning flower when she was happy, when she was his.

He'd forgotten how her body was shaped to his own, the perfect fit; how she'd maddened him with her mysteries, and touched him with her unexpected strength.

He'd forgotten what it felt like to love a woman who loved him.

Annette stirred in the bed next to Josh, one long leg swung over his.

Emma, her name played on his senses like a poem, filled his head with psalms . . .

Emma Taylor had been placed in the uncomfortable position of having to celebrate a night, which, for private reasons, she would really rather forget.

Somehow she had endured the endless line of handshakes and kisses in the air. Amidst the bobbing of cocktail hats and the flash of pinkie rings, she was given the illusion of warm friends, of easy love.

At least now that she'd seen Josh Free again, face to face, she knew it was just an illusion.

Only Josh had substance. Only he could save her from the lie of total independance. And she from the lie that he'd got over Emma Taylor, and the hold she had on his heart.

One dip into those deep-sea eyes and she had known what she'd been trying to hide: that Emma Taylor and Joshua Free were lovers in the grain, beyond whatever hurt they could inflict on one another, beyond whatever lies they'd whispered to themselves when freedom seemed dearer than love.

It burned her, oh it burned her deep inside to think that he could walk out the door with that woman, without feeling a psychic rupture, the best of him left behind . . .

'Darling, I'll take you home.' Sir Rolland held her glittery white shawl, and rested it lightly on her shoulders. 'In triumph.' One ash blonde eyebrow arched imperiously. 'You don't look very much like the conquering heroine. What's wrong?'

The candles blaze was only a whisper of light. Busboys ran about whisking serving plates and glasses away. Silverware clanked into bins. Slowly, it dawned on Emma that she and Sir Rolland were among the last of the party guests in the great room.

'It's always like this, the first time you share your music. Bittersweet. Like your first lovemaking,' he told her kindly. 'You'll get used to it.'

Emma nodded, preoccupied, her eyes the colour of sea mists.

They walked out into the soft spring night, where a streamlined limousine was waiting.

Sir Rolland lifted his languid hand to help Emma inside. When he was about to get in beside her, Emma spoke.

'Rolland, it's not going to work.'

'Hmm?'

'We don't work. As lovers I mean. We're superb as colleagues.'

'I don't understand, Emma.'

'I'm going back to England, Rolland, but not with you. Now do you understand?'

He had the grace to look surprised. 'Emma, you're just tired tonight. We'll talk about it in the morning.'

Emma bridled. His tone was vaguely reminiscent of Patrice Garden . . . 'No. I know what I need now, Rolland. Tonight just helped me see it in a clear light.'

Rolland stood tall, always lordly, always precise. 'This is goodbye then, Emma.' She had the feeling he would like to have orchestrated their parting himself. She was sorry she hadn't given him the chance. Tonight, she was sorry about so many things . . .

'Yes, goodbye.' She shut the limousine door with a metallic thud, and he backed away. 'Goodbye.'

The car zoomed off, with Emma inside.

It seemed as if she was always saying 'goodbye'.

CHAPTER THIRTY-TWO

The drizzly day of her departure from New York, Emma sat waiting in the splendid gloom of her hotel suite for Josh Free's call.

The first hour, five a.m., passed swiftly enough with Emma imagining Josh's step in the hall, Josh towering in the door, Josh proposing.

The second hour went more slowly in a review of mistakes and passionate regrets . . . about coaxing Josh to drive her to Boston, manoeuvring a reunion with Michael Garden when Josh so obviously hated the whole idea, forsaking Josh for London and the chimera of fame.

By the third hour, Emma burned with impatience and anxiety. What if Josh didn't come at all?

At eight forty-five Emma Taylor was at the airport gates with her khaki travel suit, red hot cinch and shoes, designer luggage and doubts.

It was raining, hard. Emma felt she must be the loneliest woman in the world.

And the most foolish.

She wanted to cry out loud, this is not what success is supposed to feel like. Oh God, she wasn't certain about anything anymore. What good was her new position, the whole world, if the man she loved wasn't there to share it with her?

At a maddening crawl, her limo moved up in the snaking line of cars. The chauffeur let her out to the rain-washed pavement with her bags.

In the check-in queue, she couldn't help turning and looking for signs of Josh Free, for the silver Jaguar to pull up at the kerb outside the plate glass doors.

The woman behind her prodded with a finger. 'You're next.'

But Emma could only hear Josh's promise: 'I'll help you

317

find the woman you were,' could only see him going from her with that sleek maneater into the night . . .

In the next moment, to the happy advantage of the passengers behind her who could then move up a head, Emma stooped down for her bag and peeled off from the queue.

She hurried out the electro gliding doors.

'Josh?' She turned her head, first this way, then that, seeking out her lover.

'Josh!' Her voice was more desperate now.

With the roar of the jets overhead, the airport ran into a rain-washed blur.

All of this seemed uncannily familiar to Emma as though she'd done these very things, thought these desperate thoughts before . . . The dream!

She ran towards the parking field, impeded by the binding fabric of her skirt.

'Josh?'

He had closed his umbrella. He stood with his broad back against the wind.

Heedless of the cars that nosed around the lot, snorting warm gusts of carbon monoxide and dotting the whole area with red lights, she threw down her bag and ran up to him.

'Oh Josh, I was so afraid you had gone! I was afraid you had left me . . .'

She flew into the crook of his arm, half laughing, half weeping in the now driving rain.

'I leave you!' It was only then she knew he was really there, and that she was safe. He grasped her lower cheeks with his hand, moulding the soft flesh as though he were a sculptor with a new kind of clay. His skin was slick with rain too, and the two of them shivered against one another.

'I surrender,' she laughed into his woollen sweater, the cold drops of water stinging her open lips, where he dropped avid, if haphazard kisses.

'Like I did a long time ago . . .'

Her hair crinkled like gold foil in the rain. He moved his hand over her head, sensitively, possessively, remembering.

318

'Were you really going to let me go again, Josh?' she asked in such a stricken voice that he let out a clap of laughter.

He shook his shaggy head in a spatter of raindrops. 'Don't you know me by now, woman? Sooner or later I would have found a way to get you back. When I saw you the other night I knew we belonged together, and that there's nothing either of us can do about it. We may as well accept that now and make this loving business a lot easier on both of us.'

'Why didn't you come after me the first time?' She lifted her head to look at him.

'It wouldn't have done very much good, would it? No, Emma, you had to find out for yourself that I was what you wanted. I couldn't show you, if you weren't ready to see.'

'You sound like Dr Beckstein.'

'Bless Dr Beckstein . . .' He chuckled. 'Well, that's because we're both men who love you.'

'Josh, I want to marry you! I know now I can be Emma and still love you. I can find Emma in loving you. Why didn't I ever see that before?'

'Because you'd rather make me crazy.'

'I did, didn't I? I'm sorry,' she said, unable to stop smiling, like an Olympic runner who's just crossed the finish line.

This only set off a new cascade of kisses. 'I think I'm going to have to do this, periodically, to keep you in your place.'

The rain was coming down and Emma sneezed and it was wonderful and warm in her lover's arms.

'That woman . . .?' she tried not to sound jealous.

'Oh ho, you look a little green.'

'Josh!'

'She's just someone I wanted to get on my special factfinding team. I got her.' His face was impassive. 'That's all.'

'I'm not going to inquire as to *how* you "got her".'

'Suffice to say, it did the job. And now it's over. You're the only woman I want, Emma, surely you know that by now!' He let his automatic umbrella up, with one hand.

He smiled down at her, tenderly. Then a sharp light came into his turquoise eyes like the cold green Atlantic waters into the Mexican Gulf, and he looked like the old, restless, passionate Joshua Free with whose portrait Michelle Smith had first fallen in love, a million years ago.

'Baby, I just decided we're going to take our honeymoon first.'

'Right now?'

'Why not! We're in the perfect place for it.'

Emma tossed her head, and began to laugh. She knew that she'd made the right choice. Josh was life. Josh was light.

There was no other possible man for her.

'It's okay with me, Josh. But where will we go?'

'Someplace without newspapers.'

'Or photographic galleries!'

'Right.' Josh snapped his fingers. 'I know just the place. It's an island that hasn't been "discovered" yet. Surrounded by gem-green waters, lush with high palm trees and scented scarlet hibiscus, smack in the middle of the Caribbean. The perfect paradise.'

'What paradise is that?'

'It's called the Isle of Free,' he answered slyly, 'and you and I are heading there right now.' He steered her back towards the crowded terminal gates.

'Whoa, wait!' Emma held her hands up against his chest. 'How do you know we can book a hotel room there?'

He wheeled about and hugged her close with one arm. 'Umm, you smell so good,' he licked her lips. 'And you taste good. And you . . .'

'Josh!' Emma repeated, laughing again. 'How do you know?'

His eyes brimmed with mischief. 'I know my deliciously sexy wife-to-be because . . . it's my own damn island!'

And they looked into each other's dancing eyes. And they saw reflected there the new world that was theirs.